SHE WILL DEFY

# THE VEIL

P. S. WHYTOCK

Ashlyn, Brandy, Charlotte, Hannah, and Jazmyn
Without you guys, I would have lost my shit.
Xx

ALFABORG
BEL'ONC SEA
THE FOREST OF LOST SOU
DAUÐINN MOUNTAINS
THE BLACK FOREST
ZARREN CITY

ÁLFHEIMR
EVENGILE
THE BLACK FOREST
ELDUR MOUNTAIN
THÓRSMÖRK
LLÚIN
HAMMER

# PRONUNCIATION

## Places:

**Dauðinn:** *Doi-th-inn*
**Meaning:** Death
**Origin:** Old Norse
**Dyagin:** *Die-a-gin*
Álfheimr: *Alf-eh-mer*
**Meaning:** Land of the Elves
**Origin:** Old Norse
**Bel'onc:** *Bell-on-k*
**Thórsmörk:** *Ther-sh-mork*
**Meaning:** Thor's mountain
**Origin:** Icelandic
**Eldur:** *Elled-dish*
**Meaning:** Fire
**Origin:** Icelandic
**Nal'lian:** *Nall-ian*

## Names:

**Hazen:** *Haze-en*
**Savven:** *Sav-ven*
**Brean:** *Bri-een*
**Lithônion:** *Lith-on-nee-in*
**Néefar:** *Ne-Far*
**Tatius:** *Ta-tee-us*
**Udiya:** *You-dee-ya*
**Naleen:** *Nall-lean*
**Ezra:** *Ez-ra*
**Nazar:** *Naz-are*
**Levina:** *Leh-veen-nah*
**Laudin:** *Lah-din*
**Valdren:** *Vald-ren*
**Forndýr:** *Forn-dry-er*
Åsmund: *As-mund*
**Kladine:** *Clay-din*

# CHAPTER 1

Hazen sat, staring into the flames of one of the many small crackling fires around her, the heat radiated against her skin in a comforting touch. Reaching out, her fingers hesitantly caressed the dancing tendrils, her eyes widened as they wrapped around her fingers and wrist, their touch warm and inviting.

It had all changed. She had changed. After that night, when a dragon made of fire had claimed her, she had awoken wholly different. If the flames she played with were any indication of that change.

A blaze of power kindled up her arm and through her body. If she could describe breathing or living, that is what it felt like. When the fire touched her skin, it felt like being given the breath of life. Every nerve, every cell, every component of her body was set ablaze and only banked when she removed herself from the flames.

Cool emptiness made her shiver, and Hazen wrapped her arms around her middle, looking up at the fading sky. Twilight had fallen, and the sky was a dark indigo blue. The stars were barely visible, and the moon, full and blood-red, was just starting to come out.

Her hand pressed along the tender spot on her arm where Makari had whacked her with his wooden sword earlier. They had made a temporary camp, and as soon as they'd settled, Makari ran up to her, sword in hand, and demanded that she play with him. Hazen was proud to say she hadn't dropped her arm this time and had won one out of... a dozen rounds.

It was a glorious victory nonetheless.

Thunder rumbled overhead, and she looked up at the near-cloudless sky, frowning.

"Hazen?"

Vika slipped around the fire and stood before her, a frown tugging on the Romani woman's mouth.

Hazen waved to the empty wooden chair beside her. "Do you want to sit?"

Vika had avoided her since the caravan had left. When Makari had run up to play with her, she had noted the mother staring at her and her son with terse reservation, but she didn't say anything, so Hazen had taken it as permission.

Hesitating, Vika took the seat, brushing her black hair over her shoulder. The long strands fell over the back of the chair like ink.

When she said nothing, Hazen spoke, "Vika, I'm truly sorry for last night." Vika inclined her head to look at her. "I don't know what happened. I don't know how Makari was out there, and I don't know how..." *How I saw so many of you being killed*, she almost said. "I saw... things happening, and... I'm so sorry."

It was a lame apology, but she didn't know what else to say. How could she say: *I'm sorry for not getting to your son before he was tossed like a rag doll?*

Vika's mouth pursed. If she thought the same, she didn't say. "Old magic is at play, Hazen," she said, glancing at the fire as embers sparked the sky. "Magic that predates the beginning of this world. And it wants you, for whatever reason."

"Vika—" The woman cut her a hard stare, and her words died out. It was the look of a mother protecting her child—her family.

Her face softened, and Vika let out a long sigh. "This is my family. I have no other in this world or another. I know Luca. I know he wants to offer you refuge. But please, consider my family, Makari, the other children."

She was pleading with her. Hazen's heart cracked for the Romani woman who had lived and survived so much.

Hazen placed a gentle hand on Vika's shoulders. "I understand what you're asking."

Vika gave a terse nod. Firelight danced over her high cheekbones as she turned away. Standing, she brushed a hand over her black skirt and looked down at Hazen as if she had wanted to say more. But she snapped her mouth closed and gave a quick jerk of her chin.

She was there and gone before Hazen could say another word to her. With a sigh, Hazen turned to the sky as thunder roared overhead.

Dawn barely broke the horizon when Hazen opened her eyes the next morning. There was a quiet lull in the world, but within her, there was an incessant pulsing around her bones that made her restless. Rolling to her side, arm tucked under her head, she stared at the ashy fire pit and the tiny twinkle of embers that remained.

She hadn't slept in Vika's tent last night. When she stood outside the entrance, she could hear her and Makari giggling together, and something in her ached for home. Hazen knew if she stepped into that tent, the laughter would die, Vika's eyes would watch her every move until dawn, and only Makari would get a restful sleep. So, she left her bedroll there and took up a spot on the ground beside the fire. Using a spare horse blanket under her, and another to cover her.

Despite her best efforts, she still slept restlessly. Her dreams had been wild. Filled with magic, dragons, and fire. And now, as she curled under her blanket, that same power and restlessness pulsated around her every nerve and cell.

Sighing, she sat up, the blanket pooling in her lap. Tucking a blonde lock behind her ear, Hazen gazed up at the soft indigo sky as the mist crept gently through the towering trees.

The wagons and tents were quiet, a horse nickered softly behind her as she stood.

Hazen walked over to the animal and stroked its nose as it nudged her hand. "I don't have any sugar cubes for you," she whispered.

The horse's ears twitched.

Her aunt on her mother's side had horses when she was a little girl, and every summer until she was thirteen, she would spend it at her aunt's stables until she passed from a heart attack when she was fourteen. She hadn't been on a horse since.

Hazen's fingers twitched in the horse's mane, and her restlessness worsened. She sighed and dropped her head to the animal's neck.

Birds flocked from the trees, and she startled.

Eyes to the sky, she watched the birds disappear until only three remained. Hazen squinted despite her eyes being surprisingly sharper than she remembered.

Her feet moved of their own accord, but she never took her eyes off the birds. The power in her body seemed to hum in acknowledgement. *Yes*, the power whispered.

One of the birds dipped low and then arched high, falling back and free-diving until it righted itself.

Those were not birds.

Her body was practically vibrating with energy, her chest heaving with every breath she took as her feet drew her closer to those who flew high, high above her.

The three creatures dipped from view, and her heart stuttered. Something pressed against her limbs, power, fire, *something* told her to move. To not let them disappear.

So, she ran.

That new seed of energy tore relentlessly through her. Feet flying across the ground, the forest whipped by, and she turned her eyes to the sky. The three creatures were visible between the branches before the evergreen folds knotted together. She hissed out a sharp breath.

Something called to the power within her, like calling to like. It pulled her forward. It made her feet skim the earth and her heart race in her chest. Hazen's hair was a banner of blonde behind her, low branches snagging the ends, but she didn't stop.

A deep, unrelenting roar came from within the forest, and it rang true within her. Hazen looked to her left, dodging around a tree right in front of her as she did so. The forest was a muddy blur, but within that muddle was a great fiery beast which cut through the trees like it, or the forest around it, was only shadows.

The large head of a dragon made of flames turned towards her, and molten eyes that seemed to glow connected with her own. She knew this magnificent beast. She could feel its power thrumming within her very marrow. Her dragon. The restlessness that consumed her belonged to the thing that now burned hotly within her soul. It wasn't magic. It wasn't the same as Savven or Brean or Luca or even the mermaids. It was power. Control. It belonged to the dragon who flew side by side with her. And it was hers now, Hazen let it fill her limbs, lungs, and blood.

She let it take over as she sprinted through the forest towards the creatures who flew unseen above them. The ground sloped up, and excitement began to bubble within.

The ground turned rocky. Shards of glassy black obsidian and smaller, rougher bits of basalt slipped under Hazen's feet, she caught her footing as the forest abruptly ended.

Hazen stopped herself before she went face-first into a stone wall.

Looking to her left, the dragon was gone, and she was alone. Again. Hazen looked over a shoulder to the sea of forest stretched behind her. How far had she run? The Romani camp seemed impossibly far, yet she hadn't felt she had run that great of distance at all. But all she could see were trees in every direction surrounding the towering stone face.

Turning back around, she faced the stone with an arched brow. Reaching out to touch it like a door might magically appear before her. No door appeared, but the stone was warm under her fingertips.

Power flared inside Hazen in recognition, and she sighed, hand dropping to her side. "I can't just walk through stone," she muttered as the restlessness inside pressed her to move.

The fire in her seemed to grumble, flaring once and then settling, and she snorted softly. It would seem her dragon had an attitude.

Following the curve of the stone, the forest dropped away, and her eyes widened as she rounded the wall. The earth slanted with a black rocky ground spread for hundreds of feet, travelling down and down and down until trees began to dot the descent and the forest lay at the edge far below her. The forest curved around and up the black rim until it disappeared behind the stone.

Finally, Hazen looked at the dawning sky, to the all-consuming mountain looming at her back.

*Eldur Mountain.* Just as Luca had told her.

The world shifted as something within her fell into place. An understanding, a realisation. This was where she was meant to be. Not within the forest depths or below the seas of the merfolk, or protected behind Fae princes. Whoever was pulling the strings of her fate had led her here despite all odds that she should be dead by now.

Hazen frowned. She should be dead by now. Maybe death would come within the mountain?

A flame of comfort curled within her, banishing the thoughts that brought along trepidation.

Her time gaping up at the mountain was cut short when the wind whipped at her back. The stones under her booted feet slipped as she whirled in time to see three bodies shoot down from the sky, wings flaring wide as they dropped to the rocky ground at impossible speeds. The earth trembled under her feet, but she didn't falter. She wouldn't show weakness. But her heart did pause for a moment.

Three very tall and very male figures stood, righting themselves, watching her. Black leathery wings peaked over their heads, hovering above the ground, tucked tight behind. They were not birds, and her power nudged her towards them.

The dragon's eyes opened somewhere within, and they were fixated on the three who stood before her. They were familiar to the power thrumming in her veins with kindling excitement.

They were massive in the very physical sense. Black leather clung to large muscular thighs, and their naked, muscled and scarred torsos were flexed tightly as they stood ready, waiting, watching.

The wind cut across the rocky valley, and their wings flared slightly, catching the breeze in their black leather folds.

Hazen pushed her blonde hair away as it blew across her face, wishing for one of Vika's leather ties.

The males stared at her, studying her, and she shifted under the unfaltering green gaze of the male in the middle.

*"My tribe calls them Cer Diavol, or Sky Devil. That is who you will find within the mountain."* Luca's words whispered back to her.

The one the middle tilted his head just a hair, eyes travelling down her body, assessing her. She flushed under his blunt gaze and shifted the black peasant top Vika had given her the morning prior, stitched with red flowers along the open neckline. The two at his back were stocky, made of brutish muscle and looked capable of crushing her head between their hands. But the one who observed her, whose eyes went back to hers with the faintest bit of curiosity under the scrutiny, could tear her apart. Power rippled from him. A sureness that came with being a leader.

His body was broad at the shoulders but narrowed as his hips dipped into a V. Lean and strewn with cords of muscle that flexed with every slight movement. A silver scar curved around his left hip up his back, others marring the caramel skin across his chest, and if he turned, she knew she would find them there, too. There was nothing gentle about him except for the thick mess of curly, sun-bleached brown hair that travelled just past his shoulders.

Her eyes caught something shiny as the sunlight glinted off a small gold hoop through the right side of his nose, and a gold cuff pierced through his left ear.

With the dark forest beyond him, the sunrise above him, and the two at his back, it was picturesque—in a very startling and unnerving kind of way. He was beautiful in the way war was beautiful, savage and untamed.

Something in her began to stir restlessly again, her dragon was almost annoyed at his scrutiny. She shifted just slightly to off-set the edge.

The one with green eyes held out a large masculine hand. Hazen could see the rough ridges of callouses along his palm, and she stared back up at him. He was tall—they all were—but he towered over her when he invaded her space, and it made her feel very, very small. Her breath caught in her throat, her stomach tightening when she felt the heat rippling off of him.

"Come." His voice was rough and deep, raking down her spine with a shiver of trepidation and awareness of the predator before her.

There was no question in his words. It was a command, and Hazen narrowed her eyes at him. Predator be damned. She apparently had no sense of self-preservation, but her power flared with agreement as her dragon seemed to shift and lose interest in the one giving commands. Apparently, her dragon didn't like being given orders. Hazen hid her smirk.

Amusement flared for the briefest of seconds but vanished behind a calm, emotionless gaze, and he arched a brow at her.

Hazen dared to take her eyes off them and glance at the forest behind her, where the Romani were beginning to wake. Where she knew the fires were being snuffed, horses were being readied, and tents were being packed away. Where she knew she would be safe. But what was her safety compared to the lives of everyone around her?

*"This is my family,"* Vika had said.

They weren't her family, though. No matter how much joy it had brought her in the brief time, she was honoured to experience them.

Green eyes stared down at her, waiting. Hazen suspected he would wait for however long she made him, but in the end, she was coming with them, and they both knew it.

His firm mouth tilted faintly, but when she blinked, it was gone. Frowning, she took a deep breath and held it, and when her own callouses slid over his, she released it.

The minute her hand slid into his, he pulled her close and her legs left the ground as he picked her up in his arms.

A hot flush crawled up her neck as his warm skin pressed through her clothes and his arms banded around her back, his hand spreading across her ribcage just below her breast, the other around her thighs, anchoring her to his chest. He was a living inferno, and her dragon seemed to rumble in appreciation like a cat in heat, and she couldn't blame it. The warmth eased through her muscles like water. His musk was overwhelming and intoxicating, and she forced her face away from his chest.

He looked down at her, his eyes darkened wickedly, and a cutting smile tilted his mouth. "Don't scream."

Her eyes widened at his low words, and his massive wings flared open. With one great leap, he pushed into the sky.

Clenching her jaw as she let out a sharp gasp, her arms bolted around his neck, pressing herself to him as they took flight, and the earth became a pinprick below. Hazen swore she felt his chest rumble with laughter.

Her power thrummed and roiled with excitement at being airborne. Her arms loosened a fraction as she took in the burst of orange, yellow, and red that spread across them as the sun broke the treeline and began to anchor among the clouds.

The world was a palette of vibrant colours, and for a moment, she was frozen in time, memorizing the scene before her of the mountain, the sky, the forest, and the whole world as it came to life. So that if her time were to end, or this all be a dream, she would remember the world as it was at that moment.

Luca picked up the horse blankets that lay forgotten near a pile of dying embers, his tribe a quiet buzz behind him as they packed away their camp.

He looked to the sky, the sunbeams filtering through the treetops, in the direction where he knew a great mountain stood, but he could not see it as the trees around him obscured his view.

Nodding softly to himself, he quietly folded the blankets and said to the last dying embers and the dawning light, "May your journeys be wild, and your lovers many, and may the world come to greet you with wealth a plenty."

With a rumbling chuckle and a small, content smile, Luca turned with his parting words and ambled back into the working order of his tribe. Whistling a lively tune under his breath.

# CHAPTER 2

Tatius toed the decapitated head of the once Fae warrior. His green eyes now pale in the sunlight, pupils blown wide, and skin a ghostly grey.

The top of the mountain castle was a desolate ruin of body parts and tacky blood that clung to every step she took through the grim scene.

Ravens had flocked the area, pecking at the flesh and feasting on what remained but every one of them scattered when Tatius arrived.

Despite the new day and vibrant colours overhead, death was present, and she arched a brow at the remnants, unimpressed.

Black eyes flickered to the depths of the shadowed stairwell, hearing the heartbeats within and the ones that had fallen silent the night of the blood moon. The dead outweighed the living within the mountain, and Tatius's head ticked, vanishing in the air.

She reappeared in the shadows of a cell deep within the mountain, darkness enveloped the space despite the small square of light that filtered in.

The door creaked open, and light from the torches filtered in dimly. Tatius shifted her gaze to the pregnant female sitting on the ground in a black tattered gossamer gown, her blonde hair tangled around her face, her back pressed to the corner facing the door.

Levina's eyes narrowed as a Fae male filled the doorway.

Tatius's lips turned down in a hint of disgust when she could smell the rot coming from the male. His soul was decaying within him, she knew his blood ran black.

"What do you want, Laudin," Levina spat, standing to face the male.

Laudin took a step closer but stopped when Levina bared her teeth in a snarl. "Don't."

He scoffed, ignoring her. "You're in no position to give me orders anymore."

"And yet, you'll always be a pet who takes them."

Tatius's mouth twitched with mirth, but her attention was taken when the shadows curled around her in greeting. She eyed them before brushing off their whispering tendrils.

Laudin walked into the cell, and Tatius watched his eyes linger on the small collection of urine in one of the corners. His lips curled before he shifted a black gaze to Levina. "How far the mighty have fallen," he drawled.

Levina spit in his face, and Laudin reared back.

Tatius could barely contain her snort, but it sobered when Laudin backhanded Levina across the face, and the shadows wrapped around Tatius as her rage whirled at her fingertips.

Levina staggered back, hand to her reddening cheek. Her blue eyes narrowed, throwing daggers at the male who advanced until she was pressed against the cell's stone wall. Levina instantly wrapped a protective arm around her belly, steeling her spine and raising her chin, refusing to cower to him.

Laudin brushed a finger to the handprint on her cheek, shaking his head sadly. Almost as if he could feel remorse. "Look at the violence you commit me to, Levina."

She bared her teeth at him in outrage, leaning forward and brushing his hand off of her in disgust. "Do not blame me for your atrocities."

He looked at her, disappointment sketched along his cruelly handsome face and stepped back with a sigh. "I had hoped to offer you a way out, but it would seem you've forgotten where your loyalties lay. Pity, really. Because I could love you so much better than he could."

Tatius's brows rose a fraction.

"You have never and will never know the meaning of love, Laudin," she spat. "I've told you *no* more than once before, but apparently, you fail to comprehend my meaning. So, allow me to elaborate." She stepped up to him and leaned in until they shared breath, and she could look at him in his soulless black eyes. "I would rather be flayed alive than be soul-bound to you with magic." She reared her head back and spit in his face again, this time it sprayed across his eyes and cheeks.

Murderous outrage flashed over his features, and his hand lashed out, gripping her jaw until she knew there would be fingerprints along her skin.

His teeth bared in a snarl, and he spat, "You will pay for that, I promise you."

He let her go with such ferocity she went tumbling to the ground, wrapping an arm around her belly as her back crashed into stone. Darkness flooded her when the door slammed shut.

Tatius cocked her head, eyeing the door, listening to the male's footsteps fade. *What a haughty creature. He will be troublesome in the future,* she thought idly to herself.

Levina let out a low, calming breath, straightening her body until she brought her knees up and leaned her head back, closing her eyes to the darkness.

"Are you going to hide in the shadows all day?" Levina asked softly, but she frowned after a moment and opened her eyes. "Or night… I'm not sure of the time anymore."

Tatius regarded the sky-blue eyes that searched blindly through the darkness. And she stepped out from the shadows. "It is sunrise."

Levina didn't jolt or startle; she just closed her eyes again and nodded softly. "Dawn," she murmured.

Tatius stepped up to the female, watching her silently before she knelt beside her, placing a hand on her growing stomach. She was thin, too thin for a pregnancy, especially for the babe that grew within her. Pursing her lips as she took in the bone thin limbs, bruising jaw, and purple smudges under her eyes, Tatius found herself briefly pitying the female.

Levina opened her eyes and met her with a look of pure determination. That pity evaporated, and a flicker of a smile ghosted over Tatius's lips. She would survive for the time she needed her to, at least.

"Good, I was worried he had broken you," Tatius commented mildly.

Levina's mouth pressed tight, and a coldness swept along her face, her body turning rigid. "No one has the power to break me." She leaned forward, her voice just above a whisper that filled the cell. "I give *no one* that power."

Faint whimpers and pained groans echoed within the hall beyond. The sound of nails clawing at cell doors and iron bars. Tatius listened to the chorus of death for a moment before she said, "He's going to kill you." Her eyes slowly dragged to Levina's stomach. "And *he's* going to try and kill your child."

"Let him try," dared Levina.

Tatius stood, brushing a hand along the length of her black dress.

"Is that all? You came to spy on me and then leave?"

Tatius tilted her head, staring down at Levina. "A God always checks on their assets. And you are a very big one." She waved her hand over Levina, and the female's back arched sharply as she cried out in pain.

Levina's eyes bugged, and she clawed at the ground, searching for purchase to take away the bone-shattering pain that Tatius knew was coursing through her.

When it was over, Levina lay panting on her side, hand wrapped around her now largely swollen stomach that stretched under her ruined gown.

"Wh-what did—you—do?" she asked between breaths, staring wide-eyed at her middle.

Tatius was already walking towards the shadows, feeling them wrap around her in greeting. "I need you to live," she said, looking over her shoulder one last time. "So don't disappoint me."

And then she was gone, and Levina was alone in her darkness.

# CHAPTER 3

Cool wisps of fog rolled through the forest as dawn slowly broke through the branches. Néefar opened sharp blue eyes when the fog softly caressed the stubble along his cheek. The low-hanging clouds ebbed and flowed, beckoning him to follow as they wove a path around the trees and away from his camp.

Lifting his head slightly, he looked at Savven and Brean, who were still sleeping, and stood silently. They had made camp nearing the edge of Álfheimr after travelling for nearly two days, their horses spent and needing to rest.

The forest was quiet, peaceful, and overcast in a silvery haze. Néefar let the solidarity wrap around him in a familiar embrace to years long past.

The mist parted, and Néefar's heart seemed to stop, his breath caught in his lungs as the figure of a woman cloaked in dark green appeared through a gap in the trees.

A slight smile filled with longing, love, and *home* lifted the woman's full pink mouth. And Néefar launched into a sprint, his heart speeding along with him.

Trees whizzed by, the woman was the only thing his eyes focused on as the world around him melded into an array of colours. His arms caught her to him, and he pulled her into his embrace, one hand tangling in her raven black hair while the other banded around her narrow waist, binding her to him.

"Is it really you?" he murmured desperately, fingers stroking the silk strands. He could feel the flutter of her immortal heart and the warmth of her against his chest. But still, he asked, in case his mind played tricks and she was only a figment of his longings.

Anabelle laughed gently, and the sound went straight through him with a shot of elation. He released her just enough to look down at her as she looked up at him, and he cupped her cheek in his hand. Her pale skin was cool and flushed pink against his olive complexion, and her violet-blue eyes stared up at him with adoration.

"Yes, my love, it's me." She reached up and wrapped her arms around his neck, stroking his hair and pulling him close to hold him to her.

Néefar inhaled her scent, frozen lavender filling the empty parts of him without her by his side, and for the first time in months, he felt whole.

"I've been so worried. I've missed you so much," he said, the words making his chest ache.

He pulled back, searching her eyes, his thumb rubbing softly across her jaw. She was real. She was here.

"I know," she said with a shaky breath, pressing closer to him as if that would seal the distance and time apart. "I can't stay long."

Néefar swung them around, pushing her against a tree, his grip tightening around her hips and pulling her close. His fingers tangled in her hair as his mouth claimed her in a searing, desperate kiss and felt Anabelle melt against him.

His heart pounded like a drum, and he groaned low against her mouth when he felt her fingers trail down his chest, pulling at his shirt and slipping a sneaky hand beneath it.

Growling, he yanked her cloak open and grabbed her legs, lifting her up to wrap around him. The skirts of her black dress pooled around her, and he pressed himself to the heat between her legs.

Anabelle gasped when his teeth sank into the alcove of her neck and shoulder. "Néefar!"

He loved it when she cried his name. Her fingers dug into his shoulders, and he pressed his cock against her, a low moan slipped from her pink lips, and he bent to capture it.

She pulled away slightly, breathless. "Darling, I have news. I need to tell you—"

He silenced her with another searing kiss.

Pulling back slightly, one of his hands gripped her backside while the other went to her breast, stroking a thumb over the firm peak of her nipple. Elating in the gasp that fell from her lips. "I have missed my wife," he whispered hotly against her ear. "Day and night and months being separated from you. Worried if something were to happen" —he licked up her neck and sucked on the skin until she whimpered— "that I wouldn't be there to protect you. That I wouldn't be there for you." He kneaded her breast gently, rocking against her centre until he felt her body begin to tighten. "Let me have this. Let me have you. Let me feel you. I beg."

Anabelle arched her back as he ground against her, and she whimpered, lips parting with a gasp as he freed her breast from the bodice, and the cold air made her nipples harden.

His hand slipped between them, and his fingers found her hot and wet, ready for him, and it was nearly his undoing. He groaned low and undid the laces of his front, freeing himself.

"Néefar," she begged softly, her head falling back against the tree.

Gods, she was beautiful. Bared to him and the forest, her breast offered up to him, legs wrapped around his waist, and her fingers fisted in his hair. A delicate flush spread across her cheeks, and her eyes were glassy with longing. His wife. Not his mate. His *wife*. She was his, then, now, and forever.

With that thought, he slid into her, sinking to the hilt. He uttered her name like a prayer as he filled her. Home. She was his home, and he had missed her terribly.

At their joining, Anabelle gasped and ground against him until he started to move. Slowly at first, but she made a keening cry of desperation, and he pounded into her until her breasts bounced and her head fell back. Eyes closed, her soft moans filled the air.

Gripping her backside in both hands, he pulled out to the tip and slammed back in, and he watched as her eyes rolled back in pleasure. He could feel her tightening around him, her body trembling.

"Néefar," she gasped. Chanting his name over and over again, clinging to him as he took her hard and fast and desperately.

His wife. His. His. His.

"Néefar!" Back arching, she tightened, and a low, desperate moan left that beautiful mouth of hers as she came around him, and he followed. His release barrelled out of him as he went with her over that cliff.

He breathed heavily, leaning his forehead against hers and scattering gentle kisses along her face as she turned soft, smiling eyes to him.

"I love you," she whispered.

"With all that I am," he answered back.

Gently releasing her legs, he helped her straighten her skirts, worshipping the tops of her breasts with soft kisses before straightening her bodice with a longing sigh.

Anabelle giggled, pulling a piece of bark from her hair. "This was not my intention."

Néefar grumbled happily, smiling down at her. "You are my wife and the one thing in this world that consumes me daily. I will always crave you." He brushed his thumb against her bottom lip before kissing her. "The world can wait."

Straightening his shirt and trousers, he watched her look toward his camp, the thick mist concealing anything beyond them. He knew it was his wife's doing as a sparkle of frost glimmered where the fog crept around the trees.

She frowned softly, and her look of adoration slowly turned sad.

"I have news from Tatius."

He frowned and raised a brow. "Any news from Tatius can't be good. Even good news is questionable."

"It's about Lithônion."

Néefar's blood ran cold.

The towering forest hushed at her words as if waiting on bated breath for the reveal.

Anabelle's eyes became glassy, and her whispered words cleaved through him. "He's dead."

Néefar's vision swayed, or the earth did, or maybe it was just him. He braced a hand on the tree beside Anabelle's head.

Anabelle touched his arm gently, but his head swam with memories of Lithônion coming to him with his plan. Lithônion ignoring his warnings that his plan was a death sentence. Lithônion's hope.

Hope.

And despite that hope, he died.

Néefar closed his eyes, his jaw flexing as he forced air to fill his lungs and calm the beasts within him that wanted to punch a hole through the tree he leaned on.

"My love," whispered Anabelle. "I'm so sorry."

*"Please, if Levina is alive, then there's a chance I can still bring her home. I can't do this without you, my friend."* Lithônion had begged him.

Lithônion was his friend—had been his friend—and he let him go into that damned cursed mountain. And now, it was his final resting place.

"My love." His wife's voice was soft as if approaching a rabid animal. When he opened his eyes, he saw why. His fingers had turned to sharp claws that gouged into the tree, leaving five gaping holes when he shifted his fingers back.

Anabelle placed her hand over the wounds in the wood, and they slowly healed under her touch, a lick of ice crystals coating them.

Sad, understanding violet-blue eyes regarded him, and he dropped his head to her shoulder. Her lithe fingers combed through his silver hair, soothing the pounding in his head. Wrapping his arms around her, he buried his face into her neck and held her tight to him.

"I shouldn't have let him go; I should have been firmer with him."

Anabelle hushed his words, and he could feel her shake her head against him. "No, my love, do not put his death on your shoulders. It is not your burden to bear but his own." She pulled back slightly, just enough to cup his cheek and look at him in the eyes. "The Fae are stubborn. Far more stubborn than they have any right to be, and once Lithônion made up his mind, nothing was going to stop him. You helped him prolong his life, but you cannot stop Death when it comes for a soul."

He pulled her close to him again, letting her words sink in. "Well, I can damn well try at least," he finally muttered gruffly. Tatius be damned.

Her laughter vibrated through his chest. "Yes, my love. But as we know, the God of Death is just as stubborn and cunning."

Néefar snorted and pulled away, dropping a quick kiss to his wife's mouth. "Aye, Little Gipsy, she is."

Anabelle pursed her lips in thought. "There is something else."

"Oh gods," he grumbled, scrubbing a hand over his face. "If someone else has died, I don't want to know... no, wait, tell me. Might as well."

"No one else has died... well, no one you know. Many have died recently..." Her voice became small and thoughtful, trailing off when a distant look crossed her face. Her eyes recalling the horrors she'd seen. The death.

"I'm sorry, my love." Néefar crooked a finger under her chin and tilted it to look up at him. "Share your burdens with me."

Her hand wrapped around his wrist, stroking the skin. He dropped his arm, and she took in a deep breath. Sealing away her emotions. "When all of this is over, I will lay them all at your feet, but until then, I must carry on. Despite the weight of their deaths."

While beautiful, his wife suddenly looked tired, and he wanted nothing more than to whisk her away and protect her from the darkness they were surrounded by—to tear apart the world that was slowly destroying the most beautiful and pure thing he had ever had the honour of loving. But she was strong, stronger than him by far, and he let her stand alone as she needed, offering support silently. She would not falter, and neither would he.

"What news do you bring, Little Gipsy."

A fond smile curled on her lips at his name for her, and the ache in his chest eased.

"Hazen has found the dragons and is within the mountain now."

Néefar nodded slowly, understanding. "I will inform Savven."

Anabelle looked back toward his camp, and he knew she could hear them waking. "They'll be wondering where you went. They still don't trust you… well, the witch might, but Savven is hesitant."

"And you know this, my love?" he asked, bemused.

She shrugged. "The trees whisper."

"Of course they do." He tucked a stray piece of her hair behind her ear, committing the feel of her skin to memory.

"I must go now. Before they come looking for you. There are villages that need my help."

He gritted his jaw, wanting to burn the world for separating them once again. Schooling his face, he jerked his head in a nod, dropping his forehead to hers.

"I cannot stand this separation," she murmured so softly that not even the air could hear her. Just him. "You take pieces of me with you, and I am not whole until you are in my arms."

He pulled her to him and kissed her deeply. His tongue slipped past her parted lips and tasted her, relishing in the feel of her warm body pressed against his. Néefar kissed her with every ounce of his love and affection, hoping it might brand her lips and his with the feeling of them together.

He cradled her face in both hands when he forced himself to pull back. "Soon, my love, there will be a day when we never say goodbye. Soon, there will be a day when we are never apart."

"I love you," she whispered, unshed tears making her eyes glitter in the silver light.

"With all that I am," he responded.

The bitterness of letting her go hit him as he walked away, knocking the air from his lungs. But he forced himself not to look back.

Savven looked up at Néefar as he entered the camp, the fire sparking behind him as Brean cooked a bird over the flames.

"Where were you?" Savven intoned, tossing a stick into the fire.

Néefar crouched beside the fire and put his hands up to warm them. He could feel their eyes watching him, waiting for a reply, and as he gathered his emotions, he slowly turned to look at Savven. "Anabelle came to deliver some news."

Brean's brows rose to her hairline, but Savven's face remained impassive. Barely flinching at the mention of his cousin.

Dread coiled tightly in Néefar's gut, and he swallowed down the guilt that came with it, breathing heavily through his nose.

"The first, Hazen is alive. She is with the dragons."

Brean's gasp was audible, and it cut through the silence when Savven didn't say anything, continuing to stare at Néefar like he could see right through him.

Blue eyes clashed with blue eyes, but Néefar held his ground, not looking away from his friend.

"Oh, that's wonderful news," Brean said, ignoring the tension between the males. "It's like a weight has been lifted. I truly thought she was gone, if I'm being honest."

"What else did she tell you?" Savven commanded.

His tone was low and demanding, and Néefar could feel the tension rolling off the male.

Brean paused what she was doing when she heard Savven, hovering over the fire. Her wild red hair slipped near the flames, and she brushed it back, sitting on the log behind her. "Néefar?" she asked cautiously. "Is there more?"

Forcing in a breath, he bit the words out through the guilt that pressed against his chest, suffocating him. "Lithônion is dead."

At his words, the world went still.

Brean's eyes widened, her mouth slacking in shock. But Savven... Savven became deathly calm, a withering rage filling his eyes.

Néefar had only a moment to brace himself as the Fae threw

himself across the flames, hands aimed for his throat.

The two tumbled across the ground. Dirt and limbs flew, and Néefar shielded his face as Savven came at him with every ounce of his strength. Blow after blow rocking his sides, Néefar's arms guarding what they could of his face. He wouldn't hit Savven. He wouldn't fight him. He could feel the pain behind those blows, Savven's pain.

"Savven, get off of him!" Brean barked.

Néefar grunted when a blow landed on his ribs, and his bones buckled. Grabbing Savven by the collar, he threw the male off him and rolled to his feet, chest heaving with every breath. His blood surged through his body, the beasts in him pulsating to shift and defend, but he willed them down.

"Are you done, princeling," he goaded. Smiling through the blood in his mouth.

Savven's eyes flickered but darkened with rage.

"Enough, you two!"

They ignored Brean, who stood by the fire, eyes darting between them.

Savven lunged for Néefar, teeth bared in a snarl. "It should have been you!"

Néefar kept his hands to his side and let the blow come. It rocked against his jaw, and stars splintered his vision, staggering under the weight.

"You should have been in the mountain" —another blow to his left ribs— "you should have stopped him" —another to his right, Néefar grunted when another rib cracked, and he tumbled to the ground. "You were his friend!"

Néefar focused on Savven's face above his, his snarl of rage twisting with sorrow, his dark blue eyes lighting with tears. Blow after blow until tears mingled with Néefar's blood, and he let it all come.

Savven's bloody fists slowed, and he took in a shuddering breath, eyes wide as his hands dropped limply to his sides, still straddling Néefar.

Coughing, blood spurting when he did so, Néefar heaved in a broken breath when Savven rolled off and lay beside him on the ground. He turned to look at the male who stared mutely up at the forest that loomed over them, tears streaking from the corner of his prominent face.

"Why didn't you stop him?" Savven whispered tonelessly.

Néefar gritted his jaw. He knew the old friendship between the Fae prince and the warrior. He knew the years, the trauma, and the survival they went through together—a brotherhood he would never know. "I tried—I couldn't."

Savven looked at him, pained eyes searching his for an answer he couldn't provide. When he finally looked away, fixating on the swaying of branches, he said, "It should have been you."

Turning to watch the waking world above them, his bones already starting to slowly mend, Néefar nodded softly. "I know."

# CHAPTER 4

"Behave," That's what the male with green eyes said to her before he opened a curved wooden door with an arching golden handle and pushed her into it, slamming it shut when she whirled on him.

*Behave.*

Hazen snorted, the sound echoing in the stone room. It hadn't been more than twenty minutes since he had shoved her inside, and she was getting very tired of waiting. It was as if she had an internal clock inside her head, and the endless ticking filled the sparse space with every passing second.

The flight to the mountain entrance was unfortunately short, and the companions of the male carrying her stalked into the mountain without a word, leaving them alone. They disappeared into the darkness that winded deep into the stone, lit only by fire that hung suspended by magic along the corridor.

The room was empty. Four globes of fire danced in each corner, casting the room in a creeping dance of shadows across the grooves of stone. A trickle of water creased the wall to her right and disappeared into a crack in the floor, the air smelled faintly of eggs.

*Behave.* He had said this with a faintly amused smile just before he shoved her in. Hazen wanted to smack the smugness right off his obscenely attractive face.

Gritting her jaw in irritation, she rounded on the door. Eyeing it with her hands on her hips, she tilted her head, half expecting someone or something to barge through it. When no one did, she crossed her arms, fingers drumming along her bicep.

Her dragon pulsed restlessly through her limbs. It was more like her dragon was stretching, and the power of it pressed along her bones and muscles, testing its bounds. The power within her was a very real and very living thing, and Hazen could almost hear the exasperated huff of the fire-breathing creature as she continued to stare at the door.

"For fucks sake, just open the damn door," she muttered to herself.

*"Behave."*

She stared defiantly at the door, walking right up to it, her hand hovering over the gold-curved handle. *His* voice seemed to fill the room with the command he had issued her, and she straightened her spine, sniffing.

"No, I don't think I will," she said to the phantom voice and yanked the door open, surprised that it wasn't magically locked.

The hall was unsurprisingly empty. They hadn't walked far when he had stopped her in front of the door, and if Hazen held her breath, she could hear the wind where light faintly penetrated one end of the hall.

Hazen followed that light. The path curved into a straightaway, that led to the mouth of a towering entrance into the mountain.

The wind whipped past in a clear blue sky, and as Hazen stood before it, shadows at her back and the world at her feet, she felt the tiniest inkling of homesickness ease into her chest.

How she would love to share this with her family. If even a sliver of this world.

The sky was beautiful and vast, full of light, clouds, and space. Beyond the blue, far below, was the spread of forest. Beyond that, she could see the ocean with its endless expansion.

The world, as she knew it, had significantly changed. *She* had changed.

Protected from the wind, Hazen yearned to feel it. She put ten toes on the ledge, close enough that she could feel the energy around her. Extending a hand, she reached for the wild world before her and felt the pulsing of air wrap and press against her hand, the sun's warmth on her skin.

She wasn't just the girl from Eastbourne anymore with ideals of university and failed relationships. That world seemed like a lifetime ago. Now, she stood at the peak of the world, with power in her veins and nearly a month of travelling within it and the people she had met, the friends she made, the death she had seen. Everything else seemed so mundane, and she hated that it did.

If it all turned out to not be a dream, she would find a way to bring her family here after it's all done—after the death and uncertainty of life, after the chaos. She would find a way. She could have both worlds. She would make it happen.

Retracting her hand, Hazen gave the outside world a parting look and walked back into the tunnel.

Her eyes adjusted quickly to the dim firelight, that power in her veins thrumming excitedly with every step taking her deeper into the mountains.

The hall was wide—wide enough for wings to fully expand if she thought about it—and the ceiling a towering, curved arch above her. The walls were smooth and glassy as if the stone had been polished over the years—or melted.

The latter thought gave her pause, but she pressed on when that restlessness grew insistent.

Heat filled the mountain the further she went, and she relished in it. It wasn't overwhelming or suffocating, her power rumbled with contentment.

She travelled down and down and down until a ringing sliced

the air, and Hazen's breath caught.

The tunnel opened, and she paused at the entrance, her eyes widening as the expanse of a training arena filled her vision. Fires blazed along one mammoth wall, blacksmiths were sweating over glowing metal, the ringing of hammers mixed with the collision of swords and fists on flesh.

When she looked up, the dome curved and narrowed into a bottleneck of glimmering obsidian, and along the walls hundreds of half-moon caves were cut along and up the sides of the glassy black stone. Those spaces were filled with burning fires and males who worked within them, black wings tucked in tight to half-naked bodies.

A pair of large males stumbled in front of her, grappling for purchase, sweat coating every inch of their exposed skin. She sucked in a sharp breath when one went for the other's throat, dodging under his opponent's fist.

They were *massive*. She knew they were, but her mind was still computing it very slowly.

The two paused, hearing Hazen, and she snapped her mouth closed. She couldn't help but take a slight step back when they turned intense stares at her. There was pure male power in their gazes, and they flamed bright like they were made of fire.

Her dragon perked up at their stares, and the power that rippled through her felt almost giddy with anticipation for a fight.

The one who threw the punch smirked, there was nothing kind in the way he glanced her up and down with dark brown eyes.

Pursing her lips, she stepped forward, eyes narrowing in a silent challenge.

The one who went for his opponent's throat snorted at her show of defiance. He was shorter than the one with cold eyes, but they looked like they could be brothers. Black hair, thick and cropped to their necks, dark brown eyes and light sun-brown skin. The taller of the two was cold and calculating, while the other looked as if he couldn't be bothered but still threw a mocking look in her direction when she glared at them.

"Look at this, a female for the taking. The Gods have shown us favour, brother," sneered the tallest, not bothering to question why she was there. His only interest was that she was female, her gut curdled at that thought.

"She looks like she'll put up a fight," replied the shorter.

A cold smile cuts across the tallest one's cruel face. "Perfect, just how I like it."

Hazen's blood ran cold at what he implied, and the dragon in her shifted, and she felt... *hungry.* A bloodthirsty sort of hunger filled her. She wanted to tear these males' apart limb from limb, and it took every ounce of self-control not to leap at them and drive her fingers into their leering eyes.

The tallest one advanced a single step before the ground shuddered violently. Hazen's footing slipped a fraction but she caught herself, falling into the defensive stance Savven had taught her. Her one foot slid behind her, and her legs staggered shoulder width apart, balancing on the balls of her feet. Power hummed to the tips of her fingers. Not magic, but pure, undiluted power, and she could feel the dragon swirling, ready within her when the tallest advanced another step.

Fire whipped between them with a crack and wrapped around the hand that reached for her. Tallest snarled when the flames tightened and twisted until he fell to his knees.

Hazen jolted, heart lurching, and her head whipped to the right, following that blazing rope of fire.

Green eyes were ignited with a rage that banked Hazen's inferno, her dragon settling under the power that stood there, commanding fire.

No. The males before her were not massive, not when the one to her right stood like a dragon who had become flesh and bone.

"You *dare*—"

Green Eyes twisted the fire in his fist, veins of gold cording his forearms, cutting off Tallest's words. "If," he growled, taking a step closer, wrapping the flames in his grasp, "you touch a single hair on her head" —another step and the tallest one was yanked forward on his knees— "without her consent." The entire arena had gone silent, and Green Eyes stalked slowly by her, his wings nearly touching her. "I will *rip* your wings from your back and shove you from the tallest peak of this mountain."

Tallest's face was twisted in a snarl, murder in his dark eyes. "You *dare* threaten me?" The flaming rope yanked him forward until his arm was stretched above him, holding him taunt.

Green Eye's free hand grabbed Tallest's throat; his mouth curled as he squeezed, and the male sputtered. Leaning forward, he growled through clenched teeth, "I will end *anyone* who threatens to touch an unwilling female."

"*Enough!*"

Hazen's head jerked at the sudden intrusion. The sea of bodies that had gathered parted for the two males who walked towards them.

The rope of fire vanished with a flicker of sparks, and the tallest fell forward onto his face as the male with green eyes stepped out of the way. His fury vanished behind an emotionless mask.

Hazen's eyes darted between the two males, fixing on the one with long braided grey hair and vibrant gold eyes. She knew that face, those eyes—that ancient scrutiny that befell her despite his ageless face. He was exactly as she remembered him from her dream. Though his robed tunic was dark red and gold now, he still wore black leather pants and boots.

Flicking her gaze on the other male, she sucked in a breath as black assessing eyes drilled into her. Streaks of white painted a thick black mane of hair and full black beard, deeply tanned skin adorned his harsh face, his brows furrowed in a scowl. He was dressed in all black and was the only one with wings and a shirt on. His tunic was a simple cotton shirt with laces at the neckline that lay undone.

Glancing at the males around her, they jerked their heads in a short salute as he passed them, and her brows rose a fraction. He was their leader.

"Get back to your work!" the leader commanded.

His voice cracked through the stone, and at once, everyone dispersed except Tallest and Green Eyes. Tallest, having gotten to his feet, was currently glowering with murder written on his cruel face at Green Eyes who looked utterly indifferent.

"Chief, Valdren," the two males murmured in greeting, bowing their heads.

Valdren and the clan leader halted in front of the three of them.

The male from her dreams had a slightly amused upturn to his mouth, regarding her curiously. The clan leader, though, narrowed his eyes on her before sweeping to Tallest and Green Eyes.

"Fighting amongst each other is not tolerated under this mountain!" The clan leader looked between the two, nostrils flaring with leashed anger. "Fighting over a female is disgraceful."

"Yes, Chief," they said in unison.

The clan leader's eyes finally returned to her, and Hazen stood a little straighter, pressing her mouth into a flat line.

"Why is there a female, uninvited, within our sacred mountain?" His voice bellowed for all to hear, and Hazen's cheeks tinged red when eyes turned to stare at her.

"I brought her," Green Eyes said.

"And you failed to bring it to my attention, Åsmund?" The coldness seeping into the clan leader's voice made Hazen's dragon rumble. Her dragon did not like the clan leader or Tallest.

Hazen pressed the power of her dragon down and regarded Åsmund from the corner of her eye. That was his name. Åsmund. She liked it.

"I saw her when I was sparring with Novu," Tallest said, cutting in before Åsmund could speak.

Hazen frowned, glaring at him.

Tallest feigned a look of innocence and swept a hand in her direction. "I was going to bring her to you when I saw her."

Hazen saw red and snapped, "Like hell you were, you lying bastard!"

"You do not speak until spoken to, Female!" the clan leader boomed.

She stepped forward, and her power rumbled in approval, filling her until she felt fire blaze under her skin. "I do speak! I was brought here—something brought me here, and I will find out why. You will not silence me on the biases of my sex!"

The clan leader's face turned thunderous, and Hazen swallowed the trepidation that bubbled in her throat.

A hand slyly tugged the back of her tunic, making her step back. She looked to see Åsmund gently pulling her away from the clan leader, but he never looked down at her. His eyes were shielded, staring ahead like a good soldier.

"I informed Valdren of her arrival and placed her within one of the empty rooms along the eastern entrance," Åsmund said stoically. "It was not my intention to disrespect you, Chief."

"Kladine," Valdren interrupted when the clan leader opened his mouth to snap a reply. "Åsmund speaks the truth. He did come to me when the girl was brought into the mountain because I told him to bring her."

Kladine faced Valdren, his thick body towering over the slight male who stood calmly, observing the clan leader. "I am Chief of Clan Drago. I command those within this mountain. You do not, Valdren. Remember that." The fire within the arena flickered at his words, dancing towards them as if commanded, and then settled once more.

Valdren tilted his head, slipping his hands into the long folds of his sleeves. "You are correct, Kladine, but there is one thing you forget. You do not command me. You do not command the dragon. You do not command the will of the Gods." His words were casual, as if conversing calmly with a friend, and Hazen couldn't tell if it pissed off the clan leader more or less.

The mountain rumbled in warning, but Hazen knew, this time, it wasn't the clan leader's doing. A roar cracked through the air, deep and hungry and full of threat, and Hazen felt it resonate within her. Her dragon soared in greeting, but when her eyes strayed to the clan leader's, she noted the bitterness filling his gaze before it was swept under a mask, his mouth twisting in distaste when he looked at her again.

She cocked a brow at him, waiting. Åsmund still grasped her shirt as if he did not trust her not to nose up to the clan leader and mouth off. A likely scenario as her tether of patience was beginning to wear thin.

"Thank you for bringing her, Åsmund, as I asked," Valdren said calmly, turning his gaze to Hazen, and a slight smile lifted his mouth. "Welcome to Eldur Mountain, Keeper."

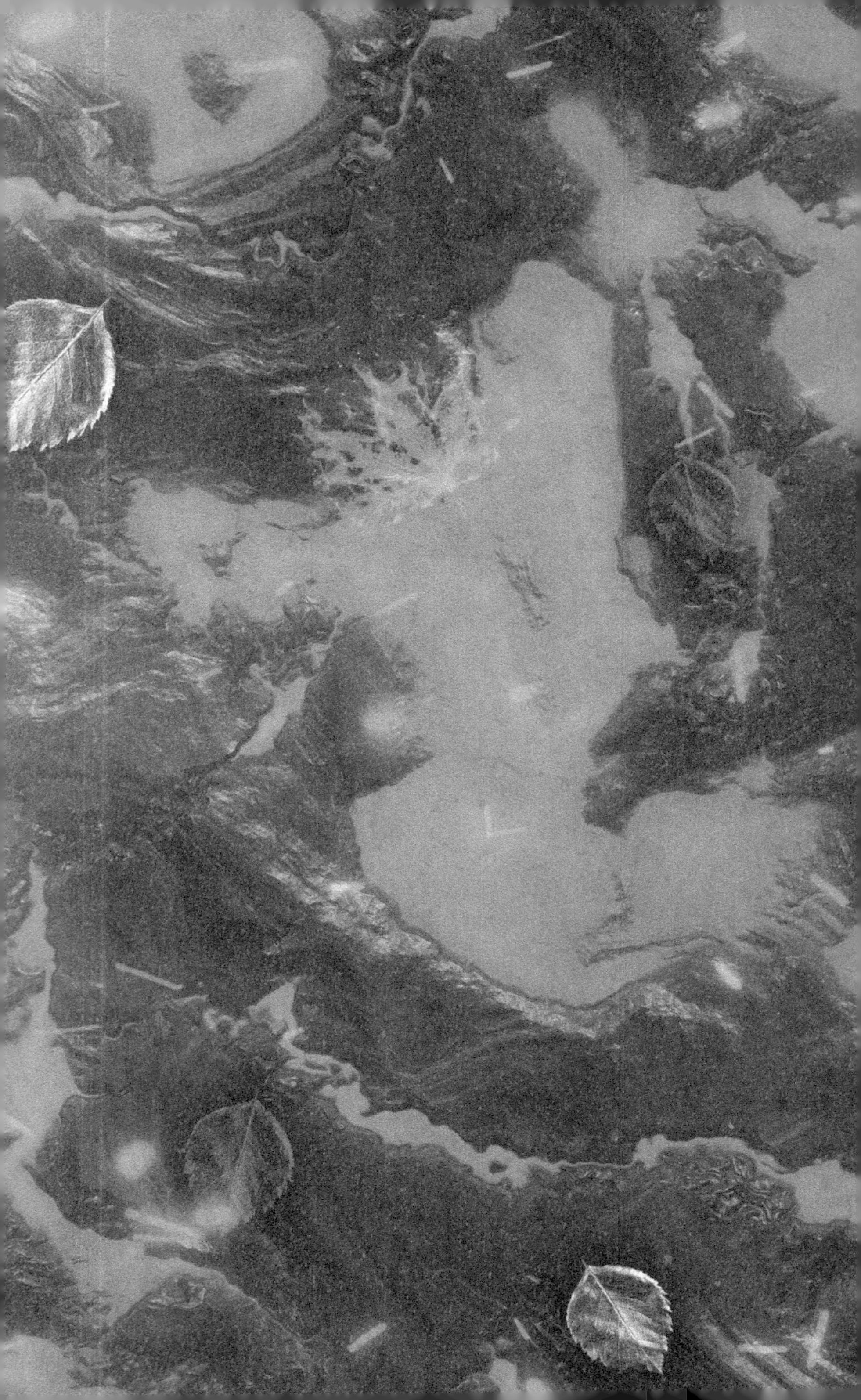

# CHAPTER 5

"Keeper?" Kladine blustered. "This *child* is a keeper?!"

Hazen let out a long, drawn-out sigh. "That's what they tell me."

"I was not speaking to you, Child," Kladine snapped.

Hazen's brows rose a fraction, biting back the words that lingered on the tip of her tongue. Åsmund's grip on her tunic tightened, and she wanted to swat his hand away, but it would bring attention to them both, so she didn't. Instead, she shifted away from him, pulling her shirt tight in his grip and hoping he would get the hint. He only proceeded to tug her back slowly. He was keeping her in line, and she pursed her lips in annoyance.

"Kladine, this *child*, as you call her, was chosen by ancient magic. Magic that created you, shaped you, and blessed you with the power you hold today. I would be mindful of your words, lest they insult that magic and the ones who created it. You never know what the Gods might do if offended." Valdren's tone was mild and contemplative compared to the warning of his words.

A red flush crept up the clan leader's neck into his beard, Hazen had to hide her smirk.

Bright gold eyes met hazel ones, and Hazen met his stare with her own, and finally, Åsmund released her tunic.

*"Hello Hazen"*

It was like a whisper brushed against her mind, and Hazen jerked in surprise at the deep, resounding voice, eyes widening. Valdren tilted his head, amusement glimmering behind his gaze.

"I was wondering how long it would take you to abandon that room," Valdren commented with a slight smile.

"I've never been one to follow orders very well," she admitted, her mouth twitching into a sheepish smile.

Valdren hummed with a soft nod of his head. "Yes, that is a trait commonly found within this mountain, you will see." His gaze flickered to Tallest. "Kain."

Tallest, or *Kain*, straightened at his name, and Hazen shook her head. A fitting name for a bastard.

"You're dismissed," Valdren said, the amusement fading when he stared the male down. There was no kindness, only order in his words.

"You cannot dismiss my own," Kladine snapped.

Hazen could see patience slipping from Valdren's face, and he gave Kladine a look that said *make it quick*.

Kladine's nostrils flared, and he jerked his head at Kain. "Find your brother and get back to your training."

Fire filled his dark eyes as he gave her a look that spoke of nothing other than his murderous intent. A smirk twisted his mouth, just enough for her to see before it vanished, and he walked past her, his shoulder ramming into hers.

"Åsmund, you too," Kladine commanded.

"No." Valdren held up a hand, halting Kladine's blustering words. "Åsmund, you will keep Hazen in your charge. Keep to your daily tasks, but she will remain with you."

Hazen finally looked up at Åsmund. His green eyes found hers for a moment, holding her gaze. Heat crawled through her chest and up her neck under his intense stare, and she let out a low breath when he looked back at Valdren with not even a glimmer of emotion on his face.

Ever the statue this one was.

"You cannot have a child following my general around all day long!" Kladine snarled.

Hazen arched a brow, looking between the three males. A general? So, he was a good little soldier. The leader of all the good little soldiers, as it turns out.

The noise of the arena faltered at the outburst, and Hazen noted the eyes darting in their direction. For a bunch of shirtless, muscled warriors, they were as nosy as her meddling aunts were. Some things were universal, magic or not.

Valdren, unphased, simply waved a hand at the clan leader's words. Nothing seemed to truly bother the male, and Hazen had to suppress her grin.

"It is the dragon's command that she be integrated into our world as the chosen successor of the keeper. Would you like to take it up with Forndýr?"

At Valdren's words, the clan leader's mouth pulled into a tight line. She didn't know who Forndýr was, but she knew that she wanted to meet them.

"If it is the dragon's command, then who am I to stand in their way?" Kladine said, submitting with a sharp wave of his hand.

Hazen regarded the clan leader, taking in the face worn down over possible centuries, weather, and war. His dark eyes met her own, but she didn't look away. Only when Valdren spoke did she finally tear away from the cold she found burning in Kladine's gaze.

"Do what General Åsmund asks of you, Hazen."

Arching a brow, she looked between Valdren and Åsmund. "I have questions, things I need answered."

Valdren nodded his head softly. "I can imagine. But in due time. Stay close to General Åsmund until I seek you out." He looked at Åsmund, a silent conversation seeming to pass between them. Åsmund nodded at whatever the male had conveyed, and Valdren turned to give her a small, kind smile. "Until our next meeting,

Hazen."

Kladine, who was stiff as a board, gave a terse bow of his head and turned on his heels. The clan leader and Keeper of Dragons walked out of the arena, one was a glimmer of elegance and steady power, while the other was a storm of shadows and simmering rage.

When they vanished into one of the corridors, Hazen let out a long, low breath.

"Well, that was interesting," she muttered.

Åsmund didn›t say anything, and when she looked up, she found him staring at her with an unreadable expression. Stoic through and through.

She arched a brow at him cocking her head. "I mean, I would say take a picture, but I have a feeling you wouldn't know what that means." When he said nothing, she huffed, laughing under her breath.

"I'll show you to your room," he said finally, his voice giving away to an inkling of emotion.

Was that amusement she detected under his mask of General?

"My room? Already?"

He nodded, a quick jerk of his head. "I'll collect you in the morning."

"You'll *collect* me?" She crossed her arms over her chest, not following him when he made to leave. "I'm not a dog to be played with when convenient."

Turning, he raised his brow a fraction. "A dog?"

"An animal, a pet to be kept," she rectified. "Are there really no dogs here?" she muttered, mostly to herself. She couldn't believe that the very animal that got her into this mess was the one thing that didn't exist, at least not to her knowledge.

A shadow of a smirk titled his firm mouth, and he stepped closer, leaning down until they were eye level and only inches separated them. "The males in this mountain, while most have honour, some will look at you like a thing to claim. To mate with. To take. And while you are in my charge, I do not want to cut down my brothers because there is a female dragon in this mountain for the first time in many millenniums."

A flush ran up her neck, Hazen could smell the sweat and heat rolling off him. Her dragon, unsurprisingly, was very content to stay close to him despite his words.

She would be damned if she was forced to stay locked in a room like a damsel. "I will not just sit around and twiddle my thumbs like an ass. So, next option. What are you doing today?" she asked brightly.

Amusement flared in those green eyes, and he straightened but didn't step back. "I'm training a new batch of soldiers who will leave in the next month for the western mountain range."

"Then I'll train with them."

This time, his brows shot up, and his flawless general mask fell in surprise. A low chuckle rumbled through his chest; she could practically feel its vibrations through the sliver of space separating them.

"You?" he asked, incredulous.

"Me," she replied with a stubborn press of her lips. "I know my way around a sword. It shouldn't be too hard."

She was, in fact, wrong.

She didn't know her way around a sword.

She was an idiot.

She was going to die. Either by collapsing from sheer exhaustion, from falling onto one of the warrior's swords, or possibly from humiliation as Åsmund glanced in her direction with a smug smirk for the umpteenth time. She was going to throw her sword at his head if he didn't stop and if she could gather the strength to toss the bloody thing.

The sword was heavy in her hands. This was not a stick she found randomly on the forest floor, a ship hook like the one Savven snapped in half, or the practice swords Makari used to duel with her. This was an actual, chop you in half, hurt like a bitch, heavy longsword.

Hazen garnered where she had gone wrong. She knew her way around a stick or a wooden sword, but a *sword-sword*. No. She knew absolutely nothing about real swords.

Sure, the footwork was the same, her body fell into the steps quickly, but the sword was *massive* and weighed nearly half her body weight. Okay, that was an exaggeration, it weighed roughly three, maybe four, kilos but her arms were not meant to swing something that heavy for this long. It took all her focus, determination, and sheer stubbornness not to drop it. Though she did drop it—a lot, her swings and defence were sluggish and slow at best.

Åsmund was leaning against one obsidian wall, arms crossed over the expanse of his sweaty chest. Hazen swallowed, eyes darting away, but slowly slid back to him as she tried not to stare at the male who looked like he had emerged from one of her wildest dreams.

His eyes trailed slowly across the soldiers training until they landed on her. He leisurely looked from the sword in her hands to the glare she was shooting him. She would have sworn a smile ghosted over his mouth, and she huffed in annoyance.

She had asked to train. She had all but demanded it. It was her own fault. Blowing the strands of blonde hair from her face, she tightened her hold on the hilt, her white knuckles pressed against the cross-guard, straining to hold the sword up with shaking arms. Her back was on *fire* and not the kind she had come to know and love.

They were running drills. There were ten 'new' soldiers, as Åsmund called them, despite them looking cut from rock, and they were divided into two groups. One group of six was set aside for sparring drills, while Hazen and the four left with her were grouped together to run over technique.

She had already caught two of them grumbling about her knocking into them, and she had to bite her tongue not to say anything. She had knocked into them, not on purpose, but her sword had tilted sideways, and unfortunately after hours of training, it felt like an anchor and dragged her with it.

Åsmund had given her the smallest sword in the arsenal, and Hazen was determined not to fail or at least die trying.

In the beginning, when she marched right into the middle of the sparring field that sat dead centre in the arena, all eyes focused on her. Every single winged male who stood around them watched her. When they saw her struggle to lift the sword, a wave of laughter rose up, and she blushed so hotly that she was sure she was permanently red.

After a few hours of this, they lost interest and returned to what they had been doing. Training eventually stopped except for the eleven of them, and the arena cleared out slowly until soon it was just them.

"That's enough." Åsmund's command was abrupt, and the sword in her hands dropped almost immediately to the ground as if held suspended like a puppet, and he had just cut the strings with those two words.

Pushing off the wall, he stalked towards them with ease. Every ounce of the leader he was rolled off him in waves of confidence and a sureness in his movements that made Hazen stop and stare.

He stopped a few feet away as the males lined up beside her.

"Well done," he said, his voice travelling up into the bottleneck of the arena. "Most of you have showed great improvement, and soon will watch over your own posts as guardians of the western range. *Some* of you have a long way to go." He glanced at Hazen with a raised brow, eyeing the sword held in her limp grip.

A snicker rose from the males around her, and she gritted her jaw, giving him a tight smile. She would get strong enough to throw this at his head, and then they'd see who was laughing.

"Put your weapons away and go wash up. You're dismissed."

Easy conversation began as the males walked away, leaving Hazen alone with the general. She shifted her feet and changed the hand holding her sword.

Åsmund watched her silently before stalking towards her. It was unnerving to have something as big as him, as masculine and beautiful, stride towards you. Her stomach flipped, and she swallowed the emotions that roiled in her gut, heat flushing across her skin. She looked up at him when he stopped with a foot of space between them.

The afternoon sunlight streamed in from the bottleneck and shone like a halo around his mass of curly hair, picking up the golden strands that wove within. He was beautiful, and her dragon perked up at his nearness.

Not that her dragon and its power had aided her in the training. It seemed the dragon chose when it wanted to train and fight.

Hazen stifled her annoyance at the power living within her when it finally showed interest in the general.

Her power thrummed with intent, and fire filled her body like her dragon was showing off.

"That was the most painful thing I have ever seen. And I have seen a lot in my long lifetime."

Humiliation doused the fire, and her dragon settled. Hazen stared up at him, craning her head back. Leaning on her sword, she put her other hand on her hip.

"Well, what did you expect? The sword is nearly as long as I am," she snipped. Another exaggeration. It came to just below her hip.

He shrugged. "I didn't think they made dragons so small. Apologies." Now that everyone was gone, he looked visibly relaxed.

She let out an indignant sound. "I am not small." And she wasn't, not by human standards, anyway.

Åsmund took a single step closer to her, his presence seemed to eat up the air between them. The oxygen in her lungs caught with a quick, sharp gasp, his chest level with her line of vision, so she had a direct view of the sweat that beaded across smooth brown pectorals and trailed down the valleys between them.

His eyes lit with laughter, watching the flush, once again, heat up her face. Pursing her lips, she looked up at him.

"I am not small. You're just abnormally large." She really needed to step back. Space, that's what she needed. She needed to put space between them, but her dragon wanted the opposite. His nearness made her dragon perk up, and that fire flared hotly within her. He sent every nerve of her body tingling with anticipation.

Despite the power and whatever it was her dragon wanted from the male, Hazen forced herself to take a step back, her heart in her stomach.

Åsmund regarded her silently, leaning down to look her in the eyes. His stare was purely male as he tilted his head and his lips curved. "Size is subjective, Little Dragon."

She felt the rumble of his words roll down her spine, and Hazen had to fight to suppress the shiver that tried to escape.

Straightening, he jerked his chin beyond her shoulder. "Come on. Let me show you to your quarters."

# CHAPTER 6

"Valdren had your room readied while you were training, but if you find something lacking let me know."

Hazen stared in amazement at the expanse of sky laid before her as Åsmund spoke. The entire wall of the mountain was missing in her room, and in its place the world dominated her vision.

Clouds extended across a blue sky, rays of sunshine penetrating white tendrils, the sun somewhere overhead on the other side of the mountain.

Åsmund stood with arms crossed, leaning on the thick wooden door. She could feel his eyes on her even with her back turned to him. Her neck prickled with awareness.

Stepping up to the ledge, Hazen lifted a hand and pressed it towards the open air. Her fingers spread across an invisible barrier, pushing firmly, it held fast.

"Can't have you sleep-walking off the side of the mountain," Åsmund intoned, bemused.

Hazen scowled, turning to him.

"You can see everything, but nothing can see you," he continued. "Dragons don't belong in stone cages."

"And yet, you live in one." Glancing around the rest of the room, Hazen noted the large bed pressed against the middle of the stone wall beside the open sky. Strewn with large pillows in shades of emerald and black with a full black quilt that looked wholly inviting that Hazen knew she would bury herself into shortly. A copper chest with hammered details and stitched leather trimming lay at the foot of the bed, and a small wooden desk sat in the far right corner on the opposite side of the room.

Her eyes strayed back to the expanse of sky. "It's breathtaking," she whispered, watching a bird fly through one of the clouds; diving and twisting with exhilaration as if playing with the sunbeams.

"Indeed," he murmured in agreement behind her, and his tone felt like a caress.

A soft knock had Hazen turning to see a head of white-blonde hair and wide, sky-blue eyes poke around Åsmund's torso. The male took up the entire doorway.

A shy smile tilted the girl's pretty face, a map of freckles sprinkled across her nose. "Hello, Miss."

Hazen tilted her head, joy filling her at seeing another female. "Hello," she said with a smile.

Åsmund looked at her, eyes dropping to her smile, and she faltered momentarily.

The girl looked between them and the room. "May I come in?"

Hazen nodded, waving a nonchalant hand towards Åsmund. "Feel free to push him out of the way."

Both Åsmund and the girl's brows shot up. The girl was more in shock, whereas Åsmund just looked like he wanted to see the girl try to move him.

Chuckling, he twisted until the arch of the gold handle on her door pressed along his back, and the girl could slip by.

"I'm Rin," the girl said brightly. "I'll be your lady's maid."

Hazen's brows furrowed. "My what?"

Rin's fingers twisted in the light blue fabric of her skirt, looking uncertain. "The clan leader thought having a lady's maid would ease any burdens that might arise."

Hazen and Åsmund looked at each other simultaneously, and Hazen scoffed. "Of course he did. Burdens for whom, though? Me? Or his general?"

Rin shifted nervously. "He didn't say, Miss."

"Of course he didn't, the old bastard," she muttered darkly. Letting out a low breath, Hazen gave Rin an apologetic smile. "I'm sorry. I'm not upset with you, Rin. You didn't do anything wrong." Stepping up to the girl, she grasped her hands between them, squeezing gently. "It'll be nice to have female company after being around this brute all day."

Åsmund crossed his arms over his chest, causing his biceps to flex. "Brute?"

Hazen raised a brow at him. "I said what I said."

Rin giggled, stifling it with the back of her hand.

"Well," Åsmund said, pushing off the door. "This brute is going to wash and go eat. Rin, I assume you can look after this one from here?"

Hazen glared at him when she noted his eyes flickering towards her.

"Yes, sir," Rin said delicately, bowing her head.

Åsmund hummed in approval, waving a hand at an identical door across the hall from hers. "My chambers, if you need anything."

Before he could close the door, Hazen stepped around Rin. "Åsmund." He paused, looking at her. "Tomorrow morning—"

"—I will be outside your door at sunrise," he finished and nodded at both of them before the door clicked shut.

There was silence between the two females and Rin sighed softly, shooting a mischievous grin in Hazen's direction. "He is so handsome," she said wistfully, turning a lovely shade of red at the same time.

Chuckling, Hazen shook her head at the girl. Rin reminded her of the girls during her school days, and Hazen felt an instant kinship with the female.

"He is handsome," Hazen concurred. "Though don't tell him that lest it goes to his head." Shifting her shirt away from her torso, she grimaced, the now cold sweat and damp clothes increasingly uncomfortable.

Rin shrugged prettily, crossing her hands in front of her blue gown. It was simple but woven with soft thread. The scoop of the neckline framed her full décolletage, long sleeves where the fabric split with a poof of white fabric underneath at her elbows before fitting snuggly down to her wrists. She was young, pretty, and looked as human as Hazen was… or had been, at least.

"He is not the most handsome, though," Rin amended. "He is *almost* the most handsome. I just like to look at pretty things." A sly smile twisted on her face, and she blinked at Hazen when she shifted her weight onto a hip and waited for her to continue. "I do have a mate, or a husband, a chosen male if you call it as such."

Releasing her shirt, Hazen looked to the expanse of sky, then to the earth far, far below it, then back to Rin. *"How?"*

Rin stifled another giggle, her face lighting up. "They take us from our villages. I live within the mountain, and sometimes I ask him to fly me back so I can see my family."

She had said this as if it were completely normal, she was excited about it even. Hazen gave Rin a scrutinising look. "They *take* you?"

The girl nodded with half a shrug. "They don't steal us if that's what you're wondering. I can see your thoughts whirling around in your eyes. They're beautiful, but they give away all your secrets."

Hazen cleared her throat at Rin's assessment. "Apologies," she murmured.

Waving an idle hand, Rin wrinkled her nose for a second and whirled towards the copper chest. "No need to apologise. You don't know my customs." Undoing the leather latch, she lifted the lid and let it lean against the bed. "Every so many years, the Drago come down from their mountain in search of a female, willing, of course. They don't just take us." She reiterated her last statement while laying black clothing items out on the bed. "If they find their female, they take us away for half a fortnight, wherever they want, and from there, we are joined." A heavy blush settled along her cheeks, but Hazen doubted it was from shame or embarrassment.

"Once returned, there is a binding ceremony within the mountain for all who mated. We are then bound by the old magic, allowing us to carry on the Drago line. Sometimes it's only one, and other times it's several."

"I'll be honest, I thought I was the only female here. I'm glad I was wrong," Hazen said, massaging the back of her neck.

Rin nodded in understanding. "Not many females reside in the mountain, and some choose to remain with their families and have their males come to them."

Hazen tilted her head. "You're chosen because they need an heir?"

"Not always," Rin said, smiling wickedly. "Sometimes the company within the mountain just isn't enough to satisfy their needs."

The words took a moment to settle, and then Hazen's thoughts went spiralling down and down and down until she flushed hotly. "Does that mean all of them have..."

Did they have mass orgies? Gods, her thoughts went down the darkest hole, and she didn't know what to do with that information.

Full, deep laughter burst out of Rin when she looked up from the clothing in her hands. "Not all of them, but some. My mate has partaken, and I have accompanied him." She grabbed a white roll from the trunk, tucked it under her arm, and three clear glass vials filled with varying shades of liquid.

Hazen couldn't help the surprise on her face but quickly pushed it down. Rin was not as innocent as she looked, and Hazen's mouth twitched with a smile.

"Please don't be offended by what I am about to say, but I think it best I show you to the bathing springs."

Hazen chuckled. "No, I'm starting to smell rotten," she said, agreeing. She wrinkled her nose when she sniffed delicately under her arms.

Rin giggled. "I wasn't going to say anything."

"Next time, please do." Hazen opened her door and waved Rin to lead the way.

"Forgive me, but can your body accommodate their... size and... assets?" Hazen asked as they took a left out her door and walked down the hall.

Rin looked at her, confused. "Assets?"

"Their wings," she clarified, taking the vials from Rin's hands when she saw her rearrange them as they slipped.

The female thanked her with a small smile before her eyes narrowed in thought. "Well, the Drago are not traditionally born, from what my mate has told me. I don't quite know their origin; it's well-kept between them, and I don't pry. There hasn't been a babe born between a Drago and their mate for us to know. I've only been bonded to my mate for fifty years, so it's all quite new still. I've tried to conceive..." Rin's steps slowed, and her voice broke a little at the words. "...I really have. I would love to be a mother, but my body doesn't listen to my heart. No matter how much I beg it to."

Hazen's heart squeezed at the pain lingering behind those large blue eyes and soft round face, so much sadness and guilt, she couldn't help herself as she pulled Rin for a hug.

Rin squeaked softly but slowly lifted her arms and hugged her back.

Hazen willed strength and understanding into that hug, wishing she could take that burden from her—to tell her it was not her fault. Her mother had suffered from infertility after they had her. She had watched her mother break down time and time again and blame herself, her body, for not being able to bear another child until one day they finally stopped trying. It had taken her mother years to stop blaming herself, to stop wearing that guilt, and it had broken her to see her mother go through that.

A final squeeze and Hazen stepped back, smiling gently down at the shorter female.

Placing an understanding hand on Hazen's bicep, Rin nodded in thanks, and they continued walking.

"After the last few centuries, I think the Drago have given up on continuing the line. They mate now for companionship, a friend, and one would hope—love. To evolve into something so much more than just warriors, or that's my hope. My mate is so much more than just a warrior once you see who he is below the sword, and scars, and brutality. He is a kind male, full of so much wonder for this world. And I love him very much."

Rin's declaration for her mate made Hazen's thoughts wander to Åsmund and what he had done just this morning... what he had threatened to do to Kain. Hazen's blood boiled at the thought of Kain's cruel smile and the cold intent on his face.

Forcing down the power thrumming in her veins, she asked softly, "Not all of them hold the same honour as your mate, do they?"

Rin shook her head sadly, bitterness clouding her pretty face. "No, not all of them, unfortunately. There are some who would hurt a female to get whatever they want. They think they are deserving of whatever they set their eyes upon."

Hazen's lip curled in revulsion. No matter what world you stood in, some things didn't change. The glass vials squeaked in her hands when her fingers tightened around their necks and threatened to shatter.

"My mate told me what Åsmund had done."

The hall curved, and the smell of sulphur made Hazen's nose wrinkle, but Rin's words made her glance at the female. The whole mountain had heard of her arrival.

"Kain is not a kind male, Miss." Rin stopped, adjusting the rolled cloth in her hand. She looked up at Hazen with steely blue eyes, her petite mouth pressed firm. "Åsmund was right to step in. He is a good general and a good male, and he does not make idle threats." She laid her hand on Hazen's, her tone low, saying, "Keep eyes on your back if he's around. Åsmund won't let him near you if you're with him, but when alone, always be aware of where you are. There are not many places one can hide within the mountain."

Trepidation rolled down her spine, sinking like a stone in Hazen's stomach. She clenched her jaw until her teeth groaned. Anger roiled low and steady in her blood, but she locked it away in the back of her mind until later, walking through the curve of a stone archway on her left.

Hot, humid air immediately coated her exposed skin, and Hazen almost moaned at the heat enveloping her. It was bliss—pure, utter bliss.

Orbs of fire lit flickering orange tendrils of light along the black glassy walls and towering ceiling high above her head. Rin led the way through the wide curved hall until it opened, and a large hot spring lay spread out before her.

Steam rolled across the top of the water, inviting and curling in the air. Stone benches were carved from obsidian, and the hot spring curved around the wall and disappeared further into the mountain like a cave system. The main pool before them was so large it took up nearly the entire floor, leaving roughly ten feet of space to walk along the ledge or sit on one of the benches. Hazen wanted to strip and dive right in.

Rin set the rolled linen on the bench closest to her and clapped her hands together, facing Hazen. "I'll let you wash, Miss, unless you need my assistance or want my company?"

Hazen huffed out a laugh and shook her head. "No, I think I'll manage. Some privacy would be nice."

Nodding once, Rin folded her hands into the fabric of her skirt. "Do you think you know the way back to your chambers?"

"Yes, Rin, thank you."

Rin lifted a finger, her face twisting in thought. "There's something I'm forgetting, but I'm afraid I can't seem to remember it… if you need to relieve yourself, you'll find a chamber through that doorway… there's something else I'm forgetting…" Rin's voice trailed off, and she pressed her mouth tightly in thought. Finally, she shrugged her shoulders. "Oh well, it mustn't be important if I can't remember it."

"Thank you, Rin," Hazen said with a small laugh.

The female bowed her head softly. "Take your time, Miss. I'll be just down the hall." And then she was gone. Spinning on her heels and disappearing in a whirl of blue skirts and white-blonde hair.

Hazen stared after her for a moment, brows raised and mouth quirked. She made a mental note to tell Rin to call her by her given name.

Rolling her head back, she sighed deeply through her nose and turned to look longingly at the hot springs that lay quiet, begging her to sink into the dark waters. There could be a monster hiding within, waiting to devour her, but she couldn't give two shits. Let the monster eat her if it meant even two minutes of bliss.

Shifting on her feet and setting the glass vials beside the water,

Hazen walked towards the doorway Rin had pointed to and peeked her head in. A normal-sized wooden door and gold handle greeted her. Pulling it open slowly, she looked inside. Her eyebrows shot up. It was a lavatory—an archaic one, but one nonetheless. Sheets of paper-thin linen lay beside it, and a stone bench held a single hole cut in its centre.

Seeing a semi-normal-looking loo gave Hazen the same effect as seeing the hot springs. She quickly did her business, savouring that she didn't have to go in the woods, hide behind trees and rocks any longer, or use leaves to clean up.

After she was done, Hazen, feeling more like herself than she had in a long while, stripped and folded her dirty clothes beside the rolled linen on the bench.

Standing naked on the ledge of the hot springs, she dipped her big toe in and nearly melted, quickly crouching, she slipped beneath the water, and moaned in happiness.

Dipping her head back until her hair clouded around her in strands of gold, she ran her hands along the sides of her face and over her hair, slicking it back. Closing her eyes, Hazen felt her muscles relax and ease in the hot water, kneading the flesh with her fingers.

If the monster in the water wanted her, it would have to be now before she melted into nothingness. Hazen moaned again, low and content in the back of her throat, eyes still closed. This was the first time since she got here that she had a chance to bathe, or long enough to wash the day's, week's, month's grime from her skin.

Eyes opening, she glanced at the vials and picked one up, eyeing the amber liquid sloshing the sides. Undoing the glass stopper, she tipped a bit into her palms. Setting the vial aside, she ran her hands together, feeling its consistency. The slippery contents began to froth in her fingers, and she didn't know if it was soap or their version of shampoo, but she chose to scrub her hair with it.

A contented sigh slipped past her lips as she washed her hair. Tilting her head back into the water to rinse. Repeating the process with another vial of thicker liquid, using it to condition her hair and the third that frothed in her fingers to run along her skin.

There was something therapeutic about finally being able to

wash her hair, wash herself, and *bathe*. It was like taking power back. She could finally face the day without the past still lingering on her skin, holding her to the deaths and grime of the past month.

The aches in her body from training eased, and the tension she had been carrying slowly dissipated.

Leaning her head on the obsidian ledge, Hazen let her body float comfortably in the water, closing her eyes.

But that bliss was short-lived when the water moved to her left. Eyes flying open, she whirled, her heart racing as her power thrummed violently. She barely noticed the orbs of fire flickering around her.

She was only kidding about the monster in the water. She didn't want to have to fight for her life, not right now. She didn't want to ruin her bath.

But it wasn't a monster. It was a male.

Green eyes stared at her from the shadows as Åsmund came around the bend in the cave and stood slowly from the water like the monster she thought would come for her. Her power banked seeing him, just slightly, but stayed within reach and funnelled through her veins like blood.

He stood waist-deep in the springs, water dripped down the expanse of muscle, through the grooves of his pectorals and down the terrain of his abs. His wings nearly blended with the shadows except for the firelight that glowed along the thin black membrane.

Hazen's eyes trailed along the wall of his chest, following a drop of water that ran from his neck down and down and down. Her eyes snapped back to his when the droplet disappeared into the water at the V of his hips.

The green of his eyes seemed to glow with fire, and the gold hoop through his nose glimmered when it caught the light. His caramel-brown skin looked like gold and the earth had come together to create the male before her. His long, curly hair hung wet around his broad shoulders.

He looked like a God. Or at least the creation of one.

Her body ignited with awareness, nostrils flaring, her hands became fists at her sides beneath the water. Rin's words floated back to her about Kain, but then she had said Åsmund was a good male, but here he was, in her bath.

A flush ran up her neck, and her face flamed.

Åsmund's eyes flickered with a glimmer of surprise when he saw her, but it was quickly masked, and his eyes, unlike hers, didn't stray from her face.

"Why are…" Her words failed, and she tried again, her mouth dryer than before. "Why are you in…" Was it her bath? Could she claim it?

Åsmund's mouth twitched in a faint, crooked smile, and he tilted his head, eyes still trained on her.

Hazen's breasts peaked when the warm, humid air grazed her skin, and she looked down. She had stood when he arrived, ready to fight a monster, and the water now pooled around her stomach. The rest of her upper body was completely exposed to him, her breasts on display. A blush burst across her whole body, and she quickly sunk beneath the hot water with a startled gasp.

His eyes locked on hers; they never strayed, and she couldn't breathe under the intensity.

"It's communal," he said, finally. His words were low, but they filled the cave regardless and pressed around her.

*"There's something else I'm forgetting."*

This is what Rin had forgotten to tell her. The hot springs were communal, and Åsmund wasn't invading her bath, and she wasn't invading his. They were *sharing* it. That thought alone made her heart drum along her ribs.

Hazen jerked her head in understanding. "I see," her voice breathless. It was all she could say, wrapping an arm around her chest, despite knowing she was hidden beneath the nearly black water.

Åsmund didn't move. He just watched her.

Swallowing, Hazen took in a low breath, feeling paralysed under his stare, her heart raced uncontrollably. There was power in his stare, the same power she felt racing through her blood, and they collided when they looked at each other.

"I'll leave," he said, breaking the silence.

He made to turn, and she stood quickly. "Wait, no." With a glance down, she let out an annoyed huff and quickly covered her breasts with an arm. A brow arched at her, and she promptly said, "I'm done. You can stay."

She wasn't done. She wanted to melt into the water and never leave. It was heaven. But she didn't want to push him out either, and she certainly didn't want to bathe with him.

Her dragon seemed to hear that thought and rumbled as if calling her out on the lie.

She ignored the annoyed dragon that pressed along her bones.

Åsmund's brow quirked again, and he gave her a wry smile, watching her eyes dart between him, the water, and her towel that lay very much out of reach.

A soft groan of exasperation welled in her throat and Hazen pursed her lips, making a circle in the air at him with her finger. "Can you turn around?"

Hazen could swear she saw him suppress a bit of laughter before he turned and gave her his back. She stared at the scars and expanse of muscle that lay between those large wings—wings that grew from flesh and melded with his skin, leaving no beginning and no end.

Using her arms as leverage, she pulled herself quickly out of the hot springs. Regret at leaving the hot water filling her, she pushed it aside, rushing to reach the roll of linen.

It wasn't a thick towel, but it would do. Hazen wrapped it around her body and tucked it tightly over her breasts. The thin fabric moulded her shape and turned partially transparent from the water.

She grabbed her clothes, held them tight to her chest, and left the vials beside the water. "Thank you," she murmured, eyeing his back.

Her words echoed back softly, and he inclined his head, his hair curling over where his wings and back were joined.

"I'll see you in the morning, Little Dragon."

The rumbling promise was as warm as the air surrounding them, and she jerked her head, nodding despite knowing he couldn't see it. She quickly walked out of the cave, her heart thudding madly.

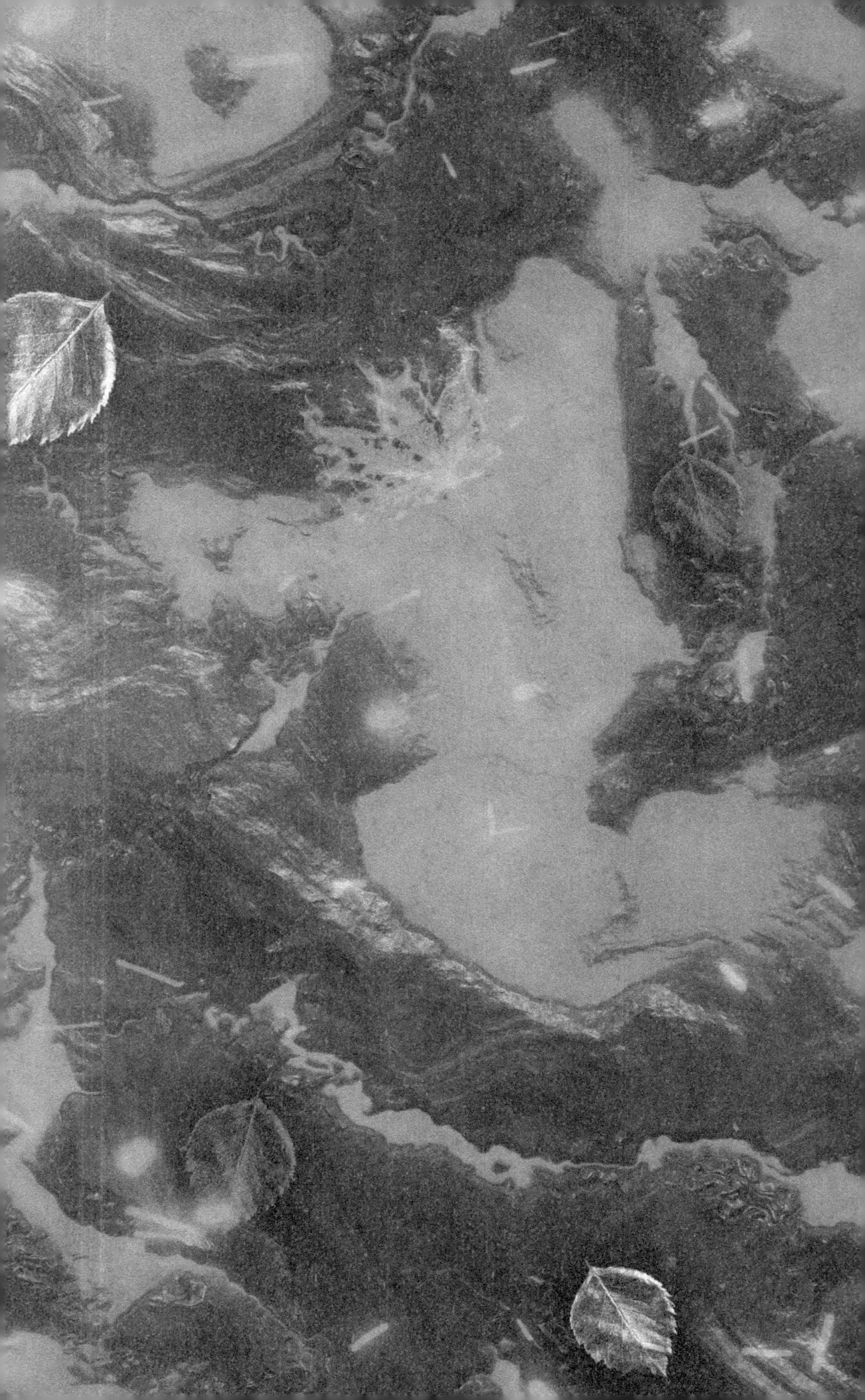

# CHAPTER 7

Brean laid a hand on the trunk to her left, amber eyes flicking up the massive tree. The Black Forest stretched before and behind them, and she knew Álfheimr lay hidden, just within reach of the dying forest.

Despite its name, the Black Forest was once lush and brimming with life. But now, as she looked at the brittle black bark crumbling under her fingers, she could feel the forest's lack of energy. It paled like its life was slowly ebbing away. The leaves on every branch were greying, and falling softly before disintegrating when they touched the ground as though their fall took too much from them to hold themselves together any longer.

The world around them was bleak and dying, and when Brean dropped her hand and looked at the prince, her mouth pressed with sympathy. Savven was looking at the forest like it was a foreign entity. Dark blue eyes wide and assessing, jaw flexing tightly as she watched emotions flicker across his face one after the other. For the first time since she threatened to turn him into a toad because of his smug smile, he looked like a child staring at his desolate home, and she knew that feeling all too well.

"It's changed," Brean said softly, eyes wandering over the graveyard of trees.

"It's my father," Savven corrected tonelessly.

Brean caught Néefar's eye, and the shifter raised a dark brow at her, his silver hair glinting in the grey light like a beacon. She shook her head inconspicuously, and Néefar turned away. Even she, who was sheltered and raised by the High Fae, knew little about their royal ties to the magic that seeped into their land. Brean knew that the Fae royalty, once crowned, are tied to the magic that flows in their lands, but if their lands were dying, then would that mean…

The wind shifted, and the forest, while already silent, seemed to still like an animal approaching its prey.

Savven took a single step forward, eyes scanning the spread of trees.

They were being watched.

Brean's stomach twisted. They were close to the walls of Álfheimr, and the Fae magic, despite waning, was still strong enough to camouflage it.

From the corner of her eye, Brean watched a dagger slip into Néefar's hand, and she turned a brief arched brow at him. His smirk was answer enough, she looked away with a roll of her eyes.

Savven went preternaturally still; Brean didn't think he was even breathing. The soft whisper of leaves disintegrating underfoot filled the silence of the forest as two Fae males appeared from beyond the magic that veiled the city of elves.

Dressed in all black, their fitted long-sleeved tunics were adorned with the gold, crossed sword and branch crest on their left shoulders. Two short swords were strapped to their left and right thighs for close combat.

"Is that you, Your Royal Highness?" one of them asked. His leaf-green eyes lit with caution and—Brean dared assume—hope.

His dark blond hair was cropped close to his head, and his hand casually rested on the hilt of the weapon to his right.

Brean's eyes darted between him and the prince. Savven's jaw flexed, she could see the tension in his body rising.

The male next to the blond, with warm brown skin and shoulder-length dark brown hair, half of it pulled away from his face, looked at Brean and Néefar with a firm, assessing silver gaze.

She didn't dare move, and she willed Néefar not to either, praying he kept his mouth shut for once in his life. She might have been raised within the protective walls of Álfheimr, but that did not make her Fae, and these males were trained to protect their walls.

"It has been many seasons since you've returned," the one with silver eyes commented.

Savven looked at their faces, his fingers twitching at his sides. Brean could see the conflict raging behind his mask and wondered if the elf prince would turn on his heels and decide coming home wasn't worth whatever it was he had to face.

Though Savven didn't flee, his demeanour changed from the reserved traveller she had met to one that could only be described as princely. His hands relaxed, and his already straight posture seemed to heighten as his chin inclined just a hair.

"Yes, Éamon, it has been some time," Savven replied to the male with silver eyes, his tone calm and calculated. He swept his gaze over the two males and then went beyond them. "What has happened to my father?"

Brean watched as Éamon and the other male exchanged glances, a silent conversation passing between them. Brief and fleeting as it was, they shared a look of hesitation.

Finally, they looked at Savven, and Éamon let out a low sigh. "It's not good, Your Highness."

Determination pulled at Savven's mouth, and he nodded once. "Take me to him."

Éamon and the other guard finally looked at Brean and Néefar, trying to decide if they would come too.

Savven made the decision for them, his voice tight and gruff, and Brean watched his throat bob as he swallowed down his emotions she saw flicker to life in his eyes. "Where I go, they go."

Hesitating, they nodded, and Éamon and the other guard turned on the heels of their black boots and began walking into the dying forest. They vanished in a blink, magic concealing them, but as Brean, Savven, and Néefar followed them across the divide, they reappeared, and the towering fortress wall of Álfheimr came into view.

The wall was as tall as the trees around them, made of thick timbers all woven together and stretching as far as the eye could see on either end. There were no gaps or cracks in their fortress, but the roots of the wall, grounded deep into the earth, were greying, the cancer spreading from the base and nearly reaching the middle.

Surprisingly, it hadn't cracked from the weight settling on the decaying foundation.

A silver cross-woven gate was raised halfway, and when Brean stopped in front of it and looked up, she found a dozen sets of eyes on either side of the gate along the wall, all trained on them. Bows held securely in each of their hands and a full quiver of arrows strapped to their sides.

The guardians of the wall were reserved and wary as they passed under the silver spikes of the gate, their skin pale in the sallow light. These were not the vibrant and robust Fae she had known as a youth. Brean's gut wrenched at the sight.

The other guard with Éamon fell away and took up a post alongside the gate while Éamon led the way into Álfheimr, Savven behind him and Brean and Néefar three steps behind the prince.

Néefar finally tucked the dagger into his waistband, and Brean refrained from rolling her eyes. However, she couldn't contain the soft gasp when she finally saw the city of elves.

It lay in crumbling desolation.

The ground shuddered, and Brean turned just in time to see the gate close and their way out sealed shut.

Her amber eyes fixed on the ashen world beyond the gate, and her lips pressed tightly as sadness twisted around her bones until her fingers furled in on themselves. The world was changing before her very eyes, and when the gate closed it felt like one door shutting and another... she didn't know if it would open.

"Brean," Savven said shortly.

She looked away slowly and finally met his gaze. They were all watching her. Understanding flickered briefly in his dark blue eyes, and he nodded his head once, just barely enough for her to perceive and turned around to follow Éamon.

"Are you okay?" Néefar asked softly, falling into step with her.

One of the massive trees lay toppled over on its side, a chunk of its side blown out where rot had consumed it. Brean could see the window cutouts and the now-destroyed room within. This tree had been a home to someone, and now it was in ruins.

"No," she said finally, tearing her eyes away from the tree. "I'm not okay."

Álfheimr looked like it was eating itself from within. A grey rot crawled up the roots of monstrously tall trees. Some were just the base, others coated entire sides, and thick cracks ran up to the semi-bare branches.

The plank bridges overhead connecting tree to tree creaked softly. Homes that were built within the colossal trunks or wrapped around their towering leafy peaks in the sky now lay abandoned for fear of collapsing.

Small dome homes made with wood, stone, and mud now scattered through the once great city between shops, leather tents, and lean-tos made of rocks and slabs of wood.

As they walked the black dirt road, males and females came to stand along either side. When Savven passed, their eyes widened, and hope slowly began to creep onto the beautifully haggard faces that seemed to be falling apart alongside their home.

There was still beauty and pride in the tiredness and misery, and the elves of Álfheimr bowed their heads when their prince finally came home to them.

The road curved and cut through the entire city, no matter how long they walked, the road was lined with the Fae, watching, bowing, waiting. And when Brean glanced back, just once, hundreds of eyes were trained on them. Strength lay within those numbers, in the set faces and straight backs of Álfheimr›s denizens.

Finally, the palace came into view, and Brean's heart dropped to the bottom of her stomach.

The four hulking Banyan trees that crowned the four corners of the white marble palace lay in fractured pieces. Where thick roots protruded from the earth and marble intertwined to merge stone and earth, chunks lay in its place. Limbs of the Banyan trees were fallen and shattered into pieces, and parts of the palace lay exposed with holes in the wall where they broke from the grey rot that coated more than half of the marble.

The rot was spreading from the palace to the rest of the city, and Brean's nostrils flared with anguish. She quickly glanced at Savven, realising that he had stopped completely. She briefly saw his hands fist and relax when Éamon turned guilt-ridden eyes to his prince.

"I'm sorry this is what you have returned to, Your Highness," Éamon said as if it were his fault that Savven's city was decaying around him.

Savven gave a barely perceivable shake of his head, murmuring, "Do not apologise, Éamon. This is no fault of yours."

Éamon nodded. "Shall we continue?"

"Yes." Savven's tone was low, but the single word sounded like he was going to face the gallows.

Brean assumed facing the gallows would have been easier than seeing the inside of the once magnificent palace he'd grown up in. Roots webbed along the walls and arching ceilings above, holding together the broken pieces of marble. The earth had overgrown the white marble walls as if coming to its aid and trying to save what was once the lustrous palace of the High Fae, breaking through the floors and intruding through the tall arching windows.

They stepped carefully over the thick limbs, and Brean looked at Néefar, who caught her eye with a raised brow. She just shook her head in dismay.

Finally, they came to large wooden doors, or half of what used to be wooden doors, for only the lower half remained. Sharp shards of wood stood where the upper half had been, jutting into the air like spikes of warning for what they were about to see.

Éamon turned, his open hand hovering over what was left of the door still towering over them in half its glory. His face was grim, his lips pressed into a firm line. "Be warned, his majesty is not all he used to be."

"Open the doors, Éamon," Savven commanded softly.

A deathly calm washed over the prince and filled the air, and Brean swallowed the trepidation boiling in her blood when Éamon pressed both his hands on the doors and pushed.

Wood groaned, and small particles splintered under the movement, like it was too much for them to handle. But they opened, scraping over the tops of low-lying stems until they stuck on a large protruding root, the gap in the doors just wide enough for them to pass.

The great hall was no longer the thriving, living thing of beauty where the Fae could gather, or the royal family could hold council. The Banyan trees that acted as pillars, their branches once tangled together with mossy vines hanging from the towering ceilings, were dead or dying. Grey rot clung to their bark, and the flowers that flourished were now just blackened remnants scattered over the root-covered floor.

Every inch of the hall was embedded in a web of stems and roots and tree branches. The ghost of moss and vines fluttered in a stale wind that whistled a melancholy tune through the long windows cut into the gleaming stone.

Brean's heart broke for Savven and shattered altogether when her amber eyes flickered up the cracked dais.

A lone king sat in one of the marble thrones, the other empty and filled with flowers that had long since died. The roots had crawled up the thrones and consumed everything that sat within. Skin grey like the rot that grew throughout Álfheimr with small stems of wood curling up and around his face, neck, chest, and limbs until he was more a part of the decaying palace than he was Fae. The only sign of colour since they arrived was the last hint of orange in the King's once fiery hair, now only a dying ember in the fire that was being suffocated.

The three stopped before the thrones, Éamon falling back so Savven could witness what had become of his father.

Brean and Néefar knew the loss of their parents, the brutality of having them ripped from them by the force of evil within people. But they didn't know this. Savven knew what it was like to lose his mother to murder, but to lose your father to grief and be witness to his decay was a pain that Brean knew she would never understand.

Wood cracked, and the King's eyes shot open.

Her heart lurched when they went directly to the male in front of her, to his son.

Savven didn't move, and Brean doubted he was breathing when a low, rasping laugh echoed in the overgrown hall. It sounded like the King hadn't used his voice in a very long time.

The King's eyes were pale green, like life was still clinging to his soul but slowly losing its grip. There was no emotion in his stare. It was empty, a void where grief had consumed him.

"The prince has returned," the King said in a guttural voice that was almost painful to hear. His vocal cords constricted around each word. But despite that, the King continued, "Do you see what you've done? Do you see what her death has done to your people? Do you see what the blood on your hands has done?!"

Savven didn't so much as twitch.

Brean's brows furrowed in confusion, the King's voice raising with each word he said.

"This is all because of you, Savven. Do you see what death becomes of your actions?" Another scraping laugh, this one cold and hollow.

Something brushed the hem of Brean's tattered skirts, and she looked down, grimacing with shock when a small branch crawled over the toe of her brown boots.

"Do you see what you've done!" the King finally screamed.

His tone jarred Brean, and ice went down her spine.

The slithering branch curled around Savven's ankle, and he forcibly kicked it off with a snarl. Turning on booted heels, the prince of the elves stormed out of the great hall, his father's cold laughter following him.

Stale cool air hit his face, and Savven took in a sucking breath, his body vibrating with the anger he held on a short leash. Running a trembling hand through his hair, he pinched his eyes shut, willing himself to calm down.

"Savven!" Brean called after him.

He had heard her follow when he stormed out of the great hall, his father's decaying voice and withered cackles seeming to follow at his back even when he removed himself from the palace—or what was left of it.

He could hear her boots on the black earth as she crawled out of the desolate ruins of what was once his home. He brought his fingers to the bridge of his nose and pinched it firmly, trying to ease the growing tension while forcing another breath.

Beneath the anger and the rage was guilt. Cold, numbing, all-consuming guilt. And when Savven pulled his hands away from his face and opened his eyes, he swore he could see the shockingly bright red stain of blood on his fingers.

Swearing under his breath, Savven staggered back with a sharp inhale and closed his eyes again, his chest heaving, heart beating against his ribs. The faster his heart raced, the quicker his breaths came, and the blood... red washed over his vision, and all he could see was his mother's face and her life seeping out of her chest where the arrow had made its mark.

The world was darkening around the edges of his vision. Black, red, black, red. That's all he could see. His chest squeezed painfully. He had come home after all this time. He had done it to himself.

"Savven," Brean's voice whispered cautiously behind him.

Her gentle hand and lithe fingers laid on his heaving back.

"Breathe, Savven," she murmured, rubbing slow circles.

Black... red... darkness... blood... his mother's blood. His vision narrowed. He wasn't breathing anymore. He couldn't make his chest work.

Brean made a soft hushing sound when something let out a distressed noise. Was it he who had made it? He couldn't tell; the world had tilted on its side, and he felt out of control. Spiralling down and down and down.

*"Do you see what the blood on your hands has done?!"*

His father's words were a consistent, demanding ring in his head. Over and over again without end.

Amber invaded the enclosing darkness. Bright, beautiful amber eyes blinked up at him, cutting through the blood and blackness. A face full of freckles like scattered constellations and kindness sketched upon a beautiful petite face that had shown him nothing but honesty, stubbornness, and perseverance. Brean was speaking to him, but he couldn't hear her. His typically high hearing had gone deaf.

She reached up and cupped his cheeks in both her hands. Her skin was soft and warm, and he leaned his face into her palm, keeping his eyes fixated on the amber invading his darkness—to the light guiding him out of the abyss.

Her lips moved again, and he fixated on her small, full mouth.

"Savven," her voice whispered against his ears, filling the space between them. "Savven, breathe for me."

His lungs filled with air as if on command, and he took in a long drag. The panic in his body receded.

He didn't know how long they stood there, but when the darkness was gone, and his hands and vision were no longer stained red with his mother's blood, his limbs relaxed, and he leaned into her touch. Closing his eyes, feeling his world shift carefully back into place, he nudged all the emotions of being home into a small box. He tucked it far, far, away into the furthest recesses of his mind.

When he opened his eyes again, Brean's mouth was quirked into a slight smile.

"Better?" she asked, her voice still low and speaking so only he could hear her.

Grabbing her slim wrists, he turned his face and watched her as he slowly pressed a kiss to each of her palms.

Eyes going wide, a bright blush spread across her cheeks, neck, and down to her breasts, and he found himself admiring the wash of colour across her freckled face.

Clearing her throat, Brean stepped back just slightly, dropping her hands. "I guess that means you're better," she said, albeit breathless.

"For now," he amended.

His head tilted, gaze roving over the slight witch, admiring her despite the ragged wear of her purple dress and brown corset. He hadn't taken the time since the ship to really look at her, but he was looking now. He would garner that amber eyes and wild fiery hair would soon be what he looked to, to guide him out of the darkness while he was home.

"What was that?" Néefar asked, coming up behind him.

Savven took his eyes off the blushing witch and cocked a brow at the shifter. "You mean, why was my father blaming the destruction of our city on me?"

Néefar gave him a dry expression. "If you want to be technical."

The bitter laugh that escaped Savven was unstoppable. "Because I got my mother killed. She's dead because of me. And my father spiralled and spiralled every day henceforth and would never let me forget it. So, I left my home to escape the blood on my hands and the reminder that I killed my mother. And now my city suffers because my father suffers the loss of his mate because of his son."

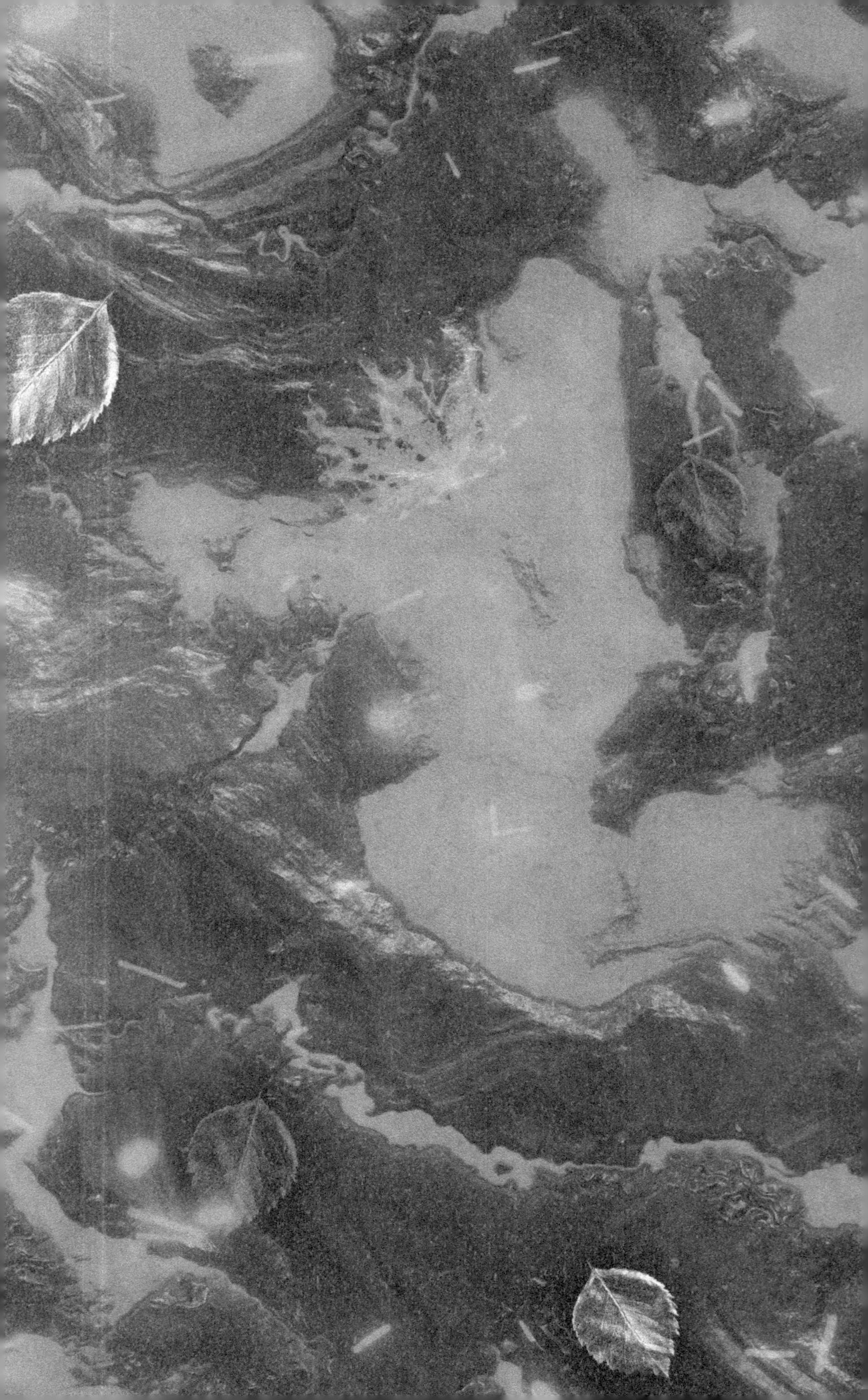

# CHAPTER 8

Thunder rolled overhead in a rainless dawn sky, black clouds formed with the promise of a deluge. Savven stood in the deteriorating arch of the balcony attached to his room. Blue eyes scanned the sky and then the forest. The wind was stale, crackling with rising pressure from the storm, or maybe it was the pressure within he was feeling. The building tightness in his chest when his eyes slipped to the crumpling palace within the city centre encased in roots and snarls and chunks of marble.

Éamon had taken them to one of the few still safely standing tree lodgings. It was on the outskirts of the city, closer to the western border. The rot hadn't gotten a chance to spread fully yet, but that didn't mean the tree was without damage.

Cracks tattooed the hollowed-out trunk. Last night, he lay in the narrow bed he was sure belonged to a child and traced his fingers along the edges of the breaks, wondering how long it would be before this tree fell along with the others.

The room was sparse. A thick, deep-seated chair carved from the same wood inside the tree—the trunk and the back of the chair created a solid piece. Brightly coloured cushions decorated it as through the previous occupants wanted to bring some sort of life back into the crumbling city. The small bed was pushed against the wall with a thick, bright orange and fuchsia wool quilt. But past that, there wasn't anything else.

Savven didn't dare sit in the chair; he could see a soft greying to the long base. The clothes Éamon had brought him lay across the arm—the army blacks, the gold crest had been mocking him since the night before. He had rolled onto his side, facing the wall to ignore it.

Rumbling thunder pulled him from his thoughts, and he sighed deeply when the stale wind caressed his face.

Turning from the sky, he fixed the neck of his uniform and tucked a stray piece of his hair behind his ear. His straight black hair was pulled neatly back into a half knot on top of his head, the rest of it lay straight down his back, sections of it braided away from his face.

The solid ground felt good beneath his toes when he stepped out of the spiralling stairwell and into the open air. And when he slowly scanned the decaying city of his people, it made something ache deep within him. Gritting his teeth, he made to walk towards the training field when amber eyes filled his vision. He stepped back when Brean popped up in front of him, dressed in the same army blacks as he was, her red hair half tied away from her face, with long soft curls framing her cheeks.

"You look rested," she said with a bemused smile.

"Do I?" he asked with a lift of his eyebrows. He felt entirely the opposite.

She shrugged. "As rested as one could be after seeing their home falling apart."

Savven momentarily allowed his gaze to wander down her body before he met her eyes again. "You look good in our uniform."

A pink blush stained her cheeks, her eyes widening before she busied herself, clearing her throat and giving him a small cheeky smile. "I look fabulous in anything, Prince," she paused, letting her gaze wander down him, "but so do you."

He tilted his head a fraction, a curious smile playing around his lips. "I like when you call me that."

Her mouth twisted, staring up at him through her lashes. "Call you what?"

"Prince."

His murmured words made Brean's cheeks turn scarlet.

"I like when you say it... it sounds... right," he intoned in a low voice, confusion flickering in his dark blue eyes briefly.

Seconds passed between them in silence, watching each other before Brean cleared her throat. "Food?"

He looked at the bread in her hands she offered up to him and shook his head slowly. "No, I find myself without an appetite this morning."

Brean looked down at the bread, frowning as she studied it. "It's all they have. They have meat when they can get it, but animals are scarce since the rot began to spread. Even the fruit trees have been affected. The fruit they bear grows rotten before it ripens." She sighed and offered the bread again. "I feel for them. It's all they have right now. You would do them a disservice if you rejected their food."

Savven's jaw flexed as he stared down at the bread. A glaring reality of his city's situation. So, he took it, his fingers brushing against her wrist softly, and slowly broke off a piece. It was soft and mildly sweet. "You're right. Thank you."

"I know," she said with a half-shrug, giving him a crooked smile. "Come on, they're waiting for you. Néefar is already there and growing restless."

They began walking, and he looked down at her with a raised brow. "Who is waiting for me? Surely, Néefar hasn't made friends."

"You'll see."

The sky overhead cast a grey shadow over the training grounds, black dirt well-trodden from years of seeing to the sparing and training of their soldiers. The training grounds were a massive open field with an archery range on one side consisting of lines of dummy enemies made from sacks stuffed with dirt and straw, and small square straw bricks with painted targets. Centre field was just a long stretch of dirt meant for hand-to-hand combat and sword training, and to the right of that was for strategy. An obstacle course spread out like a maze with traps, towering walls, and components all looking to make its user fail. Three weapons posts framed the beginning of the training field.

That was where he saw Néefar perched against the one in the middle, muscled arms crossed against his chest, olive-toned face looking impressively bored.

But it wasn't the training field or Néefar that gave Savven pause. It was the rows and rows of soldiers, both male and female, that lined the grounds on either side. They filled the training arena and the spaces beyond with bows in the hands of some, while others had swords strapped to their sides. All were dressed in the black uniforms and gold crests of Álfheimr's army.

Savven's nostrils flared when all eyes slowly turned to him. They stayed tight in formation, but their eyes fell on their crown prince one by one.

"What is this?" he asked, slowly walking through the open space between soldiers, glancing at Néefar.

Néefar was dressed like the rest of them in an all-black uniform. Swords lined a wooden bracket behind him, and the shifter turned cool blue eyes at him. He jerked his chin towards the formation.

Éamon stepped out of the ranks, the short swords still strapped to his sides for close combat, but now a bow was slung over his back, a quiver at his side. "Your army, Your Royal Highness."

He spoke loud enough for his voice to travel, and Savven's eyes darted from Éamon to the rest of his people.

"This is my father's army, your king," Savven corrected, but there was no judgment in his tone. When he looked at his people, he saw the rot consuming them. The death they were all slowly fighting. His people were thin, sallow versions of their once mighty selves, which cracked the thing inside him even more.

It was his heart. It was breaking for his home the longer he stood there witnessing its destruction. Whether by his hand or his father's, he could no longer tell.

Éamon's grey eyes didn't falter, and his face set into a look that Savven could only describe as steel. He was a soldier. He had no fear, even in the face of his prince, and the price of treason his words could hold.

"We love our home. We love our king, and we loved our queen."

Savven did his best to hide the flinch at the mention of his mother. A slight pressure applied lightly to his left hand, and he glanced down to find Brean at his side, her hand softly brushing his. She didn't grab it but shifted enough that they touched so he could feel her there. She was standing with him, he stared at her profile for a long moment before returning his attention to Éamon.

"But that love is destroying us. It is destroying the foundation of our people. What was once the great city of the elves is now merely a graveyard. But you have returned to us, the crown prince, and we will follow you. We will fight for you—"

Savven held up a single hand, though not the hand touching Brean's, and silenced Éamon's speech. "My father is still your king; I cannot overstep his reign. The laws of the Fae will not allow it. The magic tying him to our city is only broken by death, treason foreseeable by the Gods, or the current ruler stepping down. My father is consumed by the loss of your queen, his mate. His grief has blinded him, and I fear I only make it worse as it was—" his voice faltered, and he tried again, words failing him. Darkness slowly closed in around his vision, his heart rate started to falter as it quickened, his mother's gasp as the arrow pierced her heart, filling his ears.

A hand slowly slipped into his. Warm, long, thin fingers curling around him, letting him know he wasn't alone. A light squeeze had Savven looking down, and Brean's reassuring nod had him straightening and steeling himself against the memories wishing to devour him.

His people, his kin, were watching him when he turned away from the witch. Savven slid his gaze from face to face, all reserved and tired, but there was hope behind their eyes, which shined brighter with every face he looked at.

Savven could feel the darkness spreading across his lands, the emptiness in the air, and the death waiting in the shadows. He could see it in the faces of his people. He could taste the guilt on his tongue for abandoning them. So, he compressed the memories, grief, and emotions until they were tightly wound into a small glimmering ball of darkness. When his eyes returned to Éamon, that small onyx ball was shoved into an iron box within him and sealed tightly away.

He released Brean's hand and stepped forward, facing his people. "As I come before you, I am not a king, I am not a prince, I am only your kin. I stand before you as one of your own, an elf of Álfheimr. No more, no less. This rot spreads and turns our world sickly, cracking wood and crumbling stone; it destroys the very foundations we have built upon." Savven looked from face to face, seeing their hope flare with every word spoken. "But I say this now: it will not destroy us. The King can stay within his crumpling palace, but we will fight for Álfheimr, and if it perishes, then we will fight for the future we can bring!"

A solidary cry rose once, then twice, then thrice, every soldier striking his or her fist against their heart.

"I say again: I am not your prince as I stand here before you; you do not address me as such. I am Savven of the High Fae of Álfheimr. I am your kin, your blood, your brother. We are equals. We will train as equals and fight—or die trying—as equals."

Another cry followed his words, and another, and another until Savven joined them. They filled the forest and shook the rotting earth.

# CHAPTER 9

Darkness slipped and slithered across her bedroom floor, the moon glowing through the large opening in the wall. She was awake in her bed within the mountain, but her body couldn't move. It wouldn't move, no matter how hard Hazen fought. Her arms and legs were lead, and even her mouth refused to open despite the fear trying to bubble out of her throat.

Tendrils and shadows crawled up her bed, licking over her feet before crawling up her bare legs. She could feel them digging into her skin, the pain shooting to her bones, and she let out a muffled cry when they tore into her.

Eyes straining, she tried to look down her body but couldn't see past the shadows covering her torso. Hazen could feel the hot trail of her blood from every tear in her skin and could feel the wet pool around her legs. She could feel them pulling back her skin slowly, divulging into her body and looking for a place to burrow into her, to consume her.

She was back in the Abyss beneath the sea. Darkness and the demons within tormented her, destroying her.

Claws ripped into her abdomen, and a silent scream tore from her throat, her mouth jerking open. The pain was enough to make her power blaze to life, and her eyes flare with the rush; the restraints on her limbs broke, and then she was moving. Grasping at the darkness in both hands, she tore their claws from her, visibly curved talons retreating into the shadows, and with a savage snarl, Hazen ripped it apart.

Hazen's eyes flew open, and she sat upright in bed, sweat dotting her brow. Chest heaving, she looked around, the soft light of sunrise was filtering into her chambers. The black silken quilt was tangled around her naked body like she had been fighting it, emerald pillows tossed on the obsidian floor.

Running a hand over her face, she combed her fingers through her hair and took in a sucking breath. She could still feel the power rushing through her limbs, claiming her; she could still feel the tear of her skin and the pain radiating to her bones as she slipped from the bed, still naked, and walked to the wall of the open sky.

Pressing a hand to the sky, her fingers stretched over the invisible barrier. She yearned to feel the wind on her skin, to let it cool the sweat on her brow, to ease the ache in her bones and temper the power racing in her blood.

The beams of sunlight spiked through the clouds, rays of gold, red, and yellow ignited the sky. And Hazen stood, bathed in sunlight as it rose higher and higher. The warmth eased the edge she felt until her muscles relaxed and her shoulders dropped.

With a sigh, Hazen dropped her hand and turned to the bed. The clothes Rin had laid out last evening had fallen to the floor sometime during the night, the linen she used as a towel had been thrown over her trunk, and the pillows were scattered around her bed.

Pursing her lips, Hazen walked to the bed and quickly made it, grabbing all the pillows and rearranging them neatly. Her towel was dry, so she quickly folded it and left it in the trunk before picking up her clothes and fighting her way into the tight leathers.

Hazen ran a hand over her abdomen, ignoring the flash of claws tearing into her skin, and admired the sleeveless top once she had finally secured the last gold hook behind her neck. The front curved, exposing part of her collarbones until it wrapped around her throat, secured with two gold hooks, and ran down her spine in two leather strips, exposing her shoulder blades. The worn leather pants were snug, moulding to her body and hugging the high curve to her waist, and black flat-footed boots made of soft leather came to her knees.

Her confidence peaked, and she smirked softly. She felt... good. She felt rested and more like herself than ever before, even in the mortal world.

Stretching her arms over her head with a groan, she walked over to the attached bathroom she'd discovered last night. When she was done, Hazen took one last look at the dawn and slipped out of her room.

A solid wall of muscle met her as the door clicked shut. She threw her hands up to catch herself before crashing into the half-naked male, her fingers spreading over a bare chest.

Hazen let out a startled gasp, looking up. Green eyes stared down at her, a single brow raised in question. Her hand was still splayed across Åsmund's chest, the skin warm and smooth under her fingertips. Thoughts of seeing him in the bath surrounded by clouds of steam, hot water trailing over the hard ridges of his chest and abdomen flooded her mind. She yanked her hand back with a sharp breath, noticing the way his muscles tightened when she did so.

If he had been uncomfortable with her touching him, Åsmund didn't let on. Hazen's thoughts briefly went to mass orgies and her face flamed, she shook her head, banishing the thought. His head tilted as he watched her silently.

Hazen cleared her throat, putting a step between them, which only pressed the door into her back. "Why are you always shirtless?"

Åsmund's mouth twitched with amusement. "Does it bother you?"

The air grew thicker, and Hazen subtly pressed closer to the door. He was still close enough for her to smell, and she would be lying if she said she didn't like it. "No, but if I keep running into you, it might pose a problem," she said, tone more breathless than intended. Straightening her shoulders, she smoothed a hand over her braided hair and took a slow, calming breath. Finding the deepest hole she could within herself, she shoved her attraction to the male down deep and sealed it.

Spinning on her heels, she quickly turned away from him before she made a fool of herself, chin notched a little higher, walking down the hall. Åsmund fell into step behind her without missing a beat.

"What problems might me being shirtless cause?" he asked wryly.

"None, that would affect you," she muttered to herself.

"Well," he said, not bothering to comment on her remark, "you'll find that Drago do not care for shirts."

"Your clan leader wears one, though," she remarked.

Åsmund hummed lowly. "Yes, that is because he is ashamed of his scars. So, he hides them."

Hazen looked back at Åsmund, who was still trailing slowly behind her, his look still inquiring. "His scars?"

"An explosion of fire and steel ripped across the battlefield and tore him out of the air. He nearly died that day. It took him nearly a full turn of the seasons to mend, even by the hands of the most skilled healers. Now he hides the scars."

Hazen stopped and turned to look up at him fully. "That's awful."

"That is the price of a warrior. We were created to defend the land, sky, and seas. To die in battle is an honour, but Kladine's mind is a maze of thoughts that I do not think align with the Drago anymore. Time has not been in his favour since that day in battle."

"Is that why he looks... older?"

Åsmund regarded her thoughtfully before he nodded. "Yes. Time took its price when he fought death. Or rather, one of the Gods claimed a toll on his immortality."

Hazen blanched at the idea of paying a toll to avoid death, and that toll was to age in a world where age was not a concept of time.

"Hazen?"

She blinked at the use of her name and focused on Åsmund as he folded his hands behind his back, looking down the hall with a curious eye. "Just wondering, where are we going?"

Opening her mouth, she closed it and looked over her shoulder to the hallway where they had been walking. "To the... arena?"

Leaning forward, Åsmund brought his face nearly level with hers, his green eyes glinting with laughter. "You're going the wrong way."

"But I thought..." She turned and pointed silently down the hall. Had she gone left or right? She couldn't remember; all she remembered was running into his chest and that he had been too close for her to think properly.

"You went left instead of right. The conduit is in the other direction."

"Well, why didn't you say something?" she snapped, flushing hotly.

He just smirked, and his eyes darkened wickedly. "I thought you wanted to take another dip in the bath with me."

Her stomach tightened at the thought of last night. His breath fanned across her cheek and the space—there wasn't enough. Hazen swallowed when she took in a shaking breath, her skin prickling with awareness.

Power and something more thrummed through her veins, igniting her skin. He tilted his head, staring into her eyes.

"Interesting," he murmured. "They're beautiful."

She wasn't breathing now, her lungs barely moving as she stared into vibrant green eyes, noticing the glimmer of gold dusting them.

"What is?" she whispered.

His hand came up, and he used his finger to brush across her cheek, searching her face. "Your eyes, they're beautiful. I've never seen eyes like that."

Clearing his throat quickly, Åsmund straightened abruptly, the thickness in the air vanished, and Hazen forced her lungs to fill. He turned and started walking down the opposite way.

Hazen quickly caught up with his long strides. "What do you mean you've never seen eyes like mine?"

"I've never seen eyes change colour like yours."

Her heart thudded in her chest, and she reached out to grab his hand, stopping him. "What colour?"

His head tilted, looking down at her hand holding his, and she promptly dropped it. "Gold. They become gold."

Åsmund didn't say anything after that, and they walked to the conduit, as he called it, in silence.

It was empty, the orbs of fire the only light source as they walked into the massive arena. Lit along the walls all the way to the bottleneck, they glimmered like fiery stars in a sea of darkness.

"This is the conduit," Åsmund said, his voice carrying into the emptiness. "This is where we train, and above are the chambers of forgeries, where our armour, weapons, leathers, and anything we find fit are crafted. This is the heart of the mountain. And this is where you will come every morning at sunrise."

"Why?"

"To train. Your footwork is decent but sloppy, and your skill with an actual blade is frightening, but your determination is admirable." His voice carried even as he walked over to the rack of blades along the wall, grabbing one of the large ones and then plucking a much smaller, thinner sword from it. It hadn't been there yesterday.

She couldn't help but snort as she muttered, "Don't let him hear you say that." But the thought of Savven made her humour fall. She thought of Lithônion and Brean, and an ache slid into her chest. Gritting her teeth, she forced it down and watched Åsmund stalk back to her, his face turning from the amused male into a general within seconds.

"Dragons train, fight, and leave no enemy alive on the battlefield. And you will start acting like one." He tossed her the blade, she caught it by the handle with a startled yelp before it clattered to the floor.

"Didn't your mother ever tell you not to throw swords!" she snapped.

He didn't so much as blink at her, stating, "I was not born from a female. Now, take your sword and prepare. We're going to see how well you can fight with a blade you can actually lift."

She barely had time to raise her sword and widen her stance when he attacked. Hazen ducked just as his blade came down, slicing the air where she had been. He was quick, skilled, and deadly, and he was fighting like he meant it.

Raising the sword, she arced it through the air, but Åsmund deflected it with ease, flicking her blade away like it was nothing. He struck again, and she brought it up not a second too soon. Sparks danced between them, lighting up their faces before Hazen pushed back with a guttural cry, straining against his bulking strength.

Chest heaving, she grasped the sword hilt in both hands, keeping it level with her chest, the tip pointed towards Åsmund as she glared at him, teeth bared and chest heaving.

Åsmund circled her like a predator. His feet were silent on the black floors. He curled around her like a deadly shadow, and she turned with him, keeping her eyes trained on his movements.

Power, undiluted and fuelled by their fight, filled her blood, she tightened her grip on the hilt and let her shoulders relax. The fire along the wall flickered as the air grew palpable, she could feel their crackling energy around her, filling her, egging her on to ignite everything in her path.

It was subtle, but she saw Åsmund's head tick just a fraction, distracted, and she took the opening.

But she was wrong.

As she lunged, he vanished into a spot of shadows, she swung her sword quickly, slicing the air where he had just been. The glimmer of silver was her only warning before his sword clashed against hers, sparks igniting, and her sword skidded across obsidian.

She lunged for it, hand outstretched, but Åsmund's sword extended to her throat, and she froze.

"Yield," he commanded darkly.

Hazen's heart skidded along her ribs, her power tunnelling through her despite being weaponless. The roar in her ears was nearly deafening, and the fires along the walls flickered and crackled as she reached for them. She could practically feel their flames along her skin, she commanded them as they wavered towards her.

The fire answered.

An orb jetted from the wall, wrapping around her, encasing her hand. She stared mesmerised before she spun from Åsmund's blade and held up a hand wreathed in flames.

"No," she spat.

His lips curled into a deadly smile. "Good." His free hand reached for the fire on the wall, and it came at his silent command. The fire wrapped around his sword hand and twisted up the silver blade, the metal gleaming now ignited in flames.

Hazen forced herself to remain steady, her feet itching to take a step back, and her power banked just enough that the flames vanished, leaving her swordless and fireless.

Åsmund let the fire go and it flew back to the wall, joining Hazen's. The light around them dimmed again, and he jerked his chin to her sword. "Pick it up."

She did as she was told and picked up the thin blade. It was light, like swinging something made of nothing, and half the length and width of the one she had used yesterday. "Where did you get this?"

"From the trove."

"A treasure trove?" she questioned with a snort, raising her brows.

Åsmund walked to the middle of the conduit, waiting for her. "We collect weapons and whatever else we find of value after a battle and keep a trove of it. It's an elfin blade. They're small like you. I thought it would fit you better than ours."

She shook her head, walking towards him. "You have a treasure trove. You really are a dragon."

"Were the wings not enough conviction?"

Hazen snorted. "No, but it was a start."

Åsmund only hummed and waited, watching her stand before him. In the dim firelight, he was all lean, beautiful muscle with imposing strength that made her shiver. His face was hard and unwavering. "Sword up."

"Wait," she held up a disbelieving hand, "you said you weren't born from a female?" She remembered his nonchalant words, her brows raising in disbelief.

Åsmund raised his brow a fraction, his stoicism wavering into amusement before it fell behind his walls. "Sword up."

He wasn't going to deign her with an answer, but she would

get one eventually, so instead she raised her sword, eyes narrowing in on the male. She took a steadying breath and waited, her blood thrumming with building energy.

"Begin."

Hazen groaned silently when she finally crawled into her bed that night. She ached *everywhere.* She had fallen asleep in the bath and hadn't seen Åsmund again, and an hour later made herself crawl out of the hot water to her room.

Rin, bless her. She had been waiting in her room with a tray of cooked meat, a purplish root vegetable she couldn't identify but tasted like carrots, a bowl of meat stew, and a steaming hot bun covered in golden syrup for dessert.

Hazen nearly sat caveman-style on the floor and devoured her tray, but instead, she forced herself to take it to her bed and hop up on the downy quilt, and cross her legs. She was still wrapped in a towel with her wet hair hanging down her back.

Rin tried to fuss over her, but she waved the girl away, patting the bed and having her join. After a moment's hesitation, she gave in, pulled up the skirts of her blue dress to hop up, and sat across from Hazen, chatting happily about her mate and life both within and outside of the mountain. She learned Rin had three older sisters and a little brother and that she's well over a century old, which made Hazen choke on her food. It's not that she should be surprised, but Rin seemed more human than Hazen had felt lately. She nearly forgot Rin had the keen blessing of immortality, as did the rest of those within this world.

After Rin took her empty tray and dirty clothes, she closed her door softly. Hazen pulled her towel off, tossed it to the foot of the bed, and slipped under the covers. Sleep was a fast-approaching friend, and she didn't think she could resist it for much longer.

Turning to stare at the fading colours of the sunset that flooded over the mountain, the quilt tucked over her shoulders, Hazen filtered the day's events hazily through her mind, fixating on this morning when she looked at the orbs of fire along the wall and *commanded* them to come to her. She had felt the fire's energy crackling along her bones, enveloping her muscles and filling her blood. Seeing her hand wreathed in flames and not melting her skin was still as shocking as it had been the first time. Still, the power that had tunnelled through her was like nothing she had ever experienced, as short-lived as it was.

Åsmund had made her train and train and train. Sparring with her until the sunlight filtered through the bottleneck and the Drago started to filter into the conduit. Her arms were barely arms anymore by the time he called a cease and desist, and the featherlight blade dropped to the ground as though it was made of lead. Her abs hurt anytime she moved any part of her body thanks to the hours of strength training he'd forced her to do after sparring.

So, she didn't move; she took slow, deep breaths, willing herself to melt into her bed. She stared at the sky until her eyelids grew heavy and she gave into sleep.

Training was just beginning, and she knew it would only get worse.

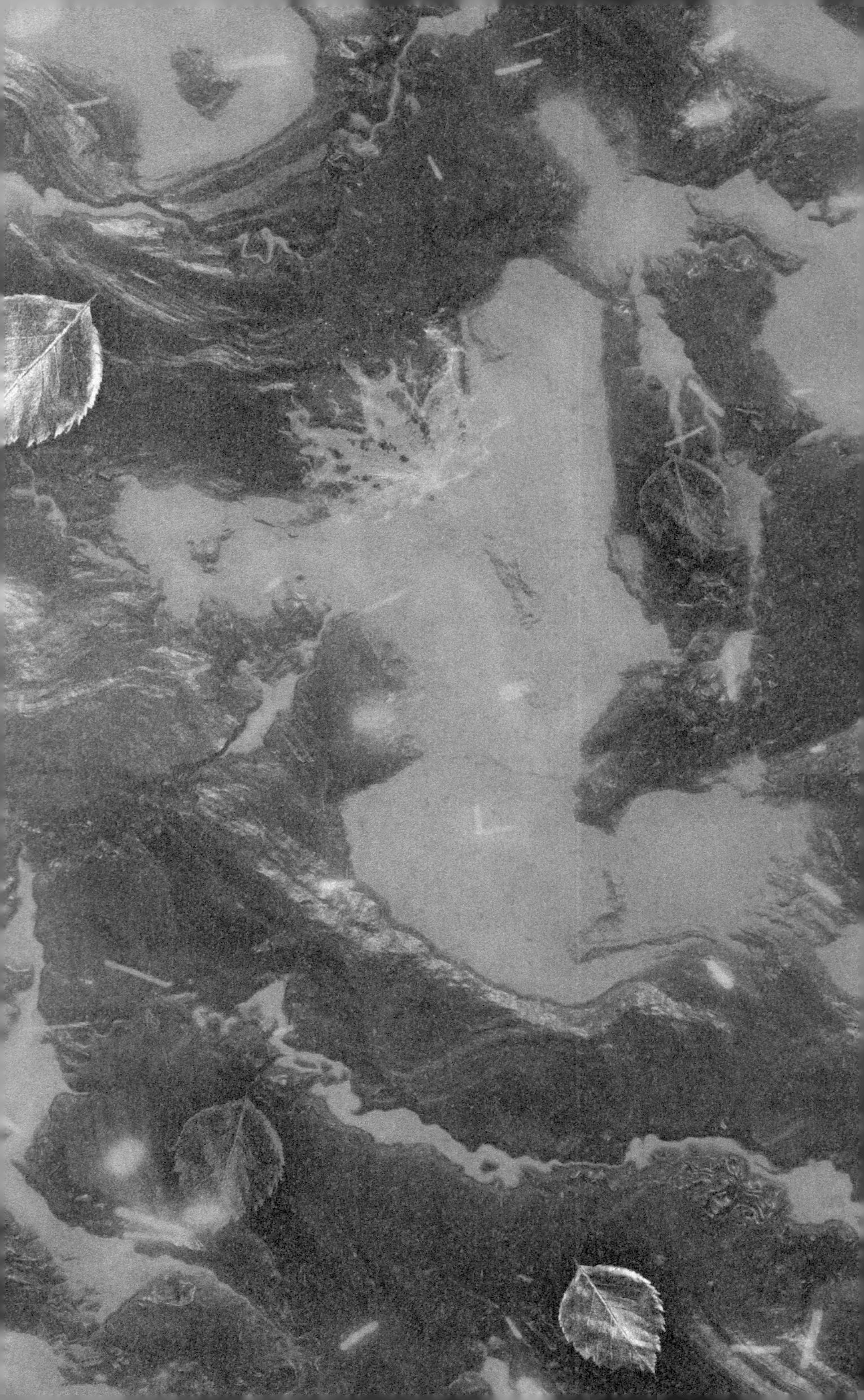

# CHAPTER 10

Rolling her shoulders slowly, loosening the burning muscles, Hazen leaned her sword onto the rack and glanced over at Åsmund.

They had met every morning at sunrise for the last couple of weeks. She stopped counting the sunrises and began to just slip into a routine. Wake up, watch the dawn, dress, meet Åsmund outside her door, spar, strength train, bathe, eat, sleep, repeat.

The first week had been hell on her muscles, but her body slowly relaxed into the training, and eventually, she could almost say she looked forward to it. Since Hazen had arrived in this world, she had shed any softness she had carried around her middle and thighs. Lean muscle tone coming through, her abs flat and firm, legs strong enough to support Åsmund's regiment, her arms toned with muscle. But she gave the actual credit to all the walking, training and… running for her life. Nothing fuelled a high heart rate like a life-or-death adrenaline spike.

Sweat dripped down her temples, and she grabbed a linen cloth from Rin, who stood off to the side. Rin had taken to watching them later in the mornings, cheering on Hazen whether she failed or not.

Hazen smiled at her. "Thanks," she said softly, wiping her brow and the back of her neck before putting it back on the tray Rin held.

She found herself having a fondness for the girl, almost like having a little sister, despite Rin being much older than her.

Rin's bright smile, pale pink dress, and braided white-blonde hair were stark in the conduit. But Hazen welcomed the support. Even Åsmund gave her a small smile of greeting every time he saw her, and Hazen, for the life of her, couldn't contain the tightening in her stomach even though the smile wasn't for her.

In the darkness of the conduit, with the whispers of early morning at their heels, it was just them for a few moments. They circled each other, watching, waiting, and coming together in a dance of sparks, sweat, and pure power.

Hazen found herself waking before dawn more frequently, ready to start the day, to see the amusement in those green eyes and the slight whisper of a crooked smile. To see the side of Åsmund he let her glimpse at when they were alone, before the stoic general came out the minute they stepped into the conduit.

During training, Åsmund was all business. But there were moments where he would watch her from across the training space, and she would catch his eye for a split second. His stare was guarded and full of emotions she couldn't place but made her breath hitch before he would look away and return to training a group of soldiers.

Then there was yesterday. Hazen's face flushed with the memory while watching the general. His curly mane was pulled into a bun at the top of his head, sweat shining across the hard ridges of his chest and dripping down and down… Hazen let her eyes wander to the deep V of caramel skin where the sweat cut a path. Her body tightened despite her better judgment.

He had her doing pull-ups on the steel bar anchored to the wall, and she had, to her surprise, been able to do three by herself, but on the fourth, as her back strained, she felt strong hands wrap around her waist. Her heart stuttered in her chest, and Hazen nearly let go of the bar like it had shocked her.

"Don't," he commanded lowly. His hand had pressed along her back with a featherlight touch that made a shiver run down her spine, stopping between her shoulder blades, his other hand still on her waist. "Pull from here," he continued, his breath fanning her heated skin.

Hazen could feel his presence against her spine, the heat rolling off him and enveloping her. His earthy musk invaded her senses, and she could barely concentrate when his hands slipped along the curve of her spine, down her hips, to her feet, where he placed them in his hands.

"Up," he ordered.

She did as she was told and pulled herself up towards the bars, her back flexing when he helped her up. She did it six more times before he let her feet go, and she released the bar with a tired gasp.

They had stood there watching each other over the small space between them, so close that she could see his skin dimpling as the sweat began to cool. Her eyes had dropped, and she noticed a new piercing in his left nipple, a small gold hoop. She had licked her lips, her mouth going dry, and when she looked up, his eyes had darkened for a moment, making her core tighten involuntarily before that guarded general slipped back into place, and he walked away.

Now, he stood in the middle of their training area, all deadly grace and power as he swung his sword through the air, his feet dancing across the floor, his black wings a blurred shadow at his back. Seeing him train was a thing of beauty, like watching Death itself dance across the world, each swing of his sword, like that of a scythe, cutting down opponent after opponent.

"General."

Åsmund quickly ceased his movements, and Hazen looked over her shoulder. A bulking Drago warrior entered the conduit, his black skin catching the firelight, face set in a severe line.

"What is it, Gerl?" Åsmund asked, walking over to the rack

where Hazen now stood, his arm brushing her shoulder when he re-racked his weapon.

Sparks ignited down her body at the contact, and she sucked in a silent breath, her body reacting despite her best efforts to control it.

"Valdren requests the female's presence in the sanctuary."

Åsmund stared at Gerl, rumbling lowly, "The female's name is Hazen."

A thrill went down Hazen's body, and she suppressed the smile tugging on her lips.

Gerl's jaw flexed at the correction, but his black eyes flickered to Hazen before he gave her a barely perceivable nod. "Apologies," he said to her.

Hazen didn't have time to wave it off before Åsmund spoke.

"We'll be there shortly. Thank you, Gerl," he said with dismissal.

Gerl nodded once, gaze flickering to Hazen again briefly before turning on his heels and walking out.

Rin's giggle broke the silence, and Åsmund looked at her with a quirk of his brow. She quickly quieted, and he looked at Hazen, who stood straighter under his gaze.

"Go cool down. The Dragon Keeper is waiting."

The sanctuary was further into the mountain than Hazen anticipated. The air simmered with heat and smelled of rotten eggs the further they went. She had nearly forgotten the smell until Åsmund had guided her into a sloping tunnel, and down and down they went.

Warm moisture coated Hazen's exposed arms and shoulders, clinging to her face and sweaty braid as the tunnel curved and a gaping mouth led them into a large cavern.

Hazen's steps faltered, her mouth dropping open. She stood in awe of the beauty that unfolded around her in an assortment of colours and life.

It was a garden, a forest, within a prison of solid stone. The towering dome ceiling arched high above them, a soft echo filling its peak from their steps. Flowers of varying specimens flooded the space in bold colours of reds, purples, yellows, and blues. Lush greenery burst around the flowers, crawling across the stone floors and up the sides of the walls until their ends dangled thickly from the curved ceiling. A singular path cut through the garden, cushioned with thick moss and small white flowers.

She looked back at Åsmund, who stood behind her, his face impassive. Raising her brows at him, she stared at him until his green eyes looked down at hers and softened. Nodding his chin beyond her, she pursed her lips, holding his gaze a second longer than needed, and turned back to the path.

Stepping diligently through the growth, fern fronds brushing across her arms as they walked, she pushed a particularly large one out of her face when she rounded a bend in the path and stopped. Valdren stood in the centre of the garden, bent over a bushel of dark red flowers, caressing the soft petals.

"Hazen," he said her name softly, his voice rich and welcoming. Standing, he slipped his hands into the long folds of his emerald tunic, floral gold stitching decorated the sleeves and hem. His long grey hair was braided down his back, gold eyes studying her openly.

She smoothed a hand over her leathers, and then her braid, she was sure, looked in disarray. "You wanted to see me?"

Gesturing to a path that branched off behind him, Valdren offered her a hand. "Walk with me?" He looked at Åsmund. "You may follow behind if you wish, General."

Hazen fell into step with Valdren, Åsmund waited before he followed a few paces behind.

There was silence. Not an uncomfortable one or an all-consuming one, just silence—the kind you found within a sanctuary, where you could mediate with your thoughts rather than be consumed by them.

Hazen let her fingers brush along a grouping of drooping bluebells, their petals like silk on her fingertips. Dew drops clung to their leaves and stems. "How is this possible?" she asked in wonder, a curling frond brushing across her open palm.

Valdren followed her gaze to the leafy blade and looked up

at the towering peak covered in rich hanging vegetation. "A mountain's life is born from adversity. It struggles to be strong—to weather the torrents that work to destroy it, and when it becomes too much, it grows peaks like daggers and roots like steel, and it withstands. And soon, the wind, rain, and storms do not bend or break the mountain… the mountain breaks them." Reaching for a soft yellow snapdragon, Valdren gently rubbed the petal between his fingers. "This garden is similar. Stone poses no life for a flower; it is a harsh environment and poisonous to something so giving. One would think that the flowers would rot, and the stone would eat them until there was nothing left but ruin."

Kneeling on the mossy path, the Dragon Keeper pushed a bundle of leaves out of the way, and seated on the ground was a small budding flower yet to show its colour, only the promise of what was to come. "So, you see, they dug their roots deep, claiming the poison as their own, and soon shaped themselves to become more than their surroundings. To become stronger."

Hazen stared at the small bud, a tiny leaf still unfurling itself from the twisting stem. "It sounds like a difficult life."

Valdren hummed in agreement, standing, the leaves falling back into place. "Aye, it is, but you're a force of nature, Hazen."

Hazel eyes snapped to gold ones, and she blinked when he gave her a soft smile.

The garden blossomed and flourished the further they walked. After what Valdren said, she wondered if the flowers had become poisonous themselves to survive. If their gentle petals brought death with their beauty.

Valdren's head tilted, and Hazen watched him nod slowly as if in silent conversation.

"They want to meet you," Valdren said.

Brows furrowing, Hazen glanced back at Åsmund, who still followed a few paces behind but looked unbothered as always. "Who?"

Valdren gently touched her arm and guided her to the right when the path branched. The vegetation began to fall away until the black stone earth fell into a steep slope of loose, flat stones, and a mammoth cave mouth opened up.

Hazen's heart thudded in her chest, looking into the expanse of darkness, feeling as small as the flowers. It was like staring into a black hole, never-ending and all-consuming and part of her was drawn to it, but the other part wanted to run away, terrified.

The ground shuddered violently underfoot, sending the loose black rocks rattling among themselves. Hazen caught herself when the mountain trembled, and her heart jerked in her chest, breath straining as she stared into the void with eyes wide and searching.

A thick plume of steam rolled from the darkness, and a growl ripped through the cave that jarred her to her bones. The orbs of fire flickered in protest.

Taking in short breaths through her nose, teeth clenched, Hazen steeled herself, the ground trembling over... and over... and over again.

Two golden eyes stared out from the darkness, and her breath stuttered, knees going weak.

*Thud.*

Gold eyes were trained on her, and Hazen couldn't look away, falling into pools of molten fire.

*Thud.*

Steam billowed out in a thick cloud, washing over her skin like a hot sauna.

*Thud.*

A great golden dragon emerged from the shadows, teeth bared. Power rippled off its massive, scaled body in waves, nearly consuming every ounce of space within the sanctuary.

Hazen's knees buckled, and she fell to them before the mighty beast with a sharp gasp.

The dragon's massive head lowered until those gold reptilian eyes aligned with Hazen's head. Teeth bared, heat blasted over her face, a low rumble filled the dome, while a deep ancient voice filled her head.

*"Hello, Hazen Solvaya. I've been wanting to meet you."*

A rush of power ignited a blazing path through her limbs and chest until she was consumed with it. Her dragon was awake. She hadn't felt the beast within her for days now as her training continued. The less she struggled through her routines and training, the less she felt her dragon. But now, the power thrummed wildly in her veins at the voice filling her head. Power called to power.

"*Stand,*" the dragon commanded.

She stood, and the dragon's head rose with her. A long hanging vine coiled around its twisting black horns, and its glimmering gold wings tucked tight to its body.

"*I am Forndýr. The last living dragon of the age and the one who called you across the veil.*"

When Hazen dared to take a step forward, a rock slipped free under her foot, and it careened down the steep slope. She watched it crash against razor-sharp black talons as long as her forearm, and the silence that followed was deafening.

Swallowing the knot in her throat when the air grew thick, Hazen ignored the tension rising and finally asked the question she had wanted the answer to from the beginning, "Why did you bring me here?" Her voice echoed against the dome's walls and into the tunnel beyond Forndýr.

"Because I told him to," a female voice drolled from the shadows.

The air grew frigid, and the shadows curled around Forndýr's thick front legs. A girl no older than thirteen stepped out.

Her black eyes were bottomless, staring straight at Hazen, her black pin-straight hair stopped just below her chin. She was pale, ghostly almost, against Forndýr's gold scales. Her phantom appearance was made more so by her black gown, hanging to the floor with long draping sleeves, that concealed her figure.

Hazen's eyes darted between the girl, the dragon, and Valdren, and she dared a glance at Åsmund, whose stare was directed at the child, his face unreadable. Still, she saw the subtle tightening in his muscles.

She looked back at the girl. "Who are you?"

A razor-sharp smile cut across the girl's full angular cheeks, her black eyes lighting. "I am Death, and you, Hazen, are my freedom."

"Tatius, now is not the time for your games," Valdren chastised darkly.

Hazen's brows shot up.

Tatius rolled her eyes. "You're lucky he chose you, Valdren." She laid a hand on Forndýr's leg, her hand dwarfed in comparison and rubbed the scales softly. "Are you sure you can't eat him? I'm sure he's well-seasoned in his old age."

Forndýr made a chuffing sound, and Hazen stared at the beast in amazement. He was laughing.

Hazen gaped at them all. "Is anyone going to explain what's going on?"

Valdren cleared his throat, and Tatius's eyes slowly slid to Hazen. Any amusement, if you could call it that, faded to reveal an expanse of nothingness held in those large eyes. A glimpse of what death would look and feel like if toyed with.

Shadows curled around Tatius, and when Hazen blinked, she was gone. The dome grew darker, and Hazen felt that familiar prick of talons on her skin, whispers from the depths of darkness that made her skin crawl. She gritted her teeth until her jaw ached, balling her hands at her sides.

"It has been an age since dragons have chosen a keeper," Tatius said softly in the shadows.

Hazen whirled. Åsmund and Valdren were gone as the night crept in around her. Something wrapped around her ankle, and she sucked in a sharp breath, looking down. Tendrils of shadows crawled up her body, and she made a strangled noise.

"Let me take you back to a time long since forgotten…"

Tatius's voice vanished into the shadows, and Hazen looked around frantically. She couldn't go back into the darkness. Lungs squeezing, Hazen brought a hand to her chest as if that would help the building pressure behind her ribs. The shadows were at her waist, and she felt their freezing touch dousing the endless inferno that blazed beneath her skin. Her dragon withered, anger coursing through her body.

The shadows covered her chest, and she could feel them whispering over her skin.

"No, no, no," she whispered frantically. As the shadows slipped over her face, her hand shot out and reached for the last ember of light before the world went black.

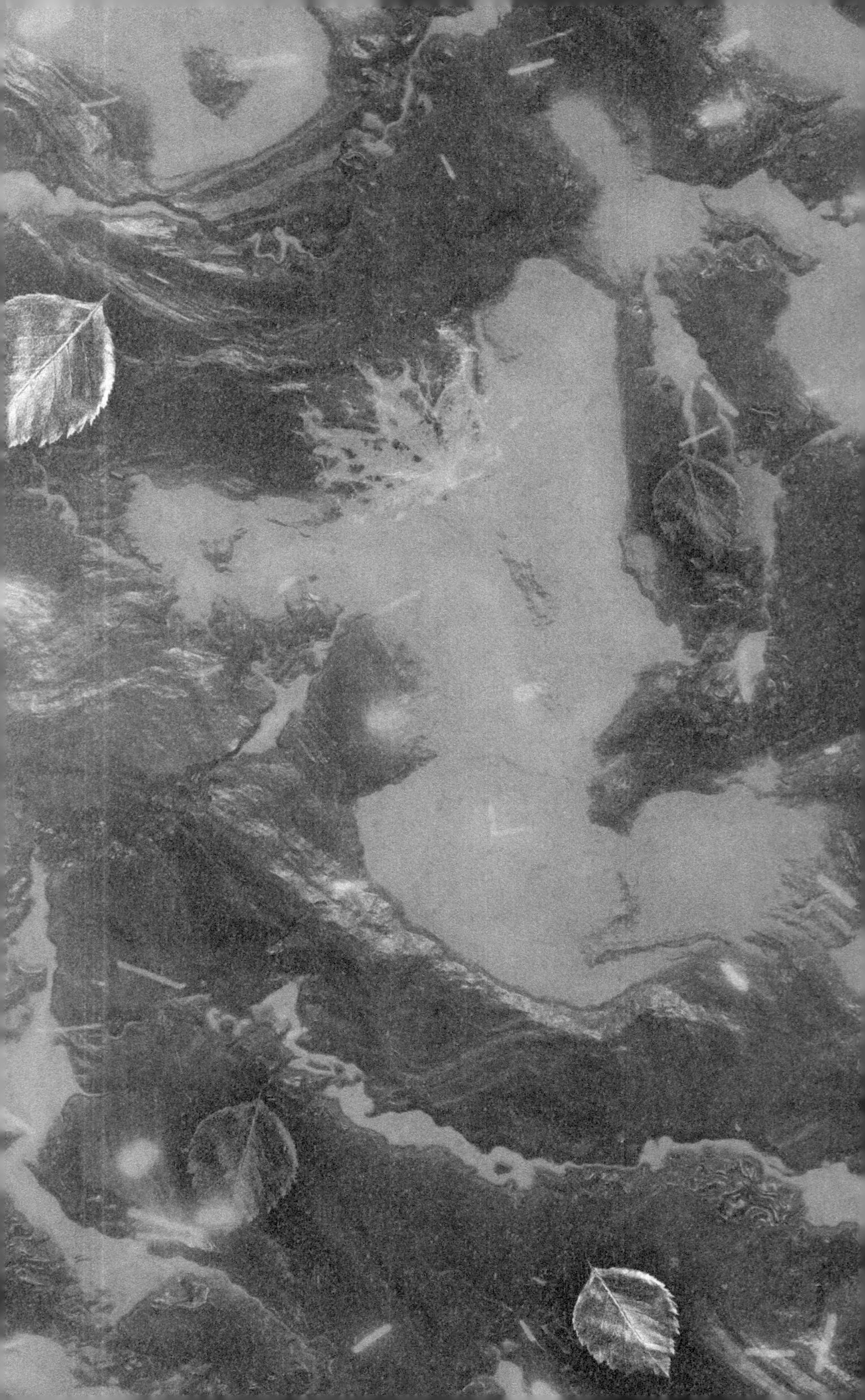

# CHAPTER 11

The light of an ember could ignite the world. Or at least a couple of feet in all directions as Hazen opened her eyes and raised her hand. The last ember floating in her palm.

It was a sea of darkness, silence stretching so tautly that it echoed back at her. Her heart was racing, her eyes strained to see into the void, but to no avail.

*"Before you knew this world, there was nothing. A vast expansion of universe beyond the heavens, untouched and untainted."*

Tatius's voice filled the abyss, and Hazen whirled, searching for the girl. A flash of light made her squint, and stars exploded into view. She stood within a galaxy.

*"This is where we come from."*

Nebulas whizzed through her torso, stars flying past her

body, planets, *and worlds*. Hazen stood in awe, her earlier terror dwindling to nothing. The ember warmed her palm, a steady glow still emanated when she raised her hand higher to light up the cosmos.

*"At the beginning of creation, we were plucked from the heavens..."*
The hand holding the ember dropped to her side as Hazen stared into space, and the story of the world unfolded around her.

Four stars fell from the glimmering expanse, exploded into existence, and light bathed the void. Four females, four *Gods*, floated in the darkness like imposing forces. She recognised the one who called herself Death—though she was much younger— and the one who guarded the Lost Forest, but she didn't know the other two. One had hair like fire and skin like snow, and the other had skin as black as night with eyes like budding leaves with whorls of silver tattooing her skin.

The Gods reached into a nebula, and each pulled a shining orb from its swirling gold and purple depths. Moulding the light between their hands, they expanded the energy until Hazen had to raise a hand to shield her eyes.

When the light dimmed, four dragons stood beside them. One so dark their scales looked black, but in the subtle light, it shone amethyst, another green like emeralds, another red like flames with black horns; but the one beside the smallest God was the one Hazen stared at. A golden dragon, but unlike Forndýr, this dragon did not have horns.

The dragons opened their sharp maws, and amber light emanated from rows of razor teeth. Raising their hands, a bright light began to grow and grow and grow between the Gods until Hazen was forced to look away. The dragons reared their heads back and loosened fire into the expanse of light.

Heat, light, and a loud boom rocketed across the universe. Hazen covered her ears against it, and the world was born.

Worlds, Gods, and dragons all vanished, falling away like stardust until the scene changed, and she stood atop a tall mountain peak that overlooked the world. The sky was bright orange and yellow as sunset split across it.

The Gods, who were now more sized to Hazen's height, stood

with the world as their backdrop, each dragon standing between them like a towering, monstrous, fire-breathing force to be reckoned with. A lone, beautiful female with white-blonde hair and almond skin stood before them, naked with arms stretched wide.

That familiar glow rippled from the dragons' mouths as they opened their impressive jaws, and a roar ripped from deep within them, loosening their fiery breath over the female.

Hazen's eyes went wide, her heart stuttering. She could feel the power that claimed the female. She knew that all-consuming sensation as the dragon took its place within her. She had been subject to this same claim. And Hazen realised what she was witnessing.

This was Rose. The first keeper.

Rose tipped her head back and screamed as her body was ignited in flames. Hazen could see the extended tips of her canines and the long slant of her ears before the fire fully enveloped her.

But she did not burn. No. The fire was claiming her—the dragon's power was claiming her.

Tatius's voice startled her when she spoke above the screams and roar of flames. *"We did not know that too much power would corrupt our creation, that the ones we shaped could not withstand. How wrong we were."*

The world changed again, and this time, the world burned.

Bodies lay half torn apart, half melted. Their mouths open in silent screams, the earth bloodied and littered with their pieces. The air was dark and covered in soot and ash, clouds of thick black smoke curled upwards, sparks from small flames igniting the sky.

She stood on a battlefield, a graveyard, and Rose was in the middle of it all, but she now had magnificent gold wings. Her skin was stained red, her white-blonde hair matted with blood, and a half-shredded robe of crimson silk clung to her body. Her hands were clawed and dripping red, and her eyes were bright gold.

*"We had thought to create a guardian of our world, one who speaks for the people, who defends them. But instead, we created a monster."*

A roar shook the battlefield, filling the skies, and Hazen knew the dragons were quickly approaching, the beat of wings heavy in the air. Another roar ripped apart the ashen world, and Hazen's heart stopped when Rose seemed to look directly at her. Rage, pity, and mourning filled those beautiful eyes before she closed them and lifted her head as the red dragon emerged. Jaws open, its black talons enclosed around her body as it ripped her head from her shoulders.

Hazen couldn't make herself look away despite the deep ache that cracked inside of her. Rose had looked… resigned to death, the fleeting look of peace before the dragon's teeth sunk into her. She had known it was too much, known the monster she had become, and welcomed the end.

The dragon took flight, and Rose's body crumpled with the others around her. However, as smoke and ash fell, light emanated from her corpse, and flames rose from her body, igniting the sky when a dragon made of fire flew from her body and took flight.

She knew that dragon. Memories of it engulfing her in her dreams and her waking to a world where power now coursed through her body, and the creature inside her roiled and twisted with it, guiding her.

Gritting her jaw, Hazen forced in a deep breath when she felt that power hum in response through her blood. "Why are you showing me this?!" she screamed.

Tatius stepped from the black clouds of ash, her face expressionless, head tilted as she watched Hazen. "Because this is where the first roots of darkness were born and where your power comes from."

The small God looked down at Rose's headless body, and Hazen's stomach rolled at her words.

"What are you saying?" Hazen asked softly, the roar of fire fading around them, her blood rushing through her ears.

Black eyes looked at her slowly, and Tatius's smile curved softly, deadly. "Rose was the beginning of our world, and you, Hazen, are the end of the age of dragons and Gods."

Her heart sunk to her stomach, hammering like a drum, her fingers twitching around the ember that warmed her skin. The small act grounded her enough to ask, "Is that why you brought me here? To be an executioner?"

Tatius looked, for the most part, amused. "An executioner? Such strong words, but no." She walked towards Hazen, lifting the hem of her gown to step over body parts. "I did not have Forndýr bring you into this world to be its executioner. I have much bigger plans for this world, and you are one of many helping me accomplish them."

Even though she looked down at the God who faced off with her, the power within those eyes, the endless abyss staring back at her while the world burned around them, made her feel much smaller. But the power in her blood shifted restlessly, and she grasped onto the feeling, rolling her shoulders back and barring her emotions.

"What plans are those? What role do you have me playing in this game of chess? Am I just a pawn?"

Tatius's laugh was soft but humourless and cold, raking claws down Hazen's spine.

"You are all just pawns to us. We created you, and the laws of magic we wove into the world sheltered you from us using you as we see fit." The humour died in her face. "But that does not mean there are not ways to move you where I need you."

Hazen felt hot rage at her words, she understood the rage she saw in Rose's eyes. Because it coursed through her body like unadulterated energy. "And what do you need from me?" she spat out.

Tatius smiled, truly smiled, and it was terrifying as smoke rolled over her. She vanished into nothing, but her voice whispered back, "You're a smart girl. You'll figure it out. You have so far."

And the fire and ash and bodies melted away, the world went dark and claimed her with it.

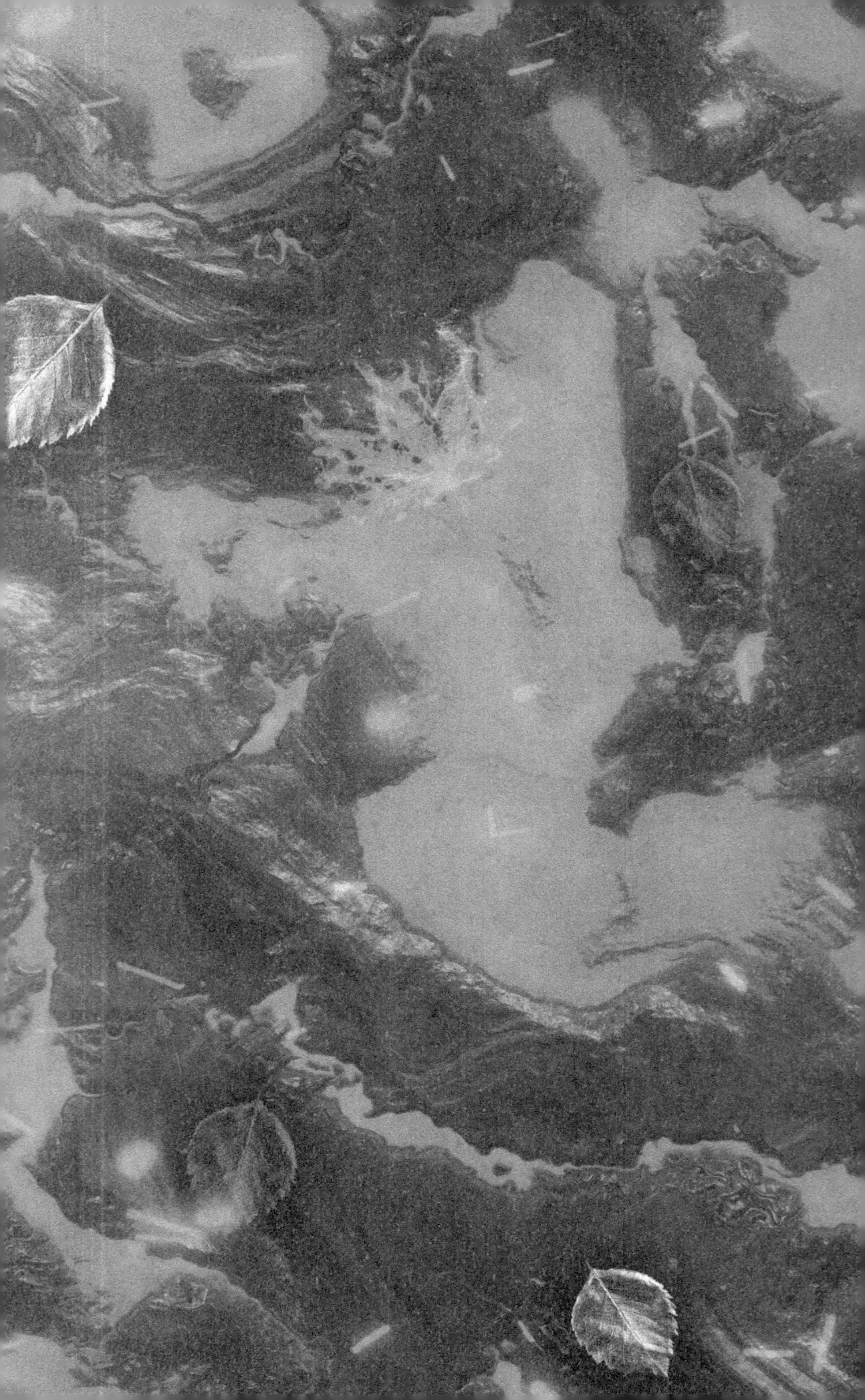

# CHAPTER 12

Åsmund stared at the silver tankard of mead in his hands, watching the amber liquid slosh against the sides as he turned it slowly in his hands. He sat alone in the dining hall at one of the four long communal tables, the floating ring of fire orbs hung overhead and cast a bright glow over the wood and stone.

He had carried Hazen back to her room when she had collapsed suddenly, swearing when he saw her body go limp and, thankfully, catching her before she hit the stone.

The sanctuary had gone cold, like death, and he could still feel the chill seeping into his skin, the fire in his blood hissing against it. Hazen had gone preternaturally still, frozen in place when the small God had appeared.

Whatever had happened, happened in her mind, her hand

twitching occasionally as she and the God faced each other silently. The God of Death, though she appeared as a child, was anything but; with eyes as cold and bottomless as the night and as ancient as the stars. She is one small creature he wouldn't want to fight, the thought of it making Åsmund shake his head. Forndýr had gone back into his hold, all of his golden glory vanishing into the darkness of his cave, leaving Åsmund and Valdren to stand there in silence, watching and waiting.

Åsmund would admit that even his patience had begun to wane, watching Hazen's fingers twitching more and more often. It was the only sign of life. He could sense the distress and anger rolling off her even though she hadn't moved in quite a long time, and it made him want to snatch her back from whatever hole the God had shoved her into mentally.

His grip on the tankard tightened, the metal groaned, at the sound he sucked in a breath and let it out with a low growl. He could feel the perfect hold of his patience chipping away the more time he spent with the female.

Valdren had stood there in reverent silence, making Åsmund want to grind his teeth. He was a general and the epitome of control, but feeling her turmoil made him want to rip them apart, which was concerning.

He didn't lose control. He didn't worry himself over a female. But she wasn't just a female, was she? She was a dragon, and her power called to him like a siren.

When he had scouted for her the day Valdren sent him and two of his soldiers out, he had felt it then. Her power was calling like a long-lost song through the trees, filling his head and limbs with buzzing energy. He had thought he was going insane, nearly falling from the sky when he felt its sharp pull towards the mountain. His soldiers had laughed at him, calling him a yearling just learning to fly, and Åsmund played it off until he saw her, and they squared off with each other.

Eyes wide and bright, like living gold; he had never seen eyes like hers before. Her blonde hair had been falling out of her braid, wild around her strong, lean face, beautiful tan skin scattered with light freckles and a delicate whorling silver scar along her left temple.

Her body was slim, strong, and sure. She held a confidence—and a stubbornness—that mirrored his own. He had felt her power rolling off her in waves, and it took all his self-control not to approach her and find out why.

Holding her had only made it worse. She was supple and warm under his hands and against his body as Åsmund flew them into the mountain. Valdren had brought orders from Forndýr to bring her, and he had. Then she had decided that wandering the mountain would be a good idea, leading her straight into the conduit, right to Kain.

The metal crumpled in his hands at the thought of Kain and his intentions with her. Åsmund looked down at the tankard and saw the metal caved in on either side, his fist squeezing the life from it, but he raised it to his mouth and took a long swig.

Kain had meant to take her, to be nothing more than a beast. There was no honour in that male. He had stopped him before from taking females in the villages, and sometimes, he had been too late. He had wanted to kill him, to end the tyranny that single male had, but he couldn't. Kladine would sooner rip his wings off and behead him before he could lay his blade to Kain's neck.

Kladine viewed Kain as a son or the closest thing to it that the Drago could have, like calls to like in that regard.

He had made Rafe's mate, Rin, bring Hazen's meals to her room or directly to the conduit during mid-day to keep her away from Kain. He didn't trust the male wouldn't try something if given the opportunity.

Her training was coming along, and he'd even found himself looking forward to the hours before his soldiers filtered into the conduit. The time when dawn was still approaching, firelight was all they had, the shadows at their feet, their breathing filling the air as they danced with their swords. She was surer of herself, her confidence growing, her feet stronger—quicker, and she no longer dropped her arm.

Åsmund's mouth quirked against the rim of the tankard when he thought of the single hit she landed on him. She had been quick, flicking her blade under his as he cut through the air directly to her chest. He had felt the sharp tap of her sword against his hip, and he had frozen in surprise as she laughed in shock.

She had laughed, and he stared at her with a small smile. He had decided right then that he could listen to her laugh for the rest of his eternal life.

"Gods," he groaned.

What was happening to him?

He knew she watched him; he could feel her eyes burning his skin across the conduit when he had her strength training. Åsmund couldn't help himself the other day and had gone to her while she was working on the bar, touching her spine and feeling the heat slip through her leathers at her hip when he held her. Having her ass in his face did nothing to help him when he held her feet, counting every pull-up she did. The torture was his own doing, he freely admitted that to himself.

But he was nearing his limit. Every inch of air between them was tense when they stood around each other, and it didn't help that he had seen her half naked, though he had made sure not to look anywhere but her face.

When he had come around the bend in the hot springs and saw her laying there in the water; breasts full and beautiful, hair floating around her like a golden sheen, her muscled abdomen dipping along the surface, the air had been sucked from his body. He had frozen until she noticed him, and he had stared at her face and then turned around when she asked him to.

That night, he went directly to the conduit and trained until he wore himself out and collapsed into his bed. The female made him crazy, but he hid it well enough. He didn't need the other males to know what kind of hold she had on their general; he didn't need her to know, either.

But Åsmund could feel his perseverance failing, and he didn't know how much longer he could withstand her pull.

"Åsmund."

Åsmund's head shot up, and he looked to his left, immediately standing at seeing Kladine swiftly approaching down the aisle of communal benches. Dressed in his usual all-black, his face pulled into a permanent scowl.

"Clan leader," he said lowly, dropping his chin.

"Drop the formalities," Kladine all but growled. "Sit."

Åsmund did and watched Kladine do the same, setting his tankard of mead aside. "What can I do for you, Kladine?"

"I see you've all but hidden the girl except during training hours in the conduit." Kladine looked at the crushed tankard but didn't say anything when he turned dark eyes back to Åsmund. "How does she fair?"

Åsmund kept his face neutral though his tone dropped, and his power flared hotly in his veins. "Do you wonder over her wellbeing or the integrity of your general?"

Kladine smirked and leaned forward, his face darkening. "I do not question your integrity, Åsmund, but I do not like animals being brought into *my* mountain without my consent. And *she* is here without my consent, so I do not wonder over her wellbeing or your integrity. I only want to know when we will be rid of her."

The air between them grew thick with warning. Kladine did not take orders well, let alone when openly commanded in front of his soldiers. The clan leader was not a humble male, and to be chastised in front of his clan because of her... it would not be something Kladine readily forgot.

Nodding once, Åsmund grabbed his tankard and took a long sip, downing the rest of the mead. When he was done, he slammed it down, wiped the back of his mouth with his hand and smiled crookedly. "Worrying over a female, Kladine?" he jested lightly. "Come now, you must have better things to do?"

Kladine snorted, the tension easing between them, and his scowl turned up in a smirk. "You're right. Worrying over a female who couldn't be more useless is a waste of my eternal life."

"Then don't think any more of her. She's my problem to deal with." The words tasted bitter on his tongue, but he swallowed it and kept the easy grin on his face.

"Kain only just brought to my attention his concerns over the female and felt it necessary I speak with you."

Åsmund retained the low growl at Kain's name. He should have gutted the male centuries ago. Now, he was simply a nuisance to him but a danger to Hazen. "Pass along my thanks to Kain," he said with a lazy smile.

Kladine's smirk dropped, and the clan leader's head tilted in curiosity. "He says you're training the girl?"

Shrugging one shoulder, Åsmund ran a hand through his long hair. "Better to train her and wear her out than to have her at my heels with questions all day."

The clan leader snorted at that and grinned. "A better male than I, Åsmund. I would have pushed her from the mountain already."

Åsmund forced himself to laugh at Kladine's words despite the roar of fire in his head. Standing suddenly, he gave his clan leader a good-natured smile and said, "Unfortunately, I must go now. I suspect she will be waking soon from her visit with Forndýr." He didn't dare tell him that the God of Immortality had also been present, lest Kladine blew the mountain apart from his rage after she had threatened to take his fifty years prior.

"She's asleep?" Kladine asked, brows furrowing.

"Something about her human blood being too weak to withstand his power," he replied tightly. It was, of course, a lie. She was powerful; he could feel it coming off her in waves, but he didn't suspect she knew the extent of it yet.

Kladine nodded slowly, thinking before he jerked his chin in dismissal.

Åsmund bowed his head to his clan leader and departed swiftly but calmly before his face gave way to the anger he could feel brewing beneath his skin.

"Are you satisfied?"

Tatius plucked a flower as they walked by a purple bushel in the sanctuary, watching it wilt between her fingers before magic glowed up its stem. It blossomed back to life, and she dropped it, disinterested. "Am I ever satisfied?"

"No," Valdren said amiably. "You always hunger for more."

Tatius's grin was nearly feral, looking at the Dragon Keeper. "Oh, hunger, I do. But not for long."

Valdren raised a brow at her and narrowed his eyes. "Whatever game you are playing at Tatius, it is a dangerous one."

Tatius snorted. "Please, save your lectures for a God who cares. Games are for children, and while I might *still* look like a child, I am not one."

The Dragon Keeper closed his eyes and blew out a deep breath. "Apologies," he murmured.

"Forgiven," she said with a wave of her hand.

"Will you please tell me what you are doing though?"

Tatius laughed delicately, and she brought up an amused hand to her mouth, looking up at him. "Oh, Valdren, where would the fun be in that?"

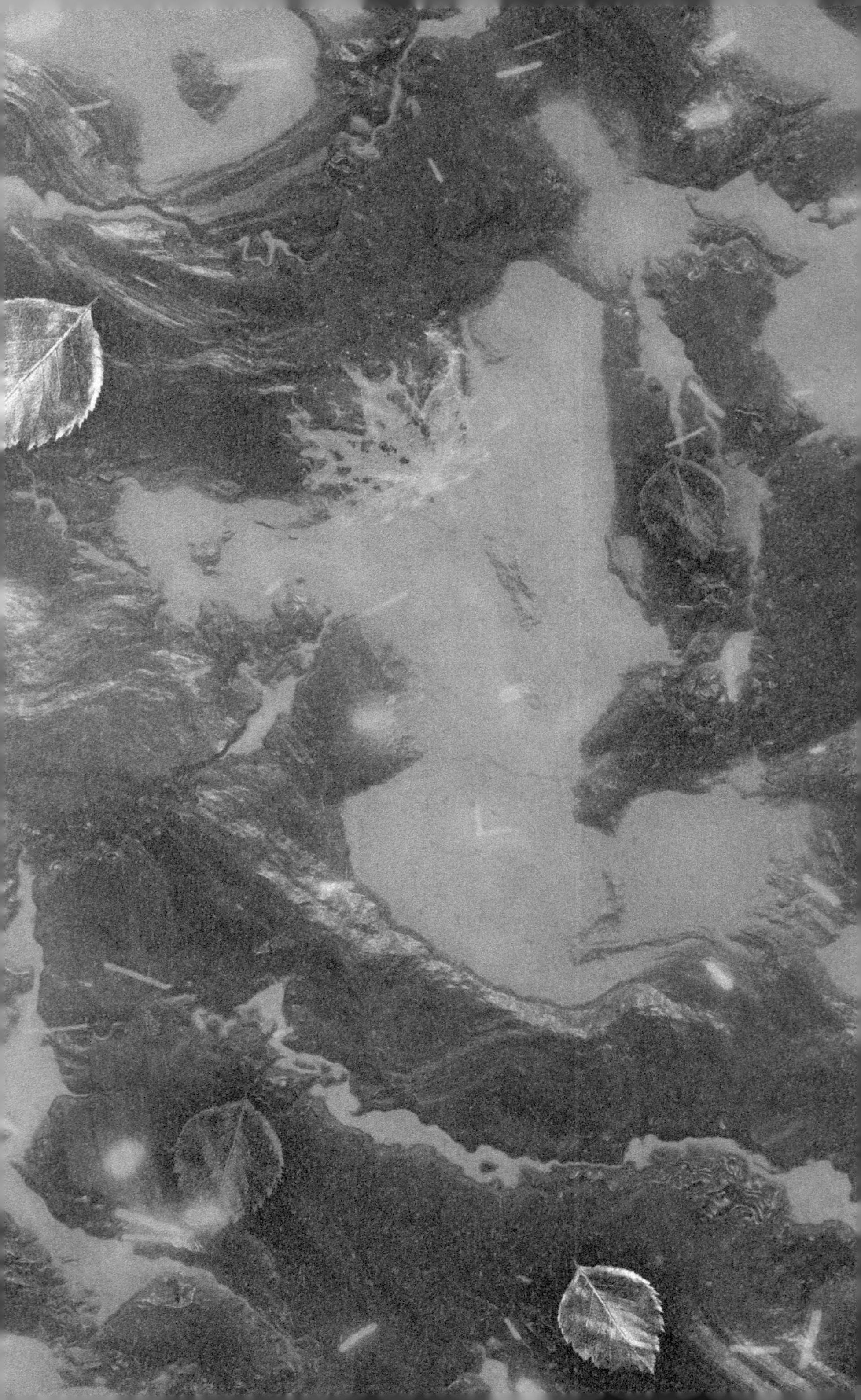

# CHAPTER 13

"You weren't in your room."

Hazen's neck prickled with awareness, feeling his eyes on her before he even spoke, her stomach flipped at the low timber. She laughed softly under her breath as Åsmund took up the spot on the ground beside her. "What a keen observation you have, General."

She sat at the tunnel entrance she had arrived through so many weeks ago, sitting on the ledge, one of her legs hanging free over the side, the other tucked under as she leaned against the glassy black wall.

When she had awoken in her room, thoughts of Rose and the death she had succumbed to both physically and mentally when chosen as the keeper of the new world infiltrated her mind; the mountain felt stifling, suffocating almost, and she all but ran to find open air. Her feet took her to the mouth of the tunnel where she now sat and hadn't moved since.

"It's dangerous to be sitting here alone at the edge."

Her lips curled in the slightest, tilting her head to regard him. His green eyes were fixated on her face, his emotions hidden beneath the flecks of gold she saw in them. "A lot of things are dangerous in this world, Åsmund."

His legs framed hers as he leaned casually back, adjusting his wings to fit in the space. One black leather-clad leg swung freely over the ledge, the other bent up, resting his hand on his knee. Hazen tried not to let her eyes wander, but the expanse of his chest took up most of her view. The little gold hoop through his nipple caught her eye, and her mouth went dry.

"Do you like what you see?"

Hazen's eyes snapped up to his, her breath catching as she flushed hotly. His deep voice was like a caress, and heat blazed in his emerald gaze, sucking all the air between them until there was only the thick crackle of energy.

"I'm sorry," she murmured, casting her eyes away.

Åsmund›s jaw flexed, and he tilted his head, leaning forward to close the space between them, his finger brushing her blonde hair away from her cheek before nudging her chin to look at him. "Don›t be sorry."

The gentle scrape of his callouses on her skin made a shiver run down her body, and she raised her hand to touch his.

He pulled back, and she instantly missed his heat. However, she didn't say anything when she saw him school his emotions.

Clearing her throat, Hazen ran a soothing hand down her leathers despite her racing heart.

A pregnant silence filled the space between them, and from the corner of her vision, she could see his gaze on her and feel its touch along the collar of her neck.

"Do you have a last name?" she asked suddenly, wishing to fill the tense silence and ease the roiling inside her.

When Åsmund didn't answer, she glanced at him from beneath her lashes, seeing his look of confusion. His firm mouth twisted into a frown, digesting her words.

"A second name?" he asked finally.

She nodded. "Yes, a name that comes after your first one. It's your family name."

His frown turned into a wry smile, and he cocked a brow at her. "Two names for one person? Are you not satisfied with just the one?"

Hazen huffed, smiling slightly. "So, is that a no?"

Åsmund tapped a finger along his knee in thought. "Drago are not created like normal Fae. We are born from fire, so a family name wouldn't suit us. And the Fae do not have more than one name simply because there is no need. Some carry titles or clan names attached to theirs, but never a second name."

His eyes were lit with curiosity when he looked at her, and Hazen admired the mossy colour.

"Do you have a second name?" he intoned.

His question had her smile falling as she turned to look at the world beyond the mountain. She did have a second name and a family attached to it, a family she missed dearly and wondered if they missed her too.

Sunbeams filtered through the clouds, sifting into their space. Light danced over her fingers as she lifted them to the warmth.

"I do, yes," she said quietly, dropping her hand to her lap. "I have a second name and a middle name."

"A middle name?" he asked.

"Humans sometimes have many names," she explained. "My middle name is a token of remembrance more than just a name."

"A name for a memory?"

Hazen smiled a soft, almost sad smile, nodding once. "My mother had a difficult time conceiving a child. Before me, there were... many attempts—many failed ones. But there was one that had stuck. It was a girl, and her name was Sophia. She would be two years older than me if she were still here."

Åsmund frowned. "I'm sorry."

Hazen shook her head, waving it off despite the tight squeeze in her chest, eyes trained on the blue horizon as if it would ground her emotions. "I never met my sister; the pregnancy didn't hold, and my mother lost her at six months. But I carry her with me wherever I go." She wasn't emotional over the loss of her sister. She had never met her. Hazen herself hadn't been alive, but knowing what it had done to her mother and the guilt she had carried with her, that is why she felt the burning of tears and the tightening in her throat.

Leaning forward, Åsmund turned his head to catch her eyes, straightening when she finally looked at him. "May I ask for all your names?"

His gaze was so sincere it made her chest ache, and she nodded with a soft laugh. "My full name is Hazen Sophia Solvaya."

"Hazen Sophia Solvaya," he repeated lowly.

The way her name slipped over his tongue like he was tasting the sounds made her breath catch, and she whispered back, "Yes."

"All your names are beautiful," he said.

She blushed under the compliment, ducking her head so he couldn't see the smile lifting her lips. "When humans meet, they shake hands and introduce themselves with their first and last name, depending on the situation. And if the situation grows romantically, they sometimes share names."

"You shake hands? That seems odd. Is it a show of strength?"

Hazen giggled, seeing his perplexity. Extending her hand, her mouth twitched with a suppressed laugh when he looked down at it, brows raised. Wriggling her fingers, she asked, "Is the General afraid they'll bite him?" She leaned in conspiratorially, a sly grin on her lips. "Don't worry, I only bite if you ask me to." His eyes darkened, and heat shot through her body, but she pushed it down with a soft sigh. "Give me your hand."

A second's hesitation was all he made her wait before he slowly extended his hand and slipped his fingers around hers. A fire ignited a path from where their hands joined, travelling throughout her body, leaving her breathless.

"Not too firm, but like this." She gently applied pressure to his hand and shook it once, then twice. "Hello, I'm Hazen Solvaya. It's a pleasure to formally introduce myself to you."

Understanding filled his face, and he gripped her hand firmly but without crushing her fingers. "The pleasure and honour are all mine, Hazen Solvaya. I am Åsmund, General of Clan Drago."

Despite the heat and tension, she felt coiling tightly in her stomach, her dragon delightfully aware of the general's presence; she smiled.

They stayed like that for a moment, his thumb brushing the pulse point at her wrist and sending her nerves scattering before Åsmund let her hand go, and she retracted her fingers. Turning to watch two small yellow birds dive through the clouds.

"I wish I could fly like them," she commented wistfully.

"You will."

Hazen snorted. "When I sprout wings?"

"You will," he restated.

That gave her pause. The idea of wings was less foreign than she thought it would be. "What does it feel like? Flying, I mean."

When Åsmund didn't answer, she looked at him only to see him stand and offer his hand. Her neck craned to look up at him. He was immaculate, all muscle and imposing power, veins corded around the arm he stretched out to her.

"Let me show you."

Those four words had her scrambling to her feet.

"Take my hand, Hazen."

It was a command, and Hazen listened.

Åsmund pulled her towards him, turning her body until her back was flush down the front of him. Hazen could feel every tangible ridge of muscle and the press of him through his leathers against her backside. Every cell in her body lit up at his touch, her skin rising and becoming sensitive at the contact of his chest against her exposed back. The scent of his musk, sweat, and spice filled her nose, and she wanted to bathe in that smell, to bury her nose in his neck and breathe it in.

Instead, she stood frozen, her breaths shallow, breasts tightening when his hand caressed her hip through her leathers and one arm banded around her middle, the other going around her chest.

They stood at the lip, back to chest, his arms tightening around her like anchors with the empty blue sky ahead.

"Don't close your eyes," he whispered, his breath fanning her neck.

And then they were free-falling.

The world opened up, and Hazen's heart stopped beating as they dove towards the Earth. Trees grew larger and larger, and Hazen squeezed her eyes shut despite his words as they neared certain death. Then, Åsmund's wings snapped open at the last second, and she jerked in his arms, shrieking, eyes shooting open. They were flying up and up and up, the forest a pinprick with every push of his mighty wings.

"You closed your eyes, didn't you?" he asked wryly against the shell of her ear.

Laughter bubbled in her chest, and a smile bloomed over her face. It was all the answer he needed.

Hazen spread her arms wide as they cut through wind, clouds, and sunlight, feeling the rush of adrenaline and… freedom. It was freedom, she felt. The elation of her dragon pressed against her bones and filled her with euphoria.

Tilting her head back against Åsmund's shoulder, she let the world fly by them as he dove them up and through thick fluffy clouds, perspiration coating their skin and drying in the sunlight when they emerged on the other side. They flew by the small yellow birds who chirped at their intrusion, through the sunbeams, and around and around the mountain until they flew above its pinnacle and the world spread before them.

Åsmund hovered them above the tip of the mountain, and Hazen watched the world she had travelled across. An acceptance fell into place as she hung there above it all. That somewhere near the sea, Savven and Brean and Lithônion were alive and well, and beneath the sea were the last resistance of mermaids who believed in a life filled with something good and kind. Somewhere within the forest below them was Vika watching Makari playing bandits, and in the opposite direction beneath the earth were two brothers and their mother who longed for a day when they no longer had to live in the darkness. A goblin who offered up his home to two strangers passing in the night, families that lived in fear but held onto hope, a blacksmith who lost his family and was clinging to grief, and a keeper who was counting on her to be something more than what she was born into.

She would do whatever it was Tatius wanted of her if it meant repaying the kindness of strangers, the death toll that hung over them, and returning the life they knew.

Arms tightened around her, and Hazen melted against his chest. Breathing in the fresh air, she closed her eyes to feel the life pulsing around them.

"What does it feel like?" he whispered.

"Living," she sighed. "It feels like living."

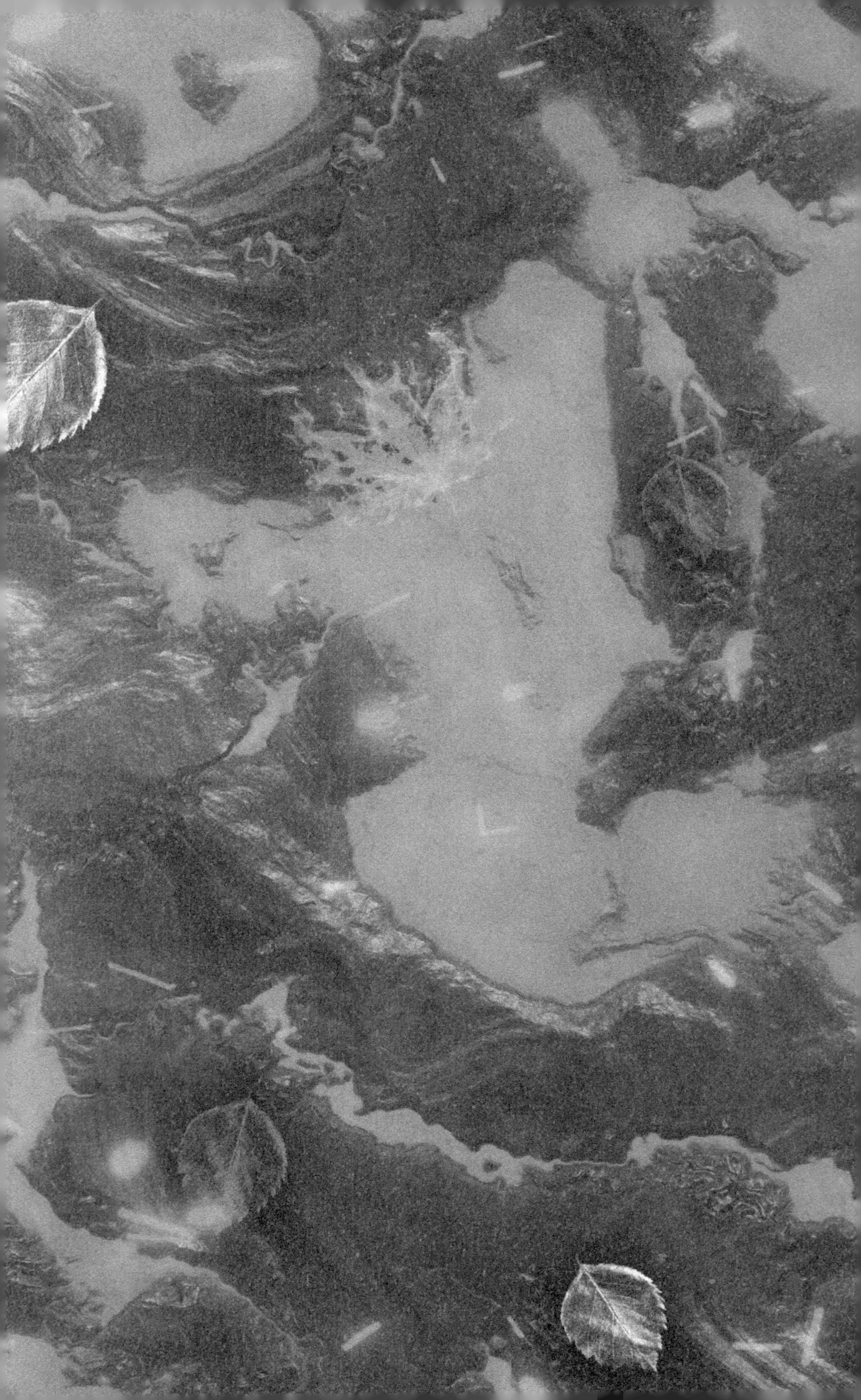

# CHAPTER 14

Swords danced, and Hazen's feet flew across the floor, sweat coating her skin like a second layer. She bared her teeth at Åsmund in a feral smile, sparks danced between their bodies as she hurled her sword up to block him.

"Look at this, Åsmund is going easy on the human. He must be losing his touch."

Kain's snide jeering made Hazen's eyes flash dangerously, annoyance ticked her jaw.

"Don't," growled Åsmund, still pressing against her blade.

Hazen's power flared hotly in response, hearing his mocking laugh. It had been a week since she had met with Forndýr and Tatius, a week for her mindset to completely change, and a week since Åsmund had taken her flying.

Things between her and the general were different but also not. The tension when they were around each other stole her breath every time. When he walked her to her door, he would stop and watch her silently before brushing her errant stray hairs away from her face with a single finger, but that was as far as it went. He was stoic as ever in the conduit and around any other soldiers, but when they were alone, his mask slipped just enough to see heat blazing there.

Kain had begun showing up at their training sessions during that time. Watching them with leering smirks and cold eyes and making comments about her strength or form. He even went as far as suggesting she was providing sexual favours to Åsmund in exchange for letting her win in the sparring ring. Enough so that Åsmund had to stop her from hurling her sword at his back when he had turned to leave.

She snapped at him for stopping her, and when he wouldn't give her sword back, she stalked off to stretch, mumbling under her breath about asshole males.

Hazen broke away from Åsmund, their swords screeching, putting space between them. Pacing, she took a long breath, her free hand on her hip, the other still holding her sword by her side.

Kain seemed to get off on her anger, his jeering was getting worse with each training session. Eventually, he brought along a couple of males, one she recognised from her first day as the shorter male he had been sparring with.

Three of them stood against the back wall, towards the entrance into the conduit. Arms crossed over their bare chests arrogantly, eyes cold and judging. Kain's mouth tilted in a smirk when she glared his way.

The conduit was full of soldiers training, the forges blazing, the ringing of weapons sparring, grunts from hand-to-hand combat, and hammers on anvils rose into the bottleneck. Yet Kain's voice was the loudest of them all, making sure any ears listening could hear him.

Hazen pursed her lips, narrowed her eyes and raised her sword. Jerking her chin, she arced her sword and spun away from Åsmund as he lunged forward, fast as a viper.

"Awe, is the princess upset at me?" Kain called mockingly.

"Ignore. Him," Åsmund commanded through gritted teeth, knocking her blade aside when she struck.

"If he doesn't" —she lunged, ducking under his arm and swinging— "shut up, I'm going to put my sword" —she spun when his blade sliced the air where her stomach had just been— "through his face."

"So violent," Åsmund mused wickedly, his teeth flashing in a smile when he blocked her attack.

"You'll never be strong enough!" Kain called. "You're just a female! What can a female do that a male can't?"

Hazen caught sight of several eyes turning their direction, and she gritted her teeth in a snarl. Her power crested into an inferno, and her hands shook with the need to suppress it. The orbs of fire flickered their attention to her.

"Concentrate, Hazen," Åsmund ordered, the steely voice of the general falling into his tone, noticing her distraction.

The power hummed deliciously in her ears, whispering for release. Her dragon stormed her limbs, filling every nerve in her body with a desire to rip Kain apart.

"Hazen," Åsmund growled, dropping his sword and grabbing her shoulder to garner her attention.

She stared up at him through lowered brows, teeth grinding together as a shrill, girly squeal emanated from the three males behind her. Åsmund closed his eyes, loosening a defeated sigh.

"Give up!" Kain shouted.

More eyes turned to them, and Hazen jerked out of Åsmund's hold, rounding on them. A storm of fury and wrath crackled in her gaze, power funnelling through her and down the blade when she flipped the sword in her grip and arched her arm back. Her sword went sailing like a dart straight for Kain's head.

Kain's eyes widened, and he dodged to the side just before the sword embedded into the stone behind him with a deafening crack.

The conduit went silent.

Kain recovered himself, and he snickered. "Look at the little human trying to be one of us. Can't even use a real sword."

No one laughed, no one so much as dared breathe.

Hazen stalked towards them slowly, the silence around her palpable.

One of the males tried pulling the sword from the stone but hissed when his fingers came in contact with the hilt and jerked his hand away, looking at the red tinge of seared flesh. "What kind of power is this?" he seethed.

Kain's eyes darted to the blade, narrowing. "Did you learn a bit of magic?"

"Magic?" Hazen intoned quietly. "No. No magic."

His dark eyes trained on her, he squared his shoulders at her approach. "A general at your back and a little training, and now you think you can throw tantrums like a babe." He snorted, crossed his arms and looked at the two males.

She stopped, looked up at him silently, and walked past him to her sword.

Kain scoffed when she passed him. "What happened to the girl who entered our world? Growing a backbone, are you?"

Taking the hilt, power immediately wrapped around her hand, welcoming her to touch the weapon, and put one leg on the wall for leverage as she pulled the sword from the stone. It slid out with a hiss.

Pivoting, Hazen regarded Kain thoughtfully. "What happened to her?" she asked, tilting her head. Her body thrummed with energy from the tip of her blade to the tip of her toes. Bringing the sword to rest on her shoulder, she stepped up to the male until they were chest to chest. Her voice was so soft only he could hear her. "She was easier to kill, so I burned that bitch."

She reached up and gave his cheek a sharp pat and a biting smile, letting her power rise to the surface just enough to know that it showed in her eyes.

Kain leaned forward and seethed through clenched teeth, anger dancing across his features. "You might be protected here because of him, but you better watch your back if we're ever on the battlefield."

His threat was too low for anyone to hear, but she could feel Åsmund's stare drilling into the side of her head.

Hazen smirked and walked away, but not before saying, "I look forward to it."

Åsmund's face was the mask of a general, but his eyes were furious, trained on Kain as the male and his two lackeys stormed out of the conduit.

"Sword," he ordered, holding out his hand for her blade.

"Please?" she snipped with a raised brow, still feeling the high of her power as it ebbed back into a state of normalcy.

His jaw ticked, he turned those blazing green eyes to her, and they instantly softened. "Please," he corrected lowly.

She handed it to him hilt first, glancing at the soldier's looking their way. There was a glimmer of respect in their gazes. Some of them tilted their heads in acknowledgement before returning to their tasks. The silence died when the conduit's activities resumed, and Hazen followed Åsmund to the weapons rack.

"Training isn't done for the day?" she questioned.

He racked her weapon, and she watched him scrub a hand over his face before turning to her. She stepped out of the way when his wings grazed close to her legs.

"Training is over." He nodded towards the tunnel. "I have something I want to show you. Something Kain said made me realise you don't know much about what runs through your blood. What consumes you when you feel such heavy emotions."

"Oh, I think I do," she muttered, thinking of the dragon that consumed both her and Rose.

Åsmund smiled softly down at her. "Let me show you what power the dragons truly have."

The air was pungent with the smell of sulphur, as Åsmund led Hazen down into a spiralling tunnel. Heat wavering in the air like a thick blanket, her bones sighed under the heavy warmth.

Down and down they went, deep into the mountain's belly, until Hazen wrinkled her nose from the smell. Once again, she had nearly forgotten that rotten egg stench, but now she didn't think she would ever forget it.

Rounding a steep corner, the ground slanted sharply, and the dimly lit tunnel began to glow like an ember, an orange light moved along the glassy stone like the reflection of water. The ground evened out, and black walls melted into a mammoth cave hosting a magma core beneath the mountain.

Its swirling pool of lava bubbled and rumbled like a living thing. The only ground to stand on was a crescent patch of obsidian roughly ten feet wide and twice as long before the sides dropped into the inferno. Hazen looked up and saw hundreds of tunnels carved into the closed bottleneck.

"It's a volcano," she breathed in awe.

Åsmund stood at the ledge, framed in fiery light, his back to her. "The Drago were created by the dragons and Gods millenniums ago to forge warriors who would withstand the rise and fall of empires. But we are not Fae. We are not little elfin princes waiting within the protection of our mountain. We defend outlying villages and the borders of our lands and fight battles when commanded to." He turned to gaze down at her, the magma banking them in heat. "We are weapons forged in fire."

Hazen reached up and flicked his nose lightly, and he startled. "You are so dramatic."

He grabbed her hand, chuckling, and dropped a kiss on her knuckles. "Let me show you."

Too surprised by his kiss, she didn't have a chance to say anything when Åsmund stepped away and shot into the air, her loose strands of hair from her braid flying around her face.

He flew across the bottleneck, hovering over the molten fire. "Don't scream."

She opened her mouth, but he tucked his massive wings in tight and dove. He dove straight into the magma.

Hazen didn't scream, but if her facial expressions could speak, they were screaming.

He was consumed within nanoseconds. His glorious, beautiful body and wings were simply gone with barely a splash from the lava. Hazen's heart skittered across her ribs before going into an outright sprint.

Eyes widening, they darted over the liquid surface, searching for any sign of him. Hazen forced in a shaking breath, panic beginning to bloom, and she toed the edge, head darting back and forth.

Fire didn't burn her, so lava wouldn't either, right? Her brain shouted for her to jump, her feet scrapping over a loose rock, and it skidded over the side, the magma hissing when it plopped in, devouring it.

"Fuck," she breathed.

Hazen sucked in a steadying breath, her chest heaving with every forced lungful of hot air she made herself take.

Oh Gods, he was dead.

He couldn't be.

*He cannot be dead.*

A thousand thoughts spiralled in her head, and she squeezed her eyes shut, forcing her mind to quiet.

She would jump.

She was going to jump.

Her toes hung off the sides.

She should have just cannonballed in.

Get it over with.

*"Coward,"* her power seemed to whisper, tunnelling into her, filling her limbs until her hands began to shake.

"Fuck it," she growled and made to leap when the core exploded in a boom that echoed throughout the chamber, and lava went flying around her like molten rain.

Åsmund emerged shrouded in magma and fire. The glowing magma slowly slipped off his body like liquid burning gold, looking every bit a harbinger of death. He hovered over the boiling pool, black wings ablaze, his hands and forearms were wrapped in cords of fire that shifted in a burning dance.

He flew to her and landed softly, the wind from his wings banking across her body when she stumbled back from the ledge. His green eyes were soft, watching her despite the wrath his presence promised.

Relief calmed the panic in her gut until hot anger flared up in its place, and she marched up to him and punched him square in the nose.

Or tried to, at least.

He caught her fist, lowered it, and held it between them. The fire wrapped around his hand, transferring to her like a snake that coiled over her skin.

"You scared the shit out of me, Åsmund," she whispered, staring at the fire intertwining them.

Åsmund brought up his other hand to stroke her cheek, and she looked up at him, watching the light of flames dance over his high cheekbones and deep caramel skin, the small gold hoop through his nose glimmering. His fingers trailed a burning path to her neck that she felt down to the apex of her thighs, her mouth parted on a breath when his thumb paused over the wild fluttering of her heart.

His eyes darkened, holding her gaze, and his hand continued down over her collarbones to her chest, where he laid his palm flat just above her breasts, and her whole body tightened under him.

"You were chosen by the dragons, forged in their flames, but you do not have magic within you, Hazen," he said, his voice low.

Her power careened through her at the touch of his flames to her chest as if proving his words true, and Hazen felt like she would burst from the pressure building. The heat, the liquid fire, the pulsing within her, and the nearness of Åsmund was all too much, so she brought her free hand up to the one on her chest and placed it over his, tunnelling it into him.

His eyes went wide with amazement, the gold flecks in them flaring brightly, she couldn't make herself look away. Hazen was completely enraptured.

The fire wrapped around his hands spread over her, tattooing her exposed skin in a web of flames. She could feel its energy seeping into her skin. There was so much of it, her power a living thrumming thing in her body as she channelled it into him, and she could feel his mend and join with hers; there was no separation of the two. She was the dragon within her, and the dragon was her, and Åsmund's essence interwove over them, and she over him. His power was nearly overwhelming, but between the two, they were balanced, joined as one, and Hazen felt it claim her as its own.

His nostrils flared as their energy was joined, his face a look of wonder, pride, and primal heat.

"You have power. Pure, undiluted, ancient power that is as old as our world, Hazen Sophia Solvaya." His words were murmured like a caress, her name sounding like honey on his tongue, and he dipped his head until they shared breath.

She could see the softness of his eyelashes and the faded scar across his eyebrow. She could feel his breath fan across her skin, making her heart race. The world around them melted into a sizzling inferno.

"We are weapons. Crafted to destroy, and, if possible… mend." A smile tilted his mouth, and Hazen's eyes dropped to it before his following words rang through her. "And you will be the greatest of us all."

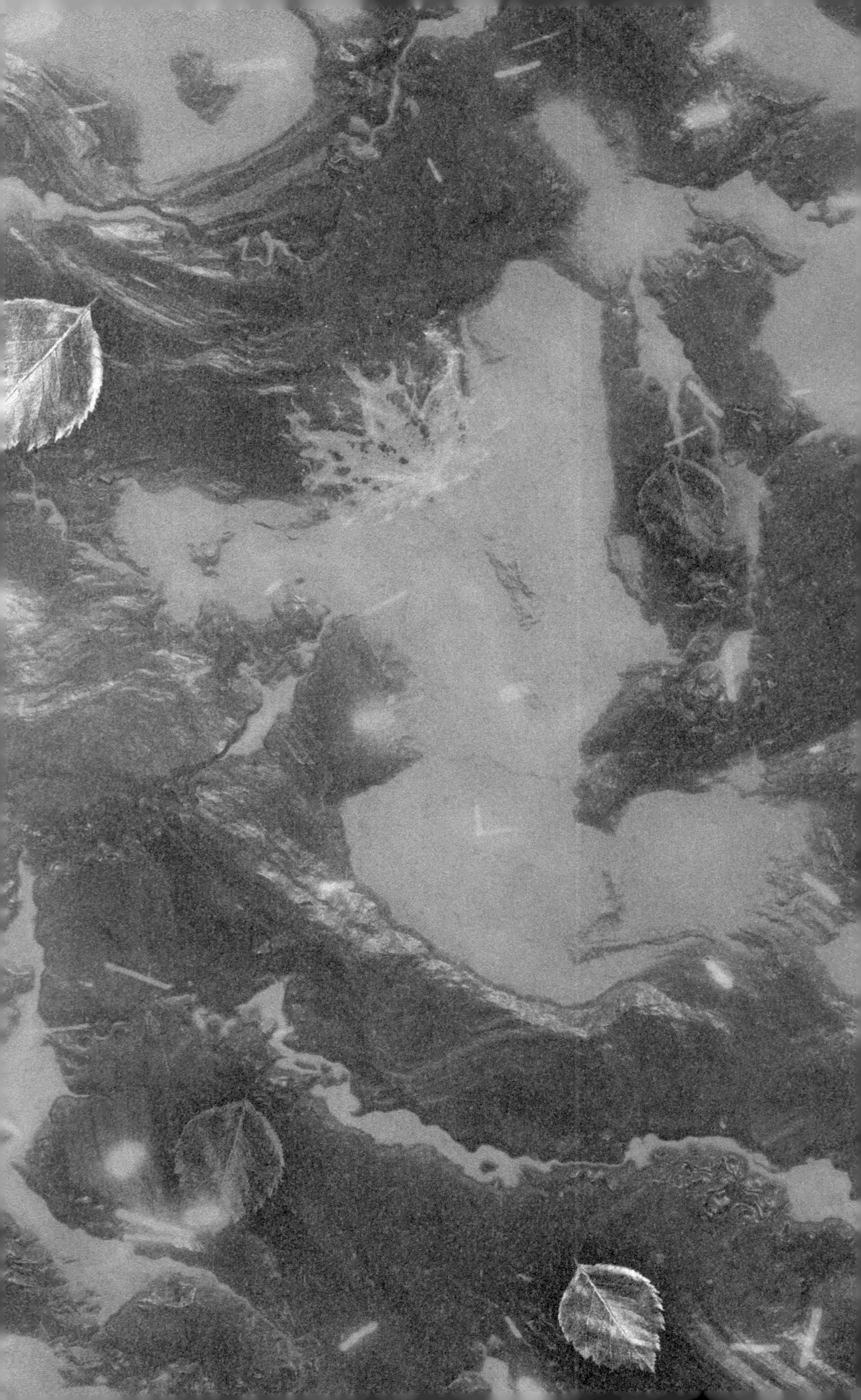

# CHAPTER 15

Brean stared at the small pouch in her hands, the grey leather smooth despite its worn state. It fit perfectly in the palm of her hand, the rounded out bottom nestled tightly in her grip. She had yet to peek inside it, fearing what the blood of the Nexus Tree might do to her if she touched it.

*"Mix it with liquid fire,"* the witch had said.

Mixing it would be easy enough, but storing it—containing something that could kill the dead or command it—was another challenge altogether.

Footsteps squelched the mud to her right, and she glanced up briefly.

"If you stare at it long enough, it might just give you all of life's answers," Néefar said casually as he leaned on the other side of the wooden table she sat at, arms crossed over his chest. He was dressed in the Fae army blacks just as she was. It was all they had to give them as the world around them rotted and every natural fibre disintegrated before they could think to use it.

Brean looked back down at the pouch, frowning, the noise of training ringing in her ears loud enough that she could barely focus.

She'd found herself coming to the training field every day since their arrival, watching Savven train with the elven army and, on more occasions, leading them through drills and regiments—though he refused to state that was what he was doing. He fell into the role of a leader as naturally as breathing; it was in his blood, and Brean was fortunate enough to witnessed it all as the days passed.

The three of them had shared the tree house for the first week, but it promptly fell ill due to rot and collapsed one day, the final crack resounding across the city like a death knell. Luckily, none of them had been in there. Now, they resided in three dried mud domes just beyond the training field, choosing to remain close to the activity and city centre.

They had all helped build them, along with several other Fae. Savven had rolled up his sleeves and got to work making more throughout the city for when more trees fell. Building homes not just for his soldiers, but their families and the citizens of his city. There was pride in Brean as she watched him fall into his role so easily; even if he rejected the title, his honour and commitment to his people were still there. This was her home just as much as it was his, and seeing him care for it despite the heaviness being home brought him warmed her heart.

But at night, when there was a storm, or she couldn't sleep, she would wander outside for a midnight stroll. Sometimes, she would see him slip into the darkness and disappear through the forest. She never followed him, never asked what he did in there. They all had their demons and handled them in different ways.

Now, she sat at one of the long tables where food was served daily to the soldiers, usually a ration of stew and bread, trying for the life of her to figure out what to do with the little pouch and the powder it contained.

Néefar's inquiring blue eyes just stared at her, and she could feel them waiting for her to answer or just say something in response.

Finally, she looked up at him, tilting her head in question. "Néefar, is there something I can help you with? I'm very busy."

He raised a brow, his silver hair gleaming in the faint sunlight through the grey overcast. Storms were more frequent now, the earth almost a near constant slush of mud.

"You look *so* busy, Witch, I just had to interrupt you," he replied sarcastically.

She gave him a small, cutting smile, narrowing her eyes slightly. "How kind."

Brean turned her attention back to the pouch, huffing when the item didn't magically give her the answers she needed.

"Have you opened it up?"

She arched a brow at him. "No, I have not."

He shrugged. "Maybe you should?"

"What do you want, Néefar?" she asked, tucking the pouch safely back into the confines of her short stays. She missed her pockets.

Néefar loosened a resigned sign. "I was hoping to find our princely friend. It would appear wherever you go, he follows, and where he goes, you magically are there. So, I was hoping to find him shadowing your skirts so I could speak with him, but alas, no such luck."

Brean glowered at the male. "We do not shadow each other, Shifter. We are friends, that is all."

The look he gave her said he believed her as much as she believed herself.

It was true that they shadowed each other, whether unknowingly or not. He was never far from her, and she found herself searching for him subconsciously if they were apart. But that did not make them more than companions. Savven was her friend; she cared for him, and she believed a part of him cared for her.

If there were feelings there, she could never act on them. Savven was a prince, and she was an orphaned witch, she wasn't even Fae.

Smiling tightly at the shifter, she looked around the training field, her amber eyes searching for the familiar head of long black hair, agile form, and solemn blue eyes.

He wasn't there.

Brean pursed her lips and looked back at Néefar, who raised his dark brows at her, the only indication that he had once had brown hair.

"What would you like me to do?" she asked indignant

Néefar shrugged again, looking wholly unbothered. "I think I saw him wander into the forest some time ago."

"Well, if you know where he is, then why don't you go find him?" she drolled, making to stand.

"I would," he sighed, feigning a pained expression, "but I promised a sparring session to Aleon."

"The blacksmith?" Brean asked.

"A wager, really." Néefar stood, and Brean followed. "A shifter against a blacksmith, best male wins."

She snorted, rolling her eyes. "You have no money. What are you betting with?"

He grinned rakishly, tugging the hem of his tunic to straighten it. "Pride."

"Of course, typical males."

Raising his palms in defence, he added. "If you find some free money lying around, let me know, and we'll wager that."

"If I find free money, I'll wager it all on Aleon," she called over her shoulder, walking towards the treeline.

"I'm wounded, Witch!"

She caught sight of him placing a hand to his heart as if she genuinely offended him, and just shook her head, looking away. If she had stared just a moment longer, she would have seen Néefar's satisfied smirk and soft shake of his head as she went to find their lost prince.

The forest was quiet. Part in reason because it was dangerous to walk among the trees now, lest they suddenly topple over from the rot and crush whoever braved the trek. Grey stained the colourful world around her, curling around roots and trunks, thick branches laying barren on the ground, having snapped off from high above. The corpses of trees long since dead toppled over on their sides scattered throughout, pieces of splintered wood disintegrating under her black boots.

A soft wind blew from the east, and she closed her eyes, hearing its whisper in her soul. She let her feet carry her in its direction. Climbing over a thick fallen trunk, she jumped to the ground on the other side, brushing the bark from her clothes.

Salt filled the air, and she took a deep breath of the fresh scent. She had forgotten how close they were to the water—not the sea, but the ocean—an endless chasm of water where the horizon kissed the waves and the sun claimed the sky every morning.

Brean remembered a time long ago when she was a girl and would escape to the very cliffs she now walked towards. She would watch storms roll in and look for a home long since lost on that horizon, hoping that maybe her nightmares were just nightmares and not memories. That the gentle touch of a woman Brean could barely remember, her face nothing more than a blur, and sweet voice with a lilting accent singing her to sleep was not just the whisps of a memory—but a dream, and one day, Brean would wake up. The crack of lightning and flash of thunder would not make her tremble, and she would not have to be strong every day of her life after. That she would still have her family. She wouldn't be just Brean the Witch but Brean McKenzie, daughter of Sorcha and Lyle Mackenzie.

Pushing the thoughts of the past back into the deep recesses of her mind, Brean stopped when she saw Savven kneeling at the cliff edge, the stormy sky above him, the tossing sea below, and the wind grazing through his blue-black hair.

He looked like an artist had painted him into the surroundings: beautiful, otherworldly, and with the weight of a kingdom on his shoulders. *The Reverent Prince* would be the image's title if it were to have one.

Softly, Brean came to his side and saw the smooth oval stone on the grassy slope. There was something carved into it in the old Fae language. Although she couldn't read it, it was easy to assume it was a name.

This was a grave.

"It's the day of her birth celebration," he said quietly after some time.

She kneeled beside him, smoothing her wild red curls back when the wind blew them across her face. "Is this where you come at night?"

Savven didn't so much as move. "You noticed that?"

"I've begun to notice a lot about you," she admitted sheepishly, her cheeks tinged pink; whether from the wind or embarrassment, she couldn't say.

He looked at her then, his expression guarded, but there was a softness to his eyes that mixed with guilt and grief before he turned back to the stone.

"She's not buried here. He—my father—burned her body and spread her ashes over the water. But I needed," he paused, swallowing, "I need something to remember, to go to."

Brean brushed delicate fingers over the engraving. "It's never easy to lose a parent, but to lose two is the greatest burden a child can carry, no matter the age."

"I'm sorry," he said, laying a hand over hers. "I know it must be hard living with their deaths."

A shadow of a sad smile twisted her lips. "I do not speak about my own, Savven."

Savven's brows furrowed. "I have not lost both my parents."

"Maybe not to death," she elaborated. "But death is almost a reprieve compared to losing a parent by their choice."

Savven's shoulders tensed.

Seeing this, Brean laid a calming hand on his shoulder. "I mean no disrespect."

His bitter laugh was clipped. "You cannot disrespect the truth. It is a harsh reality and one I must face regardless." Savven turned his face away from her, his jaw flexing tightly.

"It's not your fault, Savven," whispered Brean.

A low growl rippled through him, and she watched his hands ball in his lap.

The ocean below crashed against the cliff, and thunder rumbled with the promise of another storm. Brean tensed momentarily at the sound. Taking a calming breath, she steeled herself and focused on Savven.

"It's not your fault, Savven," she repeated.

He whirled, teeth bared, and eyes flashing. Brean's breath lodged in her throat at the sight, at the pain that filled those blue depths and the little space between them. He was so close she could nearly feel his heart racing through his chest.

"I watched that traitor Laudin fire an arrow through my mother's chest! I *pleaded* with them to run, to seek shelter! If I had been more adamant, demanded they go—"

"—Nothing would have changed," Brean cut him off quietly, bringing a hand to his cold cheek. It would seem he had been out here for a while.

Savven's eyes went wide at her words, his face falling.

"Fate is the one thing no one has control over, Savven. Your mother would have died regardless, my parents would have died regardless, it didn't matter how or when, but that it *would* happen exactly when fate designed it." She poured every ounce of compassion and understanding she had into him, getting lost in the ocean-blue eyes that began to well with tears. "You were just a son trying to protect his family. You did well, Savven. Now let it go."

He jerked his head, trying to turn away from her. "You don't—"

"—Let it go," she countered in a soft whisper, holding his face in her hands. She wouldn't let him go; she would be there for him the way she wished someone had been there for her. A stronghold that could weather his turbulent waters.

Savven snarled when she didn't let go and brought his face closer to hers. "Release me."

"Make me," she retorted.

He didn't, and his eyes searched hers.

"Let it out, Savven."

His nostrils flared.

Brean rested her forehead against his. "Let it out."

And then the sea kissed her skin as Savven let it all out. His face cradled in her hands, they knelt together before his mother's grave, the storm above opening up and washing it away.

Brean found herself staring at the pouch again the following day, scowling at it. She was leaning against a cracked half of a tree trunk, the other half behind her, beside the archery range. She brushed an errant curl that had fallen out of her braid behind her ear, stuffing the pouch back into its spot in her half stays and crossing her arms over her chest, watching the archers.

"Are you getting into trouble over here?"

Savven's smooth voice had her turning, and she gave him a welcoming smile. "Oh, always, Prince. When is a witch not in trouble?"

An arrow sunk into a straw target nearest them with a *thunk*, Brean let it steal her attention away from the Fae male next to her.

"Thank you for yesterday," said Savven quietly, standing shoulder to shoulder with her, watching the archers.

She shrugged. "You're my friend, Savven. That's what friends do."

Her neck prickled, and Brean glanced at him from beneath her lashes. Dark blue eyes were trained on her, a soft look in their depths and a clarity that hadn't been there since she had first met the prince.

A flush crawled up her neck under his stare, but she couldn't force herself to look away. "What is it?" she breathed.

"I've never met a female quite like yourself. I'm a prince of the High Fae. Most would have never cared enough to come find me."

Well, she wasn't a female, was she? Not in the way they thought. She was a woman. But he didn't know that. Brean gave him a wry smile and squeezed his hand quickly. "You need to get better friends."

Savven's face fell, and his gaze went distant.

She realised the error of her words too late, and her eyes went wide with horror. "I didn't mean to offend. I was only jesting."

He shook his head. "It's okay."

"It's not!" she argued. "I was misplaced in my speaking. I

apologise."

Savven laid a hand on her shoulder, offering her a shadow of a smile. "Forgiven."

Brean pursed her lips, hating herself for what she had just said, but turned her attention back to the archers.

An arrow sailed straight and narrow down the line, sinking into the black centre ring and coming out the back.

Néefar strolled around the archers, brows raised, eyeing the bows and stock of arrows.

"Contemplating joining them?" Savven inquired when the shifter ambled their way.

Néefar shrugged with a smirk. "I would, but I wouldn't want to hurt their pride when they get shown up by a little ol' shifter."

Brean's snort was loud and unladylike, and she rolled her eyes. "The day you best an elf is the day I turn into a toad."

The shifter's grin turned wicked, and he leaned forward, a devious glint in his eye. "Promise?"

Savven chuckled. "Néefar, the day you best one of my soldiers is the day I forfeit my crown."

"I thought you already did that?" he drawled, straightening. "With the speech and all."

Another arrow thunked into the target, on top of the arrow already there. Brean's eyes narrowed at the sharp points, a thought forming in her head.

Savven grunted lowly in response.

"I have an idea," Brean said suddenly, her words nearly a murmur.

"Is that a first for you?" Néefar asked dryly. "Don't worry, you'll get used to it the more frequently it happens."

Brean let out an exasperated huff, rolling her eyes to Néefar. "Do you ever shut up?"

"On occasion, but if an opportunity presents itself, I will take it, Witch."

"Incorrigible," she muttered.

Without telling them anything, she marched towards the target, holding a hand to the Fae female at the other end, who lifted her bow to fire another. The female lowered her arm, a frown pulling at her delicately pretty brown face, dark blonde hair pin straight down her back.

Brean stood with her hands on her hips, eyeing the target before her. Grasping the arrow shaft on top, she gave it a hard yank. It resisted, and she grunted, putting her weight into it until it finally slid out.

Finger tapping the obsidian tip, she studied the arrow like it would start talking at any minute. The shaft was made of lightweight silver metal, and the fletching was crafted like feathers but made from the same lightweight material.

"Brean."

Savven's low tone made the hair on her neck stand up. She hadn't heard him approach, but now she could feel him standing behind her.

Whirling, she lifted the arrow like it was a prize. "I have an idea!"

"Didn't we just establish that?" Néefar called, leaning against the broken tree, thick arms crossed over his chest.

Brean flicked her fingers, and green sparks flashed between them before Néefar uttered a startled curse, grunting when his body hit the ground. A root had sprung up from the rotten tree and wrapped around his ankle, quickly tugging him to the dirt and wrapping around him until he was tied up like a wild boar.

They watched him try and fight his way out, the branches only tightening with every wiggle, and Néefar spat out a curse, glaring at Brean.

"Very funny, Witch. You're *hilarious*."

She shrugged with a bright smile. "I know."

Turning back to Savven, she held out the arrow to him, and he looked at it and then back to her.

"What's your idea?" he asked, handing it back to her.

"I'm going to need liquid fire—lots of it."

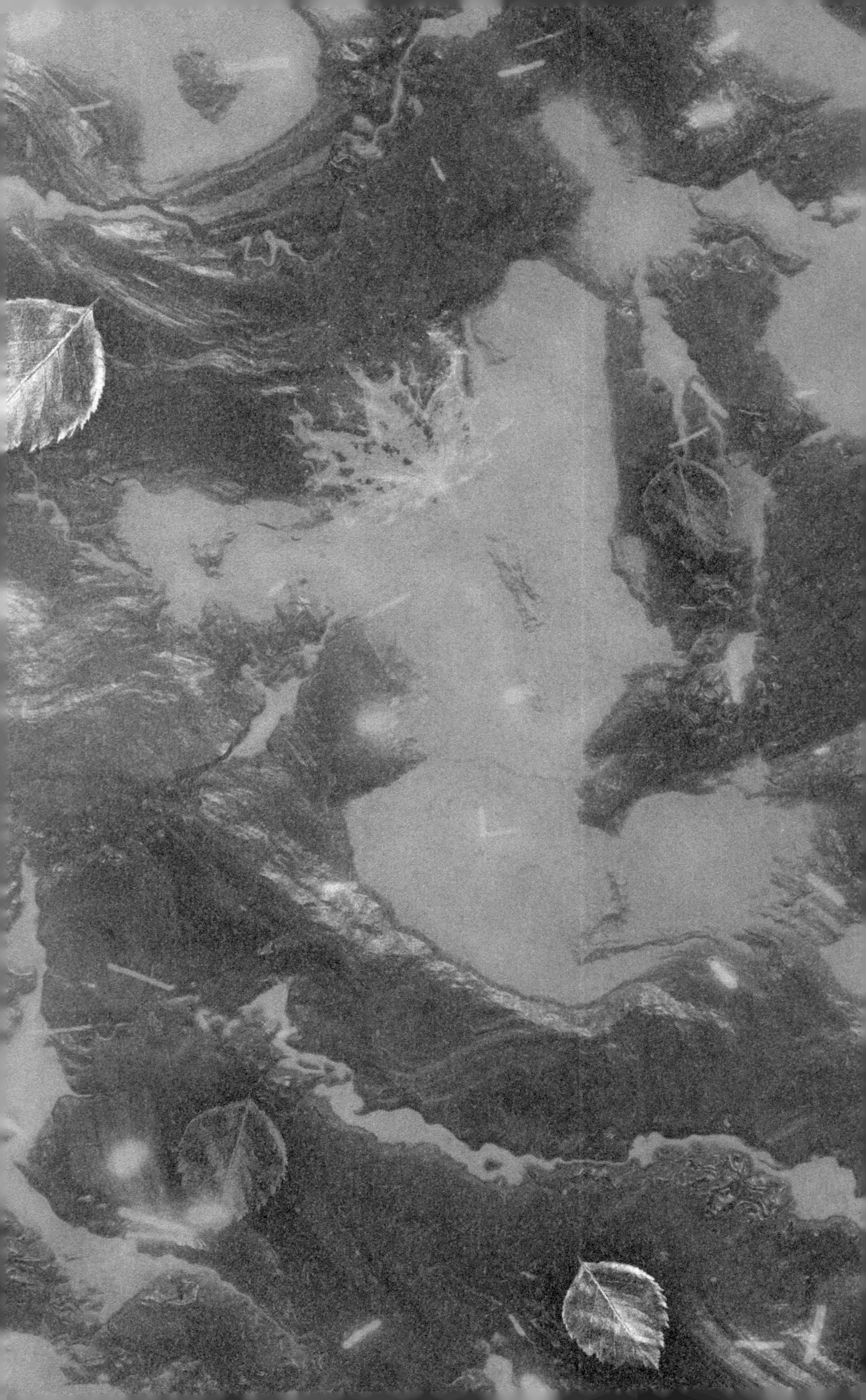

# CHAPTER 16

"Aleon."

The blacksmith looked up from his forge when Savven spoke, he looked to each of the three approaching his bench.

Dropping the pair of metal tongs onto his bench, Aleon gave them a crooked smile and wiped his hands on the front of his leather apron. "And to what do I owe this pleasure?" His honey-brown eyes darted to Néefar. "Here for another wager you're going to lose, Shifter?"

Néefar made a show of rubbing a hand over his jaw. "You have a mean uppercut, Aleon, I give you that."

Brean smirked, sliding a glance to Néefar, who just scowled at her.

"No, Aleon," Savven interjected, shooting them both a look,

"we require your services, or rather, Brean does." He stepped aside and waved a hand for her to come forward.

Aleon crossed his massive arms over his sculpted chest, his pectorals bulging under the neck of the apron. The blacksmiths in the armoury were unlike the lean soldiers. The male's body was cut from centuries of honing his craft. The fire in his forge glinted off the sweat of his tawny, bare upper body, shadows cutting along the grooves of thick muscle and scars from burns and battle. His thick, pitch-black hair was tied back with a leather strap down his back.

"And what can I do for you?" he asked, staring down at her.

Brean looked tiny compared to the male, and Savven rubbed a hand over his mouth to cover his amusement.

Unfazed, Brean cocked a brow at the blacksmith, looking up at him. "How much liquid fire are you in possession of?"

Aleon's brows shot to his hairline. "Enough."

"How much is enough?" she countered, crossing her arms over her chest.

The blacksmith's mouth quirked. "Enough to destroy this city thrice over."

"Enough to fill a river?"

Laughing softly, Aleon shook his head. "What would a witch do with that much liquid fire?"

"What wouldn't a witch do?" she snapped, her eyes flickering with annoyance.

Savven shot Aleon a look that warned him not to ire the female. He might play with fire, but the witch would turn him into some sort of creature the minute Aleon stepped out of line.

Holding a hand up in surrender, Aleon conceded with a chuckle. "Apologies, Witch. Liquid fire is stored in the vault beneath the palace." The blacksmith turned toward the crumbling marble walls, a frown pulling at his handsome face. "But the matter of the integrity of it is to be debated. I haven't stepped foot in the palace since..." his words trailed off, and he shot Savven with an apologetic look.

Savven shook his head in understanding. There was an ease in his chest where guilt had gripped him, but now it only shadowed along the edges.

"Well," Brean quipped, "I guess it's about time we checked on it."

The vault was dark and nearly in ruin. Chunks of marble and constricting roots threatened to trip or crush them if they didn't remain vigilant.

Savven held the ball of flames he commanded higher to light the dark tunnel ahead. At the end, an iron door engraved in the Fae language carved along its seams, firelight catching on its frame.

"Well, at least we know the door still holds," Aleon said amiably. "But for what lies within, I can't say."

"Wouldn't we know if the liquid fire was compromised?" Néefar asked, stepping over a sizeable protruding root.

They stopped in front of the door, the four eyeing it warily.

"If it had been, there wouldn't be a city standing, let alone its ruins," Aleon replied darkly.

Brean reached for the handle. "Then it should be fine."

Savven gripped her hand before it touched the door. Amber eyes flashed at him in the firelight. "Don't touch the door," he warned.

She looked back at the door with an arched brow, narrowing her eyes in suspicion.

Savven released her hand, and Brean stepped back and he took her place. "It's enchanted to repel anyone not of the royal bloodline. Its effect is different for each person who touches it. Boils, burns, bleeding, it doesn't matter, it all leads to death."

Néefar released a low whistle, stepping back from the door. "Well then, be a good prince and open her up."

Savven shot him an unamused look over his shoulder before casting the fire overhead to sit there suspended and took a small dagger from his waist. Without warning, he sliced it across his palm and pressed his bleeding hand to the middle of the door.

Brean sucked in a hissing breath, eyeing the weeping cut on Savven's hand, her fingers twitching to heal the wound.

"It requires blood, Witch," Aleon informed, holding out a thick arm when she made to step forward.

"Yeah, I see that. It would have been nice to have a warning before our prince sliced his hand open, though," she snapped.

"Of course, it requires blood," muttered Néefar, crossing his arms with a shake of his head.

The script on the door began to glow green, the light infiltrating the darkness behind them, bathing their faces in it. They had to look away when it flared, and then the light died.

They all blinked when the darkness returned, and the door dimmed entirely, Savven dropping his hand, let his blood drip down his fingertips.

With a click, the door opened.

Savven pushed it the rest of the way open, the iron whining under the strain of its stagnant position for the last few decades.

Before he could go in, Brean grabbed his hand as the others filed past them, Néefar shot them a smirk before ducking inside when Brean glowered at him.

"Let me heal it," she murmured.

Savven's gaze softened, and he let her take his hand in her own. A dark green light emanated from her hand when she covered his palm with her own, his blood staining her skin.

It only took moments, but when the light died, she removed her hand. The only thing left was a now thin scar.

Savven brought her fingers to his mouth and pressed a kiss to her knuckles. "Thank you," he said softly against them.

Eyes wide, Brean quickly took her hand back, wiping the blood on her leathers and nodded once. "Of course."

Pressing a hand to her back, Savven guided her into the vault, noting the heat from her skin. He smiled faintly, savouring the feeling despite their surroundings.

The vault stretched deep beneath the palace for as long as it was wide, and their steps echoed in the mostly dark chamber. Chunks of marble from overhead lay broken off within the vault, crushing bejewelled boxes and piles of gold. Heirlooms shattered across white stone floors, roots and brambles cracked the floor, reclaiming what once belonged to them.

Savven sent the fire orb to float above them, casting a dim light to guide their steps.

It was like walking through a tomb. The last remembrance of a once great city now lay beneath a desolated palace.

A stale wind blew a melancholy tune from deep within the

vault, and Savven paused to watch the darkness.

Aleon paused as well, as if hearing it too, eyeing the shadows that crept and crawled where the light didn't touch. "We should be quick about this," the blacksmith said in a clipped tone.

"He's right," Savven seconded.

"Glad we're all on the same page," muttered Néefar, picking up a half-bent gold crown, a large ruby at its centre. But promptly dropped it and stepped back when a branch crawled towards him over a pile of gold coins. The branch curled around the crown, and Néefar shot Savven a sidelong look. "Let's get what we need and go."

"It's just up ahead," Aleon said quietly, watching the shifting abyss as they moved further into the cavernous vault.

The palace cracked and the ground shuddered, Savven swallowed the lump in his throat. His heart beat harder with every step until a glimmering gold and silver vat flickered into existence when the firelight broke through the dense darkness.

It stretched nearly twenty feet sitting in the centre of the vault, a tangle of roots encasing its large rectangular body.

Savven hovered his hand over the silver top, frowning. The roots twitched as if sensing him. "Do what you must, Brean, just be quick about it."

She shrugged a nonchalant shoulder, coming up from behind to study the container. "Can I remove items from the vault without burns, boils, and death?"

Despite himself, his mouth quirked, and he raised a brow at her. "Yes, you may."

"Oh good," she chirped, almost smiling.

Savven stood back with Néefar and Aleon, together the three of them watched green sparks ignite her fingers, casting her face in a haunting glow before she aimed them towards the vat. Gold, silver, and roots glowed emerald, and with a snap of her fingers, it was gone.

Twenty feet of space wholly empty in a blink of an eye. The ground trembled violently the moment it disappeared.

"What did you do?!" Néefar snapped, stepping out of the way as roots laced along the empty ground.

"I put it in a pocket of space," she retorted, glaring at him.

"What the bloody h—" Néefar's reply was cut short when the ground cracked open.

Savven grabbed Brean and pulled her to him just as the earth split where she had been standing.

She looked up at him, her face the picture of shock. "Thank you," she breathed.

"We've outstayed our welcome," Savven said, his face tight and body tense when the ground shook again. Brean stepped out of his arms.

Aleon was backing up already, Néefar on his heels.

"You don't say!" Néefar called over his shoulder.

And then they were running as the vault began to crumble around them.

Spears of wood shot from the walls, piercing the air, and the four of them scattered, dodging chunks of marble that crashed behind them, roots that split the ground, and the growing shadows.

Savven's hair whipped behind him as he leapt over a slab of earth that jutted up in front of him. The orb of fire flew overhead, still tied to his magic, and the door came into view.

"*Run!*" he screamed to the others, glancing to his left and right and dodging under a root that came spearing for his head.

He could hear Néefar's curses, Aleon shouting when he was nearly crushed by the ceiling collapsing above him, and Brean... Savven flung his body over a marble boulder, searching for her wild mane of bright red hair. He saw her lunge through an opening in a wall of brambles, rolling out of her fall and sprinting for the door. She was smiling, and Savven felt a grin cut along his face as he raced after her.

Brean ducked under a flying stone, turning to briefly look at Savven when he caught up to her. A feral look in her amber eyes.

The door was still open, and Savven skidded to a stop as Brean crashed through the other side. He held it open, watching Aleon and Néefar fight through the debris.

"Run faster!"

Sheer determination painted over Aleon's face. The blacksmith ripped the roots off his arms as they curled around him with a vicious snarl.

Néefar was in no better shape. The earth cracked around him and caged him in. His eyes flashed in the growing darkness, slicing to Savven.

The door strained against his back, and Savven gritted his jaw, shoving his body against it when he felt it try to slam shut.

Brean stormed back into the vault, her face set.

"Brean, no!" Savven snarled through gritted teeth, the door trying his strength.

She ignored him and lifted her arms, magic dancing between her fingertips. The rubble and withering branches ceased as she threw out her hands, and her magic took command of the chaos.

Néefar's cage splintered, and the shifter was able to tear his way out. His fingers now turned to claws.

Aleon's arms freed, and Brean tore the roots from his legs.

The two males sprinted for the door.

Savven reared his head back, throwing his full strength into holding the door open. His yell was eaten by the crescendo of chaos, his muscles straining. His feet slipped on the stone floor, and he dug his heels in.

"*RUN!*" he roared.

Brean's hands began to shake, her magic faltering under the strain of the Fae King's magic. Aleon flew by her through the door, then Néefar.

Whirling, Brean sprinted through the archway, grabbing Savven by his arm as she passed and pulled them into the tunnel. The door slammed shut with a deafening snap behind them.

Doubled over, hands on their knees, they were quiet for a long time.

Savven gripped her arm, straightening. "Thank you," he said hoarsely. He could feel the marks of the door bruised into his back.

She nodded, her limbs visibly trembling.

"I hope whatever you have planned is worth it, Witch," Aleon commented lowly, eyeing the twisting bruises along his arms.

She leaned her back against the wall and scrubbed a hand over her face, smiling despite her near death and the trembling in her limbs. "Oh, it will be."

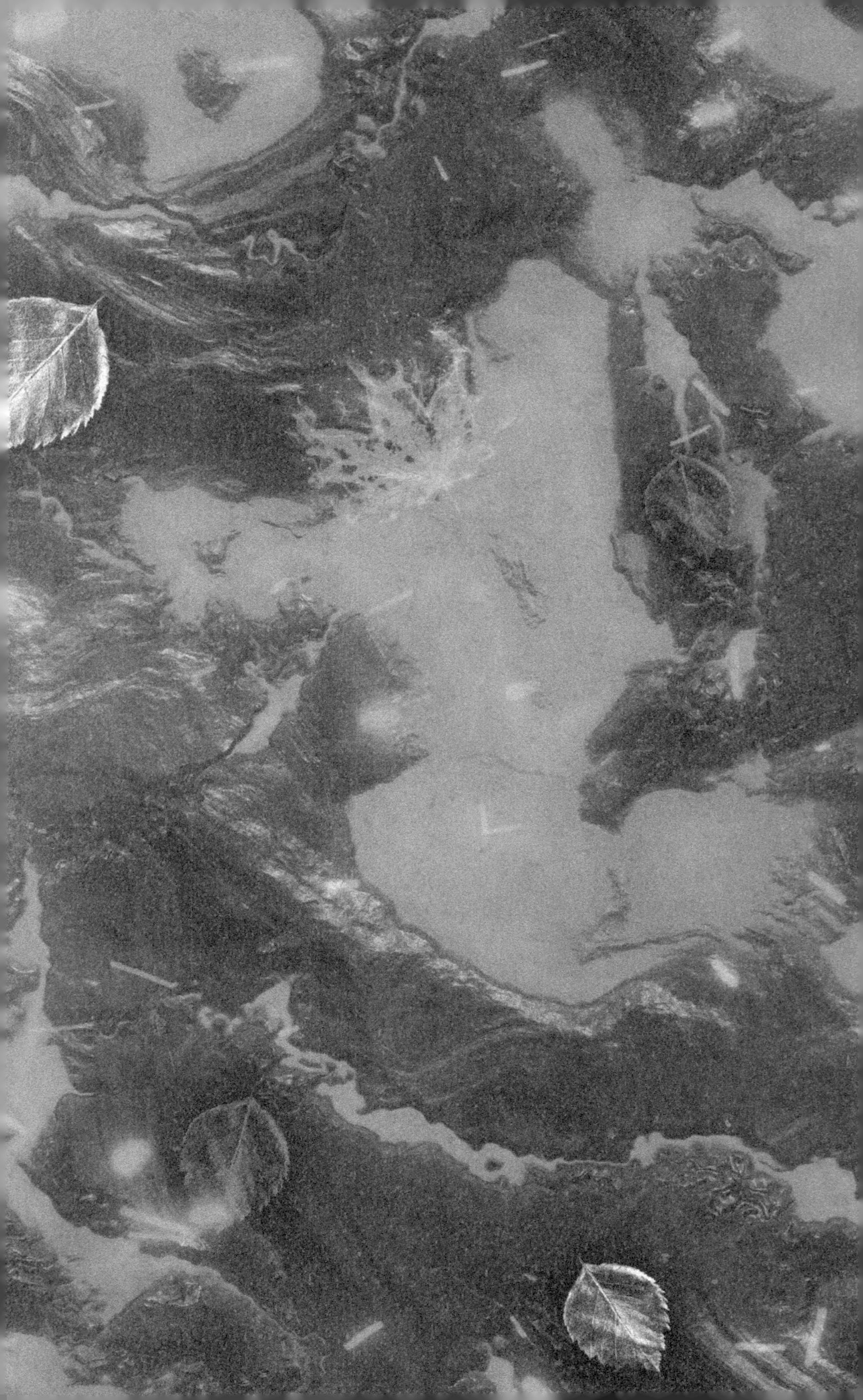

# CHAPTER 17

A dagger sunk into the stone in front of Hazen's feet. She jerked her head up from the weapons rack where she was putting her sword away, and snarled when she spotted Kain stalking towards her from across the training ring.

Shoving her sword back onto the rack, she bent, wrapping a hand around the hilt—

"—Hazen, don't!" Åsmund barked but too late.

She yanked the small blade free and weighed it in her hands.

Åsmund groaned under his breath.

The entirety of the conduit went silent, all eyes trained on them—on Hazen and the blade in her hand.

When she looked back at the male, a sinful gleam was in Kain's dark eyes, and a satisfied smile played along the curve of his cruel mouth.

"Oh good, I had hoped you would accept," Kain said smoothly.

Åsmund shadowed her back, so close that she could feel the growl rumbling through his chest.

Kain tsked, wagging a finger at his general. "You know the rules, Åsmund. Once a challenge is laid down, if it is accepted, it must be completed until one is dead or the other yields. If they refuse, the penalty is death or banishment… and since she doesn't have wings, death would be the better option—don't you think?"

"She didn't know," Åsmund rumbled darkly.

Her fingers twitched around the blade, her heart threatening to stop in her chest, and she tightened her grip. She was going to have to fight Kain. Fuck. Her power rumbled with the realisation, but the very human part of her subconscious roiled anxiously with the thought.

Kain shrugged. "That's not my problem." He turned his eyes to Hazen. "So, what will it be? Death by my hand or death by penalty?"

Hazen looked down at the dagger, weighing it in her open palm. It was a simple steel blade with a crudely hammered silver hilt wrapped in black leather.

Lips pressed into a tight line; her jaw flexed as she looked at Kain through lowered brows. She hadn't come this far to play chicken and lose. "Fight."

A wicked grin spread over his face, and he inclined his head. "This will be fun, *Keeper*."

He said the title with a sneer, and Hazen bit back her retort. She was not the keeper. Not yet, anyway.

Hazen whirled on her heels, grabbing her sword. She weighed it in her hands, nostrils flaring with a heavy breath.

"Hazen," Åsmund said quietly.

She inched her head in his direction. "I'm not a warrior, Åsmund. I'm not a soldier." Despite the power she felt racing through her bones, a healthy dose of fear accompanied it, and she shoved the dagger into her boot with a low growl.

His hand was a brand on her bare shoulder, and she turned to him, inches separating them.

"I haven't been training you to be a soldier," he said lowly. His eyes were guarded, his face set into the mask of a stoic general. "I've been training you to survive. To *live*, Hazen."

Her eyes darted around Åsmund, noting the rest of the soldiers clearing the ring until they framed it, waiting for her. "What is this challenge?" she whispered harshly. "Tell me what to expect."

"Each Drago is allowed to issue a challenge to another if they feel they compromise the integrity of our clan. Whether they feel they are a weakness, a threat to safety, or both." Åsmund cast a critical glance down her body, eyeing her sword briefly, before moving back to her face. He was weighing her odds, and she couldn't tell which way they leaned.

"So, obviously, he thinks I'm both a weakness and a threat," she bit out, narrowing her eyes on Kain when he sauntered into the ring.

"He probably also feels humiliated from the other day and means to make you pay for it."

Hazen snorted. "Of course he does, the arrogant prick. And there's no way to stop this?"

"Once a challenge is issued, it's forbidden to intervene." He paused, jaw flexing, eyeing the soldiers around them. "I can kill him." He looked up at the bottleneck. "And get you out before they try to kill me in turn."

She frowned, seeing his eyes darken to nearly black as he tried to figure a way out of this for her. "No," she bit out, frowning when she shot a glance around the general to Kain. Hazen glared at the arrogant male before turning her gaze back to the green eyes that looked torn between duty to her and his duty as a general. She huffed, offering him a wry crooked smile. "This is my fight." She wasn't about to let him win her battles or die trying.

Åsmund gripped her arms in his hands, commanding her attention. His emerald eyes blazed as his mask dropped for a second, and he whispered harshly, desperation coating every word, "Survive. That's an order."

Trepidation shot down her spine, but she jerked her chin once.

Satisfied, Åsmund released her and stepped back. "Kain is a cheat. He'll find any way to get an advantage. And in a challenge, there is no integrity. It's a fight to the death, Hazen."

She nodded again, stepping around Åsmund to face Kain, who stood at the opposite end of the training ring, sword in hand. All airs of the brutish ego-driven male that he was rolled off of him in waves.

"Do what you need to, Hazen. Fight dirty. There are no rules."

She shot him a small smile over her shoulder, her stomach flipping with nausea. "Don't worry, General, I'll claw his eyes out for you."

His jaw flexed tightly, his only emotional tell before she walked away.

One breath.

One step.

One breath.

One step.

Hazen slowed her breathing, trying to centre herself the closer she came to the ring. The soldier's eyes burned holes into her skin as she passed, and she rolled her shoulders back, inching her chin higher. Her eyes narrowed in on the male waiting for her. Her dragon was a wild thing, pressing along her nerves and muscles. Her fingers flexed around the hilt, power flooding her senses.

She was chosen by dragons. She was chosen by a God. She was not a damsel.

"If you take any longer, my immortality might run out of time," Kain said with a cold laugh, inciting a few soldiers around him to follow.

She was Hazen Sophia Solvaya, and she was going to *rip* his tongue from his arrogant mouth.

Letting a sharp smile rise along her face, she inclined her head at the male. He was handsome in a cruel way, muscled but stocky, his wings smaller and not nearly as tall and defined as Åsmund. He was, in all aspects, a lesser male than her general. With those observations, some of the tension eased from her shoulders, and her stomach settled. Kain was a cruel male; there was not a decent bone of kindness in his body, and Åsmund played by the rules when they sparred—but he was stronger, faster, and deadlier than Kain. If she could handle herself against Åsmund, then she had a chance.

They had been training all morning. She was hungry, and her

muscles were fatigued, but she had power. Too much power that sparked with interest at the prospect of a fight. A living thing that coursed through her veins that made her body feel like a well of electricity.

She stopped just inside the ring, her eyes fixated on Kain as he lifted his sword, and she mirrored him.

The air was charged, and everyone seemed to hold their breath, watching… waiting…

Kain was a blur of black and silver. Hazen swore and lifted her sword in time to catch his as it arced overhead. He shoved her back, and she stumbled out of the ring, soldiers scattering.

"Come on, I thought you were a dragon," Kain sneered, pacing the ring and watching her.

Hazen gritted her teeth and charged him, spinning and blocking his attack as he stabbed forward.

He was fast. Faster than she anticipated, barely keeping her feet under her and leaving her less than a second to throw her sword up blow after blow. Dodging, ducking, weaving, and rolling to the ground to escape his onslaught.

Whirling, Hazen's chest heaved, and she glared at him. "That the best you got?" she goaded.

His smile was insidious, his blade lethal, barely a flash of silver as they danced.

Hazen faltered, her arms shaking under his strength, and she gritted her teeth. A guttural yell ripped from her lungs as she poured every ounce of her reserved strength into her arms, leaning into her blade, heels digging in when his sword inched closer to her neck.

Kain's smile wavered, his face flicking with surprise before it vanished, and he snarled, overpowering her.

Twisting his blade, her sword was ripped from her hands, and it went sailing through the air, clattering against the obsidian and sliding just outside of the ring.

His sword swung for her middle, and Hazen didn't have time to think as she flung herself to the ground, rolling out of the fall.

Stretching out a hand, fire flew from the wall to wrap around his arm, and he stalked towards her, a murderous look on his face.

Fire danced along his tanned skin, Hazen watched the flames as her dragon screamed for blood.

"Trapped like prey," Kain said softly. "Because that's what you are—*prey*. You do not belong here. You are not a dragon." He raised his hand, now consumed entirely by fire, the flames danced over the harsh plains of his face.

Her blood ignited in an inferno at his words, her irritation peaking when she saw some soldiers nod their heads from the corner of her eye. The ember of fire within her blazed a path into her muscles until her limbs no longer shook, and she could feel her power pressing along her skin. Her dragon was gone, and in its place was an endless well of fire that claimed her. It *chose her* because it wasn't just her power—it was Rose's.

It was dragon fire.

She was a dragon.

Smiling, she inclined her head and whispered, "Come and get me."

Fire lashed out from Kain's hand, and Hazen dodged to the side when a whip of flames flew for her neck, and she latched her hand around the burning cord.

Kain smirked, jerking his hand back, but she didn't move. His smirk faltered, and he pulled the tether of flames again, but she held firm, gritting her teeth.

The flames wrapped around her wrist, licking her skin in welcome, and her power tunnelled down it, glowing with golden light until the flames began to spark. Kain watched the fire and light shoot towards him, and he stumbled back, watching it claim the fire wrapped around him. Then, he screamed.

His flesh began to bubble and burn where the fire touched him, and Hazen jerked the cord of fire towards her, Kain crumbled to his knees as he tried to release his hold on the flames.

The world around her melted away, the roar of power rushed through her ears, her eyes pinned to Kain. She was not the prey. She was not weak. *She* was the predator.

His dark eyes flashed with fear as she stalked slowly towards him, the skin of his arm burning.

"How the mighty have fallen," she intoned quietly. "The

predator becomes prey, and the balance of your perfect world is tipped." The fire wrapped around her arm, up along her neck and around her torso, fuelling the inferno within until it blazed like tattoos over her skin.

Kain whimpered, his mangled arm hanging in the air as she pulled the tether of fire still connecting them. Tears streaked down his face; his teeth bared in a silent snarl when she finally stood in front of him.

Hazen leaned forward, their faces inches apart. "Yield."

A savage snarl ripped from Kain, and his head smashed forward.

Hazen saw stars and stumbled back, blood coating her tongue. Growling, rage making her free hand curl by her side, she dropped to her knees and spun, taking the fire with her and Kain was flipped onto his back. Grabbing the dagger from her boot, fire wrapping around the steel, she threw her legs over him and pinned the blade to his thick neck.

"Yield!" she snarled.

Flames wrapped around both his hands, and he screamed, arching off the ground, but Hazen held him fast, the blade pressed to his neck, his veins bulging, skin searing where the fire touched.

"Yield or die!"

*Kill him!* Her power screamed within her.

She was faintly aware of yelling behind her, but she didn't care. Her eyes trained on the male under her.

"Kill… me," he rasped between gritted teeth, spit flying.

Hazen found herself smiling. "As you wish."

Flipping the dagger in hand, she brought it back, the deadly point aimed at his neck.

True death was something Hazen realised no immortal really knew. The figment of what lay beyond their endless lives was nothing more than a thought but never a reality. But now, black eyes flared with ice-cold fear when Kain realised she was going to kill him, and this would be his final breath.

He squeezed his eyes shut, turning his head away. "I yield!" he screamed.

Hazen's hand stopped a breath away from his jugular, the flames close enough to burn the skin below it.

He twisted his head away from the dagger, eyes still squeezed shut. "I yield!" he screamed again, his voice raw.

Her dragon twitched with annoyance, and she bared her teeth in a growl. Leaning forward, she made sure the tip of the dagger pressed into his neck as she seethed, "Coward."

Shoving off him, Hazen stumbled back, letting go of the fire. As soon as she did, it vanished, flying back to the wall where it flickered innocently.

The noise came rushing back in, but there wasn't any. The conduit was silent.

Every eye was trained on her, and she looked at them all slowly, walking towards her discarded sword. The soldiers parted, giving her space, she bit back her smile and grabbed her blade.

Åsmund was waiting where she had left him, unsurprisingly, his face revealed nothing. But there was a hint of pride in those green eyes and the smile she was hiding bloomed a fraction for him.

She stopped, her feet staggering as the fatigue finally hit her.

He took her sword, and his lips curved up slightly. "You could have killed him?" It was a question more than a statement. A question of why she didn't.

Hazen thought for a moment before shrugging. "Seeing him cower, to taste true fear, was almost better than ending him." She glanced back at the half-burned male. "And now he'll have the scars of that cowardliness for the rest of his eternal life."

"Well done."

Hazen looked back at him, startled by his words.

He gave her a small smile. "You're a better dragon than I." He pressed a hand to the small of her back, branding her, and guided her out of the conduit.

"Would you have killed him?" she inquired, her limbs as heavy as lead. She let her power dwindle to that flickering ember that heated her core. However, it still hummed a silent, more permanent melody in her blood.

Åsmund's brow ticked in thought, a dark look passing over his face as he growled, "If given the opportunity to discard clan law, I would torture him and then kill him very slowly. I would make him taste death before it even came."

A shiver went down her spine at his words, his tone frigid. "I can see why he's never challenged you."

Åsmund laughed softly.

Looking up at the general, Hazen touched his hand with hers, and he glanced down at her. "Can we go flying?"

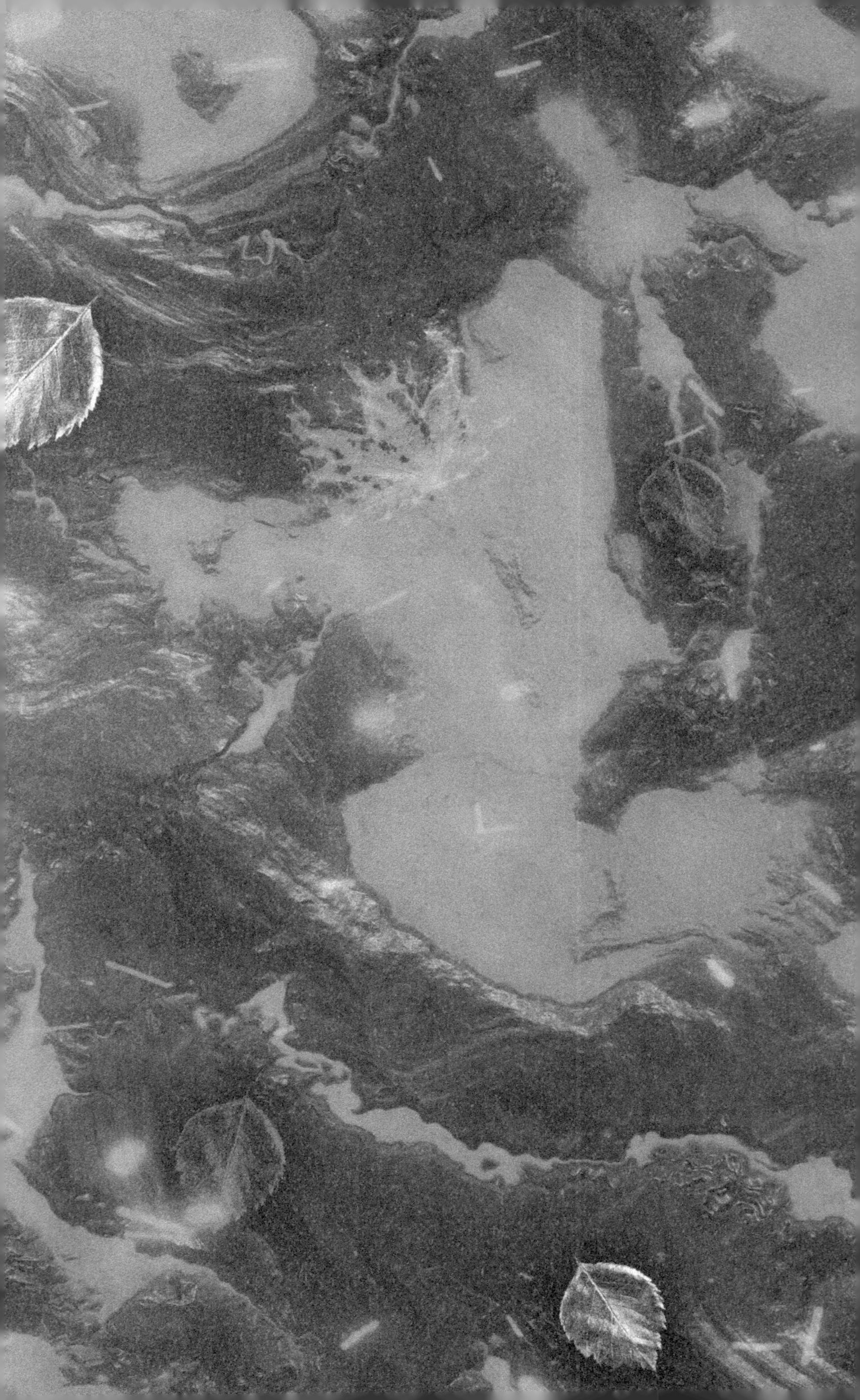

# CHAPTER 18

"Blood and stones and bones," Nazar whispered over the stone basin in the haphazard cave within the mountain's belly, shadows swarming around the black shroud he wore. "Stones… and bones and… *blood*." He twirled a long, bony finger in the crimson liquid; the owner of the blood, a bone-thin male satyr, lay discarded behind him with a gash along his neck.

Nazar's red eyes rolled to the back of his skull.

Calling the darkness from the earth, he sang to his pets, his rotten, jagged teeth bared in a smile. "Show me the one who brings the light. Show me the one whose fire cracks the night," he whispered.

*His shadows whizzed by trees and stones, turning over roots, moss, and leaves. A horse nickered when the shadows skirted around a travelling camp. A shadow paused, hissing from the darkness, and the horse reared up, its front hooves kicking the air.*

Nazar's head ticked.

*The shadow moved on, joining the rest. The earth smelled of wilting flowers, of something beautiful slowly dying. Something* mortal.

*Careening into the sky, the shadows dug their claws into the scent and followed it. Forests and mountains passed in a blur of greens, browns, and blacks until a bright blue sky filled their vision.*

Nazar gripped the ledge of the basin, black claws gouging into the stone. He wanted to see the human the little Fae lord had sent him to fetch like a subservient animal. A snarl ripped through him at that thought. He was no pet.

*Sky blue filled his vision. His shadows pierced the clouds, turning their white pillows dark and stormy when their darkness touched the light.*

He had heard the fire whisper her name in Fallúin, heard them call to the one who commanded their flames. But he had been called off his hunt by the insolent Fae who sat on his creator's throne.

The stone cracked under his grip, and the connection with his shadows faltered.

The image wavered, but Nazar dug his claws into his shadows, urging them forward faster.

*The sea spread in the distance, and a mountain pinnacle penetrated the clouds. Two figures emerged, one a male and in his arms, a female... the mortal.*

Nazar's grin cut sickly across his taut skin.

*She was cradled close to his chest, head thrown back, and a smile on her face. Her blonde hair sweeping freely behind her as the male dove and spun them through clouds and sunbeams. A look of pure adoration filled the male's gaze when he stared down at the female.*

Nazar watched in fascination when she returned his gaze, and her cheeks turned pink.

His cackles filled the dank space. "How precious," he hissed.

*The male dove them towards the ground, his shadows following close behind them. His wings flared just before they touched the trees, and he arced them back into the sky. The female laughed, a look of pure happiness etching her scarred face.*

The image wavered again, and Nazar snarled, releasing the

shadows and pulling himself out of their depths. Releasing his claws from the basin, the stone shuddered and broke in two. Blood, stones, and bleached bones spilled out, pooling at his feet.

*"NAZAR!"*

Nazar let out a low hiss as his name was screeched through the dark castle.

*"NAZAR!"*

Wrath flooded his undead body, shadows rising like curling smoke around the thin fabric he wore. His bones clicked, and he curled his hands into fists, his short black claws digging into his sallow flesh. If he could bleed, blood would have coated his hand.

The shade vanished into smoke, reappearing in the great hall, he walked through the gathering mists. Darkness curled around an obsidian pillar, the air pulsating with his temper.

Laudin leaned against the wall behind the throne, twiddling a dagger in his hands. He straightened when he saw Nazar.

Ezra, the damned Fae, sat strewn on the dark throne, his hands laid out and tapping against the silver armrests. His black eyes flickered to Nazar when he showed himself.

Lips curling back, Ezra sneered, "It took you long enough."

Nazar made a show of bowing his head, staring up at him as he did so. "Apologies, My Lord."

Ezra scoffed, waving a dismissive hand. "Useless."

Eyes rolling to the back of his head, Nazar straightened and willed his demons down as they hissed from the depths of the shadows circling the hall. The Fae on the throne paid them no heed, not when Nazar could feel the demons swirling beneath the little lord's flesh and bones.

Ezra's head twitched as if hearing the demon's beckoning, and his snarl filled the hall. "Quiet!"

Laudin stood up, putting his dagger away.

Lips curling in a heinous smile, Nazar watched the Fae unravel behind his eyes. The demons whispered murderous thoughts, demanding blood. He could hear them call to the little lord, could hear their claws gouge into his bones.

Ezra jerked forward, hands braced on the throne, his chest heaving and eyes wild. *"ENOUGH!"*

The demons settled, slithering back into the darkness.

Nazar hovered within the border of shadows, head inclined, waiting.

Ezra stormed off the dais, a flurry of black stalking towards Nazar.

The shade regarded him the same way a predator regarded pray. "My Lord?" he drawled in a low hiss.

"My army is ready to be dispatched to every city and hovel," Ezra spat, his head twitching as the demons began whispering again. But they weren't whispering to the Fae, and Nazar listened to their slithered words—to their cravings. "Hundreds of Dökkálfar at my disposal. The world will taste my power; they will follow me, or they will die."

Humming softly, Nazar's bony finger stroked a shadow, it curled softly around him. "I do not think that is wise, *My Lord.*" The title was like poison on his black tongue.

Ezra stepped closer, invading the shadows that curled around Nazar, their tendrils wrapping around the Fae male with silent hunger. He leaned his head forward, his teeth bared as he spat, "You do not *think.* You are under my control, my command. Laudin will dispatch my army, and you will follow *his* orders. Do I make myself—"

His words ended abruptly, choking on the last sounds, Nazar's claws wrapped around his pale neck.

"—Crystal clear, *My Lord,*" Nazar finished for him, his blood-red eyes glinting. "I would not move if I were you, little Fae."

Laudin had made to move but froze at his words.

The shadows screamed from the darkness, tearing apart the Fae in his hand. Nazar inhaled the delicious scent of fear that rolled from the male. He showed the rows of razor teeth, his black tongue flicking out to taste the air. He groaned low, leaning forward to drag his tongue up Ezra's face.

"You taste delicious," he said leisurely.

Ezra fought against him, baring his teeth. His nails dug into Nazar's skin, tearing the flesh, and the shade chuckled lowly.

"You think you can hurt me?" he growled. His red eyes began to glow, and the shadows around him crawled across the floor until the ground moved, and a low hissing filled the air. "You cannot hurt me!"

The air pulsated with power, and Nazar flung the Fae across the great hall with a savage snarl. Ezra crashed against the throne, his body crumpling on the top step of the dais. Stalking towards the male, hand outstretched like a snake that had caught its prey, Nazar pinned Ezra into the throne with dark magic, his back arched against the edge of the seat.

The temperature dropped in the great hall, Ezra's ragged breath misted in front of him as Nazar slowly climbed the steps. Hovering over him like Death, Nazar's limbs lengthened, his bones crackling in the palpable silence.

"Wh-what… do… yo-you… w…" Ezra's face turned red, then purple, as Nazar's shadows constricted around his throat like a serpent.

"What do I want?" Nazar questioned. He leaned forward, his teeth scraping the Fae's arched ear. *"Everything."*

With those words, Nazar stabbed a clawed hand through his chest.

A soul-splitting scream wrenched from Ezra, and Nazar let his hold loosen just enough so he could hear its symphony.

Blood spurted from his chest, while Nazar's hand dug through the cavity of bone and muscle, relishing in the smell of life ebbing away around him.

Wrenching his hand from Ezra's chest, Nazar stared at the mass of darkness curling and seeping from his fingers like living tar.

A gurgling came from the Fae male, blood trickling from his gaping mouth. Pupils blown wide with pain, Ezra stared at Nazar with horror. The shade returned it with one of malice.

Nazar returned to the shifting darkness in his hands, stroking a bony finger through the mass. "Thank you for caring for my pets, but it is time I collect on my debt."

The shade stumbled back from the throne as the mass of darkness crawled up his arm, coating every inch of skin it touched in a thick black tar until he was coated from head to foot. Nazar's eyes rolled back, his arms stretched wide, his pets reclaiming him. Sinking beneath his flesh, runes carved into his skin with ancient scripts, from his temples down to his ankles. Every inch of his skin was inscribed, oozing with the black tar until the last tendril slipped beneath, and the runes glowed from within.

Power radiated through his bones as his demons reclaimed their places, and he soothed a hand over his white hair, grinning.

"I think," he drawled, rounding red eyes on Ezra, "it is time for a new dark lord."

Ezra choked on his blood, trying to speak and failing.

Nazar tutted. "Don't speak. It'll only make you die faster, and I much prefer to watch you suffer. The scent is intoxicating." He took in a deep inhale for added measure, pleasure contorting his features before his face split into a hungry smile. With a flick of his hand, Ezra's body flew from the dais and cracked an obsidian pillar, his body crumbling at its base.

The shade turned his attention to Laudin, who still stood frozen behind the throne, eyes wholly black now. Nazar's head clicked to the side in thought.

Before he could say anything, Laudin dropped to a single knee, bowing his head, his dirty blond hair obscuring his face. "Whatever pleases My Lord, I will do."

"Disloyalty is my favourite trait in a pet. They taste so much better when I finally eat them," Nazar commented.

Laudin didn't move.

Cackling, Nazar extended a hand to the shadows clouding around his feet, and they crawled up his body. "Rise, little Fae." Laudin rose, his face impassive. "Ready my army, we're going to pay a visit to a little mortal." The male didn't move, and Nazar's hand twitched. *"GO!"*

Laudin nearly sprinted from the great hall, the wooden door slamming shut behind him.

Shadows misted his skin, healing the runes into black scars along his pale flesh and dissipating until they once again curled at the hem of his robe as he climbed the steps of the dais. Turning, he stared down at the expanse of the great hall, a smile curving his mouth, and he took his seat on the silver throne.

"I'm coming, Little Human," he sang in a low whisper, his eyes rolling back as he delved into his shadows. "I'm coming for you."

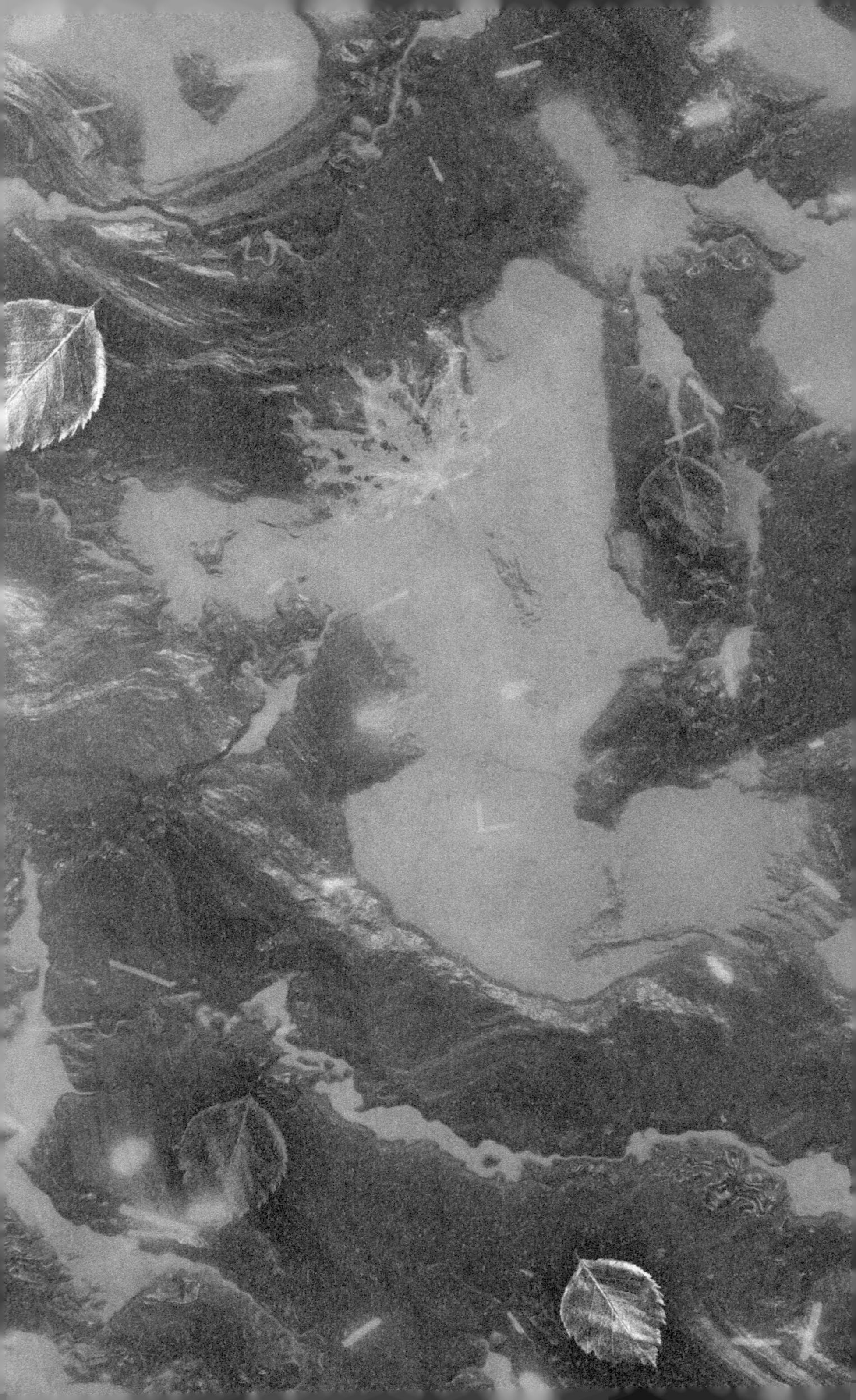

# CHAPTER 19

She stood in a dark forest. Everything was grey, like ashen coal. It fell like snow, coating everything it touched.

Hazen extended her palm and hissed in pain when the ash touched her skin. Withdrawing her hand, she glanced up, feeling its sting along her exposed skin.

There was no fire. Only ash. The forest was as it always is, but the life... the life had been sucked from it.

Hazen stepped forward, and the grass at her feet broke away, crumbling beneath her weight and turning to dust. She touched the bark of a tree she passed, and the weight of emptiness, of death, consumed her. Where her hand brushed, the tree collapsed, she yanked her hand back with a harsh gasp.

So much death, but not in the way they knew. The colour had been sucked from the world, though it still held the illusion of living. What stood now was a pale comparison. Frail and ashen, waiting to break.

Soot coated her vision, clinging to her eyelashes, she brushed it away. Hissing when her skin burned, she looked down to find the back of her hand red from the pain.

When she looked up, the world had changed.

Hazen now stood on a field littered with bodies, and a gasp of horror ripped from her. Those who were slain upon the ground and those who stood statuesque with battle armour adorning them, weapons at their side, lay all around her. Winged beasts who should defend the skies were grounded, wings broken.

She could see familiar faces from a distance, and her heart stopped before it began to race. Hazen sprinted through the battlefield, blonde hair flying behind her, ash coating her fighting leathers when she brushed against a frozen body.

They were spaced apart, but she saw them all, stopping before one very familiar to her.

A crown adorned Savven's strong brow, his blue-black hair braided away from his face and half tied back. His teeth were bared in a savage snarl, and a thin sword was held between both hands mid-swing.

"I guess the boy found himself," she whispered into the ashen world, remembering the story he had told her about the little boy who lost his home, his family, and in turn, himself.

Her eyes moved onto Brean, who was just beyond Savven. A bow was in her hands, and an arrow was nocked at the ready. Her eyes glinted with steely determination, her lips pressed tight, and her wild mane of red hair tamed haphazardly into a braid.

Hazen gently reached out and touched the witch's cheek softly, choking back a sob as she watched her disintegrate under her touch.

Hazen's heart raced like a drum beneath her ribs, every breath wrenched from her lungs painfully, her skin burning. She stepped back, shaking her head. She was surrounded by a nightmare she could not control. She was surrounded by death, by something that drained every ounce of light from the world and left nothing but dark, decaying ash.

"No," she whispered, stumbling back.

Everywhere she went there were faces frozen in time and void of life. Hazen spun on her heels, losing her balance. A cry seized her throat as she *fell through what was once a Fae soldier, now diminished to a cloud of ash... and then another and another and another.*

*Head pounding and pulse racing, Hazen's world spun out of control, and she fell to the ground, squeezing her eyes tight.*

Hazen awoke with a start, bolting upright in bed, sweat drenching her naked body. Her heart raced, beating wildly under her skin. Swinging her feet over the side of the bed, Hazen clung to the edge of the mattress, forcing in deep breaths until her heartbeat slowed, her body still buzzing with adrenaline.

Hair clung to her shoulders and cheeks, and she pushed it away from her face with a shaky hand. Standing, she grabbed her still-damp towel and tried to wipe the nightmare from her skin

She walked over to the open wall, the sky outside was lit in a dreamy blue and black by a silver quarter moon, full clouds suspended in the air, and the chaos of stars expanded above.

How she wished she had wings to fly. The walls at her back felt like a prison, and her skin itched to be free of it. Hazen put a hand to the invisible barrier, her fingers spreading over it. She stayed there for a breath before she yawned and turned to go back to bed.

Blood-red eyes filled her vision, and Hazen let out a terrified scream, tripping over her feet. A face that only evil knew stood inches from her. Pale skin, scarred in black markings, stretched taut over a bony demonic face, a row of rotting jagged teeth smiling at her from the growing shadows in her room, consuming everything they touched. The moonlight reflected his white hair as he stalked closer to her, his limbs unnaturally long.

She had seen him once. His face filled her memories of a village burning, and... he had been hunting for her. The shade. Nazar.

Chest heaving, her back pressed against the invisible barrier, her eyes darted around her room, landing on the door. Her power was burning in her core, a livewire in the darkness, and she tried to think of a way out.

The demon clicked his tongue as if sensing her thoughts. "That wouldn't be wise."

Hazen lunged, swinging a hand at the shade. He stepped away from her blow with inhuman speed, and she took the opening. Running for the door, hand outstretched for the golden latch, her fingers brushed the metal before shadows banded around her ankles. Her head smashed against the floor, dragging her away from her only escape.

"No!" she screeched, fighting the darkness that curled around her ankles and wrists like shackles.

The shade vanished into mist, and Hazen's eyes searched her room, the last sliver of moonlight fighting its way into the void. The shadows began to pull her into the abyss, and her nails dug into the hard stone deep enough to gouge lines across the surface. Her nails split, bleeding, but she gritted her teeth, digging them in and twisting her body. The shadows constricted like living things, branding her skin, and tugged harder until her hands slipped, and she was pulled into the abyss.

Red eyes glowed from the darkness, and Hazen's throat seized with terror.

"I'm coming for them all, Little Mortal," the shade hissed, his voice echoing around her.

"Who—who are you?" she whispered jaggedly, fixating on the glowing red eyes that tilted slightly.

"I am the night," the red eyes came closer, "I am the shadows that play where the sun does not go. I am the darkness that lingers beneath your bed while you sleep. I am the darkest part of your nightmares that torment you. I am the one that *feasts* on your fear."

Hazen blinked, and the red eyes vanished.

"How mouthwatering you smell."

She screamed when the words were pressed to her ear, and she jerked her whole body away, though the shadows still held her hostage.

Loud cackles filled the abyss, and Hazen's chest heaved with shallow breaths, hands going sweaty.

Ice-cold fingers wrapped around her throat, squeezing, so cold that it burned her skin. A guttural cry ripped from her at the pain, her dragon roaring within, fighting the cold slowly seeping into her body.

"*Shhh,*" the shade soothed.

Jagged whimpers fought free, Hazen's arms straining against her manacles.

"It will all be over soon," he cooed. "I'm afraid you and I cannot co-exist in this world, Little Mortal. The darkness cannot exist in the light, and you must be extinguished. I can feel it, your fire— your *light*."

Claws dug into her throat, letting blood spill and pool around her. Hazen gritted her teeth, holding onto the tether of power that fought off a cold death.

The ember flickered when it felt the first lick of the shade's darkness, flaring hotly. Hazen's body went rigid, and then she relaxed, closing her eyes, ignoring the pain that pulsed through every cell in her body. Holding tight to the ember, she focused all her energy on it, and it flared again, the cold pausing, assessing.

Again.

Again.

The shade squeezed tighter, snarling when her body began to burn. And the mark on her left shoulder, which she had nearly forgotten, began to turn hot. Her muscles stretched, and something inside her felt ready to burst free from her back.

She gripped the ember tighter.

*Again.*

Her body hummed deliciously, fire weaving through her muscles, fortifying them, and with a snarl, she ripped out of her restraints. Her skin glowed like an ember in the darkness, and she grabbed the shade's hand at her throat.

"You will die!" he screeched, his voice filling the abyss.

Slowly, Hazen peeled back his claws, one by agonising one, detaching from her neck. A scream ripped out of her from the pain, but his hand came free, and she used all her power to throw him off.

"Fuck you," she spat, and her power flared to life.

A scream rent the air, and Åsmund startled awake, going for the obsidian dagger at his bedside table. His eyes scanned his chambers briefly, clearing them of threats. As soon as he realised the scream had not come from his room, he stood quickly, and threw his pants on.

It was eerily quiet, his body tense, ready for a fight. Had he imagined it?

Another scream, a female's scream, had him running from his chambers. Door banging against the wall, he paused in the hall, and his heart stopped. Something feral and protective reared itself inside of him. For the first time in his very long life, Åsmund felt genuine fear.

Shadows swarmed Hazen's door, on instinct he threw out a hand. Fire shot from the wall at his silent command, and he used it like a blade to slice through them. The shadows shrieked and dispersed, while he charged through her door.

Hazen's chambers were ice cold, he flung the fire into the darkness that consumed it. They scattered where the light touched, and he followed it, cutting a path to her bed. But she wasn't there.

Another scream and a faint glow of light emanated from the abyss. He snarled, and let his power wrap around the flames. Fire exploded across the darkness just as beams of light shot through.

Åsmund shielded his eyes.

The light dimmed, and he blinked through the spots in his vision. He willed the flames to break apart and light up the ceiling, casting her chambers in a low glow that touched every corner—not a trace of a shadow left standing.

Hazen's naked body was curled on her side, her blonde hair turned golden under the fire, and her skin… glowed from within.

His breath caught, taking in the sight. Noticing the faint red bands around her wrists when her hands curled around her head protectively. A tattoo of wings glowed brightly against her left shoulder, fading quickly. At the sight of the imprints of red around her neck and the small deep punctures towards the back of her hairline, dried blood staining her neck, a dangerous growl rumbled through his chest. The fire in the room flared along with his power, his vision zeroed in on the marks.

He took two strides to cross her chambers, kneel, and gently pull her into his arms.

Hazen jerked when he touched her, but he murmured her name

softly, and she stilled, opening her eyes at his voice.

"Hazen," he said slowly, drawing out the sound. He said her name like a prayer, relief flooding his senses when her vibrant gold eyes locked on his. His nostrils flared when he saw her power swirling in those molten depths.

The moonlight filtered into her chambers, catching the angled plains of her face. He brought a hand up to stroke down her cheek. When she sighed faintly in response, his chest squeezed and his heart stuttered, an overwhelming urge to wrap her in his arms and fly them away from here. To keep her protected and hidden away from the darkness. His body went taut when the glow of her skin brightened, her body grew hot like a living flame. But she didn't burn him, though he did burn all the same, but not in the way that hurt.

She looked beautiful—she *was* beautiful. Åsmund had never seen such beauty, such wilful determination, in one female. He had met many females in the surrounding and outlying villages and posts. Pretty, some even stunning, but none had made his eyes stray to them. None had made him anxiously await each sunrise or yearn to catch her stare whenever she was near, or touch her no matter how slight... or cast aside his duties as General.

He'd watched her train, learn, and fight to survive every day in a world that, if moments ago was any indication, wanted nothing more than to see her dead. But she was resilient, brave, determined, and stubborn above all. And he loved it. He loved seeing her embrace her power, embrace the dragon within. She called to him like the sky, and he wanted to answer her song in flight.

Shifting his weight, no matter that she was naked in his arms, he stayed kneeling on the floor of her chambers, his wings spread protectively around them.

Her glow began to subside, her eyes still locked on his, she slowly brought her palm to his cheek. Åsmund couldn't help himself. He leaned into her touch, his eyes never straying from the gold in hers. The heat of her skin faded but didn't wholly leave, leaving her warm and soft against his bare chest.

"Åsmund," she whispered. Her voice was so faint it was barely a sound as her lips moved, forming his name. "Åsmund," she said again, more audible this time. Hazen licked her lips, her fingers slipping back to curl into his hair.

Desire shot through him, and he bit back the groan at her touch. He would not allow himself to dive into those feelings, not right now. His abs clenched, his cock hardening the more her fingers moved through his hair and down his neck, grazing his skin like the finest silk. This woman would be the death of him.

Grabbing her wandering hand in his own, he couldn't stop himself. He brought her fingers to his mouth and kissed their tips. "Let's get you to bed," he said.

She wasn't glowing anymore, and her eyes were no longer molten, but they weren't hazel either. They were just gold now and utterly breathtaking.

Scooping her against him, Åsmund stood, ignoring the touch of her breast against his hand. Hazen curled into his chest, her head leaning into the hollow of his neck.

"You smell good," she muttered, nuzzling the skin.

He huffed, smiling faintly. "Do I?"

"Mhm," she hummed, nodding her head.

Åsmund lowered her to the tangled black sheets, carefully tidying them around her and pulling them up to cover her full breasts. She curled into them on her side, eyes closed.

He stared down at her for a moment before walking to her open door and checking the hall. It took him a heartbeat to walk across, close his door, and return to hers before closing it behind him and latching the bolt.

His dagger lay discarded on the floor. He must have dropped it when he went to her side. Picking it up, he tucked it into his waistband and turned to check on her but halted.

Hazen's eyes were pinned to him. Fully awake with clarity in that gold gaze.

"You should sleep," he commented. "I will stay by the door." He would sleep on the ground if he needed to, but after what he saw, he wouldn't leave her, nor would he sleep.

"I can't," she intoned, blinking before scooting over and moving the blanket back. "Not by the door."

He blinked, frozen. It was... not a command, but not a request either. It was just a statement, and she waited for him.

"Are you sure?" he asked carefully.

Her lips twitched, the first signs of her usual self since he found her. "I wouldn't have said anything if I wasn't."

Åsmund inclined his head. "Apologies, Little Dragon."

"Accepted. Now come here."

Padding on bare feet, he sauntered towards her, pausing at the edge.

Her eyes flickered to his pants. "You can't wear your training leathers. Who knows how sweaty they are."

He groaned silently. "I have to, Hazen."

She let out a deep sigh. "If you must."

"They're clean."

"I just wanted you naked."

A low growl did escape at those words. "Now isn't the time for that, Hazen."

Hazen shrugged, watching him slide beneath the blankets, fixing his wings to rest beneath him, immediately she curled around him. Her hand slid over his abdomen, a leg hooking over his, and she wiggled her head onto his chest when he settled back against the mound of black and green pillows.

"I disagree," she murmured. "I'm naked."

"That couldn't be helped," he countered, chuckling.

"Fair enough."

Åsmund looked down at the woman in his arms, stroking his hand lazily across her bare shoulder down to her elbow. She looked up at him, her hand on his abdomen coming up to tug on one of his loose curls.

"What happened?" he finally asked.

She didn't say anything, curling the strand around her finger.

"Hazen—"

"—There's a creature called Nazar. He's a shade," she said, cutting him off.

When he didn't say anything, she sighed, dropping her hand to his chest, ghosting over the piercing at his nipple. His jaw flexed, but he didn't move or say anything. He just waited.

Her finger traced around the piercing, nestling tighter to his side. "He said we couldn't co-exist in this world. That he could feel my power—my light is what he called it. That he would extinguish it..." her voice trailed off, and Åsmund watched her stare out into the night sky, her hand dropping from the piercing to curl around him.

He tucked her in tight to his side, his hand still tracing up and down her arm. "What else happened?"

She was silent for a long while, and Åsmund looked down at her to see if she had fallen asleep. Her gaze was fixed on the sky.

"It was a nightmare," she murmured. "He brought so much death; it was consuming. Eating away at me, and I knew that if my flame went out, I wouldn't wake up."

Fear shot a chill down his spine, and he swallowed down the primal need to protect her. To hide her away from all of it. Like a dragon protecting its trove.

"So, I didn't let it go out," she continued quietly. "But the darkness is no longer coming, Åsmund. It's already here, and we're about to feel its wrath."

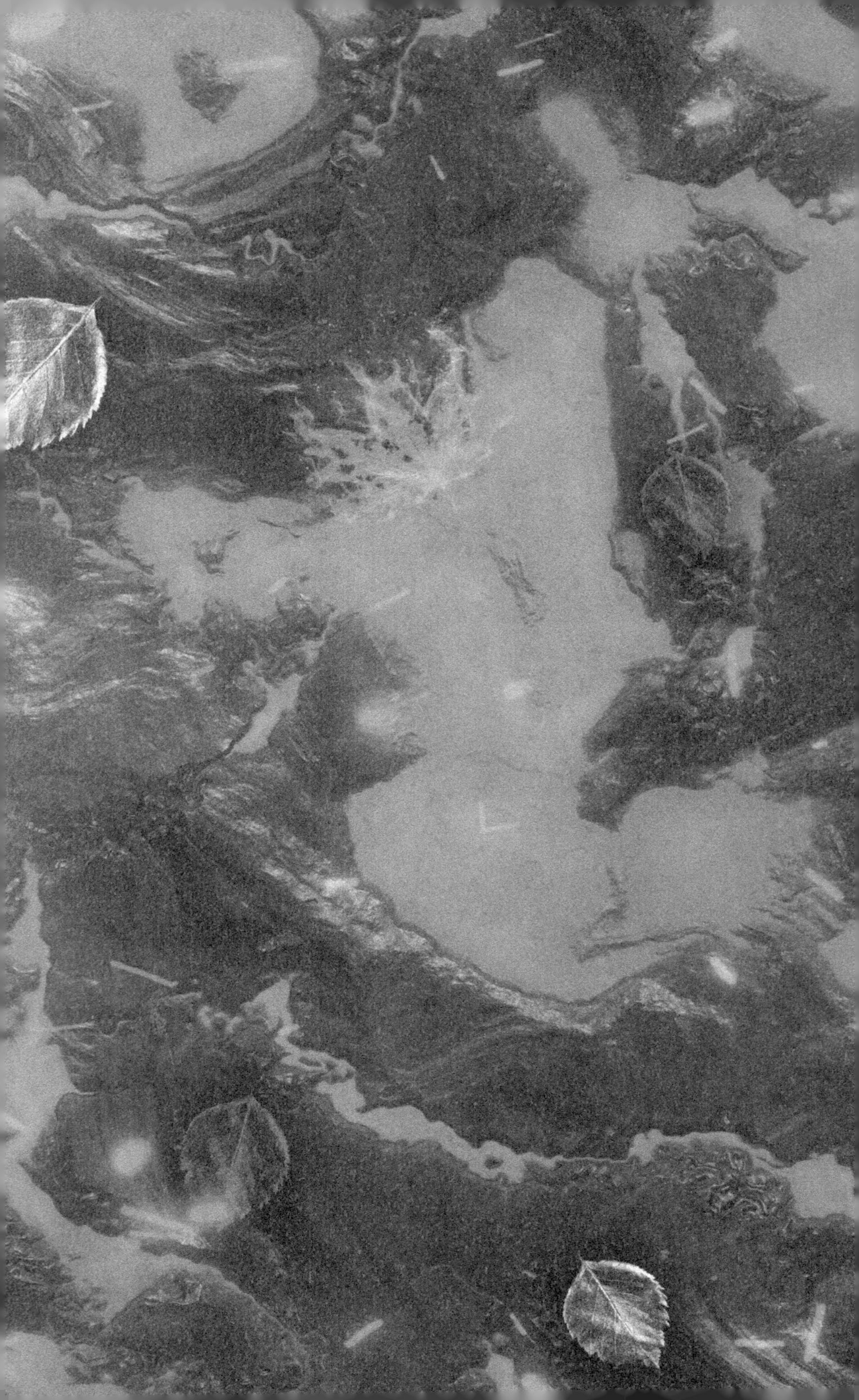

# CHAPTER 20

"You mangled one of my own, and now you want me to aid you in this fairytale?" Kladine blustered, his face red and his dark eyes flashing in warning.

Hazen snorted, shaking her head. "He challenged me, or did he fail to add that crucial detail?"

They stood in a massive council room big enough to host a dragon, Hazen suspected that's how it was designed, to host the dragons that once ruled the skies so long ago. The sky lay behind the curved golden council table where the clan leader was seated, dressed in his usual all-black. Hints of dawn framed his back, lighting against Hazen's face.

She and Åsmund had laid there in her bed until the sky began to lighten to indigo when Hazen sat up, uncaring of her nudity, and kissed his cheek before slipping out of her bed to bathe. She had felt his eyes burn into her back as she grabbed her towel, wrapped herself in it, and walked out. It had taken every ounce of self-control not to ask him to join her, but she needed to think, to gather herself before she faced the day.

When she had returned, he had his boots on, and his hair was half up in a knot at the top of his head, standing in front of the sky. Those green eyes fixed on her the moment she stepped through her door. He was the most stunning male specimen she had ever seen. He made her want to be more, to be better. He was also infuriating, but that was part of his charm, wasn't it?

He had taken her to hold council with Kladine at her request, leading her to where she now stood in her fighting leathers, Kain's challenge dagger strapped at her thigh, blonde hair braided back, exasperated and annoyed, staring pensively at the blustering male. Åsmund stood by the door, leaning against a tall pillar, ankles crossed and impressive arms folded across his broad chest. She had sworn him to silence, and he just gave her a shadow of a smile and nodded.

"You mangled his arm! Even the best healers cannot restore its full function!" he snarled, outraged. "He is maimed!"

She raised an indignant brow. "And that's my problem, how?"

Kladine's eyes bugged, and he slammed a fist down. "He would be better off dead!"

"I disagree," she drawled. "Let him know what it's like to be helpless. Besides, I gave him the option, he chose to live."

"Get out!"

Hazen's brows shot to her hairline as his voice thundered in the council room. "No."

The clan leader's eyes flashed in warning as he stood slowly from his seat, sunlight catching his dark salt-and-pepper hair. "That is a command. Get. Out."

"No," she said simply, staring into his dark eyes and letting power rise in her own.

Kladine whipped his head to Åsmund, rolling his shoulders back, his wings flaring the only inclination of his growing anger, and he inched his chin up when addressing his general. "Remove your ward, General." He paused before rectifying his statement, "No. Remove her from my mountain entirely." He rounded on Hazen with a cold smirk. "I wish to be rid of her. You are not Drago. You do not belong here."

Hazen stalked towards the council table, holding his glare when he narrowed his eyes at her. She let her power rise to the surface, feeling it press and mould itself to her body until they were one. "You're right. I am not Drago. I am not one of you." She placed two hands on the table and leaned across it until they were face to face. "I'm better." His face turned purple from rage, and she smiled sweetly, leaning away. "I'm trying to help, Kladine, and you're making it very difficult."

"Your dreams are not visions," he sneered, leaning back into his seat, airs of arrogance rolling off him.

The redness had faded around her neck and limbs, but the punctures were there. The marks of Nazar's claws would scar, and it would be set as a permanent reminder of what happened here. Pulling her braid to the side, she exposed the left side of her neck and the four red grooves at her hairline.

"Those mean nothing."

She snarled and lunged forward. "They mean everything! You hate that I'm here. You hate the change I bring, but deal with it!"

"Females cannot be trusted!" he snapped, then shut his mouth, his nostrils flaring.

Hazen's irritation dwindled slightly, and she regarded the male coolly. "You were hurt." She said it as a statement, and the clan leader's mouth curled back into a sneer.

"Females lie and betray. Their tongues are deceitful. I do not need you pulling my general into your fairytales. You will not be the ruin of my clan. I will not allow it!" His fist banged against the gold table again, making the neck of his shirt slide open to reveal a sliver of puckered flesh.

Her eyes narrowed on the mangled skin, her mouth twisting. "Did you really get those scars in battle? Or were they from your lover?" Hazen asked softly.

Kladine's eyes flickered with dark warning, nostrils flaring, and jaw flexing tightly. But he didn't say anything.

Åsmund shifted from the corner of her eyes at his clan leader's silent admission. No one knew the truth.

Hazen walked away, looking around the room. Her eyes travelled to the towering ceiling, the beautiful pillars, the glassy black walls, and then to the general who watched her every step. His eyes glued to her with fire in them, even as his face remained impassive. Her heart stuttered under his stare, and she quickly looked away, rounding back to the clan leader.

Sunrise was beginning to break the sky, storm clouds in the distance, light streaking through it in soft blue beams that filled the chamber.

"I'm sorry someone hurt you," she said gently.

Kladine's jaw flexed, and she held up a hand when he made to speak.

"Love is powerful, as is lust, but betrayal tastes the same no matter what you feel for them. But you cannot hold the actions of one over the actions of all. You are hurt, Clan Leader. I am a woman, a female, and you see me as the female who betrayed you. But I'm not."

She glanced at Åsmund and saw him watching his clan leader like a predator marking its prey. She knew then if Kladine tried anything, Åsmund would be the first to shove him from the mountain—without his wings. But the clan leader was too busy staring at Hazen to notice the dangerous silence coming from his general.

"I was brought to this world for a reason," she continued. "I have faced creatures and beasts from nightmares. I've nearly drowned, been eaten, tortured, and starved. I have not fought across this world to be told my warnings are only fairytales." Her face hardened, and she stood straighter, letting her power fill the room. Her skin began to glow again. It was different, a new kind of fire that filled her veins, and she relished in it. "You may be allowed to hide away in your mountain, but I cannot. So, either you heed what I say and do your *duty* as Drago, or stand by with your thumb up your ass while the world burns. Choice is yours. We are heading to Álfheimr. You can either be a part of the change or not at all, but change is happening with or without you." She tilted her head to the side, eyeing him coolly. "What side of history will you be on, Clan Leader?"

"Well, that was interesting," Hazen commented a little later as she and Åsmund walked through the halls to their chambers.

"Not interesting. Impressive. I stand in awe of you, Little Dragon."

His words made her giggle, and she glanced up at him, nudging his arm with her shoulder. "One night of seeing me naked, and you've gone soft?"

"No," he rumbled. "Soft is not a word I would use."

Heat and desire flushed through her body, and suddenly, the hall felt too small and her leathers too tight.

His green eyes darkened, and he growled low and primal. "I can smell your desire, Hazen."

Hazen's breath stuttered, eyes going wide. "You..." Words escaped her, and she swallowed.

His hand touched the small of her back, warm and possessive, before he reached across her, forcing her to stop. Chest level with her head, she licked her lips when his light brown skin filled her vision. Her breath fanned across his pectorals, she watched as his muscles rippled, and her hand found itself grazing the warm skin of his hip.

"Go inside, Hazen," he commanded lowly.

A soft click, and she turned her head to see her door swing open.

Hazen rounded back to Åsmund, her hand still on his hip. He stared down at her, his brown and blonde curls framing his handsome face. A face currently warring between his own desire and duty.

He jerked his chin gently and stepped back. "Go."

"You're too noble for your own good," she muttered.

That made him smile, and Åsmund gave her a cheeky grin. "One of us has to be."

With a disappointed sigh, Hazen walked to the doorway,

pausing at the threshold. "Åsmund," she said tentatively, "do you think any will join?"

Kladine finally relented but had been clear that he would not join her, neither would Kain—that she was glad of—and that he would not command his Drago to go with her, though they had free will to do so if they chose.

Hazen had accepted his terms and quickly left the council room before he could change his mind.

"No matter who shows and who doesn't, you will always have one by your side." He reached out and stroked a stray hair behind her ear, his thumb brushing the curve of her jaw. "And I will act as a hundred soldiers in their place if need be."

Chest heaving, Hazen stared up at the male before her, searching his eyes before briefly glancing at his lips. They looked soft and firm, and she wanted nothing more in that moment than to drag his head down and kiss him. She did not need a legion if she had him. They would fight side by side, him in the air and her below. But they would fight together.

Åsmund waited for her to close her door, and when she did, she leaned back against it, heaving out a sigh, trying to regain some semblance of control over her emotions.

Hazen glanced at the rolling storm clouds filling the sky and the rain that fell heavy against the invisible barrier between her and the elements. Lightning lit the clouds, and thunder rumbled violently in response. The world beyond was an illusion through the storm.

Going to her trunk, she knelt before it, opening the copper lid. Shuffling extra training leathers aside, glass vials with suspicious blue and purple liquids, and extra linens, she found a jar of ink, an old quill, and rough parchment. Standing with her things, she knocked the lid shut with her hip and went to the small wooden desk.

It took a couple of tries and a few more curses, but after a while, Hazen could finally write a coherent sentence without making a dot of ink explode over the page. With that, she went to work writing a letter to Savven.

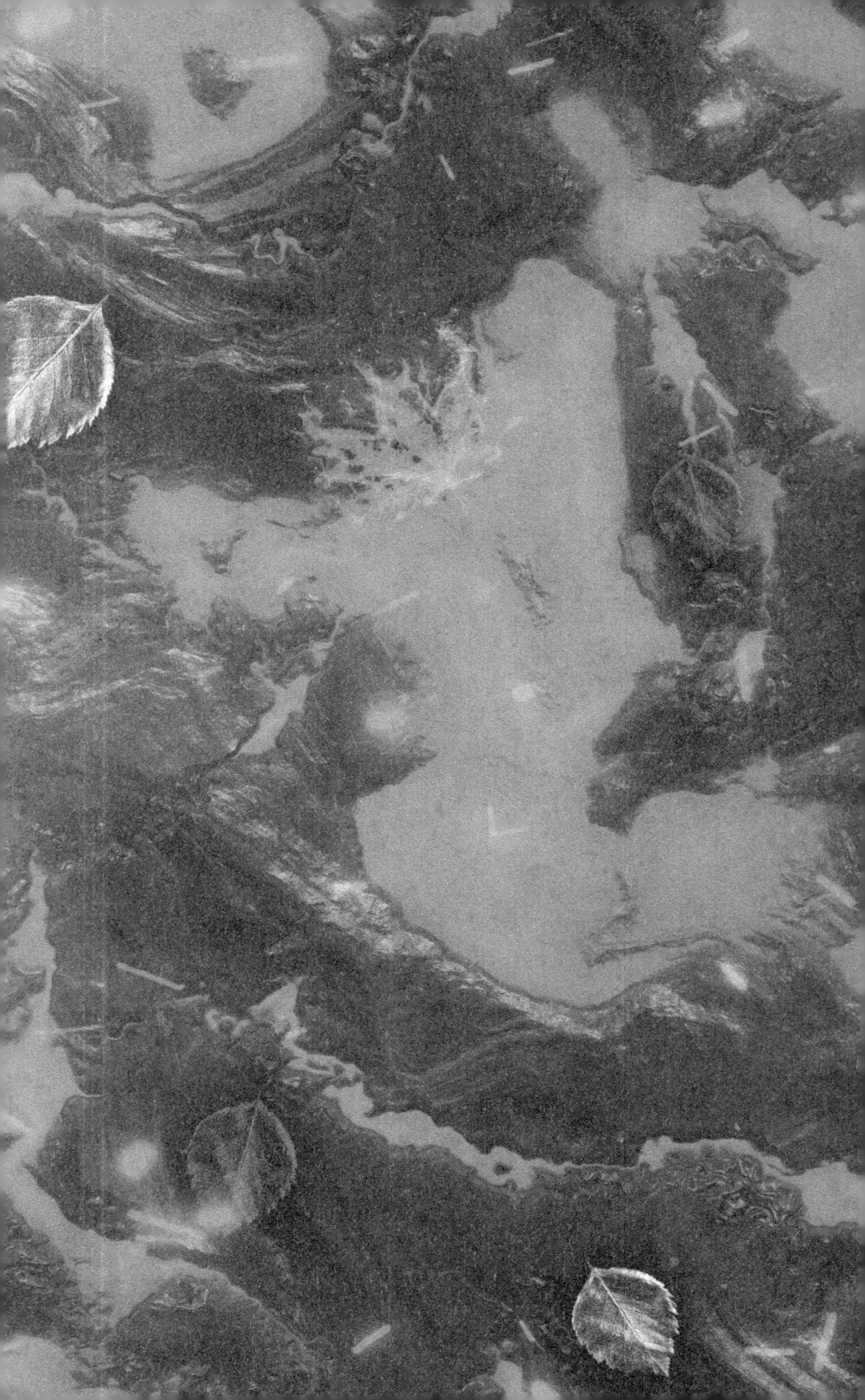

# CHAPTER 21

*"Forgive me."*

Those words echoed through Ezra like a death knell. He lay discarded on the dark floors of the great hall beneath the silver throne where he had dragged his body, trying and failing to make it to the doors leading to Levina's chambers, bleeding out slowly. Dark magic clung to the fist-sized hole gaping in his chest, slowing his body's healing so he would eventually bleed out and die. Ezra welcomed it. Death. When the cold finally stopped being cold, the pain receded, and the memories... the memories stopped tormenting him. He could rest in death, finally be free of the torment. But for all he had done, his soul... he feared there was nothing left to save.

*"Forgive me."*

Ezra squeezed his eyes shut, tears slipped from their corners.

It was a nightmare, wasn't it?

The last two hundred and eighty years had been only a nightmare. He prayed to the Gods that it had been. That every death by his hand, every demon he could feel crawling along his bones, scarring his insides, every drop of blood he consumed to keep them fed. It was all just a nightmare.

But it wasn't, and a pained sob broke free from his throat, blood gurgling past his lips in the process.

It wasn't a nightmare. *He* had been the nightmare.

"No-*o*," he cried out into the silence. His words echoed back at him, and he blinked when darkness flared the edges of his vision for the second time that night or day; he couldn't make sense of time. Not that it mattered. Nothing mattered but the impending death, and Ezra willed it to claim him faster.

Instead, the darkness filled his vision, and he fell into his memories.

*Battle erupted around him, and he charged the wall of darkness and all the creatures it held within with a single loud cry. With his sword tight in his grip, he cut through a charging minotaur with ease. Dropping to his knees and spinning, he brought the blade to the backs of its knees, and the creature went crashing to the ground. The earth thudded at its weight, Ezra got to his feet and slid the blade through its neck in a single movement.*

*A dwarf next.*

*Then another.*

*A centaur.*

*A satyr.*

*Then, it was just bodies and blood, and he was a storm that sliced through them. But they kept coming, and the darkness loomed ahead. His eyes went wide when it crashed over them like a wave. The world went black.*

When he opened his eyes, Levina was there. Her beautiful face and sky-blue eyes made his heart seize in his chest. She was his friend first, but also the female he loved. He would turn worlds over for her if she asked that of him.

But this wasn't Levina. Not the Levina he knew and loved.

The Levina in front of him laughed in his face when he pushed her away, reminding him of the rejection he had received only a few months prior.

His Levina didn't care for him that way, and he understood despite the break in his heart. He would love her from afar, turn worlds over for her silently from the shadows, and be content with that.

"You will fall, or you will jump," the now demon creature said in a rasping voice.

The world shifted, and the darkness disappeared. Ezra was standing back on the battlefield, but everything was frozen in time.

He saw Néefar, his hair still dark, teeth bared, mid-swing of a sword. The blow was directed at a Harpy with talons aimed at his chest. Wings flared wide, and the female face twisted in an ugly snarl.

"Such an interesting turn of events," said a causal female voice—a child's voice.

Ezra whirled and found the God of Immortality, dressed in a black gown hung loosely around her with long sleeves. Her black hair fell bluntly to her shoulders. She regarded him with calm, bottomless, dark eyes. He dropped to a knee, bowing his head.

Her laughter made him look up.

"I see the Fae have trained you well, Ezra."

Opening his mouth to answer, he quickly closed it.

She sighed, exasperated. "Stand up."

He did, his leathers soaked in blood and dirt now. "What is the God of Immortality doing in a battle?" It was a brazen question but one he couldn't help asking.

"What wouldn't a God of Immortality do in a battle?" She snorted as if he had asked a stupid question. "I am Death, Ezra. I am the fine line between your immortal soul and the end it faces. The God of Immortality, of life and death." She snorted again, rolling her eyes. "So many titles you have given us, given me. Just call me Death. For that is what I am. Or Tatius. Either will do."

"You're here to collect souls?" he asked, eyeing the body at his feet.

"No," Tatius mused, frowning when she glanced around the

battlefield. "Souls corrupted by darkness do not taste as good."

"You… eat them?"

She waved a hand. "That's neither here nor there. These souls will await passage when I return to the realm of the dead. But what I need is standing right in front of me."

Black eyes trained on him, and Ezra stood straighter.

"Me?" he asked, brows knitting.

"You," she echoed with a Cheshire grin. "I have a choice for you. A fork in your fate, if you will."

"I thought the Gods couldn't—"

"—interfere." Her eyes turned sharp. "I'm aware. Thank you. But that is why it is a choice, and not me making it for you… though I so wish I could. It would save me time and be so much easier. I have done what I could to aid her and change the prophetic tone of fate, but not being able to use you as I see fit is truly a bother sometimes."

Ezra shifted the blade in his hand, glancing at the God of Death up and down. He jerked his chin once, unease coiling in his stomach. "Ask what you must."

"Anabelle is going to die," Tatius said simply, almost bored.

He made to speak, but she shot him a dark look that told him not to interrupt her. He closed his mouth, jaw flexing as his fingers twitched nervously.

"Or you will take what is meant for her," she continued. "That is your choice. Let her die, and the world burns. Or you take the darkness and become the monster for the sake of the world."

The blood in Ezra's veins froze, his heart seemed to stop entirely. "What?" he breathed. It was all he could manage through the pounding in his head.

Her head tilted, and despite her youthful appearance, she was the predator, and Ezra was caught in her snare.

"As much as I like to bend my own laws, I cannot force you to choose a path. I can only tell you the outcome for both and let you choose accordingly."

"Anabelle dies, and the world as we know it falls. Or I take what was meant to kill her, and I… become the thing that destroys the world."

Tatius shrugged a shoulder, raising a brow at a decapitated body, toeing it with a black slippered foot. "I have plans, and I don't want to see them disrupted. I have a lot invested in them. So do your God a favour and choose accordingly." Her thin lips pulled into a cutting smile when she returned her focus to him.

"Why is Anabelle going to die. I thought she gave away her mortality."

"Yes, but the keeper ceremony has not been completed," she quipped in an irritable tone. "One must not be without the other. Be chosen by spirits, blessed by the dragons, and drink from the Cup of Life. She has done two of those things; the circle is incomplete, and she can still die from one of Balwin's attacks. But you, my immortal creation," she took a step closer to him, "will survive."

"And still damn the world," Ezra snarked, his tone growing icy. The God of Death wanted him to take a killing curse and damn the world in the process.

"No. Not if I have my way. I simply want you to become a monster for the sake of the world."

"How convincing. You could ask anyone else, why me?"

"Because I have plans for the others, and you are so conveniently here." Annoyance filled those black eyes, and Tatius's thin lips pressed into a tight line. "I find my patience has grown thin. I've given you a choice. Now make one."

"I can't!" he argued.

Thunder clapped overhead as the small God grew irritable. "You will because that is your fate! Choose a path, Elf. But know this: no matter what you decide, many will die. Whether by your hand or not, that fate cannot be avoided. Their death is written in the galaxies. Stand by and watch, and die with them, or be their executioner and save many in the process."

Ezra's chest heaved with strained breaths, and when he blinked, the God of Death was gone. Though her voice floated around him, stating in an unbothered tone, "Take the shifter with you. It'll give her something to hold onto as death becomes the new keeper; it kills her weaknesses with fury. It's quite amusing to watch, really."

The noise of battle rushed in around him, and he spun, ducking in time to avoid being cleaved in half by an axe as large as his torso.

A choice. He had a choice.

The world bled around him. Black shadows and mist consumed the dead, growing stronger with each body and soul and ounce of blood it consumed. His mind was a frenzy of thoughts, ultimatums, and outcomes. The outcome was the worst of it all. The world would die if he didn't. But the world would still die if he did, but by his hand. No, that wasn't right. Only some would die, not all, but he would be the reason for their death.

Ezra screamed in frustration, slicing through an attacking centaur, the heavy body crashing behind him. Blood coated his vision, and he let out a pained cry. He would be the cruel version of death. The cold nightmare the denizens of this world feared when they closed their eyes.

The demon spoke true. The darkness knew what fates the God of Death had laid plan for him.

"You will fall, or you will jump."

A guttural sound ripped from him, and he charged for the forest, gripping Néefar as he passed. "Come! Anabelle needs our help. She's in danger!"

Néefar didn't need convincing. At the mention of the keeper, the shifter went sprinting with him into the cover of trees.

He saw Anabelle up ahead, thick black shadows separating him from Néefar. But Ezra only ran faster, his heart racing against his ribs like a drum. His impending future was a looming dark cloud ahead. There was no light at the end of this—not for him.

Balwin's darkness, nothing more than shadow magic and demons, split the air like an arrow. Anabelle whirled away from the illusion of her dead mother, but not soon enough. Balwin's aim was true, and the space closed in fast.

Ezra willed his feet faster, chasing death, and at the last moment, threw himself in front of her.

Time seemed to slow, stretching into an eternity as his eyes connected with her violet-blues. Anabelle's face was the picture of shock, and in her gaze, his mind flashed with clips of his life, from being a child to everything that led him here, to this moment.

Pain erupted through him as Balwin's mark found its place, directly at his heart. White hot fire tore through his chest, and he let out a low grunt. The only sign he felt anything.

He opened his mouth and forced out the words, "Forgive me." Then, he fell into an abyss of darkness, and the world around him vanished.

Tatius appeared in the dark, empty halls of Dyagin castle. A stale air hung like an overcast cloud, and she sniffed delicately, wrinkling her nose at the tang of rot that filled it.

Her bare feet were silent on the black stone, as she walked through the solid wood doors to the great hall as if they weren't there. Head tilting a fraction, she eyed the body at the bottom of the dais.

Flames flickered in the iron sconces hung on obsidian pillars as she walked down the middle of the aisle. Stopping when she stood above the Fae male, his blood, no longer the black blood of the fallen Fae but red, weaving a path from his body through the grooves in the stone, leaving him pale, his ink hair clinging to the sweat dotting his brow. A large gaping hole cratered the centre of his chest, and she saw the dark magic clinging to its edges every time his body tried to heal itself.

"Interesting," she murmured.

The male's eyes shot open, and his dark stare found her own.

"Hello, Ezra," she intoned. "It's been a while."

Ezra made to speak, but he choked on the blood coating his tongue.

She watched him force his head to the side, his life essence dribbling out of his mouth.

"A-am... I... do-done," he whispered brokenly, pink saliva dripping from his lips.

Tatius took pity on the male and knelt beside him. "You did well, Ezra." She put a hand over the dark magic, feeling it respond to her touch like she burned it.

"Let... let me... d-die," he sobbed, tears trickling from his bleak eyes. "Plea-se."

"And let your soul go with regret weighing it down?" she commented with raised brows. "How heartless a God do you think I am?"

He tried to speak but choked on another wave of blood that had rushed into his mouth, sucking in a ragged breath when his lungs cleared.

"It's better that you didn't answer that," she amended.

Tatius laid her hand over the gaping hole, feeling every pained breath he sucked in. He would die eventually if she let him, but the regret she felt clinging to his soul was all-consuming, and her face twisted in revulsion. Regret tasted almost as bad as the black rot used to corrupt souls.

It took only a thought from her, and the wound knitted itself together from the inside out, his blood reversed and seeped back into his body. Even the fabric of his fitted black tunic wove itself back together.

Ezra's eyes flared as life filled his body, and he sucked in a loud breath.

"Better?" she asked, watching him lay there, staring up at the towering black arch.

He turned his head slowly to look at her. "Why?"

Tatius snorted. "Because your regret is not becoming. Do away with it, and I will grant your wish to give you death."

"What do you—"

Before he could finish, she smiled and snapped her fingers.

At the snap of her fingers, the world went black, and he squeezed his eyes shut, fearing he had returned to the hellscape that had been himself and the demons that consumed him.

Sweat broke out along his brow again, and his heart rate sped up, his breathing a loud pulse in his ears.

A bird chirped, and his rapid breathing froze. Not the caw of a crow, or the squawk of buzzards waiting to feast on remains, but a chirp. It chirped again, and Ezra opened his eyes.

He lay on his back in a forest, bleak light filtered through greying tree limbs. He felt the soft earth beneath him.

His fingers brushed along the dirt, feeling every grain roll under his skin. Leaves fluttered in a soft breeze, and Ezra reached a hand for it, for the feel of the wind on his skin.

As it grazed his outstretched palm, tears burned his eyes once again. Sitting up, gaze fixed on the world above, he inhaled the smell of the forest.

It smelled like his faint memory of home, but a stale, dying scent was attached to it.

*Home.*

He hadn't been home in a lifetime.

Ezra crawled to his feet. His muscles and bones felt hollow and breakable after years of being feasted on by Nazar's demons. Leaning on a tree for support, he looked at his surroundings. He stood in the middle of a dying forest. Cracks formed along thick tree trunks; some felled at their base, and others split in half. But it was home. Despite its appearance, he knew those trees. It was like a faint image of a life he no longer remembered, obscured by a veil he wished to tear down.

This was home. He knew it.

He turned left, then right, stopping as his instincts urged him forward.

*"Because your regret is not becoming. Do away with it, and I will grant your wish to give you death."*

Ezra took his first unsteady steps, sealing away every roiling emotion that formed in his gut. He would go home. Even if they killed him for what he had done, he would go home.

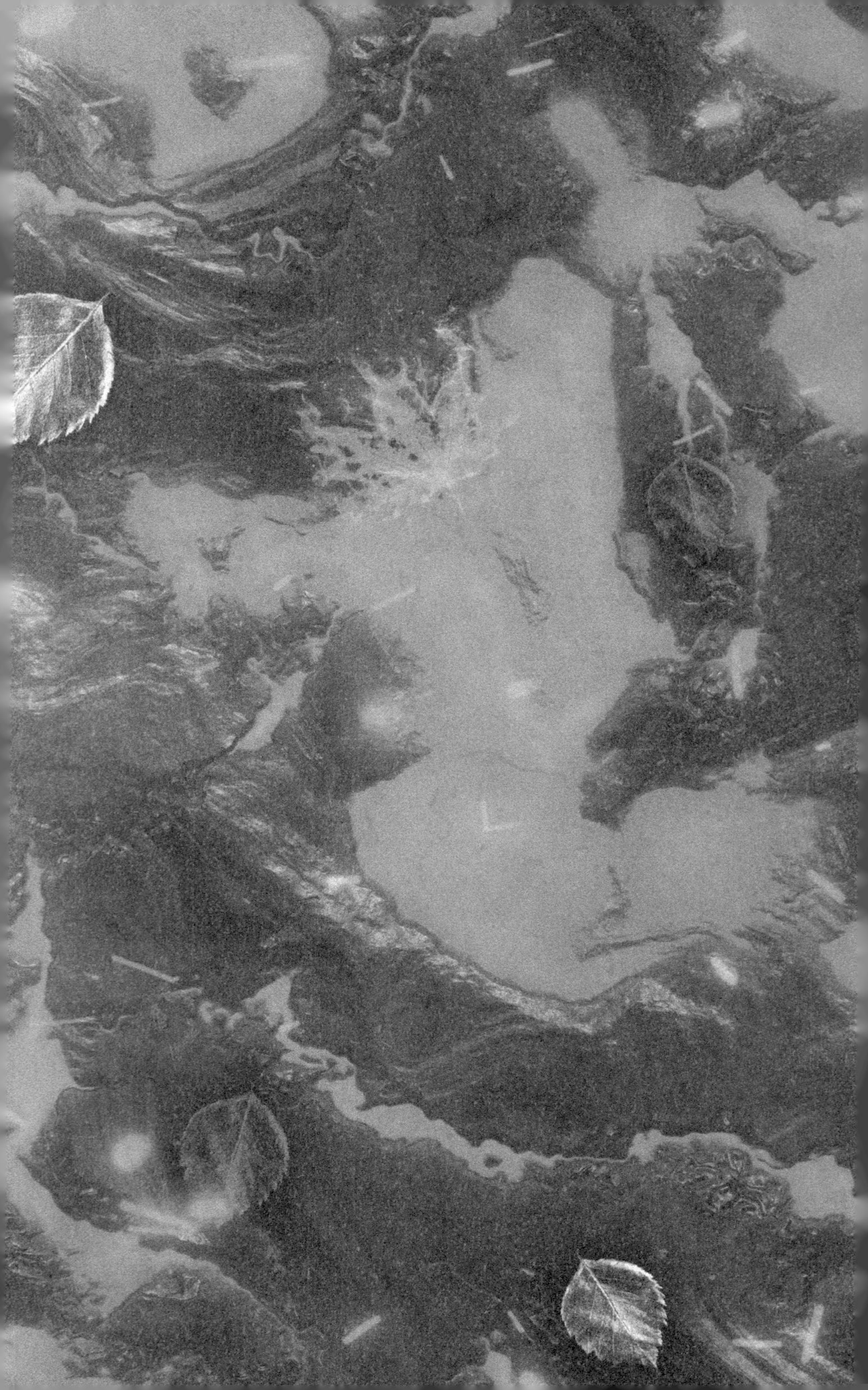

# CHAPTER 22

Nazar stood naked on the ledge of the Dyagin walls, overlooking the forest below. A blackening sky threatened from above, despite the stagnant wind.

Throwing open his arms, jaw lengthening unnaturally, he loosened an ear-splitting scream that sliced through the air. Thunder roared overhead, and the animals below screeched in return.

The runes on his flesh seeped with black tar down his body and over the side of the wall. Clouds rolled overhead, and the wind began to roar. His white hair whipped behind him as darkness rose like coiling smoke, forming a swirling pool of shadows.

He stepped forward, and the shadows swallowed him as he fell from the castle walls. The world went dark, and he landed on the other side in a crouch. Straightening himself, the shadows he walked through moved up his body and draped over him like a robe. He glanced at the towering, tangled wall that barricaded the Forest of Lost Souls.

"You are not welcomed beyond these walls, Shade."

The soft, melodic voice of the forest queen came from behind him.

"Nal-*een*," he cooed. Nazar's head clicked sharply to the side, his black tongue wetting his mouth, blood eyes gleaming at the female who emerged from the tangles, dressed in emerald strips of fabric that draped over her slight breasts and between her legs, leaving expanses of light green skin exposed. "You cannot interfere. Even the dead know of the chains that bind the Gods."

Her moss-green gaze considered him briefly, and he gave her a cold smile.

Closing his eyes, he inhaled deeply, his tongue lashing out to taste the air. A rich floral sweetness coated it, and he hummed low in the back of his throat, returning his stare to her. "I've never feasted on a God. Come closer," he whispered, eyes darkening with hunger. "Let me sink my teeth into you."

His words did not phase her. Naleen walked towards him with calm, calculating regard.

The shadows around his feet shrank back at her approach, and Nazar's hand twitched with a jolt of uncertainty as one of the four creators of this world stalked towards him.

Naleen peered at him, studying him.

Nazar snarled. "Either open your walls, or I will rip through them. The choice is yours."

A slight smile ticked on her beautiful face, her soft pink hair falling over her bare shoulders. "I will let you pass. But hear this, Shade: if you find yourself lost, my pets will take great care in ripping your head from your shoulders and tearing at your carcass until all that is left is a shell."

Nazar hissed out an oath, and venom shot towards the God. When the darkness vanished, she was gone.

Her voice came from behind him, whispering, *"You may enter."*

He whirled around, the forest empty behind him save a creeping white mist that curled over the floor.

Wood cracked, and he turned slowly, watching the forest entrance open.

Cackling softly, a dark smile cut its way across his face. Nazar's shadows crawled through the opening, disappearing into the thick fog that coated the dead woods.

"Come, pets, and let us play."

# CHAPTER 23

At the sound of her chamber door opening, Hazen sat up from her desk. Having fallen asleep, her quill hung loosely between her fingers. Blinking the exhaustion away, she glanced at Rin as the girl slipped into her room.

Her hair was artfully braided back, gold clasps in the white-blonde strands. She was dressed in a long, dark, rose-coloured gown with fitted sleeves that draped open at her wrists and plunged between her breasts. A shimmering swath of gold fabric lay in her arms, which she carefully laid on Hazen's bed.

"Rin?" she asked, groggy, setting the quill aside.

Rin gave her a beaming smile and quickly walked over to her. "Did you fall asleep writing?" she giggled, eyeing the parchment on the desk. "You remind me of my eldest sister, Talia. She writes stories and will always fall asleep in the midst of them."

Hazen made to roll the parchment, but Rin stopped her.

"You need pounce powder for the ink to set it," she explained when Hazen shot her a questioning look.

Going to the trunk, Rin's gown swirling around her, she opened the clasp and began to rummage through it. After a moment, she pulled a small clear jar out with white, chalky powder and walked back over to the desk. She quickly sprinkled some of the powder over the parchment, and blew the residual away.

"There, that'll do it," she said brightly, lifting the parchment and shaking it lightly before rolling it up and handing it back to Hazen.

"Actually," Hazen said slowly, "I need to get that to someone quickly."

"I can do that," Rin said with a small smile. "I can use one of the carrier birds. Who is it going to?"

"The Prince of Álfheimr," she said, adding quickly, "I don't know where he is or if he's alive, but we were travelling to Álfheimr before we were separated. If he is alive, then he might be there."

Rin hummed in response, her smile turning reassuring. "Don't worry. The carriers will find him. They're very clever."

Hazen's chair scraped the stone, as she pushed it back to stand. Her body ached from her nap, and she stretched with a low groan, hearing her bones pop. "It's almost dinner," she commented, catching the sunset trying to cut through the storm clouds.

At that, Rin brightened considerably, and Hazen didn't think that was possible. "Yes! And you will be dining with the Drago tonight."

"What?" Hazen breathed, stilling.

She hadn't dined with anyone but Rin since she'd arrived, sticking to her chambers per Åsmund's orders. Not that she minded much. After training, she rarely had any energy left to do much other than sleep, let alone verbal sparring with a group of males who barely tolerated her.

But the thought of dining with Åsmund and the other males now made her pause. Almost excitedly so.

Rin floated to the bed, looking at Hazen over her shoulder. "It's tradition."

"What is?" Hazen asked, following her.

"To feast before war." Rin perched on the bed, tucking one of her legs beneath her. "Åsmund spoke to the Drago. He gave them an option. Stay or fight." Rin looked down at her hands, her fingers twisting in her lap, smiling sadly. "My mate goes with you. I do not know who else. But you will have him at your back."

Hazen laid a hand over Rin's fidgeting ones. "Rin."

The girl looked up at her, tears brimming her wide blue eyes. "Look after him," she begged softly. "I do not know where you go or who you fight, but I plead with you. He is a good male, a kind male, and I love him very much. Bring him home to me."

Another crack formed along her heart, one of many since she arrived in this world, and she bent, wrapping Rin in her arms. Hazen soothed a hand over her hair and down her back, squeezing her gently. "I'll do my best," she said.

Rin nodded against her shoulder, pulling back with a sniffle. "That's all I ask."

Gold caught the corner of Hazen's eye, and she looked down at the satin fabric. It was like liquid metal against the black quilt. "What is this?"

Giggling, Rin clapped her hands, giddy. "General Åsmund selected it and had me bring it for you to wear tonight. Isn't it beautiful?"

Hazen's brows shot to her hairline. "I'm wearing this tonight?" She fingered the material, watching it slip like water over her small callouses.

Hopping off the bed, Rin walked around Hazen and grabbed a linen towel from the still open trunk. "Go bathe. We have work to be done before the feast."

Hazen didn't have much say in the matter, with Rin shoving the towel in her arms and pushing her out of her room. When the door shut behind her, Hazen stared tentatively at Åsmund's door across the hall. She wondered if he were in there now, or maybe he was bathing. A sly smile curved her lips, and she made her way to the bathing chambers.

He wasn't in the springs, so Hazen made quick work of washing. Freshly cleaned and wrapped in a new dry towel, she was seated in the chair by her desk and turned to the sky for natural light, the rain had stopped during her nap.

An assortment of small clay jars and tiny glass pots were spread across her desk, Hazen had peaked inside a couple of them and was thankful Rin knew what she was doing with them, because she couldn't make heads or tails what any of it was. The writing materials were stowed away before she returned, and she was informed that her letter had been sent off with a carrier.

Rin hovered over her, smudging something glittery along her eyes, cheeks, and shoulders. She used a piece of kohl on her waterline and black tinted oil on her lashes, a look of concentration twisted her petite face as her tongue poked out between her lips. Hazen had the distinct thought of what it would have been like to do her makeup every morning before class with these small jars, suddenly grateful for the ease her makeup palette provided.

Her damp hair was already nearly dry in the warm air when Rin turned her attention to it. She ran a wide-tooth comb through it and pulled at the strands, sometimes hard enough to make Hazen wince.

When she was done, she produced a small misshapen mirror and set it on the desk.

Hazen paused, not looking at the mirror. What would she see? She hadn't seen herself in a month. Would she recognise herself? Steeling her emotions, Hazen looked at her reflection and sucked in a breath.

Rin had braided thick and thin sections of her hair to interlay with her sun-bleached strands, tying back half of it into a small, messy bun. Two braids draped on either side to wrap around the back, whisps of hair framing her face... her face, Hazen looked at the woman she saw in her reflection for a long moment. The scar from the sea witch's poison marked the left side of her face, the curling whorls stark against her deeply tanned skin. Gold dust swept her eyelids, around her tear ducts and under her eyes. Rin had applied it to her cheekbones, highlighting their sharp curve. Her lips were painted with tinted oil, giving them a deep, rosy look, but her eyes... her eyes weren't hazel anymore; they were almost entirely gold. A glimpse of power kindled in them, making them light in the growing darkness.

Standing, Hazen backed away, staring at her reflection. Dropping the towel, she stared at her naked body, adorned only in the small amber necklace. She knew she had gotten stronger, but seeing it was entirely different. Her legs were lean but defined, her stomach flat, and she could see the shadow of abs in the firelight. Her arms were strong and trimmed. She held herself differently, too. Shoulders back, head high. There was an air of confidence around her… an air of power.

But what stood out the most was her as a whole. She looked less human and more… feral, not entirely Fae. Just untamed.

Turning, Hazen looked over her shoulder to her reflection, her fingers reaching to trace the now barely marked skin. The brand that looked like wings and a web of knots had looked like a bruise in the beginning but faded almost entirely. Now, there was only a faint white scar you could barely see.

She smiled at herself, turned back around, and glanced at Rin, who held a hand to her mouth, hiding her grin.

"You're beautiful," Rin finally burst.

Hazen reached for her hand, offering her a soft smile. "Thanks to you."

Nearly an hour later, Hazen stood nervously in front of her door, hands twisting in the fabric of her dress. Realising what she was doing, she dropped the fabric and smoothed a hand over the metallic gold front.

The dress clung to her body like water, moulding to her breasts and the dip of her waist until it trimmed the floor, barely-there straps wrapped around her shoulders to the undersides of her arms. A long slit exposed her right leg when she walked, and the back dipped low, nearly to her tailbone. The front was draped with soft folds that exposed the rise of her breasts every time she breathed. It was the most beautiful thing Hazen had ever worn, and she felt entirely exposed.

Rin had brought matching gold satin flats with delicate chains of gold that draped around her ankles. And when Hazen saw herself in the mirror for the second time that evening, she stood in awe.

Closing her eyes briefly, she sucked in a breath, gathering her nerves, and made to open the door when a knock came.

Her heart jolted. She felt like she was going on a first date.

Hesitating, her hand hovering over the handle, she exhaled and shook her head softly. "Come on," she murmured to herself. "Don't chicken out now."

Grabbing the handle, she unlatched the bolt and swung it open.

Her heart stopped fully.

Åsmund turned at her door opening; he was truly the most devastatingly handsome male she had ever seen.

He wore his regular black leather pants and boots, but what caught her stare was the black fitted tunic. The sleeves were crafted to hug every muscled ridge, with a laced V-neck that hung loosened and undone, exposing the expanse of light brown skin and sculpted pectorals. Simple gold stitching wove into the hem and sleeves, gold tips on the points of his enormous wings. His curly hair hung long and wild around his shoulders.

Seeing him clothed was the equivalent of seeing him half-naked for the first time. Breathtaking. He was the thing of fantasies, the type of male writers wrote about in their pages. His high cheekbones, firm mouth, and strong jaw were nothing compared to the gold-flecked emerald eyes that darkened as they swept over her with burning appreciation.

His gaze was like a physical touch, and every inch of her felt electrified. Where he looked, her body came alive. Her dress did little to hide her hardened nipples, when she caught his gaze stopping there and darkening, her core tightened.

Jaw flexing, he brought his gaze back to her.

"Change," he said roughly, his voice hoarse.

Her brows shot up, and a startled laugh slipped out. "What? Why?"

Åsmund rubbed a hand over his mouth, hunger in his gaze. "That is not a dress. That is a death wish to all who look at you."

Hiding her grin, she stepped forward and looked up at him slyly, closing the distance. "Is that your way of saying I look beautiful? Well, thank you. You are quite stunning yourself, General."

"You are beyond beauty, Little Dragon," he rumbled. His hand came up and grazed along the gold shimmering on her shoulder, his fingers trailing down her arm. "Remind me to tell Rin she outdid herself."

"I'll pass it along," she said, bemused, fully aware of his fingers tracing a leisurely path that made every cell in her body come alive. "Shall we go to this feast?"

Åsmund looked like a male ready to feast, but not the kind they were going to. He looked at her like a male starved, and she was his last meal.

Her body hummed in response, and she took in a shallow breath. "Don't look at me like that."

"What can I say," he commented, jaw flexing, "dragons like shiny gold things."

Hazen's lips quirked.

Her general, the thought gave her brief pause, wondering when he had gone from general to *her* general, took a resigned breath and stepped back, holding out the crook of his elbow. "Come, we have food to eat, and I have soldiers to fend off."

Her laughter followed them down the hall.

Pain lanced through Levina like lightning, and her eyes shot open in the dark cell. The pain receded, and she relaxed, placing a soothing hand over her stomach. "It's okay, Little One. Your mother is here with you." Usually, a tiny foot or little hand pressed along her insides, but all was silent.

Frowning, Levina cradled her stomach and slid her legs under her to get to her knees before using the wall to help her stand. Her stomach was round and heavy but not as large as it should be, and the weight made her brittle bones ache. The fatigue in her body had her swaying when she straightened. They fed and watered her once a day; from it, her limbs were thin and her skin sallow. Her baby was growing while she withered away, and Levina pushed away the thought that there might be a chance she didn't survive this. She had to.

The stench of urine and faeces hung like a thick cloud; the

smell alone made her gag, and she covered her nose and mouth, stumbling to the door.

Her dress hung in shredded swaths of black gossamer fabric, a layer of grime coated her skin, melding her with the stone chamber that housed her. Leaning against the thick wood, she glanced into the hall, breathing in the semi-clean air, and stared at the only sign of life—a flickering flame in an iron sconce.

She stayed there long enough for her eyes to droop shut, and she slumped against the wood, still holding fast to the door.

Another bolt of pain shot through her, across her stomach and wrapped around her lower back. She gripped the bars, her knuckles bleaching, and a pained moan slipped through gritted teeth as she doubled over, cradling her belly.

When the pain receded, Levina slowly righted herself, panting. Fear crawled down her spine. She gripped the bars with one hand so tightly that her knuckles went white immediately, her other hand was holding her stomach with the utmost tenderness.

"You can't come yet, Little One. It's not time," she hushed, her voice cracking and desperate.

But Tatius had changed that, hadn't she? Her womb had grown after the last time she had seen the God. Speeding up her pregnancy.

Lips wobbling, Levina blinked back the tears that burned her eyes. Fixating on the dancing flames, she pressed her lips together.

She would not cry. She would not be afraid. She would be strong.

She chanted it repeatedly until it filled her prison like a song.

"I will not cry."

"I will not be afraid."

"I will be strong."

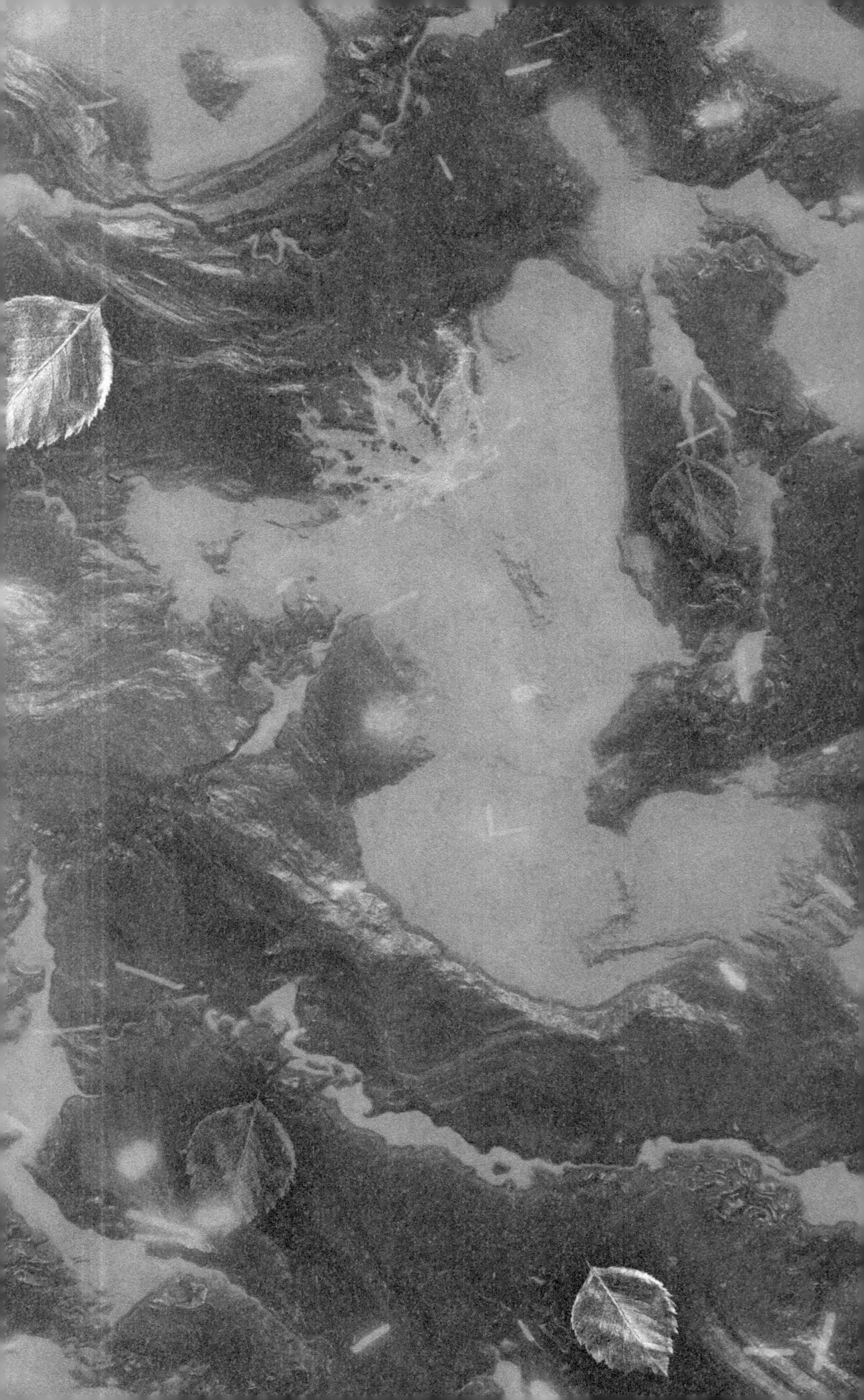

# CHAPTER 24

Music filled the hall, and firelight danced above in a floating corona that lit everything in a beautiful glow. For the first time since she arrived, Hazen saw more females than just Rin and herself.

Couples were grouped together, females communing with one another, all dressed in beautiful gowns of varying styles. Most males wore black or dark coloured tunics in an array of deep greens and blues, but they all had in common the gold tips on the crest of their wings.

Her gown, as Åsmund had told her when she asked, was of the High Fae variety. She had snorted and rolled her eyes at him.

"I don't need to know which of your lovers this belonged to," she had said.

"Jealous?" he murmured in her ear.

"Not in the slightest." Lies. It made her a little jealous.

His only response was a teasing smirk as he told her a dragon never reveals the depths of their treasure trove but that the dress now belonged to her.

She had to look away from him when he told her that and was saved by the music and laughter greeting them.

Four long communal tables framed what she supposed was a dance floor. Benches were occupied by various soldiers, and in a corner were three females draped in white gossamer fabric that, when it caught the firelight, showed the silhouette of their naked bodies beneath. The three females held instruments resembling a violin, a mandolin, and a flute.

A lively tune filled the air, reminding Hazen of her summer travels to County Tyrone as a child. Her slippered foot tapped in time to the jig, and females ran to the dance floor, twirling and dancing to the music.

Hazen beamed, laughing when she saw Rin drag her mate, a handsome male with close-cropped chestnut hair and dark brown skin, to the dance floor. He grabbed her by the waist and began to spin with her, laughing when she tilted her head back and flung her arms wide, her white-blonde hair wild around her. And Hazen knew she would always remember her that way, in that moment, and she tucked the memory securely away.

As they walked through the hall, every eye turned to regard them silently before returning to their conversations.

Åsmund directed her to the table at the front, with four high-backed wooden chairs in the centre. Valdren sat on the far right, with Kladine seated beside him.

The Dragon Keeper looked at the couples and single males who drank and ate with a shadow of bemusement on his ageless face. He wore a long black and gold ornate robe, his grey hair pulled back in an intricate knot.

Kladine stared on, unimpressed. His black eyes shifted to her as they walked towards the table, and she notched her chin slightly higher.

"Clan Leader," she murmured in greeting, sitting when Åsmund pulled out her chair beside Kladine.

His eyes flicked to hers, and he tilted his head just barely. "Keeper."

Hazen paused, rearranging her dress around her, and slanted a look at him. She hadn't forgotten what was expected of her, but she had done her best not to think about it either. And now a weight dropped into her stomach. "I am not The Keeper, Clan Leader."

"Yet," he corrected curtly.

She turned to watch the dancers, leaning back into her seat, heart beating in time with the mandolin. "That is a decision I have yet to make."

Kladine scoffed, shaking his head.

Hazen raised a brow at him. "You disapprove?"

"Of course," he snapped, his hand curling into a fist on the table.

"Of course *you* would," she quipped with a press of her mouth.

A male passed with a tray laden with meats and fruits and placed it in front of her and Åsmund, who had taken the seat beside her. Hazen pulled a slice of steaming meat and an assortment of fruit onto the gold plate in front of her.

"Being keeper is a responsibility that is not lightly given. If you reject it, you spit in the face of the dragons—of the Gods!" His voice had risen enough to have eyes looking their way.

Hazen gave Rin a tight smile when they locked eyes. She silently communicated that she was fine, and Rin nodded once, glaring at the clan leader for good measure. Stabbing a slice of light orange fruit with her utensil, she brought it to her mouth, chewing on Kladine's words as she ate. It tasted like a peach, and Hazen smiled at the familiarity of home.

"Do you not care that you tarnish a tradition as old as our world?" Kladine hissed.

Swallowing a piece of meat she had selected to try next, Hazen shrugged. "Let me ask you a question, Kladine."

"It's *Clan Leader*," he spat.

She looked him dead in his eyes, unphased. "Quite frankly, I don't give a shit."

Kladine's face turned red, his eyes bulging at her frankness.

"If you lived as you do now and then suddenly one day it

changes, and the world expected you to give up something that was so innately *you*. What would you do?”

“I would do as expected of me,” he barked.

“No, you wouldn’t,” Hazen replied calmly, popping another piece of fruit into her mouth. She made him wait until she swallowed to continue. “You don’t like change. Your role as clan leader is like my mortality. It’s who I am, and making a decision based on life or death takes that away. It’s not a role I take lightly.”

Nostrils flaring, Kladine rounded on the dancers, fixating on them before turning thunderous eyes on her. “It is tradition!”

“Tradition be damned. It’s time to make a new one.”

Slamming his fist on the wood top, the plates rattling, Kladine stood abruptly, his chair nearly toppled over.

“They chose wrong when they chose you!” he snarled and stormed off in a cloud of rage.

Åsmund let out an exasperated sigh before chuckling beside her. “I remain in awe of you, Little Dragon,” he muttered, his eyes full of mirth when she glanced at him from beneath her lashes.

A low cough caught her attention. She found Valdren watching her with bright eyes.

“Good evening, Valdren,” she said politely.

He tilted his head at her, smirking with amusement. “Good evening, Hazen.”

“Apologies for that.” She waved a hand to where Kladine stormed off.

“No need,” the Dragon Keeper said, chuckling, and turned to watch the dancers.

The music changed to something soft and lulling. The one female who played the mandolin set it aside and began to sing of the night and day, her voice enchanting the dancers, who parted and circled their partners as if transfixed in a dream.

Åsmund’s chair scraped the stone floor, and he stood.

Hazen looked up at him, and he offered her his hand and a small smile.

“Dance with me?”

“I don’t know how,” she whispered, though she slipped her hand into his.

He leaned in close, admitting lowly, "Neither do I."

Unable to stop the giggle that escaped, Hazen pressed her fingertips to her mouth and let Åsmund guide her to the dance floor.

"Finally, something you're not good at," she teased.

Smiling faintly, Åsmund bowed his head at her, and she mirrored him. The dancers twirled, and Hazen's head followed them, watching their movements.

"Put your feet on mine," he murmured in her ear, slipping an arm around her lower back.

Skin flushing, she swallowed, eyes fluttering when his breath skimmed the sensitive flesh of her neck. "Are you sure?" she asked, breathless.

"Do as I say, Hazen."

Hazen nodded and stepped carefully onto the tops of his boots.

Åsmund anchored her body flush against his, every inch of him shaping itself to her. Hazen could barely think, feeling his heat radiate over her skin, her breasts pressed against his chest.

His hand took hers, and then they were dancing.

The hall was a blur of firelight and colours, but Hazen only had eyes for the general who held her as if she were an extension of him. She pressed onto her tiptoes, holding onto him, neck craned to stare up at the green eyes that never left her own, and their world narrowed to just the two of them.

When the music slowly drifted off, they stayed there, pressed against each other, eyes locked as the world slowly crept back in around them. His fingers trailed up her naked spine, slowly brushing her hair over her shoulder, and Hazen shivered.

A lively tune started up, and dancers began moving around them. Hazen stepped off his boots, but he didn't let her step away, instead his fingers curled around her waist, keeping her close.

"Can I ask you something?"

Åsmund quirked a brow but remained silent.

"I should have asked sooner, I should have…" she trailed off, pursing her lips, glancing at Rin and her mate. "Do you have a mate? Or a female you're interested in?" Hazen nibbled on her lip, blushing from her question. She didn't think she would ever ask those exact words, but now she anxiously awaited his answer.

His eyes softened, and he leaned forward, his cheek skimming hers. "I wouldn't have lain in your bed with you naked if I did."

Bellies full and feet aching, Åsmund and Hazen found themselves strolling leisurely to their chambers sometime later. Their smiles soft, her arm looped through his, and the silence welcoming.

"You lied, by the way," she commented casually.

Åsmund hummed, slanting a look in her direction.

"You can dance. You said you can't."

He chuckled in response. "I can't dance. But I can follow the music just fine. It's similar to fighting."

Hazen snorted. "You would reference fighting."

"War is nothing but a dance between two enforcing groups, both volleying for the lead. Neither one knows how to follow."

"I can follow," she replied stubbornly.

Smiling wryly down at her, he asked, "Can you?"

Shrugging, she laughed lightly. "If it interests me."

"You'll be the death of all the Fae," he replied, amused. "They live to enforce hierarchy. If you are not born into your role or selected, you follow those who are."

"I guess it's a good thing I'm not Fae then."

"No, you're better than that. You're a dragon. And dragons do not conform."

Hazen went to reply about the irony in his statement when a cold laugh broke out, and they paused.

Åsmund cursed under his breath when the laughter sounded again, and Hazen let out a long-drawn sigh. She knew that laugh. It had echoed behind her for half of her training sessions.

"I should have killed him," she muttered darkly.

Growling in response, Åsmund took her hand and dragged her to an alcove up ahead. Pressing her into the shadowy space, his arms bracketing her head, wings flared slightly to shield her from view, he leaned forward, their bodies nearly touching.

To anyone passing, they would look like a couple that snuck away to find some privacy.

"I can handle him," she whispered.

In the shadows, everything seemed heightened: how he smelled, how her body tightened and became overly sensitive, how much she wanted to drag her hands through his hair and kiss him.

"You shouldn't have to," he intoned darkly. "Not tonight."

Footsteps resounded behind Åsmund, followed by laughter on the other side of his spread wings. If she ducked her head under them, she would have been able to see the toe of Kain's boot.

"Finally lost your little pet, Åsmund?" Kain remarked with a snicker.

Åsmund›s face turned dangerous, and he growled in warning. "Can you not see I am busy, Kain? Go bother someone else."

"Better you than I," Kain continued, ignoring him. "How bothersome to be stuck with such a useless creature. She'll die in the first moments of battle, so don't worry, you'll be rid of her soon."

Hazen sucked in a sharp breath, her own anger rising.

"Is that what you thought when you challenged her? That she makes an easy death to add to your tally?" Åsmund scoffed, keeping his tone unbothered despite the brewing anger in his eyes. "Correct me if I'm wrong, but didn't you misjudge her skill a little bit? Now, do me a service and go away. I'm busy."

"She won by pure luck," Kain snapped, the orbs of fire flickering.

"I hear you'll never use your arm again." Åsmund was goading him, his face a mask of fury.

Hazen cupped his cheek, giving him a reassuring smile.

An animalistic snarl ripped from Kain. "That little bitch maimed me, but I will get her back for that tenfold. Just wait."

A bitter smile cut over her face, and she dropped her hand, her annoyance sparking. Åsmund shook his head at her in a quick jerk.

"Don't," he said, barely audible.

"She is not a dragon," Kain continued, ignoring the growing tension in the air, "more like a witch with her fire that burns Drago. Fire does not hurt us, and that is because she is not one of us, and you will be grateful when I slaughter her in her sleep."

She was a storm of shimmering metallic gold and fury as she pushed Åsmund away and marched right up to Kain, spitting, "Why don't you say it to my face, coward?"

Kain stepped back in surprise but quickly caught himself. The two Drago behind him flinched when she appeared.

Hazen bared her teeth in a savage grin to the two behind him, rounding it on the male with the mangled arm that lay in a black leather sling. He wasn't wearing a shirt, allowing her to see the puckered flesh, scarred over with varying shades of mottled pink and white, deep grooves wrapped like a snake around his forearm where it had constricted around him.

"Well, at least you still have it," she said sweetly.

A wide, salacious grin cut across Kain's cruel face. "Whoring yourself to us already? My turn next? I'll let him stretch you out for me."

Hazen made a show of stepping back, arching a critical brow at him. She looked pointedly at the bulge in his leathers. "Huh," she said thoughtfully, "I didn't realise it was big enough to use? I thought that's why you were so angry all the time."

Åsmund's chest pressed along her back, shaking subtly with repressed laughter.

Kain's face turned dark red. "You dare—"

"—I do," she cut in. "You challenged me due to bias of my sex. But from where I stand, you are not only insufferable but now useless." She stepped closer to Kain. "Now, do *me* a service: go back to the rock you crawled out from under." Hazen lifted a hand, and the fire came to her outstretched fingers, dancing around her palm. "Unless you would like me to mangle the other one? How will you jerk yourself off then?"

He bared his teeth in outrage, wings flaring wide and causing the two behind him to step back lest they get hit by them. "I do not take orders from a female!" Despite his heated words, his eyes flickered with fear at the flames.

Hazen huffed out a dark laugh. "Good thing I'm not a female. I'm a *woman*."

Regardless of the fire furling around her wrists, Kain advanced a step towards her, malice on his face.

She had to give it to him. He had some balls—tiny ones—but they were there.

Åsmund's wing curled around her one side. His growl filled the hall, and the fire around them wavered towards the male pressed to her back. Murderous power radiated off him in waves.

A debate raged over Kain's face as if weighing whether he should or shouldn't make do with that single step and the threat it held. But instead, he sneered at Åsmund and stepped back. "What a good little subservient animal you've turned into, General."

And then he was stomping down the hall, the two following closely behind.

"What am I going to do with you?" Åsmund remarked once Kain and his lackeys were out of sight.

She smirked, letting the fire go back to the orbs. "Spank me and call me a good girl?"

He turned her by her shoulders to look at him, his eyes dark green and intense. "Come again?"

A wide expanse of muscle filled her vision; their bodies nearly touched, and with every breath, she could feel her breast graze his chest. The friction caused her nipples to tighten and desire to shoot through her body. She should take a step back, she should, she… looked up into his green eyes. They were nearly black, and it made her breath hitch.

His gaze drifted to her mouth, lingering, before trailing down her neck, where her pulse pounded wildly in her throat as if he could hear her racing heart, and then back to her eyes.

"I'm just teasing you," she said, albeit breathlessly. "I'll behave."

"Promise?" he asked darkly, lifting a hand to stroke a strand of blonde hair away from her cheek.

His thumb grazed along her skin, trailing down to her bottom lip.

When he rubbed it over her mouth, she couldn't help herself. Her tongue darted out, and she flicked the tip against his thumb.

Åsmund's low groan surged through her like fire, and he gripped her by the waist, whirling them and pressing her against the stone wall. His wings shielded them from onlookers, a single orb of fire hovered above their heads, igniting the plains of his face in a golden glow above her.

Hazen's body was flush against Åsmund's, his arm banded around her waist, keeping her in place. His heat seared the skin beneath her dress, and she wanted to shed the minuscule fabric between them.

"I can't promise I'll behave," she breathed, amending what she had said.

"Don't tempt me to do things a good general wouldn't do," he growled in warning, his eyes nearly black with desire.

Her lips curved into a sly smile, whispering into the space between them, "A good general knows how to play in the dark without getting caught."

Åsmund's hand dropped from her lips to her neck. He squeezed gently, fingers wrapping around her throat like a collar, and her eyes fluttered shut. Moaning lowly, she arched into him when his knee slipped between her legs, her core going molten.

Bending his head, his breath fanned across her jaw and to the sensitive flesh by her ear.

Hazen felt his tongue taste her skin, and her whole body ignited. The flames above them danced as her power spiralled inside of her, rising to the surface and heightening every delicious thing he was doing.

Slipping a hand up her exposed thigh, he lifted it and pressed his hips to her centre. He was rock hard against her, and she pressed into him, causing him to groan deep and long.

"You will be the death of me, woman," he growled.

Hazen practically purred when he called her woman, and she felt his cock twitch in response. Raising onto her tiptoes despite him holding her thigh, she pressed her body to him, sliding against the thick length of him as she did so. Her mouth hovered just below his as she whispered, "What a beautiful way to die."

The hand at her throat slipped to the back of her neck, locking her where she was, and he lowered his head—

Laughter cut like ice through their fire, and Åsmund jerked back, though his wings still shielded them from view until a pair of soldiers passed them.

Catching herself when he released her leg, Hazen straightened her gown, trying to steady her breathing.

When they were gone, Åsmund curled his wings in tight and stepped back.

It wasn't cold within the cave, but Hazen shivered at the lack of body heat she was already missing. Her body throbbed almost painfully. His touch was branded on her. She could still feel his fingers wrapped around her neck and around her thigh, and she wanted him to put them back. But looking at him and the primal way he stared down at her, she said nothing. Didn't move. Barely breathed.

The air was charged between them despite their interruption.

Nostrils flaring, his eyes became nearly onyx. Hazen was certain he could smell the arousal on her.

"Go to your room, Hazen."

Her chest heaved, and she pursed her lips into a flat line. That was the last thing she wanted to do.

"Go," he continued, almost pained, "and lock the door."

A lock wouldn't stop him, but she knew he wouldn't come. She knew he wouldn't change his mind. Sighing, she shook her head. "Your honour will be the death of me."

Gathering herself, she left him standing there. Hazen could feel his eyes boring into her back until she was out of sight. And when her door was locked and the dress a pool of shimmering gold on her floors, Hazen slipped between her covers and let her hand wander between her legs to the wet heat that sat pulsating in anticipation.

She pictured Åsmund's hand between her legs, his tongue, his fingers, his cock. All of it.

And when she climaxed, it was his name she moaned.

Åsmund stood in the hall between their chambers. His cock was punishingly hard, and his heart raced in his chest as he forced himself not to move.

He had followed shortly after he made her return to her chambers, counting the moments until he had himself under control. He would have taken her there in the hall, of all places. He had let his guard down, forgetting where they were for a moment. Allowing himself a taste of her, she nearly brought him to his knees. He wanted to worship her, to make her scream his name—but not in the hall, let alone the mountain where he had a duty to uphold.

But now... all sense of duty and propriety vanished. When he had gotten to his door, he had smelled the heady scent of her arousal. The thick sweetness that hung in the air. He wanted to devour it all. Lick every drop of it up and share it with no one until it coated his face, tongue, and cock. He wanted all of her all over him, and it was taking everything in him not to break her door down and ravage her.

The metal handle of his door groaned when his grip tightened considerably. Hearing the breathy moans slip through the door, and a sharp gasp followed by his name on her lips as she came, had the handle bending as he squeezed it harder.

Åsmund stood there between their rooms for a long while until he got his heart rate under control. Forcing himself to take a long breath, he found the willpower to shove into his room and bolt the door behind him.

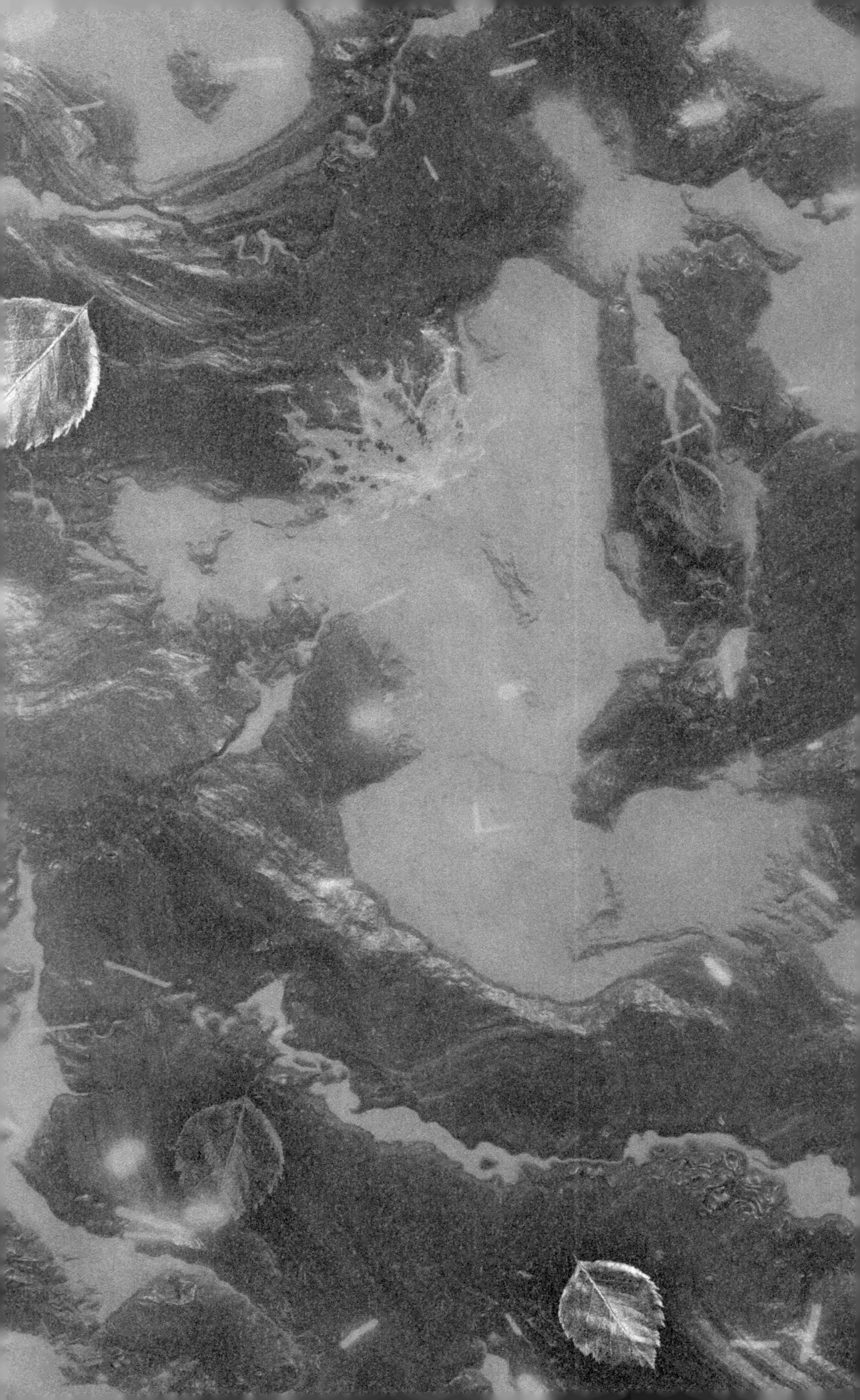

# CHAPTER 25

Nazar watched the ground under him turn to ash as he stepped through shadows into a moor of tall grass. He paused to inhale the stench of rotting life that crawled from the black mist, a portal between The Lost Forest and the world beyond.

Chimaeras and harpies took to the sky with screeching wails as minotaurs and gorgons followed in his ranks. The undead and demonic crawled and floated through the portal with dark curiosity. A Cerberus, twin to the one felled nearly three hundred years prior, snarled as a Harpy flew overhead. The winged creature screeched and drifted higher into the sky, away from the three heads and their salivating maws.

Hundreds poured out of the shadows, filling the green and gold world around them that slowly greyed at his presence.

He sensed Laudin step out behind him, the Fae sniffing the air and standing just behind Nazar as hundreds of undead Fae walked from the portal and followed the dark creatures of the Lost Forest.

When Laudin made to move, Nazar's hand lashed out across his chest, claws sinking beneath the Fae's skin and halting him. "Go back to the castle, and make sure Ezra's bitch doesn't try to escape."

Laudin's eyes flashed black, darting between Nazar, the portal, and the hundreds that stalked towards the forest.

Leaning into Laudin, Nazar let his tongue drag along the male's face, tasting the darkness beneath his skin.

"Go," he hissed into his ear.

Jerking back, Laudin snarled and stormed through the portal and disappeared. Then the portal winked out of existence.

Nazar returned his attention to the world before him, hovering his scarred hands over the earth. Slowly, a black mist, like smoke, began to rise; and where it grew, the world turned to ash.

He let it rise and rise until he released it, and it shot to the skies. White clouds turned dark and thunderous, lightning spiderwebbed overhead. Where the darkness had lifted from the earth, it now stood brittle and dead, its colour sapped completely.

As the death of the world began to feed his demons, Nazar smiled faintly. "Let us begin."

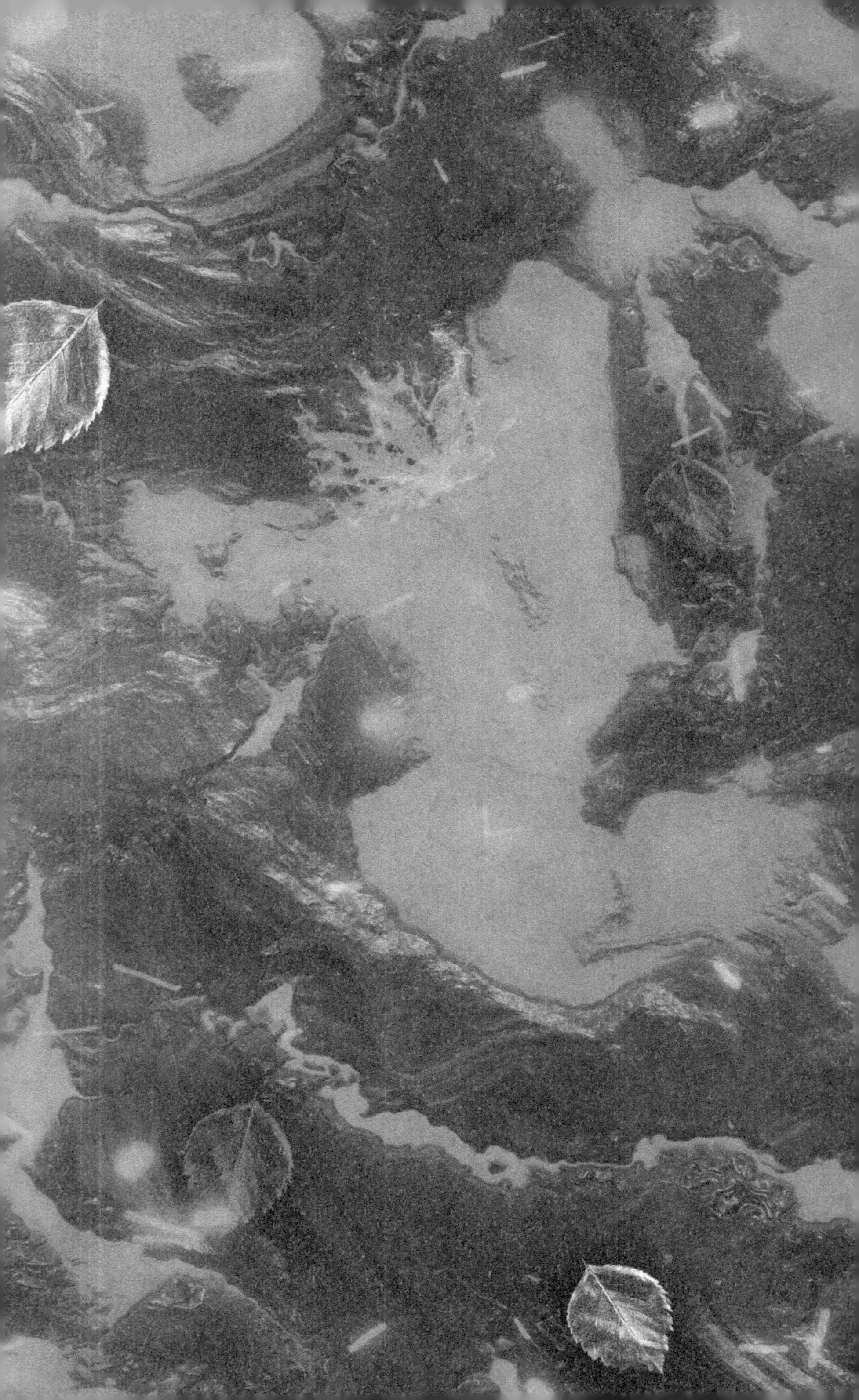

# CHAPTER 26

Hazen pressed a hand to the barrier between her and the world. The sky splashed in deep crimson. Despite only a couple hours of sleep, she had awoken before dawn and found herself standing before the starry sky, watching it shift from night to day.

Dressed in her black leathers, hair still semi-wet from her bath, and French braided back, Hazen watched the world. Change was coming. She could feel it down to the marrow of her bones, like how the air changes before winter's arrival or just before it rains.

A frown tugged at her lips, and she wished she could make the trepidation vanish, but it only coiled tighter in her gut.

Relenting, she dropped her hand with a sigh and walked to her door. With a last glance at her room and the painted sky, she walked out.

She hadn't said goodbye to Rin, but last night, in its own way, felt like a farewell to her. Hazen was tired of the forced farewells, she felt like a shadow coming and going from peoples' lives, never having a proper moment of goodbye, and though she had the opportunity, she couldn't bring herself to utter the words to the small blonde female. If Rin cried, Hazen knew she would cry, too, and that was the last thing she needed.

When the conduit neared closer, Hazen's heart sped up, her palms turning clammy. She didn't know how many would join them. Even so, she told herself that if none did, and it was only Åsmund and Rin's mate, that was all she would need.

But a small smile bloomed on her face when she entered the training arena.

"Well, I would have been content with just you, but this is better," she said casually, walking up to Åsmund.

Her general stood before a group of ten Drago soldiers, sorted into two lines of five, all standing at attention for their general.

Åsmund's hair was pulled back into a bun, a gold glimmering plate of armour wrapped around his chest, an imprint of the two dragons stamped into it, wings flared and facing away from each other. The armour left his arms and shoulders bare for his black wings; he wore matching gold wrist guards on his forearms. Åsmund's sword was secured down his back, black leather straps crossing over his chest, and daggers strapped to each large thigh.

Every soldier was dressed and adorned similarly, their stares wavering to her as she approached them.

"It's hard to move a mountain overnight," Åsmund replied, turning when she walked around him. "But those who came are loyal to a fault."

She met every one of their gazes, acknowledging them. "That's all I need." Hazen met the gaze of one male she recognised, and she walked up to him. "What's your name?"

"Rafe," he said simply.

"Rafe, I promised your mate last night I would try to bring you back to her." Hazen looked at them all now. "I make that promise to you all. I cannot guarantee life. But I will promise to do all that I can."

"Death in battle is an honour, My Lady," Rafe said. "My mate knows this."

She smiled almost bitterly. "But your mate is also a strong, beautiful, and equally terrified female who loves you, and is worried she might lose that love. Do not take that for granted—any of you."

Stepping back, she raised her chin a fraction, letting her power wash over her. "I want to know the names of those who decided change was worth risking their lives for." She would remember this moment in her history, the moment she could feel the world shift, just like the seasons.

And one by one, they each gave her their name.

At the last name given, Åsmund stepped up to her and held open his arms in invitation.

"May I?" he asked.

Her heart softened, warmth seeping into her eyes, and she nodded. "Always."

Åsmund bent and scooped her into his arms. Her hands laced behind his head just before his wings stretched wide, and he shot towards the sky.

When he flew into the air, Hazen caught a glimpse of the clan leader melding into the shadows. Their eyes locked, and she swore she could see a look of regret in his eyes before he became too small for her to register.

The conduit's bottleneck widened, and the red-painted sky neared closer and closer until wind whipped across her cheeks, and the world opened before them, expanding in every direction for as far as she could see. The top of the volcano an enormous crater despite its small appearance within the stone walls.

One by one, the Drago shot into the sky. Black wings were washed in red as soldiers were bathed in the first light and flew towards the brightening horizon.

Hazen's eyes were fixed on the land, sea, and sun beyond. *"Follow the horizon, Hazen. It'll lead you home,"* her father had whispered to her one summer when they went fishing. She had worried they would get lost in the ocean, and her father only chuckled, kissed the top of her head, and told her to set her eyes on the horizon. Those words meant something entirely different as she pursed her mouth into a firm line of determination.

An explosion cut the sky, and Åsmund held her tighter, angling his wings sharply, turning around. The twelve of them hovered in the air, watching in silent awe as Forndýr burst through the volcano's top in a shower of molten lava. Valdren seated on his back, his face fierce, and Hazen could see a smile lifting his cheeks.

Forndýr dove towards the mountain, wings tucked tight, and claws bared. Before he crashed, the dragon arced up, flaring his wings, and his talons dug into the stone, boulder-sized rocks crumbled beneath him. Arching his golden neck high, Forndýr spewed fire into the sky, and a roar rattled her bones and trees below.

*"We will join you, Keeper,"* Forndýr's ancient voice filled her head.

While her eyes were fixed on the sight before her, Hazen still sighed at the title but said nothing against it to the dragon. Lest she offends him. *"We fly to* Álfheimr,*"* was all she said down their mental connection.

Forndýr ascended, flying ahead of them, leading the way to the city of elves. His gleaming scales were a beacon to all who pardoned a glance to the sky.

Hazen gasped. "Look!"

Drago flew by them, Åsmund turned to where her eyes were fixated.

Darkness rose like plumes of smoke from the ground below to the sky above. Light and dark formed a divide between them. Shadows creeped over the forest in thick tendrils. Birds scattered in the distance, flocking to the sky, and Hazen's heart nearly broke when she saw them consumed. They never reappeared.

Nazar had warned her.

He was coming.

He was coming for them all.

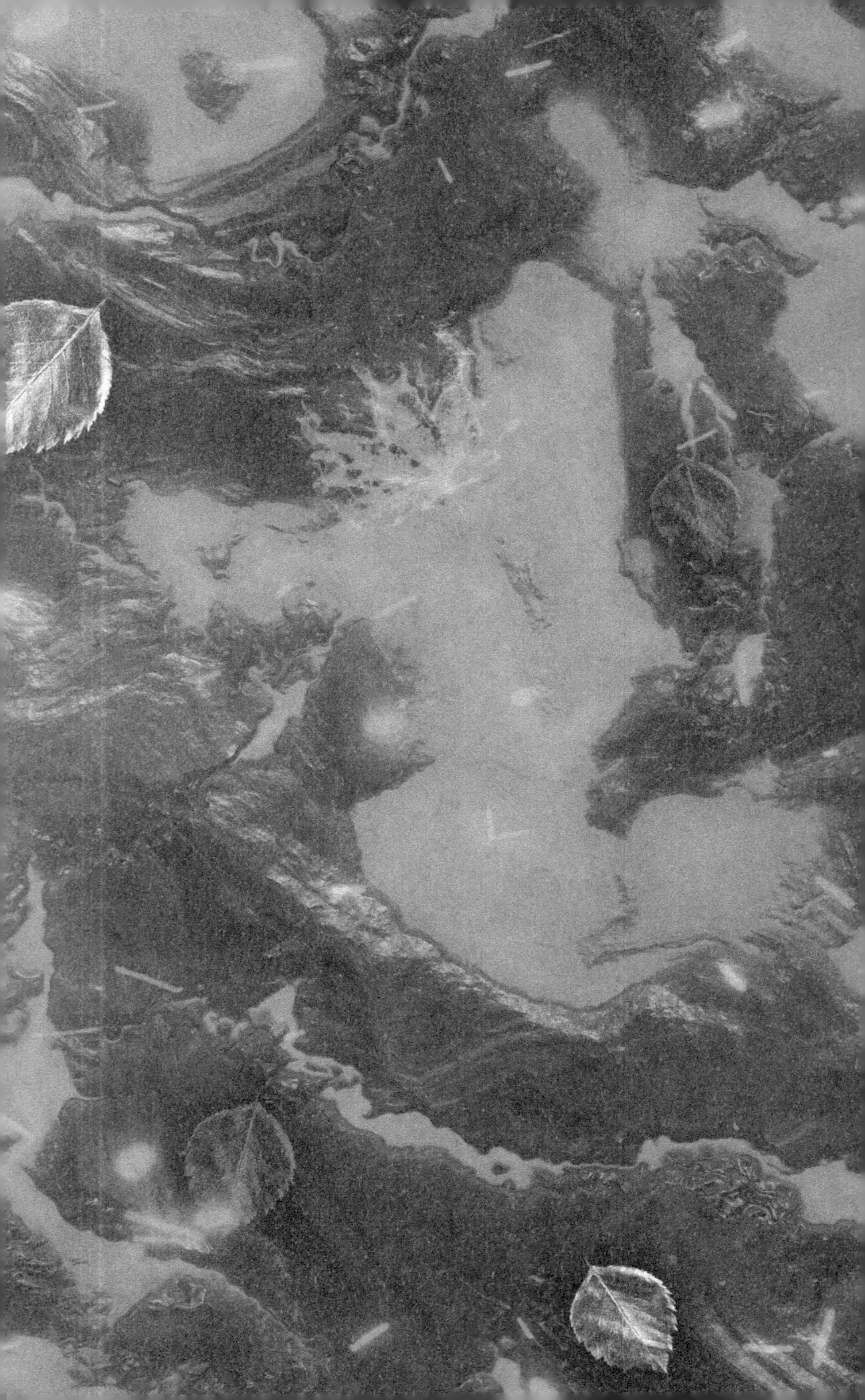

# CHAPTER 27

Savven stared down at the small, rolled parchment in his hands
for the third time that morning since he received it by a bright
yellow canary, the handwriting legible but sloppy:

*Savven,*
*I hope you're alive.*
*I'm going to Alfh*

There was a bold scratch through the attempt at writing
Álfheimr and two small drops of ink beside it. Savven smirked.

*"The city of elves. So, if you are alive, meet me there—if you're*
*not already. Is Brean with you? I hope she is. I liked her. But I'm not*

*writing to catch up. Do you remember the shade? He paid me a little visit. What an asshole. But Ezra is… I don't know what happened to him, but I don't think he's a threat. Maybe he was never a threat, not the way you believed. But Nazar is a living nightmare, Savven. He is the darkness you spoke of, and he passed along a warning just before he tried to kill me: 'I am coming.'*

*I hope to reach your home quickly. I will be accompanied by, hopefully, more than one Drago soldier. But the imperious bastard who likes to call himself clan leader has a lot of influence over these males— understandably so. But change is a foreign concept to them, and I fear that is all I symbolise.*

*Change is coming, and it is only about to get worse.*

*I hope to see you soon.*

*Sincerely,*

*The annoying human.*

His mouth twitched involuntarily.

*The annoying human.*

Rubbing a hand over his mouth, Savven found himself shaking his head while chuckling.

"What has you so amused?"

Savven, who leaned a shoulder on a tree he suspected was nearing its breaking point, slanted a look to Néefar, who strolled casually in his direction.

"Found my hiding spot so easily, Néefar?" Savven was just in eyesight of the crumbling palace, hidden in a copse of trees away from the training field.

Néefar tapped a finger to his nose. "Luck has it; I can be selective about which animal part I want to use. Wolves have a wonderfully heightened sense of smell."

"Wonderful," Savven drolled before holding up the rolled parchment. "We have guests arriving soon."

Néefar leaned on a tree opposite him, crossing his arms over his muscled chest, the fabric of his black tunic pulling tight. "I hope they bring good news."

Savven followed the shifter's gaze to the palace, his jaw flexing. "It doesn't appear so."

There was silence, and before long, Savven could feel Néefar's gaze on him. Their eyes clashed in a sea of blue, one dark, the other light.

"I'm sorry," Néefar said quietly. "For deceiving you."

"Are you though?" Savven looked away, his mouth a flat line, brows furrowed in thought. "Something tells me you would do it again."

"I would—"

His admittance made Savven frown at him.

"—But that does not mean I am not sorry." Néefar ran a hand through his silver hair, letting a breath out through his nose. "We might not have had the years of friendship you two shared, but Lithônion was my friend, too. And I help my friends because they're the only family I have left. Anabelle understood this and did not stop me, in fact she encouraged me. You," Néefar swept a hand to the broken palace, "with everything that has happened, I had hoped you would understand as well."

"He could have come to me," Savven snapped, guilt roiling in his gut.

Néefar scoffed. "Could he? From what I heard, Prince Savven has been hiding for many, many years." The shifter's face softened, and he pushed off the tree, facing Savven. "Pain is a bitter friend, and I understand it all too well. You are not alone in that. Lithônion also knew this. *That* is why he didn't seek you out. He knew what you blamed yourself for and the risks of going after Levina. He didn't want to add his death to your shoulders. Lithônion was thinking of *you*, Savven. Because that is what family does."

Guilt turned to grief, and Savven found his eyes burning. He quickly blinked and looked away.

"I'm sorry I destroyed the map," Savven said softly.

"It's okay. I understand why you did it."

Savven willed the tears back, turning to Néefar. "Anabelle will find you again."

"I know," Néefar stated, a light filling his eyes at the thought of his wife. "I've sent a raven to her with word of my location. She should be arriving any day."

Chuckling, Savven shook his head. "Good. This is her home

too… or whatever is left of it."

The light dimmed, and Néefar glanced between the palace and Savven. "Your father is wrong to blame you."

"My father's grief is only the guilt of what he thinks he could have done differently," Savven corrected solemnly. "But he avoids it and places blame on me. Because it is easier than just facing reality. The truth was that there was nothing he could do, no matter how much he could try to alter fate. I see that now. And I cannot fault him for it."

Néefar held out a hand to Savven, his face turning serious despite the hope lingering in his bright blue eyes. "Forgive me, friend?"

A hint of a smile curved Savven's mouth, and he grasped Néefar's forearm. "Brothers."

Later that day, a horn sounded, singling the approach of something nearing their borders. Savven waited in the open, desolated space of his city. What was once towering with trees, homes, and shops now lay in ruins—just crumbling and nearly flattened, the earth reclaiming what was once theirs.

Brean and Néefar stood at his back on either side. Éamon and several other soldiers stood in formation behind them. Brean shifted restlessly on her feet, Savven glanced over his shoulder, raising a brow.

"Sorry," she mumbled, a blush staining her freckled cheeks and settling.

Gold light cast over them before a shadow fell from Forndýr's massive wings, blocking out what little sun they had as he glided overhead. Several pairs of wings came into view next, flying over the treetops.

Forndýr circled twice, coming lower and lower until he flapped his wings, gusts of air blowing across their face and unsettling the ground. Then the massive dragon landed with a mighty thud.

Drago soldiers dove to the ground, righting themselves quickly and landing one after the other in low crouches. Standing, they fell into formation.

Savven counted ten, his eyes darting from each face, searching for one in particular. He frowned, not finding her.

Another Drago walked around Forndýr as the towering dragon tucked his wings into his body. A female held in his arms. Green eyes locked on Savven, assessing. He watched the Drago soldier set his eyes on the one he cradled closely, those same eyes softening before he lowered her to the ground.

Hazen stared back at him, her gaze entirely gold, and there was a wildness she hadn't had before. She looked different. A white scar mapped the side of her temple. Her hair was bright blonde, braided back, and her skin was warm and tanned. Dressed in black leathers, she prowled towards him, lean and muscled.

There was an agility to her steps, a confidence that peaked when she stopped before him.

"I have a bone to pick with you," were the first words out of her mouth.

Savven couldn't help the small smile that curled his lips. "Oh?" he asked.

She crossed her arms over her chest, her shoulders bare, and he noted the mark on her shoulder was barely visible anymore. "Why didn't you tell me there were sea dragons and psychopathic sea witches?"

His brows shot to his hairline. "Excuse me?"

"Oh," she held up a finger, "it gets better. Said psychopathic sea witch tried to imprison me at the bottom of the damn sea in a nightmare. And she gave me this." She waved to the scar along the left side of her face. "That was a lot of fun," she said sarcastically.

Closing his eyes to reign in his amusement, he opened them and gave her a crooked smile. "It's good to see you too, Hazen."

There was an ease of relief that filled his chest when he had gotten the little scroll early this morning. But now, seeing her alive lifted a burden he hadn't realised he had placed on himself.

Hazen threw her arms around him and squeezed him tight without warning. "I'm glad you're alive," she whispered into his ear so only he could hear.

Startled, Savven slowly lifted his hands to wrap around her and hugged her back. He noted the Drago who carried her watching them with a guarded expression. Forndýr and Valdren standing silently in wait.

"Likewise," he whispered.

Hazen stepped back, her eyes landed on Brean, and she threw herself at the witch.

Brean laughed and squeezed Hazen tightly to her. When they parted, the two females looked at one another, smiling.

"Black is a good look on you," Brean commented, eyeing her up and down slowly.

"You should see what else looks good on me," Hazen said lowly with a smirk.

Brean glanced over Hazen's shoulder, and Savven watched her look at the Drago soldier with the green eyes before her face turned mischievous. "Oh, I bet it does," she sniggered.

Hazen swatted the witch with a gasp, laughing. "Not that, Brean!"

The witch chortled wickedly.

After a moment, Hazen looked around, her eyes searching every face, and Savven knew with a sinking gut who she was looking for.

"He's not here," Savven said softly.

Hazen looked up at him with confusion. "What happened to him?"

"He made a choice and paid the price for it."

A darkness crept over her face, digesting his words. "I'm sorry," she said finally. Her face pinched with sympathy, and she touched his arm gently.

Savven shook his head, stepping aside. Clearing his throat, ready to take the attention off him, he waved a hand towards Néefar. "May I introduce our resident sea dragon?"

Néefar glared at him, and before he could say anything, Hazen's face morphed from sympathy into a mask of fury. Power glinted in her eyes, and her skin seemed to glimmer with light.

Savven stared in amazement, knowing he wasn't the only one, he could hear the soldiers shifting restlessly behind him. They had never seen power like that before.

She stormed up to him faster than Néefar could react, and her fist connected with his jaw.

Néefar's head snapped back.

Forndýr growled at her show of violence.

"Do you know how many died because of you!" she yelled, chest heaving, ignoring the dragon. Unaware that Forndýr had lowered his head closer to the ground, teeth bared in the slightest. If she could grow fangs, Savven would swear she would have torn the shifter's head from his body with the rage he saw in her eyes. "Everyone on that ship, besides us, died! Because of *you*." The last word was spat at Néefar, who was straightening himself, rubbing a hand over his already bruising jaw.

The Drago who had carried her approached and laid a hand on her shoulder. Hazen's chin ticked in his direction, sucking in a calming breath. The soft glow from her skin vanished, and the power that curled in her eyes settled.

Jaw flexing, Hazen turned back to Néefar. "Stay out of my way, or I'll drown you myself."

He heard Brean snort.

When Hazen looked at Savven, it was with eyes that carried the weight of the world in them. She was so unlike the woman he met in the forest. "We need to talk. Now."

Savven locked eyes with Valdren and the dragon before returning to Hazen and nodded. "Follow me."

"She has a mean right jab," Néefar grumbled as Savven walked away.

Brean laughed, full and rich. "That was worth every irritating moment with you."

Néefar snorted. "I don't think she'll really make do with her threat."

"I would *love* for you to find out and see."

Hazen sat perched on top of a long wooden table beside a massive training arena, legs crossed, one boot on the bench while the other tapped the air. She had just finished explaining everything that had happened since they were separated, and just hearing it vocally made her feel exhausted.

At some point during her journey, she had just accepted that this was her reality. The people she met, the creatures she saw, and whatever crazed path the God of Death had put her on. But hearing it all out loud put a different realisation in her mind, Hazen wondered if she would ever go home.

"Are you sure?" Savven asked.

Blinking, pulled from her thoughts, Hazen looked at all the faces around her. Forndýr was curled over two sections of the training field and appeared to be sleeping with the forest backdrop behind him. He wasn't nearly as ferocious as she thought a dragon should be, and she briefly wondered why he had come with them. Valdren stood stoically to Savven's left, his presence offering little substance to why they were there. Brean leaned on a worktable to his right, her face twisted with a plethora of different emotions. Néefar sat yards away from her on the same table she perched on, eyeing her on occasion as if he was concerned she would make due on her threat.

And then there were the soldiers. Too many to count. All loitering around them, listening to her tales, Hazen felt exposed under their gazes and almost wished they could return to their mountain. To her familiar stone walls and view of the sky. To her training and little moments with Åsmund.

She glanced briefly at her general sitting on the bench beside her legs. The tops of his leathery wings pressed against her thigh, his green eyes met hers. The grey light caught the gold hoop through his nose, glinting, his skin looking like warm caramel.

Hazen shrugged, turning back to Savven, who was waiting for her to reply. "I would say *as a heart attack,* but you wouldn't understand."

All eyes turned to her in question.

"My point made," she quipped.

"It makes sense," Néefar said lowly, leaning forward to rest his forearms on his knees.

Hazen slanted a look at him.

"You didn't see him, not how I did," he continued. "Ezra wasn't… stable. His mind wasn't his own. But the shade," Néefar paused, shivering with a look of disgust as if remembering the undead creature, "I've never come across something so vile."

"I would have to agree, unfortunately, with the sea dragon," Hazen drolled.

Néefar scowled at her.

She ignored him.

"I watched this shade slaughter an entire village just to find me and then try and kill me again because he said that the two of us couldn't co-exist." Hazen scrubbed a hand over her face, tired. "I understand Ezra has been a tyrant. Villages have burned because of him, people have died, families torn apart... but what if..." her voice trailed off, and she looked at the ground.

Something the God of Death had said to her filtered into her mind.

*"You are all just pawns to us. We created you..."*

"What if he's just a pawn piece on a large chessboard?" she murmured, almost in a daze. "What if it wasn't Ezra who did those things, but the one who created him into the monster? What if it's been Nazar all along?"

There was silence, and Hazen glanced up.

All eyes were locked on her, different emotions passing along their faces and the faces of the soldiers beyond them. Then the uproar of chatter rose, and Hazen let out a long-drawn sigh, leaning into Åsmund's touch when he pressed against her. He hadn't said anything since they arrived. Hazen suspected the general was assessing everyone and placing them into different boxes of assets versus weaknesses; that thought alone made her mouth twitch upwards.

The voices grew and grew until they were too loud in her ears, and she closed her eyes, focusing on her breathing as her heart picked up speed. Despite the arguing, the world went silent. The only thing filling her ears was the quiet intake of her steady breaths and the *thump-thump* of her heart.

A soft humming, like a female's voice, filled the stillness. It was quiet, melodic, and familiar. There was magic in that pull, which had Hazen opening her eyes as if in a trance. Turning her head to the forest beyond the training field, the pull got stronger. The humming was coming from within, and her brows furrowed.

"What about the ceremony?"

Those words pulled Hazen out of her trance, and she blinked quickly, snapping her head to Néefar, who had asked the question.

The arguing trailed off, and then she was once again under their scope. She felt like a science experiment.

"What ceremony?" she finally asked, playing dumb.

Brean shifted on her feet, speaking up. "If what you say is true, and you are to take over the role of keeper, then the ceremony must be held before Nazar reaches us."

"Why?" Hazen couldn't help the bite in her tone, regretting it when she saw Brean flinch. Pursing her lips, she sighed, softening her tone. "I mean, why does it have to be now?"

"Because your body is still mortal."

All eyes turned to Valdren. He hadn't spoken since they arrived; he simply observed, standing there in black leather and a golden ornate top wrapped around his slim torso with wide sleeves. But now, his gold eyes were locked on Hazen.

"If we face Nazar, then you will die."

She uncrossed her legs, leaning forward, elbows braced on her knees. "Is that so bad? Or are you all that afraid of death?" Would she go home then?

Forndýr raised his head, growling in warning. *"You will watch your tone when speaking to the Dragon Keeper, Human."*

Hazen stood, rounding on the dragon, ignoring Åsmund's hand that made to stop her. "Might I remind you that you have been absolutely no help since I arrived. Except to give me this lovely gift that I had to figure out on my own, without your help. So, you'll forgive me if my *tone* isn't to your liking."

Forndýr's head snapped forward, baring his long, razor-sharp teeth as he bit the air in a warning. *"I might be old in my days, Human, but I will still eat you if provoked."*

Loose strands of her hair blew back from his scalding breath, and she could smell the sulphur rolling through the plume of smoke that blew from his nostrils. "No, you won't," she challenged. "You don't even want me to die fighting, so what makes you think I believe that?"

Hazen rounded on the ones who watched her with wide, horror-stricken faces. Åsmund's was just exasperated, and she nearly laughed when she saw it. But sobered quickly when she looked at Valdren, who had tucked his hands into the folds of his gold sleeves.

"Is that why you came? Not to help. Not to fight. Just to pass along the title? And then what, you'll leave and let us handle the rest?"

Valdren sighed, his face looking older in the pale light. "There is a fine balance that one must tread. Forndýr is part of a long lineage that dates to the first dragons and the last of his kind. The rest were slaughtered while still eggs, Tatius saved him. Gifting his egg to me to protect. When he hatched and chose me to be his rider, I was bound by a vow to protect him until the end. The last dragon. He has a duty to fulfil with you as keeper, but dragons are not bound by honour to fight in battles if they have no desire to."

Hazen stared at the male silently, her face void of emotion. And then she said, "No."

"No?" Valdren's face fell into confusion.

"No," she echoed.

Tension grew in their inner circle, and a hush rose within the soldiers around them.

As if sensing the growing unease, Hazen watched Savven whip around to the Fae soldiers.

"That's enough for today."

The Fae paused, and Hazen could see they wanted to stay. She snorted silently. Nosy people.

"Go," he barked.

It took a minute for the training field to clear out, but when it did, he looked back at Hazen and jerked his chin in a short nod for her to continue.

"What do you mean '*no*'?" Néefar drawled.

Hazen pinched the bridge of her nose. She could feel a headache coming on. Dropping her hand when the pressure subsided, she said, "Exactly what it sounds like. No. Full sentence."

"Hazen… I don't think they understand," Brean said softly, her own understanding lighting her amber eyes.

The soft feminine humming filled her ears again. She could feel it pressed against her back, the tug of its gentle nudging. And for some reason, it centred her.

"I am not accepting the role as keeper," she said as clearly as she could, not daring to look at Åsmund. She didn't want to see his face when she rejected an immortal life. She couldn't. It would add another crack to her heart, and she didn't think she would survive it.

Stunned silence filled the air. Even Forndýr, when Hazen glanced over her shoulder to raise a brow at him, just blinked slowly as if processing.

"So, you," she said to the dragon, "and you," she turned to Valdren, "can go back to your mountain. As you can see, your services are no longer needed."

*"That is not how this works, Human!"* Forndýr snarled in her mind.

Hazen looked back at the dragon. "I don't really know how it's supposed to work in your world. But in mine, I get the choice. I was told I had a choice. So, I'm making mine."

*"None have ever rejected the immortal cup!"*

"Well, I'm glad I could be your first," she snipped, adding silently, *you old annoying lizard.*

"Hazen…"

She looked at Savven, her mouth pressed into a tight line, waiting for him to chastise her as well.

"Why?" was all he asked. There was no judgement, just curiosity.

Why not be immortal? Why not live forever?

Because she wanted to go home. Because she missed her family. Because she didn't want to conform to their ideal just because it's what is expected. Call her stubborn, or naïve, or *human.* She'll accept them all. Because that's who and what she was.

A shadow of a smile passed over her mouth, and she looked at her friend. "Because I don't need to be immortal to be strong." She looked at Valdren, adding, "If you don't like it, then you should tell the Gods to go pick someone else."

A plume of steam blistered her back in warning from Forndýr, a rumble cresting through her mind. She pointedly ignored him.

"You could die," Néefar said, almost bored of the conversation, his eyes roaming the training field as if searching for something.

She sighed, nodding in agreement. "Yes, well, I haven't yet, despite their tired attempts. So, they'll have to try harder."

Brean caught her eye, and the witch's gaze shimmered with a sad sort of knowing in them. A tight, watery smile curled her mouth, barely nodding so no one noticed. Hazen watched the witch with curiosity. Something about her expression made it seem she understood why Hazen didn't want to give up her mortality.

The soft humming started again, and the mark on Hazen's shoulder began to warm. Her power pressed along her bones, and a tightness formed in her back again as if the space was growing too confining.

"Besides," Hazen continued, ignoring the uncomfortable sensation. "You have Anabelle."

"You have Anabelle for what?" asked a soft, clear voice.

They all whipped their heads to the left as Anabelle walked towards them, dressed in all black. Hazen guessed it was Álfheimr's uniform, as Savven, Brean, and Néefar were all dressed similarly.

Her blue-black hair hung freely around her beautiful pale face, soft arching ears poking through the folds, violet-blue eyes lit in curiosity.

"Thank the Gods," were Néefar's hushed words before shoving off the table. In three strides, he met Anabelle and pulled her into his embrace. He kissed her like a starving man, his hands tangled in her hair, and Hazen's brows shot to her hairline.

When they pulled apart, Néefar leaned his brow on hers. Hazen felt like they should give the couple some privacy, though they appeared not to mind when they turned back to the small group. Néefar visibly relaxed.

"Hello, Valdren. Hello, Forndýr," Anabelle said softly with a smile.

Clearly, the ancient lizard had favourites. He'd perked up when her voice entered the space.

Savven gave Anabelle a brief hug when she walked towards him. "Cousin, it's good to see you," he said.

"I wish it were under better circumstances," Anabelle admitted solemnly.

He nodded in agreement. "This is Brean," Savven said, turning to introduce the witch.

Brean smiled kindly at Anabelle, bowing her head at the introduction.

The Keeper regarded the witch. "It's a pleasure to meet you."

Néefar didn't wander far from Anabelle's side. However, he let there be distance when she approached Hazen, the male glaring at her over her shoulder.

"Hello, Hazen," she uttered with kindness crinkling the corners of her eyes. "I'm glad you found your path."

Looking at Åsmund from the corner of her eye, Hazen smiled faintly. But that smile fell, and she rolled her shoulders back, speaking so everyone could hear her. "You have a keeper already. You have Anabelle."

When Hazen met her eyes, Anabelle didn't say anything, but she inclined her head softly, and that was all Hazen needed.

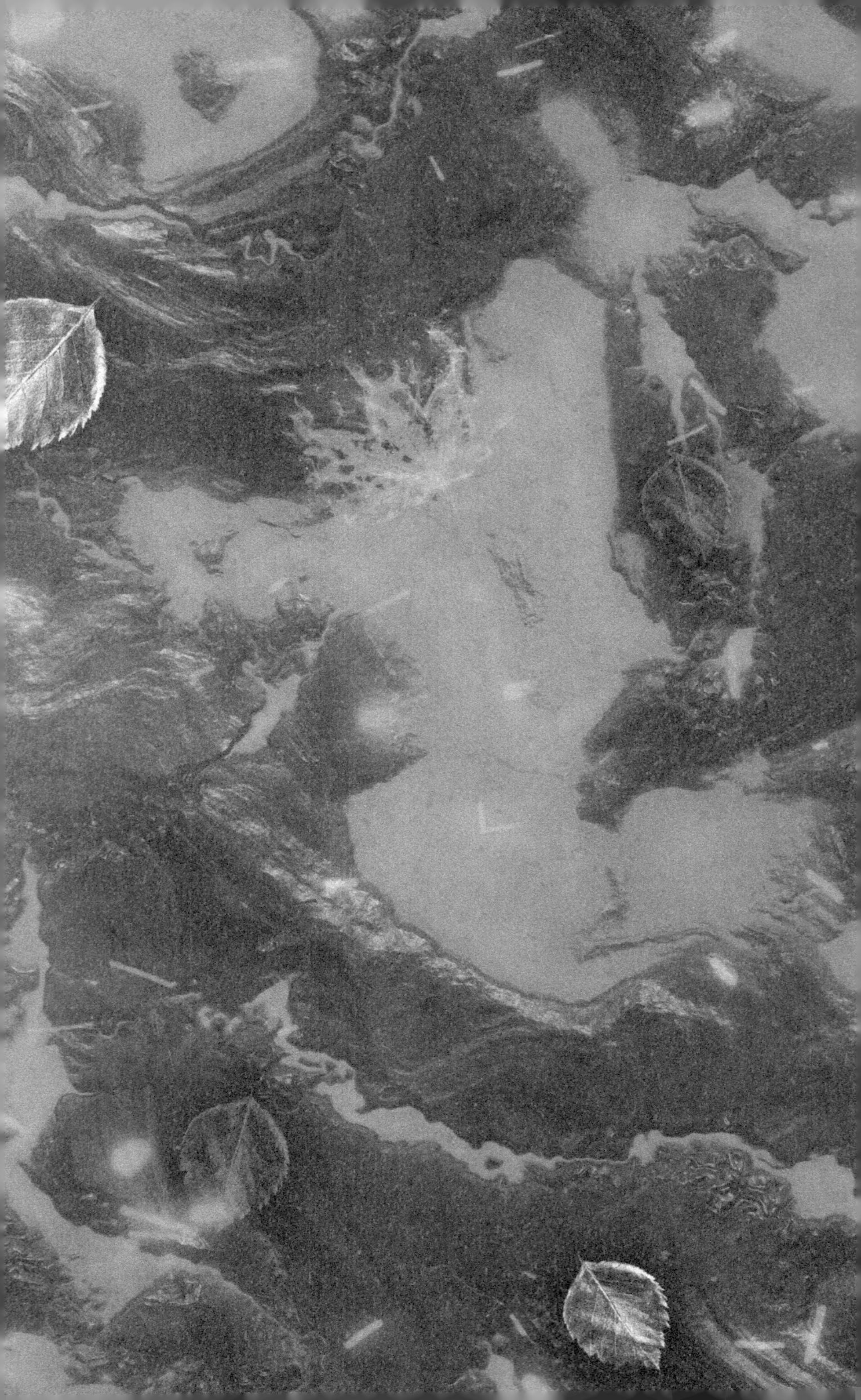

# CHAPTER 28

His bones gave way under him, and Ezra cried out when his face smashed into the earth. Cheek pressed into black soil. With every sucking breath, he tasted bits of dirt that clung to his mouth, saliva dribbled out in an attempt to rid it from his tongue.

A guttural sob shook his body, hot tears streamed down his face. A broken branch pressed painfully into his abdomen, and nausea rolled through him.

With the last bit of strength, Ezra heaved himself up just before he vomited blood over the ground.

Panting, he stared wide-eyed in horror. A face floating beyond the fog of memory he had. The owner of the blood. The last *meal* he had to satisfy the demons.

Nausea roiled again, and this time, when he threw up, it was acid. It burned the taste of copper away, and Ezra sat back on his heels, head tilted to the sky, sobbing.

"Please," he begged brokenly through his tears to the Gods, praying they were listening. "Please give me the strength to see my home one last time, to see my family."

He was so close. It was like a siren call, tugging him to them. He wanted to see them. He *needed* to see them. If just to plead his eternal atonement before he died.

The stale wind brushed his wet cheeks, and he closed his eyes.

Ezra's muscles trembled violently, unable to hold himself, and his body collapsed beside the emesis.

His vision began to darken around the edges, and he blearily saw booted feet running towards him.

A hiss and the boots skidded to a stop.

"It's Ezra," a voice said disbelievingly.

"Get the prince!" someone snapped.

And then Ezra's vision went black as he fell into a welcoming abyss. Praying death followed soon.

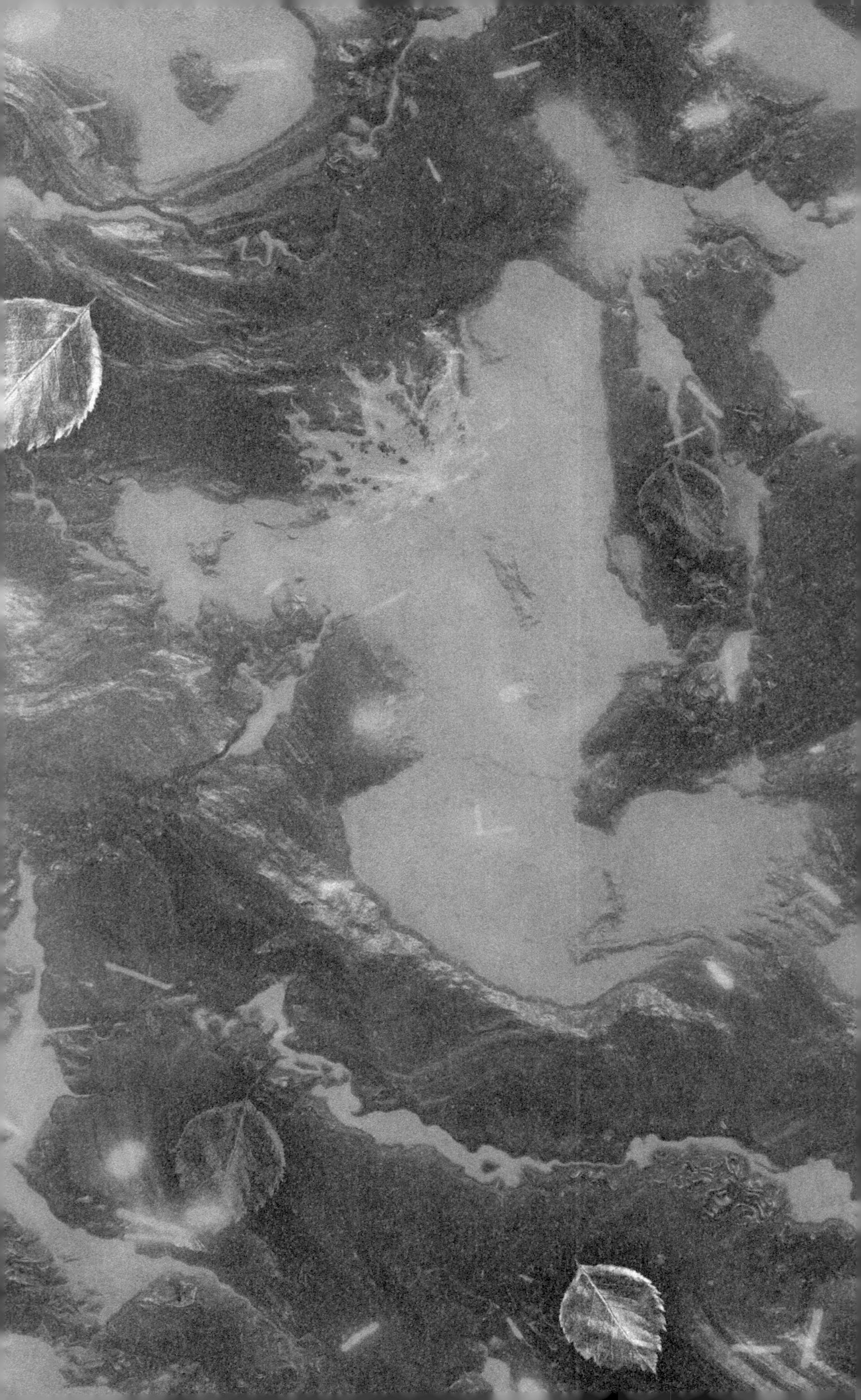

# CHAPTER 29

Savven nearly hit one of the wooden posts of the city's wall when his eyes locked onto the thin body crumpled on the ground just beyond their borders, ink-back hair concealing the pale, angular face he knew lay beneath. Bracing himself on the greying wood, Savven took a cautious step forward, his heart thudding wildly.

Four border soldiers stood around the body, bows aimed at it, waiting for his orders.

Towering trees surrounded the male like gravestones, waiting to claim him for themselves as they died, too. Dim grey light filtered through the scarce branches, lighting over the one who had made nightmares come to life for the last fifty years.

Savven stopped between two trees, the body still a few paces ahead. But he couldn't make himself move any closer.

Footsteps crunched behind him. He had nearly forgotten his friends when one of his guards had come sprinting towards them.

*"I... it's..." The Fae soldier's head darted around them, trying to force the words out. "It's Ezra," he finally managed.*

Savven hadn't waited. He took off in a dead sprint without so much as a heart beat's hesitation.

They had begun to argue amongst themselves over Hazen's declaration and refusal to become the next keeper, let alone cast away her mortal life. But if he were being honest, he didn't care. He didn't care about the dragons and Gods anymore. He didn't care about their traditions. He didn't care about what was expected of him *or* Hazen or anyone. He just wanted to survive this and rebuild his home. Nothing more, nothing less.

But now, his friends slowly approached from behind, and Savven stared pensively at the body, his right hand shaking at his side.

Soft fingers curled over his own, soothing the tremors, and he glanced down at Brean, who stared back solemnly.

"Ezra!" Anabelle gasped from his left, stomping past him. "Remove your arrows," she snapped at the guards.

The guards looked at Savven tentatively.

He jerked his chin, and they lowered their bows, taking two steps back. Giving Anabelle space as she fell to her knees before the body.

Savven saw Néefar stop and fold his arms over his chest, watching his wife with guarded eyes.

Anabelle hovered a hand over the body before gently brushing the black hair back.

Ezra's face was sallow in the light, his cheeks sunken as if he had been starving, he was dangerously thin. If it weren't for the subtle rise and fall of his chest, she would have declared him dead.

With trembling fingers, Anabelle rolled Ezra onto his back, brushing off the dirt that clung to the side of his face. She undid the laces at his neck with quick pulls, looking for something. Spreading his collar wide when the laces gaped open, exposing his chest. It was smooth and pale.

Tears streaked down his cousin's cheeks while Anabelle laid a hand over the unmarked skin. Whatever she had been looking for hadn't been there.

"Bring him to the healer's quarters," Savven said lowly, eyeing his old forgotten friend. "And bring the binding manacles."

The guards nodded, slinging their bows over their shoulders.

Anabelle used the back of her hand to wipe her tears. She stood slowly, stumbling back when one of the four soldiers lifted Ezra's body into his arms, the other three framing his back in a protective half circle.

When Savven turned, he paused, seeing Hazen watch the body as it was walked by her. Her gold eyes slid to him, an undercurrent of power held within her stare.

"It looks like the King got captured by his pawn," she commented before turning and following the small procession.

Savven understood her meaning well enough.

Álfheimr city had gone deathly quiet when Ezra's body had passed through. Every eye was trained on the limp figure held between the guards. Every emotion differed on each passing face: fear, hatred… sorrow. Sometimes, a combination.

The guard discarded Ezra's body onto a stiff woven cot inside the large hut made from dried mud and straw, a thatch roof kept in the heat from the cast iron hearth in the centre. Similar beds lined both sides of the hut, all empty except for Ezra.

Using the manacles another guard brought, they shackled both of Ezra's wrists to the steel frame of the cot. The runes engraved into the cuffs glowed blue before fading.

"What are those," breathed Anabelle, pulling a silver stool to Ezra's side and taking a seat.

Néefar lounged in the cot beside Ezra's, getting comfortable as his wife tended to the unconscious male. A frown tugged at his mouth, and he crossed his arms but said nothing.

Brean hovered by the entrance, her face neutral, arms wrapped around her middle. She caught Savven's eye briefly, giving him a tight smile as if sensing the emotions running through him.

"They're manacles with binding runes carved into them. They bind his magic so he can't use it," Savven explained quietly, turning away from the witch.

Anabelle waved a Fae female over, asking for a bowl of water and a cloth. The healer's eyes went wide when she saw Ezra, and she paled but nodded and scurried off.

"That's barbaric, Savven," Anabelle said hotly when she finally turned back to him.

"It's necessary."

"He's barely a shell of himself. His magic would allow him to heal."

His jaw flexed, teeth grinding together. "Exactly."

"You can't mean to let him die!" She stood abruptly, the stool toppled violently behind her, but it didn't fall.

"I mean to find out why he's here and what he wants," Savven replied in a steely voice. Every bit of his princely title slipped through his words. "Until that time comes, and he has proven he is no threat, he will remain in these manacles."

"Savven—"

She made to argue, but he shot her a stern look, and the words died on her tongue.

The pain he saw in his cousin's eyes made him soften his tone as he said, "My father is in no position to safeguard our people, so I must be the one to make those decisions."

Anabelle collapsed onto the stool, taking Ezra's hand in her own.

The healer rushed to Anabelle's side with a copper bowl and a stack of cloths, which she placed on the small silver table beside the bed.

Thanking the female, Anabelle grabbed a cloth from the top, dipped it into the water, and ran it gently over Ezra's sweat-dotted brow.

"Hazen was right," Savven said quietly, the embers popping in the hearth filling the silence that followed. "Nazar has taken power."

Hazen walked away from the healer's hut. She hadn't found it in herself to go in. Stopping just outside the door when they had all walked inside, and watching the leather flap over the door fall into place.

Åsmund had pressed a warm hand to her lower back, his breath fanning her neck, murmuring into her ear that he had to speak with Forndýr and Valdren. She nodded faintly and heard him walk away, taking the comforting heat with him. She knew she would have to talk to him about what she had decided, the thought had her heart tugging painfully in her chest.

Before she had slipped into the woods, she had eyed her general and the Drago, who stood with him, conversing with the massive dragon and his rider. A plume of smoke had puffed out of Forndýr's nostrils a second later at Åsmund, and Hazen slipped into the woods.

Now, she walked through the forest just beyond the edge of the training arena alone. Hearing the soft humming again, like an echo in the distance. It was pulling her closer. A tug on her soul, on the power that filled her bones.

The broken woods were quiet. There was a reverent stillness to them, and Hazen paused, glancing up.

Clouds formed overhead; she could see them rolling through the half-bare branches, leaving a bitterness in the air. Rain was coming, she could smell it.

Familiarity tugged at her heart, and she turned her head to the left, eyeing the forest in that direction. She knew these woods, like a memory of a memory.

Before she could walk in that direction, she felt a presence at her back, and she closed her eyes, her heart squeezing painfully.

Åsmund stood behind her in his golden cuirass, watching her. His beautiful green eyes guarded behind the mask of the stoic general.

"Åsmund," she whispered.

Despite the facade, his chest heaved, giving away the emotions rolling through him. "Forndýr and Valdren have left. With you refusing the immortal cup and your role as keeper, Forndýr has deemed his presence unnecessary."

Hazen took a step closer. He mirrored her.

"Please understand," she pleaded in the silent forest. She didn't give a damn about the great dragon or his keeper. She only cared about the dragon in front of her, the male who captured all her innate attention.

When she said she wasn't taking on the role of keeper, she pointedly kept her eyes away from her general. To see the look on his face when he found out she was choosing to remain mortal. To die—whether now or years down the road. It would have been too much.

His eyes searched hers, his wings flaring slightly. "Why didn't you tell me?"

"Because I didn't know for certain until I said it aloud and because I didn't want to hurt you." Her lips trembled, and she gritted her teeth, fighting back the building tears.

Åsmund shook his head, a curl slipping out of the bun to frame his face. "Do you really think I give a damn?" he asked harshly, taking another step closer.

Her brows pinched, and a hot tear escaped down her cheek. "I'm sorry." And she was. Because she was human and he wasn't.

"Do you think I care about how long or short our lives are?" Another step. Anger filled his gaze, lighting the gold flecks in his eyes. "Do you think I am so worried about how much time we have?" Another step, and another, and another.

Hazen craned her neck to look up at him. All the bravado she had melted away, and all that was left was a woman who had slowly begun to fall for the male in front of her, just to tear away any possibility of a life together.

Åsmund's large hand lifted to cradle her cheek, and she leaned into his warm touch, his thumb brushing away the stray tears.

"You, foolish woman," he whispered. His words filled the breath of space separating them. "I will follow you to the end of time and across worlds if necessary. Where you go, I will be. No matter if either of us dies, I will cherish what we have been gifted."

She sucked in a sharp breath, her eyes pouring into him. "Åsmund—" She had barely whispered his name when his mouth claimed hers in a kiss that illuminated the world around them.

His mouth devoured her, his hand slipped to the back of her

neck, bringing her closer. Hazen arched her body into his, feeling the warmth of his skin sink into her. She held onto his massive shoulders as the world spun and spun and spun in a torrent of colours and emotions that rocketed through her.

Growling against her mouth, Åsmund's teeth nipped at her bottom lip, and she gasped. His tongue slipped through, tasting her, and she yielded to his demand. Submitting to him.

He kissed her until she was dizzy and breathless, and every part of her ached with a need for him that they had denied within the mountain. When he broke away, panting, his breath feathered across her cheek as he leaned his brow against hers.

"I am yours," he whispered against her lips.

"Mine," she echoed. And then she was wrapping her hand around his head and dragging his mouth back to hers.

Hazen didn't think a kiss could ever feel like this. Like bliss, and passion, and fire all at once. But when Åsmund kissed her, the world stopped, the burdens disappeared, and there was just them.

He broke the kiss momentarily to bend and grab the backs of her thighs, lifting her up. Hazen wrapped her legs around his waist, and then his mouth was back on hers. Claiming and desperate.

Walking forward with her wrapped around him, Hazen's back pressed soundly against a tree. Åsmund's hands wandered over her body in a trail of fire that made her back arch into his touch. His fingers grazed over her taut nipples, and she gasped into his mouth when he pinched them through the leathers.

It was too much. She needed more. She needed him. Damn everyone and what they needed from her. What she needed was this, was him, in every way possible. But for now, she would claim this moment, and if fate deemed them a future, she would have him in that, too. Body, soul, and name.

Breaking the kiss, Åsmund trailed his lips down her jaw and across her neck. His tongue doing wicked things to the sensitive flesh under her jaw that made her core ache. Hazen reached behind her neck, yanking at the clasp that held her leather top together. It opened, and the neck fell.

Åsmund paused, looking at her with darkened eyes, desire blazing in them but affection mixed with that desire. A softness.

"Are you sure?" he breathed, his nostrils flaring, and she knew he could smell her arousal.

"Please," she begged, her breath fanning his light brown cheek.

He didn't need to be told twice, his jaw flexed a second before he claimed her mouth again, and with her pressed against the tree, his hips holding her in place, he used his hands to yank her top down.

Her breasts tightened at the first brush of air, falling free of the leather.

Åsmund pulled his mouth away, his gaze settling on her chest as her nipples peaked, aching for his touch. She arched toward him, silently pleading for him. His hand came up, thumbs brushing her nipples, and Hazen moaned at the jolt of pleasure that went through her.

"Åsmund," she breathed.

He leaned forward, his teeth biting down on her neck, and her eyes went wide with the mix of pain and pleasure. He had marked her, and she thrilled at that thought. A strangled whimper left her lips when he dragged his tongue over the bite and brought his mouth to her ear.

"Say it again," he whispered, and then he pinched her nipples at the same time.

"Åsmund!" Hazen gasped. She was going to combust under his touch, and she arched against his fingers.

"I want to taste you," he growled against her mouth.

She whimpered, nodding her head.

He unhooked her legs from his waist, and she slid slowly down his body. Feeling the steel press of him along her aching core. Feet on the floor and breathing heavily, Hazen kept her eyes locked on his as he stepped back and watched her undress.

Hazen didn't care that they were in the forest or that the training field was just in the distance. All she could see and hear was the pounding of her heart and the hungry male who stared at her as if she were the most decadent thing he had ever beheld. A dragon looking at his treasure.

She preened under his gaze, taking her time with her boots and pants, wiggling out of the top until she stood naked before him.

The apex of her thighs was wet with arousal, her breasts straining for his touch again, and her core throbbed with desire. She needed him to touch her, to taste her, as much as she wanted him.

Åsmund's nostrils flared, smelling her desire, and his dark eyes trailed down her body slowly, lighting her skin in a blaze.

"You're beautiful," he whispered roughly, his throat bobbing.

"Then make me yours," she whispered back.

His growl was primal as he took one step and knelt before her. Green eyes trained on hers, Åsmund lifted her legs, one at a time, to his shoulders until her glistening centre was level with his mouth. His wings snapped out, and she knew without looking up that her body was concealed behind their large span. She was his and no one else's.

Hazen barely took in a breath before she felt the flick of his tongue on her clit, and she let out a strained moan, hands going to his hair. Her fingers messed up his bun and tangled in the now loose strands, anchoring him to her. Then he was devouring her, and her eyes rolled back as he flicked and sucked at the centre of her desire.

Fingers digging into the bare flesh of her thigh, Åsmund ate her like he had been starving for centuries. He released one of her thighs and used that hand to trail along her ass and down to the wetness that coated his mouth.

His finger pressed along her entrance, and Hazen bucked her hips, pressing the back of her hand to her mouth, covering her moans.

"Don't," he ordered lowly, looking up at her, hearing her muffled sounds. "I want to hear you come undone. I want the world to hear my name on that beautiful mouth when you shatter."

Hazen lowered her hand, nodding with a whimper, and Åsmund's feral grin was the only warning when his finger pressed into her, curling into the spot that made her see stars. His other hand came around, pushing along her lower abdomen, and she felt the tension beginning to form in her core. Tighter and tighter, like a band ready to snap.

He added another finger. Moving in and out of her wet heat, his mouth sucking on her clit, and when he nipped at it lightly with his teeth, the band snapped, and Hazen shattered against his mouth. Screaming his name.

When she came down from the high of her orgasm, he softly lowered her legs from his shoulders, she braced herself on the tree behind her, her breath coming in ragged gasps.

Hazen opened dazed eyes, her mouth parted and panting. "Please," she whispered to the male still kneeling before her. He looked like a male worshipping a Goddess, his eyes nearly black with desire, chest heaving, and her release on his mouth. "I want all of you."

He stood, his hands trailing up her sides with feathered touches.

Her fingers followed up his armour, finding the black leather straps across his chest and undoing them. Åsmund pulled his sword and the casing from his back and laid it at the foot of the tree. Next were the gold buckles of his cuirass on either shoulder. Åsmund caught it before it fell and laid it beside his sword.

Hazen grazed her fingers along his chest, skin rippling wherever she touched. She stopped at the little gold hoop through his nipple, and she bent, kissing along his pectorals until her mouth found his nipple, and she tugged the hoop with her teeth.

Åsmund's groan was deep, his head falling back, hand wrapping around the end of her braid.

Smirking, she flicked her tongue along the other nipple, her hands trailing to the V at his hips and tugged at the laces at the front of his leathers. Slowly, she undid them, pushing them open. Keeping her eyes fixed on his, Hazen reached her hand beneath and gripped him. A shudder rolled through Åsmund, but he didn't move, letting her have her moment.

The weight of him was heavy in her hand, and when she pulled him out, his cock stood thick and proud, the tip dripping. With a shaking breath, she dragged her hand up the impressive length of him, wiping her thumb over the tip. Smiling faintly when he groaned, his eyes rolling back in pleasure.

She made sure he was watching when she brought her thumb to her mouth and sucked it clean, tasting him.

That was his undoing, and he grabbed her by the hips, lifting her up. She wrapped her ankles behind his back as his wings sheltered them from view. Dragging the tip of his cock through her wet heat and over her throbbing clit, until he was lined up at her entrance.

She combed her fingers through his now loose hair that tumbled around his shoulders, bringing her mouth to his and murmuring, "All of me belongs to all of you, Åsmund."

And then he was slipping inside of her. Stretching her with every inch of him, and when he was seated at the hilt, stretching her until she thought she would burst, he pressed his brow to hers, whispering, "To the end of time and across worlds."

As Åsmund claimed her body, soul, and heart, Hazen clung to the now. Savouring every kiss, every touch, every press of him, not knowing when one moment might be her last.

And when they shattered together, the forest was their only witness.

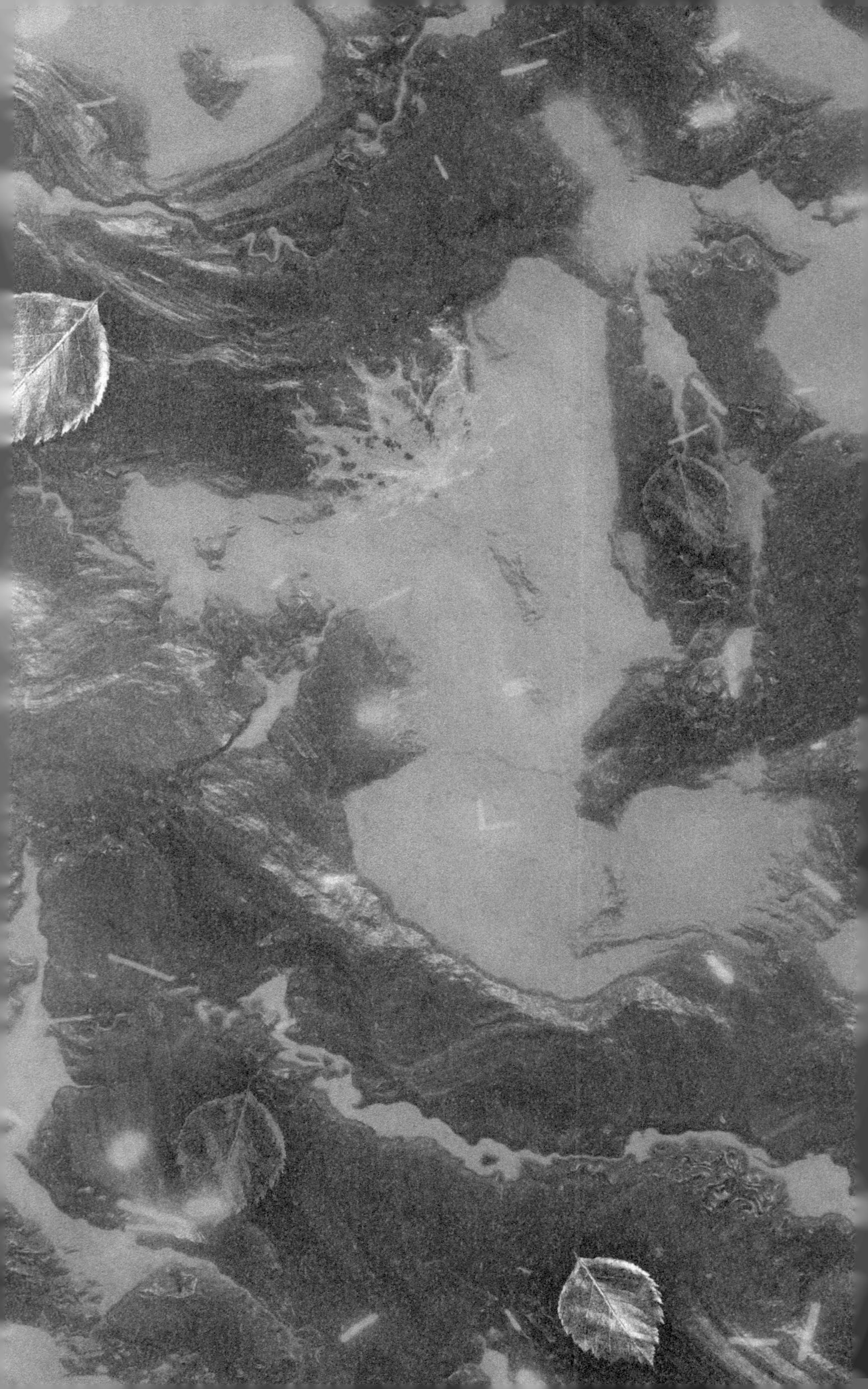

# CHAPTER 30

The night had fallen quickly. Multiple fires flared brightly through Álfheimr with Fae soldiers and their loved ones gathered around them. A fiddle played further back, and laughter carried through the air.

Seated on the ground, Hazen leaned back between Åsmund's legs, who sat on a half-rotten log, his hands gently massaging her shoulders. The glow of the fire played off her hands as she reached for the flames, and they flew at her silent command.

Laughing softly, she watched it dance through her fingers and smiled when it curled around her wrist and began to spark.

Åsmund's wings curled protectively around them as he leaned forward, his mouth brushing her ear, whispering, "You're getting better at that, Little Dragon."

"I had a good teacher," she replied, shivering when he brushed her loose hair aside and pressed a chaste kiss to the spot behind her ear.

Hazen noted the Drago soldiers seated around a bonfire like theirs, smiles on their faces and deep uproarious laughter pelting the night.

"Do you mind that they see us?" she asked curiously, looking up at Åsmund.

He spared his soldiers a brief glance before he shook his head at her. "No. I care little for what they think of me now. And if they care, they know better than to say anything to me. You are mine, and I will make sure the whole world knows. I spent too much time upholding my duties as General and not enough time doing this." He dropped his head, his hand sliding from her shoulder to cradle her jaw as he kissed her deeply.

"Get a room!"

They broke apart, and Hazen turned a murderous glare at Néefar, who dropped onto a wooden bench. He had a crooked smile, and his blue eyes gleamed with mischief.

"Feel free to hit him," Anabelle commented, straightening her blouse and sitting beside him.

Her face was flushed and hair dishevelled, Hazen could only guess what they had been doing.

"My husband knows no bounds to his teasing," Anabelle continued.

Néefar put a hand to his chest, giving her an exaggerated pout. "Wife, you wound me. I thought it was part of the charm you so loved?"

Brean, gazing up at the stars beside Savven or trying to as the clouds rolled above, turned a sceptical brow at Néefar. "There's a charming bone inside of you? Where? Because I have yet to see even a glimpse."

The shifter gave her a cutting smile. "I reserve it for only the ones I think deserve it."

Snorting, Brean rolled her eyes at him. "Please, don't change your mind on my account. I don't need your charm. Your irritating presence is more than sufficient."

Anabelle touched her husband's chest, shooting him a warning look. "Behave," she muttered lowly.

Grinning wickedly, he leaned forward and whispered something into her ear that had Anabelle blushing.

Hazen shook her head, smiling faintly at the flames in her hand. Embers and sparks that looked like starlight illuminated her face as she let the familiar power within rise to the surface. Her power merged with the fire, and it flared brightly. Hazen stared transfixed at the little flame that danced in her palm.

"That's a neat trick. Is that all you can do?" Néefar asked casually, throwing a stick into the fire.

Sucking on her teeth, Hazen stared up at the male through lowered brows. "Can you only shift into a murdering sea dragon?"

"No. I can shift into anything so long as I know what it looks like beforehand." Néefar's smile fell, and he turned serious. "I am sorry about that day. But there was a reason for my actions."

Hazen leaned forward, Åsmund's hands ceasing their ministrations on her shoulders. "You can justify and make excuses however you like. But there is never a reason to blatantly take innocent lives. They could have had families or loved ones waiting on them. Full lives ahead. And maybe it's my human nature talking." She shrugged. "But there is never a good reason for what you did."

Everyone went silent, and Hazen caught Savven's eye as she leaned back into Åsmund.

Savven tilted his chin at her, and something *almost* like pride glimmered in his dark blue gaze.

"I suppose you're right," Néefar remarked. He grabbed the silver cup at his feet and lifted it to the sky. "To the souls lost at sea."

Those with cups grabbed them, toasting to the fallen, and drank.

Åsmund toasted and passed his cup to her, Hazen drank the wine in it, setting the empty cup aside when she was done.

"All right!" Néefar called, pouring more wine from a leather skin. "It's time for you to sing, Witch! I know you can, and it's the least you can do for being a pain in my—"

Anabelle smacked Néefar upside the head. "Do not goad her! If she turns you into a lumpy little creature, I will simply laugh and not feel the least bit sorry for you."

Savven snorted at that. "Please. It'll be the most entertainment I've gotten in such a long time."

"You wound me. Both of you," Néefar said with false ghast.

Anabelle just stuck her tongue out at him. Néefar's laughter was a deep rumble before he pulled her close and kissed her deeply in front of them all.

Hazen could hear Savven grumbling about them needing to find a room, and she couldn't help the grin that bloomed. Some things didn't change between worlds, no matter how divided they stood.

Anabelle, swatting at her husband when he tried to pull her back, stood and smoothed a hand down her pants. "If you will all excuse me. I'm going to check in on our guest."

Savven's scowl was fleeting, but not before Hazen caught it.

"I'll come with you," Néefar said with a sly smirk.

Anabelle only rolled her eyes and walked away, shaking her head as her husband followed.

"You don't have to sing, Brean," Hazen said.

The witch only shrugged. The firelight made her look more like a dragon than Hazen and Åsmund. Her amber eyes glowed in the light, and her hair shifted like a living fire. "I don't mind. There's a song from my childhood my mother used to sing to me before..." her words trailed off, and a far-off sadness filled her eyes. Clearing her throat, she opened her mouth, and a soft melody began to fill the air.

"Of all the coin that e'er I had..."

Hazen froze, listening to the soft burr and lilting accent that came with her words, like the voices of people long since lost that were finally free. Her eyes were fixed to the flames as she continued to sing, and while the words were slightly different—older, Hazen knew the song.

"...they would wish me one more day to stay..."

She sat up, seeing Åsmund look at her curiously from the corner of her eyes, and softly began to sing with Brean.

"...goodnight and joy be with you all."

Brean looked up at Hazen with brimming tears in her eyes, and Hazen knew within her bones that she and the witch were the same.

"...Come fill to me a stirrup cup, goodnight and joy be with you all..."

Darkness called for him. The remnants of Nazar's pets left behind a shadow of their talons and hissing commands that made Ezra cower in his dreams. He stumbled through the shadows, swiping through the black mist over his mind. He had wandered through those tendrils of fog for longer than he knew, and when Nazar had stolen back his demons, nearly three centuries had passed. Because time, when lost in the mists, had no meaning. It was just endless darkness and torment.

His heart rate picked up when he felt the prick of claws on his forearm. He turned sharply, facing the darkness. There was nothing there. Ezra glanced at his forearm, no tears marked the sleeve of his black tunic.

Claws suddenly raked across his back from nape to hip, and his spine arched sharply. Ezra screamed against the fire that exploded across his back—

He jolted awake, arms seizing as the manacles restrained his movements.

"Ezra, it's only a dream," hushed a soothing voice.

Panting, his dark eyes wide, he fixed his gaze on the glow of embers in a hearth, letting the light smooth the nightmares from his mind. When the darkness rescinded, his muscles relaxed, and he fell back into the cot. He was sweating, and his limbs started to shake as the heat cooled.

Someone stood and sat beside him, and then a damp cloth was pressed along his brow.

His vision, which had been hazy when he awoke, cleared. Anabelle sat at his bedside. Her face was equal parts gentle and sorrowful. Her brows furrowed slightly, and her full mouth twisted into a frown.

He tried to reach for her hand, his tongue lead in his mouth when he tried to speak, but the bindings at his wrists held fast, and he was too tired to fight them.

"An… na… bel…" he said brokenly. His throat was full of sand.

Violet-blue eyes snapped to him, and she set the cloth aside and reached for something. A metal cup pressed to his lips, and Ezra choked on the strong herbal liquid but drank it down until his tongue unstuck from the roof of his mouth.

"Anabe… lle," he tried again. His voice was still rough, but the sounds came easier.

"Don't talk," she whispered, soothing a hand across his cheek with the damp cloth again. "It's just after midnight. Try to go back to sleep."

The water felt good on his skin, and his mind wanted to dive back into the darkness. But he fought it, fixating on her.

"I… am… sor… sorry."

Anabelle clicked her tongue. "You should be conserving your strength."

"I… am…" he took a steadying breath, holding her stare, "… sorry."

He needed her to know, to say the words, and to know she *heard* him.

"Ezra, please," Anabelle pleaded, her eyes glistening in the dim light from the hearth.

Someone else stood, and Ezra jerked his head, his heart leaping in fear.

Silver hair, dark olive skin, and bright blue eyes stared down at him. "Hello, Ezra," Néefar said calmly, regarding him.

Images tore from the fog that covered his mind. Visions of Néefar in the great hall of Dyagin, of Levina and what he had done to her… and the last face in his mind made him seize: Lithônion as his head toppled from his shoulders.

A pained wail tore from his chest, his eyes fixed on Néefar as memories of everything he had done spun through his mind one after the other. Of every face he slaughtered and plea of mercy he ignored.

"I'm sorry," he sobbed. Chanting the words over and over again until they filled the space.

"I'm sorry."

"I'm sorry."
"I'm sorry."

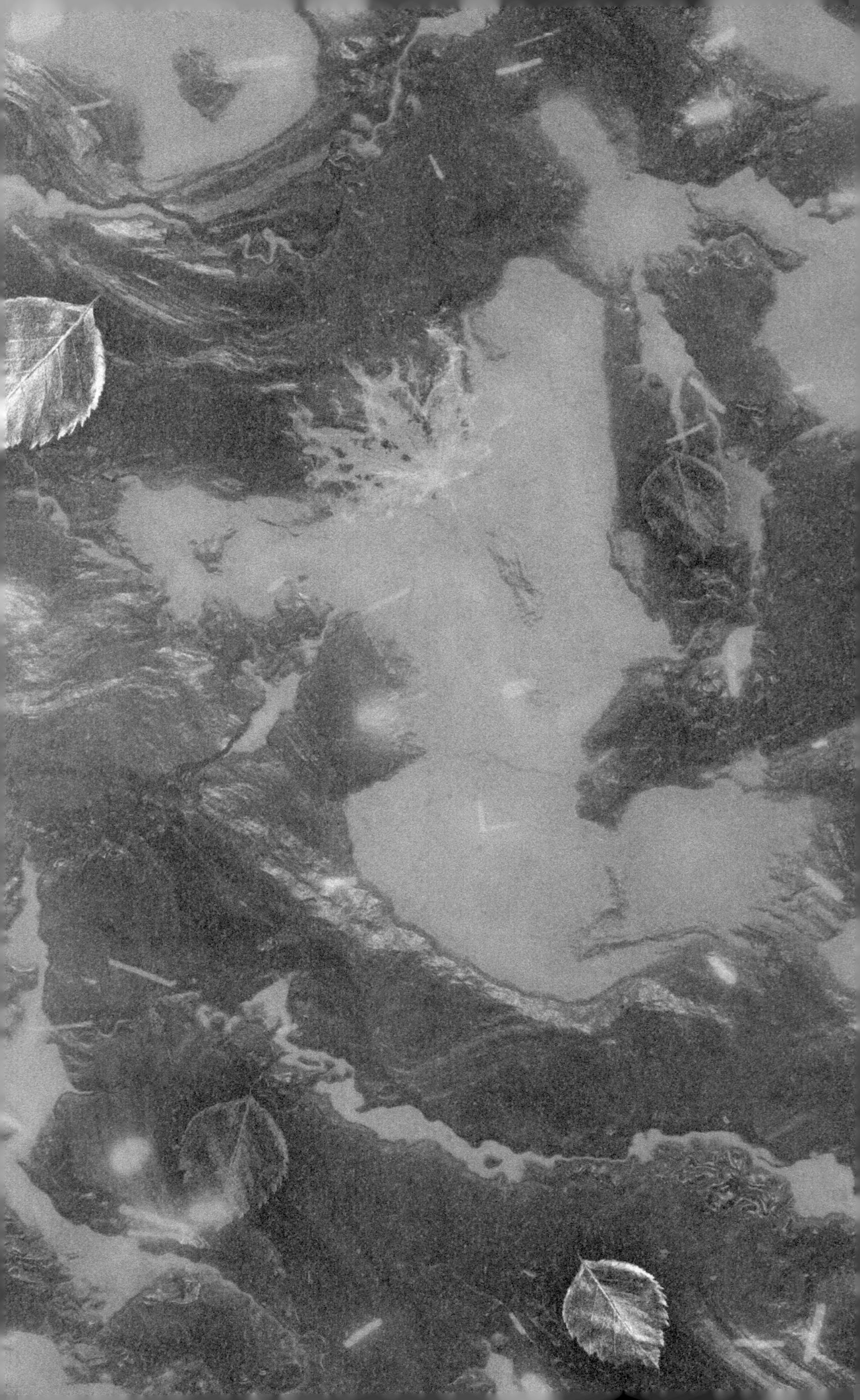

# CHAPTER 31

The morning colours were suffocated by the turbulent sky above as Nazar stepped into the expansive, vibrant moor, the black storm following behind him as if he commanded earth and sky.

His white hair was a beacon in the shadows at his back, and his bloody eyes scanned the tall stalks of golden grass before him, whipping violently in the heavy winds.

Shadows slithered past him, slowly crawling through the tall field. Where they touched, the grass died, its long stalks turning to ash.

The trees were a crescent around his army of undead Fae and dark souls taken from the Lost Forest, the sea to his left, and a large black still river cut through the moor into the woods.

Nazar eyed the river with a sharp, rotting smile, head tilted.

He walked towards it until he toed the edge and inhaled, sniffing the scent. They had mixed something into the water, something they had hoped might stop him. His eyes followed the river, which stopped just before the cliff's ledge and cut into the forest.

Less of a river and more of a moat.

He smirked.

He had waited almost three centuries for everything to fall into place. For Balwin to make do with their bargain. He had died before he could pay his debt, but he had transferred the darkness to the elf, and then Nazar had seen the world he could have. The world he could take his fill of until there was nothing but hollow bones left.

The Fae could have their moat and their little tricks. But he would feast on them and take his time doing so. Until every soul begged for mercy across their world, and then, he would devour them, too.

But there was one that he wanted most of all. One that the fires called to, one that could destroy all his hard work and centuries of waiting.

Nazar lifted his chin, his head angling to the sky as his eyes rolled back. Black as night, tar seeped from the runes carved into his flesh. He released the leash on his demons, and they shot into the forest.

Searching for the light he craved most.

The light of the dragons.

A violent tremor had shaken the earth at sunrise, but that wasn't what had pulled Hazen from the mud hut and the warmth of Åsmund's arms. He had woken when she had and made to follow, but she lightly pressed him back onto their bedroll and told him to rest. She only needed to stretch and let her mind settle.

When he frowned, she had kissed the worry from him. Soon, those kisses turned feverish, and he had her stripped of her clothes and rolled her under him before she could think to protest. His tongue did wicked things to her body until Hazen was sure she would combust. She had to cover her mouth as he took her. Running her hands over his wings as they flared, his growl of arousal making her do it again with more confidence. He had bit down on her neck, marking the skin on the other side, and she had shattered, muffling her scream as she came around him, and he filled her with his own release.

After lying there in dazed bliss, she laughed softly, kissing him when he protested, and stood and dressed in her leathers, quickly braiding her unkept hair back, whispering that she would be back soon. Now, she stood just beyond the training field where she had first heard the soft feminine humming, just as she did now. It pulled her further into the woods, and Hazen let her feet follow that direction.

Thunder clapped overhead, and Hazen jolted, watching the sky turn black. Something bitter filled the air, and she wrinkled her nose. Determination filled her, and she pushed on. Walking further and further into the forest.

The trees she passed were familiar. Pressed so tightly together, she had to watch her feet at times as they made to trip her. They were massive, their bark black as night despite the greying of their roots and the cracks that wounded others.

The forest opened, the trees grew further apart until they formed an aisle, their trunks rising like massive pillars on either side. Hazen stopped, her breathing filling the silent air.

At the end of the aisle was a stone altar that sat catatonic, and the feminine humming filled her ears like a siren's call, urging her to walk towards it.

One step, and then another, and soon Hazen stood before it. Her hand hovered over the rough surface, and her eyes darted to the engraving in the stone before glancing at the forest beyond the altar.

"Where are you?" she whispered on a breath.

She didn't know who she was speaking to or what she was looking for, but she knew something was listening and waiting for her to find them.

"You brought me across the veil." Hazen stepped around the

altar, her eyes scanning the still forest. "You've been calling for me since I arrived in Álfheimr."

The lulling hum that filled her ears drifted off, and a stillness overcame the forest. The world held its breath, waiting, as Hazen stepped forward. Letting her power rise to the surface, that familiar warmth cascaded through her muscles, and the world became translucent.

Veins of gold glimmered beneath the earth, a shadow cast over the ones connected to each tree, suffocating the flow of life. What little flow there was dripped from the branches, and she held out a hand, watching a tiny droplet of gold fall into her palm.

Beyond her hand, the webbing of veins vanished suddenly. Hazen tilted her head, hand dropping to her side.

"There you are," she whispered, walking towards the break.

Her black boots toed the line, and Hazen reached out a hand. With her power thrumming in her blood, she could see the air shimmer in front of her. It felt like liquid when her fingertips grazed it, and it wavered with a faint prism of colour that quickly disappeared.

"I see the question you hold in your heart, Mortal," said a soft, lulling voice.

Hazen inclined her head over her shoulder, sparing a glance to the figure beside the altar. "You're the one I've been hearing?" she asked.

"I am Taleana."

Hazen whispered her hand over the shimmering air before turning. A female with almond skin, long copper hair that cascaded down her back, and eyes like burning embers stood patiently beside the altar in a robe of ornate emerald silk, watching Hazen with keen curiosity.

"You're one of the four Gods," Hazen stated.

Taleana nodded her head in silent confirmation. "And you are the one who holds the first light."

Hazen didn't disagree with her. After Kain had challenged her, she had begun to suspect that her fire wasn't just fire, and Taleana had only confirmed her suspicions.

"It was never meant to come down," Taleana commented,

walking towards Hazen. "But you want to know if it's possible?"

The power in her pulsed at her back, making the scar on her shoulder burn. Hazen shifted her feet, feeling the uncomfortable sensation dig into her muscles. Ignoring it, she asked, "Is it?"

Taleana looked at the open air behind Hazen, thoughtful. "I cannot answer that."

"Do you know what will happen if it does?"

"No."

Hazen's gold eyes clashed with bright amber ones, nearly red in colour, and she held the God's stare.

"Magic is a living thing and can be both creator and destroyer. If the veil comes down, there is no telling what path it will carve for itself." Taleana waved a hand across the air, and it rippled in greeting. "The world beyond is not a kind place."

"Neither is this one," Hazen said simply. "So maybe it's time for a change."

Smiling faintly, Taleana's eyes flickered to the sky, watching it before she met Hazen's gaze and vanished suddenly.

The bitter wind caressed Hazen's cheek, and she turned, frowning at the God's sudden disappearance. There, gleaming atop the stone altar, was a thin sword with a silver and gold twisted hilt, a dragon's head at the end, and a ruby for an eye. Below the sword were the words etched in a language Hazen didn't know.

"They mean 'all ends have a beginning'," Taleana whispered in the wind. "It is the first blade of creation. May the sword serve you well."

Hazen slowly slid her hands around the hilt and raised it before her. It was heavier than the one she trained with but easy to swing as she cut the air, her muscles sighing with the use.

Thunder cracked through the world, so loud that treetops shook with its power. Hazen jolted, taking two steps back from the altar, her eyes scanned the sky. Lightning spiderwebbed across black clouds, and a chill crept into the forest. Her breath clouded in front of her.

Darkness slowly crept in through the trees, crawling across the ground. Hazen turned, scanning the area around her, widening her stance as she let her training kick in. Her magic pulsed under her skin, making it glow faintly and come to life, wrapping around her wrist and up the sword.

Shadows shot forward, slicing the air by her face, and Hazen stumbled back, her blade cutting the air as another came shooting towards her. Centring herself, she gritted her teeth, and when she swung, her blade cut through the next shadow that came her way. It exploded into black mist with a screech that pierced her ears, another taking its place quickly and another and another. Each vanishing when her blade, wrapped in the first light Taleana had described, cut through them.

The darkness began to creep around her feet, and Hazen stumbled back, heart hammering against her ribs. She watched as the trees slowly sapped of colour around her.

Claws reached from the abyss and gouged into the stone altar, leaving four deep grooves.

Chest heaving, her head darted around, staring into the darkness. Cackles and shrieks split the air, and Hazen's blood turned to ice.

They had run out of time.

Turning on her heels, blade at her side, Hazen sprinted from the forest as Nazar's piercing howl rent the air like a death knell.

Silence hung like a death shroud over the great hall in the broken palace. Thick roots, snarling branches, and knotted brambles still encompassed the hall from floor to narrowest peak in the towering ceiling. Parts of the sky peeked through the growths, and rain began to sprinkle in from overhead.

Savven stood in the middle of the great hall, preternaturally still, staring at his father's corpse.

The King was seated upright, covered in a weave of roots that seemed to meld with him until flesh and wood became one.

The earth quaked at dawn, and Savven awoke immediately, feeling a new weight settle onto his shoulders. He knew at that moment that his father's heart had ceased beating.

He had left his hut and walked to his old home, to the shadow of a once grand palace. Carefully stepping over thick roots and under low-hanging vines, he pushed through the narrow crack in the broken doors to the great hall and found his father as he was now.

Savven felt the steady trickle of what was left of his city, its magic and life, slowly filling him. His father's grief had nearly destroyed these lands and their people, and the magic was almost obsolete.

Pursing his lips, Savven straightened his already perfect posture as if his father's imperious gaze was still alive and narrowed on him.

He had endured thirty-five years of his father's cruelty and anger after his mother's death. Grief was the sword his father had wielded, and guilt was the blow Savven was dealt. Thirty-five winters until he had finally left his home and didn't look back. Until now. It had taken fifteen years and forced circumstances, but he had come back.

Now, the Fae King was dead.

His jaw flexed as he walked slowly towards the throne, climbing the dais and stopping before his father. Pain flooded his chest, and his eyes burned as he stared down at the once-proud king.

He wasn't always a cruel father or a negligent king. Once upon a time, he loved his son and his people. But that had been a long, long time ago.

"I missed her too," he whispered into the eerie quiet, his words followed by the drip of rain. "And I missed you." Bending forward, Savven braced a hand on either side of the throne and kissed his father's cold cheek.

When he straightened, he noticed the faintest smile curved the corners of the King's mouth, and peace settled his proud brow.

Savven swallowed the knot in his throat. "I hope you find each other in the next life."

A horn split the air.

He stilled. The horn blew again, twice more, and his blood ran cold. It was the call to arms.

With a final look at his father, he stalked from the palace and didn't look back.

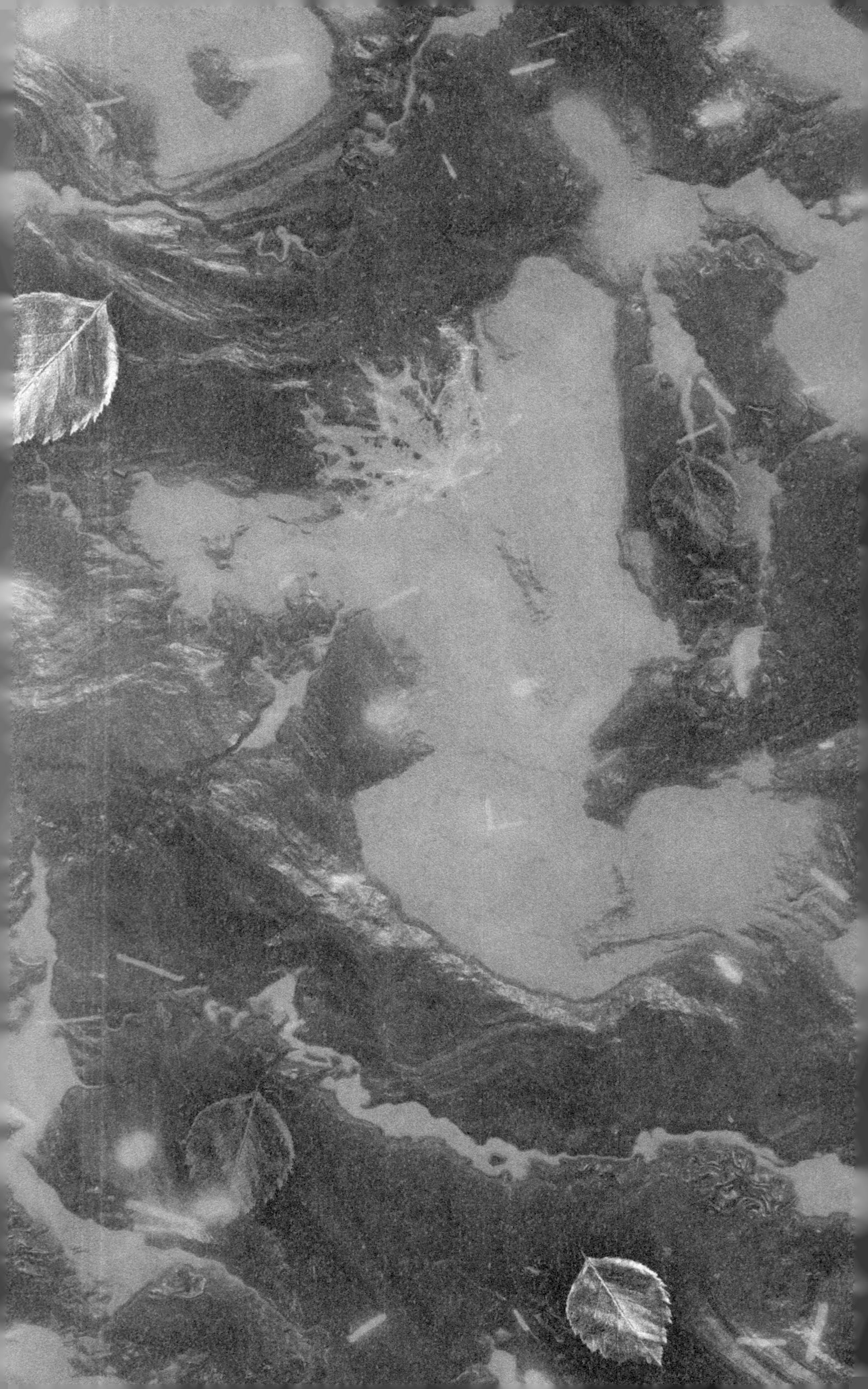

# CHAPTER 32

The sky was nearly black; not even a faint glimmer of the sun could be seen. Rain carved down Savven's face, dripping from his lashes and nose, his hair plastered to his skin as Savven's feet pounded into the muddy streets. When he rounded the bend to the training field, he skidded to a halt.

Carts had been rolled out with weapons, his soldiers created orderly lines, passing swords and bows down the channels. Each one fell away at the end of their line to run to one of the three formations they started.

The Drago stood ready in two lines of five, gold cuirasses and wrist guards gleaming, massive black wings tucked tight into their bodies, with swords strapped to their backs. Åsmund stood off to the side with Hazen, who held tight to a gold sword, securing a gold cuirass of her own against her torso. Savven watched him lean down to say something in her ear, and a blush stained Hazen's cheeks, forcing Savven to look away from the intimate moment.

Bright red hair caught his eye, and he watched Brean grab a bow from one of the carts and a full quiver of arrows. Her hair was braided tightly back, and she was dressed in the elfin blacks. She was impressive as she slung the bow across her back and strapped the quiver to her left hip, determination furrowing her pretty brow. Savven stood momentarily in awe of the witch; she was a soldier, surviving the war this world waged against her since childhood, and now, she was prepared to fight in his army, for his people.

"Savven!"

Savven's head jerked to the right, seeing Néefar sprint towards him, dodging two soldiers as they ran to their formation.

"Nazar is here," Néefar rushed once he got to his side. "The shade found Hazen, and she fended off his shadows until she could get here to warn us."

Savven's chest tugged with deep-rooted emotions when he looked at the field of soldiers, friends, and allies. Anxious understanding twisted in his gut, coiling with his new sense of duty. These were *his* soldiers now, *his* friends, *his* allies. "And where are his shadows now? Where is Nazar?"

Néefar pointed towards the sea moor to the west. "The shadows receded in that direction."

"Which is perfect because I have a pretty little surprise waiting for them," Brean commented darkly as she strolled over, fixing the leather strap of the quiver to hug her inner thigh.

Savven allowed himself a moment to track her movements before he pulled away and scanned the area. "Where's Anabelle?"

Néefar's jaw muscle twitched, his eyes darkened looking every bit the conflicted husband at the mention of his wife before he pointed in the direction where Nazar's shadows had vanished, and Savven looked closer at the wooded area. "She's holding our boundary."

There, just within the copse of trees, was his cousin. Blue and gold shimmering magic flared from her as she raised a barrier of ice between them and the shadows. The demons within the darkness throwing themselves at the ward, testing it.

The drums of war began their rhythmic pounding as the last of his soldiers fell into formation. A soldier from each formation came forward, brought a long curving horn to their lips, and blew. The horns filled the air with the beating drums, Savven's skin prickled with the thrill that came just before a fight.

Thunder crashed as Savven stalked towards the three formations, every single one of the soldiers had their eyes trained on him. Rain drenched them to the bone, swords strapped to their hips in the two outlying formations, and bows held tight in the grips of the formation in the middle.

"The King is dead!" he called into the waiting silence.

None of the soldiers showed any sign of remorse or surprise. They had felt the ground quake at dawn, and they had buried their king long before Savven had returned to them.

Sealing away his emotions, Savven walked down the line of soldiers. "We go to fight an enemy we know nothing of. This creature does not fight by the laws of Fae! It does not fight with honour! It wants to take our lands, destroy our homes, and kill our people! I implore you to raise up your swords! Let loose your arrows! Defend your land and protect your people! LET THEM FEEL OUR WRATH!"

As one, the soldiers struck their chests with their fists, over and over again, chanting in time with the drums, it rose like a song into the deluge.

Hazen stood beside Åsmund, Savven's speech still carried in the bitter air as drums and horns filled the rain.

Åsmund faced the Drago soldiers, his face set in steel, back straight. He looked his soldiers over from wing to boot. And he said only three words that had Hazen smirking darkly:

"Burn. Them. All."

Savven's soldiers were trained and skilled, she had no doubt, but after training with the Drago, she knew that these ten males held the same strength as the two hundred at her back.

Fire flew from hissing torches along the training field at the Drago's silent commands, wrapping around their arms and up their wings. Wicked smiles cut their faces, and excitement lit their eyes as their wings flared open, and as one, they shot into the sky.

Hazen rounded on Åsmund. "Are you going to join them?" Her heart was its own war drum, one that was going to beat right through her chest.

Åsmund lifted a hand to her face, stroking his thumb along her cheekbone. "Yes," he said softly.

She nodded shakily, taking in a staggering breath. She could do this. She could fight. She would fight. Smoothing a hand down the thin gold armour along her torso he had surprised her with, she nodded again, more firmly this time.

Åsmund lowered his hand and gripped her by her shoulders, making her look at him. His eyes were bright and intense. "I will find you in this world or the next after all of this." Leaning forward, he kissed her hard and claiming, and it left her breathless. Pulling back, he leaned his brow on hers, whispering harshly, "Remember: I did not train you to be a soldier, so do not fight with honour. Live, Hazen."

She gritted her jaw against her nerves, knuckles bleaching around the hilt of the sword in her hands, and nodded. "I will."

He kissed her once more before he released her and stepped back. With one last long look, her general shot into the sky. Fire trailing behind him at his command and igniting his wings.

Cold rushed in when his heat vanished, it left Hazen shivering in its absence. Tugging at the ridged collar of gold around her neck did nothing to alleviate the anxiety she felt tunnelling into her body. Luckily, the armour wasn't too heavy and moulded to her body like her leathers had. Secured at the neck and travelling the space between her shoulders to leave them bare.

Savven called his soldiers to march, and Hazen stepped back, watching them tread into the forest. She gazed at Savven as he stalked towards their enemy with predatory intent, his brows lowered, mouth pressed firm. He grabbed a sword from one of the carts, dressed in only the army blacks, and joined the ranks of his soldiers.

Hazen fell behind him, watching Anabelle up ahead cast a silver light through the forest. The light let them tunnel through the shadows that twisted and curled around the trees, snapping them in half. And while the shadows didn't press against Anabelle's magic, they didn't flee from it either.

As they walked further into the western ridge of the forest, Hazen watched the shadows slither by the edge of the light, waiting. Staring into the darkness, she saw claws and faces appear and reared back, startled.

Disfigured faces with cutting smiles, twisted with black leathery skin and sunken cheeks. Creatures that looked like they could have once been human or Fae, now sat with eyeless sockets in their skulls, jagged teeth, naked skeletons, and thin bodies that were black as tar.

It was not just shadows and creeping mists. The darkness was a shroud for the demons within, and they were waiting for them as if contained on an invisible leash.

Hazen licked her lips, tightening her grip on the sword. She took a shallow breath, her stomach knotting as she forced herself to calm down.

She would withstand this. She would fight. She would live dammit.

"It helps if you don't look at them," Anabelle murmured, falling into step on her left and casting a sideways glance at the shadows.

Hazen looked away from the demonic face holding her stare and at Anabelle, her brows going up. "You look…"

"Different?" Anabelle offered with a sharp smile.

"Dangerous," Hazen corrected.

The keeper's canines were longer and sharper, and they looked like they could tear into her flesh without a thought. Her nails had lengthened to claws, and frost coated the black sleeve of her elf army uniform. Her dark hair was pulled back into a tight braid, exposing the watery script tattooed into her skin along her neck, and the tips of her ears were swept in delicate points. She looked deadly.

They silently followed the drums before Hazen said, "Do you

ever get used to it?"

Anabelle sent her an inquisitive look.

"Feeling like this is all a dream?"

"Sometimes I think I'm dead."

Hazen's mouth twitched. "What?"

"The thought crosses my mind occasionally," the keeper said with a shrug. "Maybe I did drown in that pond, and Gallian didn't save me like I thought. Maybe this is our afterlife."

Hazen took one look at the demon staring at her—or rather, the hollows of its eyes staring at her—and shuddered. "If this is our afterlife, then I want a do-over."

Anabelle looked at the demon, her mouth pulling down at the corners. "But then I remember all that I've lost in this world and realise it couldn't be a dream, and I couldn't be dead. Because even in my dreams, and certainly in death, I could never be so cruel."

Hazen slipped her hand into Anabelle's and squeezed it gently.

The further they walked, the more stale and lifeless the air became, and soon, the trees began to thin. Salt air filled Hazen's nose, and beyond the trees was the sea and a vast moor.

The Fae filed out into two rows. Archers at the rear, foot soldiers at the front. The line split as their king walked to the head. Hazen followed him through, Anabelle at her side. Brean already stood at the front with an arrow loosely nocked, her eyes fixated on the shadow rising from the other side.

Åsmund and the Drago hovered above them, the push of wind from their wings comforting Hazen's frayed nerves. She briefly looked up, finding bright green eyes locked on her. She nodded once, and he looked away.

Stomach turning over, Hazen watched with wide eyes as the shadows rose like a tidal wave and parted to reveal an army of demons and undead creatures. At the front of them all was a face made from nightmares. Blood red eyes fixed on her, his white hair like a torch in the sea of dark grey.

There was a long, black river that stretched from the cliff's edge into the forest. "What is that," she asked in a hushed voice.

"Their funeral," Brean uttered, her eyes narrowing, fingers tightening around her bow.

Nazar spread his arms wide, and they watched in horror as his jaw lengthened unnaturally and a screech from the deepest regions of the underworld cut the air.

The darkness at his back rose higher and higher into the air, and a mighty roar bellowed from its depths. A dragon made of smoke and ash dived out of the shadows.

"Fuck me," Hazen uttered.

"All you have to do is say, *please*," Néefar commented casually, strolling up beside her. His eyes lit with excitement, and his focus was on the dragon arcing high into the sky on smoky wings.

Hazen closed her eyes slowly, taking in a deep, calming breath. "Now is not the time to try my patience."

His crooked smile was enough for her to raise her sword and press the tip to his crotch, glaring at him.

"If you have to stab him, please do so somewhere less vital," Anabelle commented, sliding a sly look at her husband.

"Traitor," he shot back with a swaggering grin.

Hazen snorted despite the situation they found themselves in, her nerves easing, and lowered the blade.

Néefar stepped around Hazen, grabbed his wife and kissed her once.

Anabelle was locked on him as he stepped several paces away from them. An easy target in the swaying grass of the moor.

"I'll come straight to you, Little Gipsy!" he called.

And Hazen watched Anabelle's smile tighten, her gaze turning watery before she blinked it away.

Two seconds spanned before Néefar began to shift. Growing larger and larger until Hazen craned her neck, staring up at the face of a massive dragon with long, razor-sharp teeth. Gold horns curved back from the top of his head; glowing reptilian sapphire eyes stared back at them. Black scales, each rimmed with gold, as large as dinner plates, covered his ginormous body. A long tail with spikes as long as her arm covered the end, swishing across the ground.

Néefar craned his head back and let out a deafening roar.

Hazen quickly covered her ears, the earth rattling beneath her.

Spreading massive black leather wings, Néefar shot up,

disappearing into the turbulent sky above. Åsmund and his soldiers close on his tail, and they, too, disappeared.

"Brean," Savven said lowly.

Hazen knew that tone; it was a command.

Brean's eyes flashed green, as the end of her arrow caught aflame.

Nazar screeched again, and the army at his back began moving forward, falling into a sprint. Their hungry snarls filled the moor.

With each breath, Hazen's chest rose rapidly, watching Brean draw the arrow back. Waiting, waiting…

The undead approached swiftly. Some ran on all fours, their limbs contorting unnaturally, while others were surefooted, causing unease to trickle through Hazen.

Brean still didn't loosen her arrow. Eyes trained down the shaft.

They neared the black river, splashing as they entered its calm waters.

Still, her arrow did not fire.

At least a third of his army filled the length of the river now, and as they made to climb out, Brean finally released her arrow with a single breath.

The flame flew straight and narrow across the moor, right for the river.

And then the world exploded.

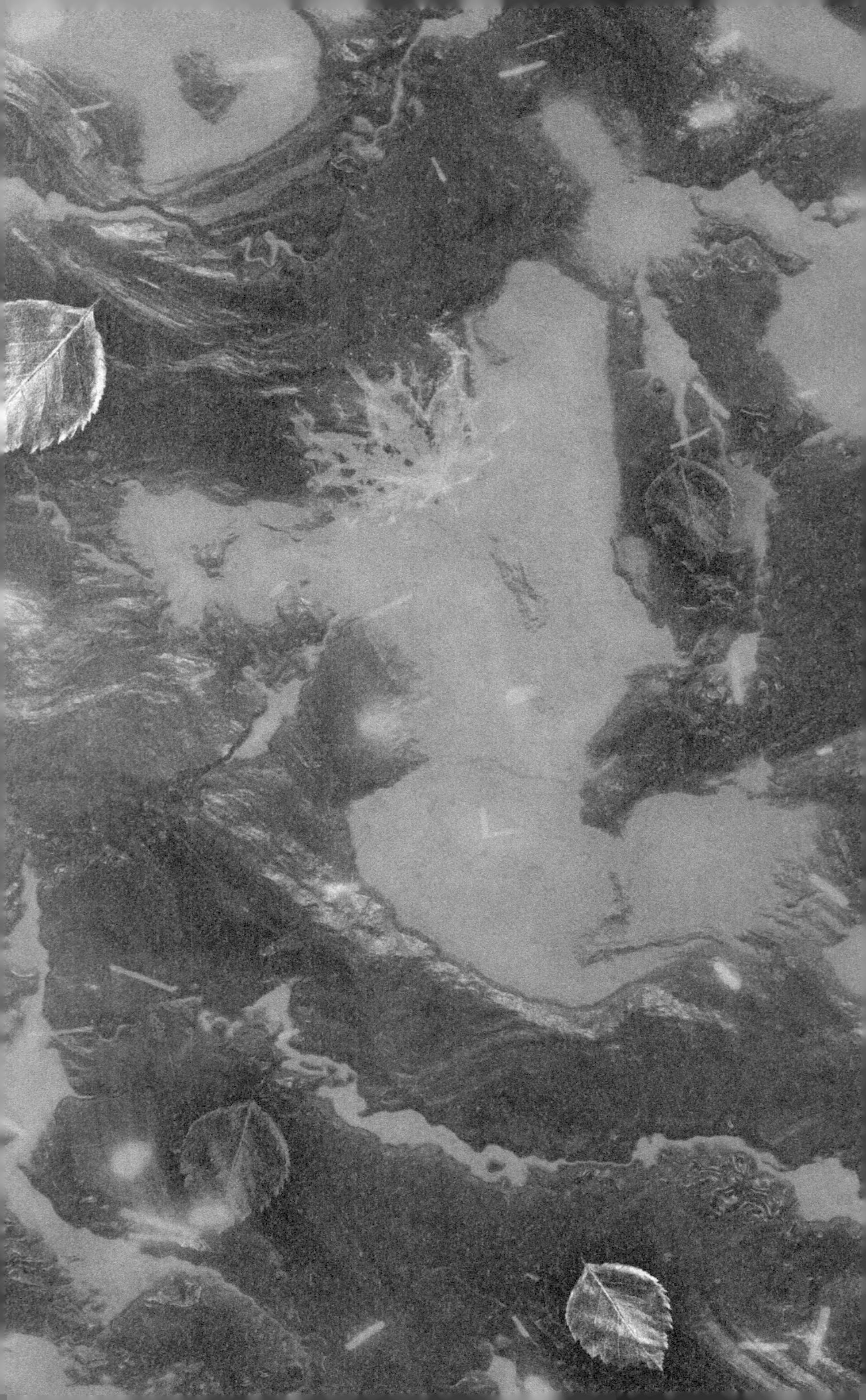

# CHAPTER 33

Hazen was thrown back from the explosion. Ears ringing, she shook her head in a daze, trying to clear her wavering vision and stumbled to her feet, grabbing her discarded sword.

A long crater now cleaved the moor, smoke rising into the wet air.

At Savven's command, archers loosened a cloud of arrows into the sky. The arrows sailed true, filling the chests of Nazar's surviving army. But the arrows did nothing to stop them. Their bodies jerked at impact, stumbling to the ground, but they slowly crawled to their feet. Some snapped the metal ends off with brute strength, and others pulled them free, dropping them.

She didn't have time to think or speak, only move. Running headfirst into the fray. A cry tore from her throat. Foot soldiers charged behind her, Savven at their head, they met Nazar's army in a clash of talons and swords.

Fire ignited black clouds, blue lightning streaking through them as two dragons battled overhead. Drago soldiers unleashed fire and steel onto their opponents in a chaotic symphony.

Hazen ducked under the lunging arm of a male faun. His eyes were glassy and white, matching the markings that were carved into his pale chest. She found her footing and swung her blade in a clean arc through the faun's neck, her feet dancing around the body as it crumpled.

Screams of terror filled the air, Hazen panned the area, quickly surveying their enemy. Nazar's undead didn't carry weapons. Horror was etched on the soldiers' faces when creatures of all species of nightmare lunged for them. Tearing apart the Fae limb for limb.

Something hard slammed into her back, and the ground rose up to meet her. She caught her fall just before her face made contact with the sodden earth, her bones crying at impact, but she looked over her shoulder in time to see a female soldier slice her blade through a near skeletal-like demon with taut black skin. The demon paused, looking down at his torso, then a dark grin spread across its face, showcasing a mouth full of razor-sharp teeth. It lunged for the female, but her scream was short-lived before it tore her throat out.

Rolling to her feet, she let her power rise to the surface, feeling its demanding press along her bones. A fire that shone brighter than flames and sparked in the grey light wrapped around her wrist and down her blade.

Taking note of her, the demon, who was crouched on all fours, looked up from the female's neck, her deep red blood dripping from its pointed chin, eyes black as night.

Hazen barely had time to shift her stance before the demon lunged. Jaws snapping an inch from her face, she screamed, fire fuelling her body, and her skin began to glow brightly.

The demon shrieked, head jerking back, and threw itself off her.

Stalking towards the creature, with a savage snarl, she lifted her blade and stabbed it through its chest.

White fire sparked the tarry skin, and the demon's cry split the air as it burst into flames.

Hazen watched, wide-eyed, the withering body fall to her feet and still. Heart hammering with the knowledge that her power could kill these things, Hazen dove deeper into the chaos in a blaze of fire and light.

Ezra's eyes flew open. Hearing the sounds of battle far off in the distance, his heart sped up.

Nazar had come.

Fear seized him, and he looked down at his hands, they were still bound in the manacles. He tested them, they held fast, they would with his strength nearly that of a mortal. He felt as though death was lingering nearby, waiting for him in the shadows.

Gritting his teeth, he pulled harder, the weak muscles in his arms bulging. He relaxed, heaving in a breath, and then tried again.

The cot posts groaned, and Ezra threw his whole weight into pulling at the restraints. A healer appeared, and she squeaked in surprise, seeing what he was doing.

"Undo them," he demanded in a rough voice. His throat felt like sandpaper again.

"I cannot," she said quickly, not daring a step closer. She looked young. Far younger than him, her wide brown eyes were filled with fear.

He yelled through gritted teeth, trying the manacles again and feeling them muffle his magic and everything that made him innately Fae. "Then break them! I need to help them!"

The cot joint shifted, and his eyes fixed on the weak point. He pulled at it desperately, but it didn't move further.

"Please!" he begged.

Pursing her lips, the healer scuttled forward. Hovering just beyond his cot. "You must promise not to move until I'm gone." Her hands were shaking by her sides, Ezra couldn't fault her for it.

He had turned their world into a living nightmare, she had every right to fear him because of the horror he had inflicted.

He nodded, a quick jerk of his head, and relaxed into the cot.

Bending, the healer grabbed the chain between the manacle on his wrist and the one bound to the cot post. It glowed blue in her hand before it broke in half.

He was free.

She did the other one and practically ran from the hut as soon as it broke.

The manacles were still bound around his wrist, but he was free.

He could hear the battle raging on, forcing him up, he stumbled to his feet, his body barely holding him upright. Still, determination filled his bones with enough strength to stagger forward.

He would get to the battlefield, if it was the last thing he did, and it very well might be.

Mud, blood, and rain sprayed across Anabelle's face, her magic shooting down a Harpy as it dove towards her, claws and talons poised for her chest.

The creature shrieked, and its body crashed into the ground as it turned to ice, sending the dead around it flying.

A cut marred her cheek, strands of her hair clung to the sweat beading her skin, blood speckling her face like black and red freckles. Death surrounded her. Their death toll was greater than the ones they fought, Anabelle swallowed the spiral of fear that shot through her, threatening to consume her entirely.

Above her, she saw Néefar quickly arc back, claws digging into the side of the dragon made of smoke and ash. But he simply went through it as if it didn't exist. When the shadow dragon's teeth snapped towards Néefar, Anabelle had to force herself to look away.

Ducking under an attacking minotaur, Anabelle lunged for a forgotten sword, whirling, and sunk it into the beast's neck. She yanked it out, blood splaying, the beast toppled sideways.

Another and another, they all fell. Whether by sword or magic, they all met the same end. Their skin turned to ice and shattered on impact while she moved to the next attacker and then the next after that.

She couldn't see the sun or tell how long the day stretched, how long they fought. Despite her immortality, her bones were tired, but she kept fighting. She couldn't stop, and she wouldn't because stopping meant death, not only for herself, but everything and everyone that she'd sworn she'd protect.

Anabelle saw Savven fighting his way through a large grouping of demonic creatures. They were all clawing their way towards him at once. Leaping one after the other for his exposed neck, face, and any limb they could reach. But no matter how many times he sliced through them, they didn't fall.

She sent her magic sailing, poised like a dagger of icy light, the demons scattered when it punctured through their dark bodies. Sending them flying through the air.

Savven nodded his thanks, eyes darting over her shoulder. "Behind you!" he screamed.

She turned to see a Cerberus, its three heads snapping for her, she lunged to the ground just as one of its jaws clamped down where her shoulder had been. Grime coated her skin, and Anabelle felt its hot breath upon her as its teeth grazed her back.

"Another one!" she griped, getting to her feet. "You've got to be kidding me!"

The music of battle filled his ears, and Ezra knew he was almost there. His hobbling turned into a staggering run, his breaths coming in shallow pants, eyes fixed on the tree line.

Once, there was a time when battle would make his blood sing. He loved the thrill of a fight, he loved to train, he loved his brothers and the soldiers he fought alongside.

But that was a different life. One where he hadn't turned into a monster. One where he could smile and be content, knowing he lived a life dedicated to duty and honour.

That life didn't exist anymore. He was no longer General to the army he charged towards or Captain of Álfheimr›s Guard. He was just Ezra. As his feet picked up pace, he knew he was running towards his death. But it was a death he'd welcome if he could turn the tides in favour of his friends.

Skidding to a stop outside the sea moor, he watched as his kin fell. Torn apart, devoured, screams still etched on their faces. It was a slaughter.

The flare of magic caught his eye, and he saw Anabelle sprint from the hungry maws of a Cerberus. Her magic hit the creature in its middle head, and it froze.

Ezra watched a minotaur pick up a discarded blade, its black eyes fixed on Anabelle. Dread filled him with icy terror. And then he was running, sprinting into the horde.

A demon gripped Anabelle's arm, and she screamed, feeling its nails sink into her flesh. Blood poured down her bicep, and she yanked her arm away. Her hand coated in ice, her curved nails glinting dangerously, and she swiped it through the demon's neck, tearing out a chunk.

The demon screeched, clawing at its throat where ice had begun to spread. It fell to its knees, covered in glimmering hoarfrost.

Whirling, Anabelle froze. A minotaur charged straight for her, a sword held in its beefy hand. It was too close; she could nearly feel its rancid breath on her face. The fighting pressed in around her.

A deafening bullish roar ripped from its snout, black eyes glinting, it lunged the sword at her as she raised her hands in a shield of ice.

Ezra's face filled her vision, and memories of the past replayed in her head as history repeated itself.

Pain widened his eyes, the battlefield went silent around them. Something sharp pressed into her chest, and she could feel blood running down her tunic, her skin stinging with pain. She heard screaming in the distance, and Ezra's body twitched.

Anabelle's gaze slowly went to the sword tip pressed into her sternum and followed it to the centre of Ezra's chest.

The noise of battle rushed in as Ezra's knees gave out, and she realised she was the one screaming. She was screaming his name repeatedly. Hot tears cut down her dirt-streaked face, the rain mixing with them.

With a guttural cry, Anabelle lunged around Ezra, eyes turning gold, and all her senses became feral. Before the minotaur could pull the sword from Ezra's back, Anabelle flung herself onto the beast.

It reared, startled.

And before it could pull her away, Anabelle's claws dug into its neck, tearing at the skin and blood-matted fur until its roar came out a gurgle, and it bled out.

She hopped off the minotaur before it toppled sideways and darted back to Ezra, quickly falling to her knees. Seeing him grabbing the blade, the steel cut into his flesh and blood dripped down the manacles still attached to him.

"Ezra," she soothed, halting his hands. "Let me take the manacles off."

His eyes were wild, and he grabbed her hand as she went to freeze them off, stopping her. Ezra opened his mouth to speak, but bright crimson was the only thing that came out, dribbling down his chin.

Understanding webbed inside Anabelle, and she felt the sting of tears again. "Ezra," she sobbed, pulling him closer.

His face was ashen, blood bubbled up in his throat as he tried to breathe, pooling at the corners of his mouth.

She cradled his head in her arms, soothing the pain that furrowed his brows. "I'm so sorry." Hot tears spilt down her cheeks, her heart fragmenting when she felt his life slipping away.

Ezra met her stare and brought a cold hand to her cheek, feebly brushing her tears away.

That only made her cry more, and Anabelle pressed a desperate kiss to his brow. "Please," she begged. "Please live."

When she pulled back, Ezra's dark eyes glinted with his own

tears, but they were steadfast. His hand dropped to hers, guiding her fingers to the blade.

The fragments of her heart shattered at his silent request, but she swallowed and nodded. "Okay," she breathed, pressing another kiss to his temple. "Okay…"

His hand gripped hers firmer, and she stared back at him. His eyes were desperate, searching, pleading with her own as if saying something silently to her.

"It's okay, Ezra," she murmured, her voice shaking. "I forgive you."

And then she pulled the blade from his back in one clean movement.

The hand that held hers fell to the ground, lifeless.

# CHAPTER 34

Åsmund flew high above the battlefield, dodging the multiple heads of a chimaera on his right. He let his fire go, and it whipped with a crack across the lion head of the beast.

Flames erupted along the black mane, its ruby-red eyes trained on him. Its dragon tail spewed its own fire, and Åsmund flew out of the way, wings tucked tight to his body. Free falling towards the ground.

Bodies on both sides moved below him, unaware of his presence, his wings flared right before he hit the ground. With the chimaera breathing down his neck, he grabbed the sword from his back, wrapping his fire around it and met the beast halfway.

They clashed together in a tangle of talons, wings, and fire.

Åsmund had the distinct awareness of his soldiers fighting

above him, even when teeth snapped close to his face and the beast's rancid breath curdled his senses.

A yell slipped between his gritted teeth. As he shoved the creature away, talons caught his arm, adding another trophy to his collection of scars.

Lunging, its dragon tail whipped towards him. He grabbed it in one hand, muscles straining at the beast's strength, and his sword sliced the air. The chimaera screamed in agony, black blood spurting from the severed limb.

Using the distraction, he punched the fire blade into its skull. Wings going limp, the beast fell off his sword with a sicking sound and crushed the ones below it when it slammed into the ground.

Fire rained across the drenched sky, thundering clouds rolling over them, lightning marking their path in deadly streaks as it flashed thrice and pierced one of his Drago through the back. Åsmund watched him fall from the sky, dead before he landed.

Dragons warred above them, filling the air with their mighty roars as they came tumbling, tangled together, from the sky in a flurry of wings and shadows.

The shifter snapped at the beast's neck, but his maw went through it. Shadows ebbing away before knitting back together. The shade's beast was playing with the shifter, dread filled Åsmund at the realisation.

Sword in hand, he shot towards the dragons, fire tangling around his limbs like armour, and flipped the hilt in his hand. Arching it back, he thought of Hazen somewhere far below him and let it sail as the shadow dragon latched around the shifter's neck and *tore*.

A pained scream filled the air from the black and gold dragon, and if Åsmund had tried to discern it, he would have thought it sounded like a name. Sapphire eyes went wide, and the shifter fell away from the shadow dragon who released the chunk of his neck it had torn off.

Åsmund's blade sunk into the shadow dragon's head as the shifter crashed to the ground with a mighty, earth-rattling thud.

Flames engulfed the black head as the sword went through it. The beast screamed, head thrashing, and the fire soon vanished.

Red eyes fixated on Åsmund with murderous intent.

Swearing, Åsmund shot into the sky, the dragon just behind him.

It wasn't fire that spewed from its mouth, but pure darkness and Åsmund realised too late that this beast was linked to the shade as its black-as-night talons curved around his torso, crushing his cuirass.

Ribs cracked and shattered under the pressure. Åsmund snarled through the pain, thrashing and sending wave after wave of fire into the beast. But the flames were eaten by the darkness, and the massive head of the shadow dragon lowered to his level, teeth bared with a warning rumble, his wings taking them higher and higher until they broke the torment of clouds, and the blue sky opened up above them.

Åsmund's chest concaved in the dragon's grip, blood pooling in the corners of his mouth, but still, he fought. His muscles bulged in his arms as he strained to tear the talons away. The fire inside him flared and exploded at his command, penetrating every shadow around him until the air grew thin, his fire snuffed out entirely. He could feel his heart racing in his chest, eyes scanning for a way out. A way to live. But there was none. It was just open air.

His scream was defiant and filled with rage as he stared at the dragon with a twisted snarl. "Do your worst!"

The dragon's jaws snapped for his wings and tore them from his back.

The world went still, silence ringing in his ears as pain radiated to every bone in his body, and his back seized, his mouth gaping in shock.

The dragon released him, and then he was free-falling.

Anabelle watched in horror as Néefar's body hit the ground. She could hear his bones break at the impact, earth spraying in every direction, and bodies disappearing when he fell atop them.

She was sprinting towards him before she realised what she

was doing. Slicing her way through creatures who didn't die at her blade but stumbled away, providing a clear path towards her husband.

Light flared from the fallen dragon, and she saw him shift. His naked body was beautiful, broken, and covered in the grime of battle.

She willed herself faster, her breath coming in short, gasping pants that were too loud in her ears, her heart threatened to burst out of her chest. She just had to make it to him. She could save him. She had done it once before.

A demon entered her path, and she flung it away with her magic, sprinting harder. A strangled cry tore her throat, and she dropped to her knees beside her dead husband, hands shaking over the chunk from his neck that was torn out.

His once bright blue eyes were dim, pupils blown wide. Silver hair tinted black and red, his olive brown skin was painfully pale. He had bled out quicker than his body could heal him—before she could reach him.

Silent horror sliced down her body with great waves of grief, her world went mute.

Hands tore at her arms, and she jerked away from them, only for claws to dig into her hair and limbs.

Demons surrounded her back, Anabelle screamed in rage as they wrenched her away from her husband. Fighting wildly, they held her fast, pulling her in every direction. Bones snapped, and flesh ripped apart. A scream as wild as a banshee rent the air, and her magic burst in a great wave from her core.

But too late. Anabelle felt her right arm tear from the socket as the creature holding it flew back from the tidal wave of power, her arm in its claws.

Sobbing, Anabelle collapsed to the ground, bleeding out. She didn't feel the pain, adrenaline and shock numbed her completely. Making to stand, her ankles gave out. They had been dislocated. The ground jarred her knees at impact, and her only hand left caught her fall.

Sobbing through her teeth, tears mixing with her blood, she crawled through the sodden ground. Using her arm as leverage, her nails dug into the mud, her knees propelling her forward one at a time, over bodies, fluids, lost weapons, and finally, her husband.

Anabelle gripped his hip and heaved herself on top of him. Sobbing as she trailed desperate kisses across his bare chest. Trying to funnel the last of her magic into him. But it didn't work, and she leaned her brow against him, wailing. The sound was lost. Her body didn't have enough strength to make any noise.

"I love you with all that I am," she sobbed silently.

The world became a hazy reality around her, and she didn't care. She clung to Néefar, holding him with the last morsels of her strength, until slowly, the darkness crept in around her vision, and the keeper died.

# CHAPTER 35

Hazen was dancing. Her bones ached, and her arms were coated in blood and dirt, rainwater streaking through it, but she moved just as Åsmund had taught her. Keeping to the balls of her feet, she spun around a towering minotaur, one of his black eyes bleeding out around an arrow lodged in it.

Ducking its advance, she sliced the weapon across its abdomen and then up its chest in two quick flurries.

Its clawed fingers came down and struck her across the left shoulder. Hazen lurched forward under the blow, pain jarring her bones, and stumbled out of the way as the minotaur fell face first into the earth.

Another fell, and another, and Hazen saw no end to this. Her breath was ragged in her ears despite her training, she didn't see the demon at her back.

Slamming forward, she hit the ground hard enough to see stars. With a groan, she tasted mud and copper, she grimaced, rolling to her back. The demon leapt into the air with a screech, landing on top of her.

Before the creature could dig into her, a sword cut through its neck. Hazen quickly shoved the body off. Eyes meeting Savven's fleetingly, she nodded her thanks.

He jerked his chin and ran towards the bright red hair Hazen saw in the distance.

Shadows crawled over the grassland, which was now less grass and more trampled earth and ruin. The tendrils of darkness were ebbing closer and closer to her, so Hazen dug her fingers into the dying earth.

Fire travelled through her, down her fingertips, and into the ground. The rush of power consumed her, and she let out a wild scream. The earth pulsed with life, the ground exploded with fire and light, and the shadows vanished.

Staggering to her feet, she rounded on the masses ahead of her, behind her, and beside her. There were too many of them.

A solid object cracked against her skull, and her vision faltered. Hazen stumbled once then fell to her knees, moments before she felt a foot kick her spine in. The ground rose up to greet her again, heart thumping loudly in her ears she lay there on her stomach. With blurry vision, she watched those around her fight to their deaths, the tang of copper and grass and mud on her lips.

Cold fingers wrapped around her shoulder, claws dug into her already torn skin, pain igniting every cell in her body, warm blood trickled its way down her arm.

Hazen stretched out her hand, lunging for the hilt of her sword just as the one grabbing her threw her onto her back. Her eyes landed on Nazar's death-white face, and she sliced the blade across his stomach without a second's pause, making contact.

Nazar stumbled back, holding a sickly pale hand to his wound, shock marring his taut face.

Hazen rolled to her feet despite the thumping in her head, her left shoulder aching and screaming with every movement, blood gushed from the gashes, but she held fast to her sword. She looked at the shade through the downpour of rain.

Drawing the sword back, she stabbed it into his heart and watched his look of surprise turn into a fiendish smile.

Her blood froze in her veins.

Nazar vanished into black mist, his heinous smile lingering. All that was left was her blade, pointing into the air.

"Are you so afraid to die you need little tricks to win?" she screamed into the open.

*"You cannot kill what is already dead,"* whispered his slithering voice.

Hazen whirled around, ducking in time to avoid the tip of a blade bearing down upon her neck. She lunged her sword up and sunk it into the sternum of a milky-eyed satyr before drawing it out and slicing its head from its shoulders. The dead couldn't live without their heads.

She felt her blood run down her arm, hot and sticky, as she searched for Nazar. Stumbling through the bloodied masses, her eyes fell on Brean, her hair a beacon in the wet gloom, Savven at her back, both fighting off undead monsters of their own.

Glancing up, she searched the skies. She had seen Néefar fall and the shadow dragon rise high into the clouds. But she hadn't seen Åsmund, and she prayed silently to whoever was listening that he was at least alive.

The skin on her neck prickled, and slowly, Hazen turned. The world went eerily quiet as blood-red eyes met gold ones across the moor.

Nazar stood beside the tree line to the east, and she knew he was waiting for her.

Heart racing, she ran towards him. Fighting her way across the moor. The grime of war splattered across her skin so thick that Hazen feared it would leave a permanent brand on her flesh.

Freed from the confines of the battlefield, Hazen stood small in comparison to the forest. The black woods stretched high above her, dwarfing her and everything else that came within reach.

There was that sense of change she had felt the other morning. It was etching itself into her very fibre, preparing her. The mark on her shoulder turned hot the longer she stood there, and Hazen flexed her back at the sensation, ignoring the tearing pain from her wounded shoulder.

With a last look back at the faces she had come to love, despite not finding them in the horde, she took a deep breath and stepped beyond the forest line.

The sounds of battle were muted like a veil had been placed over the forest. Hazen was surrounded by a grey, decaying world. Her hand stretched out and touched the rough bark, watching it crumble beneath her fingers like ash. Images of a nightmare that seemed from a lifetime ago filled her mind, and she clenched her jaw, sealing away her emotions as she witnessed her dream become a reality.

Ash surrounded her. It made up the forest floor, the sparse grass that grew, the towering trees. It slowly sucked the life away, feasting on what remained. The lifelines that flowed beautifully in streams of gold under the earth were now black, and Hazen forced in a breath.

"Where are you?" she whispered, her voice seeming too heavy in the numb silence.

The stone altar came into view. Nazar stood before it, scratching his black claws across the top.

Red eyes glowed faintly in the greyness, snapping to her, a smile carved up his scarred cheeks at the sight of her coming to him.

"I was waiting for you," he intoned softly. Dark tendrils of mist and shadows dripped down his body. Hazen had to repress her shiver of fear.

She eyed the strange markings etched over his skin and the tar that seeped from them, visible through the near sheer shroud he wore.

"Are you too afraid to face me on the field?" she sneered.

His bony hand whipped out, and the air coiled tight around her. Hazen's chest squeezed painfully, she felt her ribs break, stealing the breath from her lungs when her feet left the ground. Nazar's fingers curled, and white-hot pain speared through her limbs before he flicked his wrist, and her body slammed into a wall of trees.

The air loosened its hold on her, sending her crashing to the ground and slumping forward. She sucked in a ragged breath, moaning when her broken ribs shifted painfully against her dented armour.

She scrambled to her feet as Nazar stalked towards her. Bile rose in her throat at the overwhelming pain that accompanied her every movement. Eyeing her discarded blade, Hazen leaned on the tree she had slammed into, feeling it slowly give way under her weight.

Nazar's hand snapped out, claws dug into her neck, his nails tearing away her flesh.

Hazen's screams travelled the forest, pain shooting through her body like hot livewires.

"The undead do not fear anything, Keeper!" he snarled.

Her eyes widened, seeing black shadows ripple across his skin. Then his words sunk in, and a slow cutting smirk slipped over her lips despite herself and the iron grip he had on her throat. "Didn't you hear?" she rasped, chuckling. "I'm not the keeper."

Red eyes narrowed on her.

Hazen couldn't help but laugh, feeling the power in her veins build and build until it erupted, and her skin glowed with its surge. Biting through the pain, she reared her head forward and smashed it against Nazar's face. Hazen heard his nose crunch. Willing strength into her limbs, fire and light wrapped around her hands as she slowly pried his claws from her neck. One by one. The thin bones in his hand snapped under her grip, and Nazar screamed in outrage.

Fire ignited her blood, she shoved the shade with every ounce of strength left in her, the shadows vanishing in the light. He stumbled, and genuine shock sketched his horrible face.

Wiping the back of her hand across her bloody mouth, Hazen staggered to her sword. Bending slowly, she kept her eyes on Nazar and grabbed her weapon, straightening.

Nazar laughed coldly, waving a hand over his nose the cartilage fixed itself with a loud pop. "For one that claims not to be the keeper, your magic surpasses you."

"It's not magic," she spat, raising her sword. "It's pure power.

And I'm going to use it to cut your ugly head off your fucking body."

Chin raised at her threat and a sneer on his face; black tar trailed Nazar's skin as his essence was drawn out. Shadows took up his image until she was surrounded by at least two dozen of him.

They all grinned wickedly back at her, pointed and salivating, and asked, "Which of us will you cut down now?"

Black mist shrouded the ground, crawling its way towards Hazen. Skin prickling, the air turned frigid, and she felt her insides begin to freeze, her fire wavering faintly within.

Without warning, the shadow figures lunged.

Hazen raised her sword, slicing through one and watching it disappear, only for another to take its place. Nazar's cackles filled the air, and they all leapt for her.

Another.

And another.

And another.

Until Hazen stood panting, the dented cuirass pressing painfully into her side, her arms wavering to keep her sword up.

"The dragons chose *you*?" Nazar sneered, laughing softly. The sound was like nails down her spine. "My, my, my, how pitiful. I guess the Gods do have fallibility, and so do their precious dragons. So much *power*, and you don't know how to use it."

Hazen's heart stuttered, but she tightened her grip around the sword. From beyond the murderous faces, she saw the real Nazar cock his head and watch her like an animal watching its food. The smile he sent her way made fear burn inside of her.

"Goodbye, Chosen One," the real Nazar said.

She had a brief image of him walking away before his shadows all smiled in the ashen world, and the darkness shot for her like an arrow. Hazen barely took in a sharp breath before they consumed her, and the fire within went out.

Levina sobbed. Baring her teeth when pain erupted across her pelvis and back. She let out a muffled scream, clamping her hand over her mouth. Sweat coated her body, dotting her upper lip and dripping down her neck.

She held the iron bars of her cell door in a death grip, bowed over, cradling her belly when the pain receded. Panting, she stared at the black floor. Her body began to shake, feeling the pressure building again, and she squeezed the bars until it felt like she didn't know which would snap first, the bars or her hand.

Footsteps filled her cell, and through the wave of building pain and pressure between her thighs, she was vaguely aware of Laudin hovering by her door.

"What do you want!" she screamed through clenched teeth, feeling the need to push. Her voice carried in the cell and through the tiny bars of the door into the hall.

When she looked up, Laudin watched her with entirely black eyes.

Panting, she screamed again, her jaw threatening to snap, but she kept her eyes on the male. If he so much as made to enter her cell, she would tear him limb for limb.

Laudin smiled faintly. "When the babe is born, I'm going to enjoy killing it in front of you. And then I'm going to leave you here to rot with its corpse."

The darkness in Levina reared its ugly head, she could feel the demons she repressed over the years trying to crawl out. But she shoved them down and snarled, "If you even breathe in my baby's direction, I will tear your lungs from your chest!"

He snorted softly, and she watched him back up to lean against the wall across from her cell. Arms folded and black eyes gazing into her little prison. "I'll be waiting."

Her retort died on her tongue when the pressure became overwhelming between her legs. Crying, she bit down, doubled over, and fought the urge to push. Her screams tore the air.

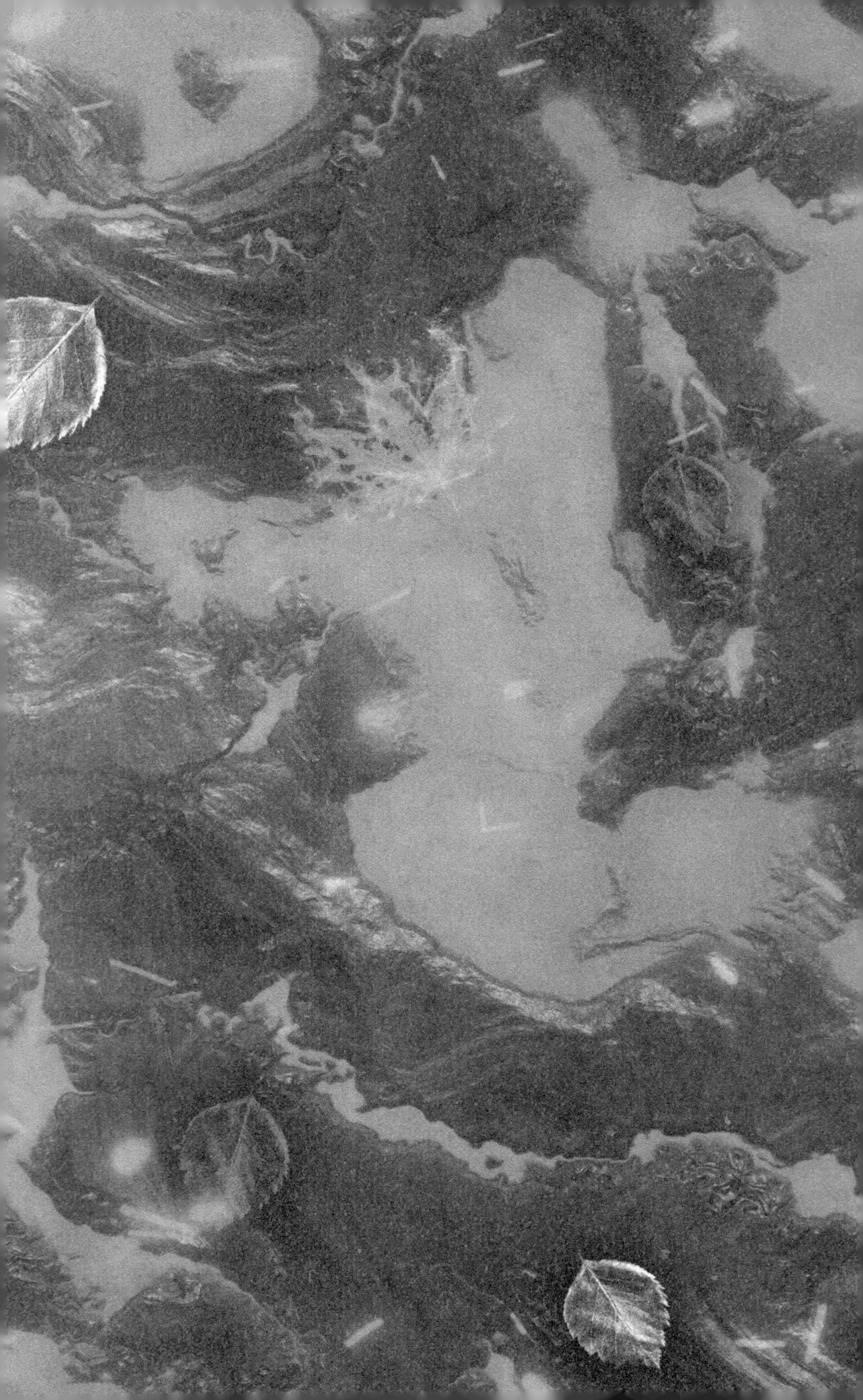

# CHAPTER 36

Savven ripped his sword from the chest of a gorgon. The half serpent hissed violently, arms outstretched. It swiped for him, and Savven spun out of reach. Bringing his sword around, the blade carved a clean line through its upper torso, and he watched the life blink from existence before the gorgon's body parted in two.

Grime from battle mixed with sweat. It had stopped raining, and the ground turned to slush under his feet. The moor was a tangle of trampled grassland and death that threatened to trip him if the bodies didn't first.

He watched his soldiers fall and his friends die, and the demons kept coming like a tidal wave. Muscles fatigued, his magic doing nothing but shielding him from the inevitable as jaws and teeth came snapping for him. He couldn't do more than raise a shield of magic around him before he parried with a blow of his own.

Looking over his shoulder, he saw the familiar red hair and amber eyes narrowed with ferocity. Brean was a constant at his back. For every body he laid down, she followed. Having discarded her bow in the fray for a sword, they had made their way through the onslaught together.

Brean met his gaze. Exhaustion danced behind the adrenaline he saw in her stare, her freckled face coated in streaks of black and red. She had never looked more stunning and dangerous.

She shot him a quick smirk before whirling out of the reach of an undead Fae female whose sword arced over her head. She cut the female across the knees, and she went toppling to the ground. The female bared her teeth at Brean, and Savven watched the witch cut the smile from her face.

When the female didn't move, Brean looked over her shoulder at him. The wicked grin on her face fell, and her skin blanched. "Savven!" she gasped.

Savven frowned, quickly following her gaze. The colour drained from his face, and a stone dropped in his stomach.

Nazar stepped from the tree line, his white hair and red eyes visible even from where they stood in the middle of the moor. To their right was the crater left from Brean's trap.

At the rise of his outstretched hands, darkness shot from the ground. Like the chaos of a thousand storms, thick clouds of poisonous shadows rocketed through the air.

Savven watched, horrified, as those who still lived fell, and all of life was extinguished. He whipped back around, Brean sprinting towards him. He met her halfway and pulled her to him, wrapping his arms around her petite body and using his back as a shield.

"Close your eyes, Brean," he whispered against the top of her head, pulling the last dregs of his magic up to make a shield around them.

Her fingers balled into his shirt, and she craned her head back to look at him. He held her stare, drowning in the fiery amber depths, even as the darkness consumed them, shattering the magic, and they fell into the abyss.

*It was warm. Whatever afterlife she was in was warm and bright, Hazen had to blink several times when she opened her eyes. She stood in a forest filled with long-limbed birch trees, their orange and yellow leaves fluttering in a warm breeze. The ground was soft with black dirt underfoot, Hazen's booted feet wiggled back at her when she looked down. She was dressed in her black leathers, hair loose down her back and untangled. The armour was gone, the grime was cleaned, and her bones were whole.*

*"Hello."*

*A familiar voice was met with an unfamiliar face as she turned.*

*A female with small, delicate features and startling green eyes stood before Hazen. She wore a beautiful gossamer lavender gown, braids interwoven through golden hair that fell loose down her back leaving the tips of her arched ears poking through.*

*The female clasped her hands in front of her. "I'm assuming we are blood-kin. You're in the Haven."*

*Hazen studied the female carefully, head tilting in thought. "Grandmother?" They shared similar features. Despite the colouring of their eyes and the softness of the other female, Hazen could swear she was looking into a mirror.*

*Beaming, the female stepped up to her. "Is that what I am to you? A great mother?"*

*Laughing under her breath, Hazen said, "Something similar. You are my father's mother and my... elder."*

*Humming, the female nodded her head in understanding. "I see. Well, what should I call you, my greatdaughter?"*

*The title alone made Hazen laugh freely. Weaving through her loose hair, the wind carried her laughter into the golden forest. "Hazen," she said, gathering her amusement.*

*"Hazen, my greatdaughter, I am Adanessa. Welcome to the Haven."*

*A thought pressed on her mind, and Hazen asked, "Am I dead?"*

*Adanessa smiled softly. "Yes, in a sense. Not quite gone, but not quite there, either."*

*Hazen brushed her fingers down a stalk of fluttering yellow, orange, and red leaves. "What is this place?"*

*"It is a token of our magic, our essence, passed through the females of our line. We imbue a seed of our magic into a gem, and each generation is tasked with carrying or protecting it."*

*Hazen's hand went to her neck, but the necklace was gone.*

*Adanessa noted her movements and smiled knowingly. "You would find it missing if you were wearing it because you are within its confines now."*

*"I'm in the necklace?" Hazen clarified, sceptical.*

*"Well..." Adanessa paused, thinking. "Part of you is. Your body isn't."*

*Hazen looked up at the blue sky, thick fluffy clouds floating overhead, and then at the stretch of willowy trees spanned in every direction. It was beautiful here, untouched and untainted.*

*"Think of this place as a refuge for your soul," Adanessa continued. "Something terrible must have happened for you to come here. The Haven is reserved for those of our lineage who need protection."*

*"Something terrible did happen," Hazen murmured.*

*Her grandmother waited patiently, watching her with a small smile.*

*"I have to go back," Hazen said grimly. "If I don't, then Nazar wins."*

*"Well, if you go back, then you're going to die," said an unimpressed female voice.*

*Hazen whipped around, and her heart nearly stopped in her chest.*

*Rose stood leaning against one of the trees, dressed in a simple, nearly sheer white gown draped across her collarbones. Long split sleeves showed off her toned arms crossed over her chest. The long branches swaying in the wind half obscured her face, her light almond skin and pale blonde hair glowing in the sunlight. Gold eyes assessed Hazen with open judgment.*

*"She's right." Adanessa stepped up beside Hazen tilting her head at the first keeper. "Hello, Rose. I was wondering when you would show yourself."*

*"I'm sorry, what?" Hazen demanded, looking between the two females. "Why is she here?!"*

*Rose scoffed, pushing off the tree. "The Haven is passed from female to female in the lineage. Who do you think created it?"*

*Hazen's eyes went wide, and she shook her head in denial. "You're not saying... you can't be... I barely know my grandparents on my father's side. Now you're saying I have an ancient bloodline that started when the world began?"*

*"Just because you don't know the past doesn't mean it doesn't exist." Rose prowled towards them, a look of cool assessment on her stunning face. She was beautiful in an unearthly way. She had large gold eyes, light blonde brows that slanted up, and a narrow jaw framed by high cheekbones.*

*"You've murdered thousands," Hazen said slowly. "Tatius showed me." But even as she said those words, her heart ached. She had seen Rose's eyes before her death. She had seen the sorrow and her relief.*

*"Tatius showed a version of the past," Rose snapped, a wave of simmering anger behind her molten gaze. "My soul hears the stories from beyond the Haven. About me. About what apparently happened. A jilted lover, greedy, power-hungry, a disgrace, the reason the keepers are now half-breeds of the Fae."*

*The term half-breed made Hazen flinch despite herself.*

*Rose's laugh was bitter and harsh in the beautiful forest. "What they don't know is that the Gods and their pet dragons regretted not allowing themselves control of their own creations. So, they put their powers into one of them and tried to see if they could find a way around their own laws. But that much power in one not created for it calls for destruction." Regret and that same sorrow filled her stare, and her jaw worked as she chewed on her following words. "They made me into a weapon and realised they couldn't control me like they had hoped. So, when the Fae rose up with armies at their commands to bring me down, and I slaughtered them all, the Gods were forced to kill me themselves and face their defeat."*

*Flashes of history filled Hazen's mind with what Tatius had shown her. The death, the bodies, the blood, and Rose standing in the middle of it all.*

*"Tatius is the God of Death, and she is playing her own games. So, for whatever reason you're here, she has a hand in it. And it is why you were filled with the first dragon fire. My dragon fire. You and I are connected, Hazen. By blood and by condemning circumstance."*

*"But it's not fire, not just fire," Hazen corrected, shifting her weight.*

*Rose shook her head. "No. It's not. It's first light mixed with the first dragons' fire. It's the power of creation."*

*"That's why it burns even the Drago." It wasn't a question. Hazen had suspected for a long time that her fire wasn't just fire but something entirely different.*

"The Drago." Rose snorted. "They were created by the dragons and were the last army to try and kill me. But their thoughts of victory soon changed when they realised I was now part dragon as they were and held power that could burn them."

Hazen glanced at the air behind Rose, remembering her gold wings. They weren't there. "Where are they? Your wings."

"Hiding. Like yours."

Brow's knitting, Hazen tilted her head in confusion. "I don't have wings."

Rose turned her left shoulder and pulled down the neckline of her gown. The light brown skin was marked with a silver scar that looked like a web of wings crawling down her bicep, over her shoulder, and across her back. "You have one, too."

Hazen turned and showed her left shoulder. An identical scar tattooed her skin.

"If you had taken the immortal cup, you would have seen the full extent of your power and true form for yourself."

She gave Rose a tight smile. "Well, cry me a river. Because it's over and done with now."

Sighing, Rose turned to Adanessa, who stood quietly by Hazen's side. The first keeper's expression softened. "It's time for us to go, Adanessa."

Adanessa's smile turned beaming, and she grabbed Hazen's hand, holding it warmly between them. "I hope to see you again, Greatdaughter."

Before Hazen could open her mouth to reply, Adanessa vanished in the wind that gently blew.

"You refused the immortal cup. You're a fool for that, but," Rose paused, thinking over her next words, "I can respect it. The Gods cannot control what they do not have. Your mortality is your greatest shield from their power. You are still free to decide what happens because you are not bound by Fae law."

Shifting, Hazen regarded the first keeper from head to foot, cocking her brow. "What would happen if you helped me? Would you cease to exist? Would I become immortal?"

"Yes, I would cease to exist, but I have lived a very, very long life in this Haven, and even my soul grows tired. And no, you wouldn't become immortal. I don't quite have that power, unfortunately. Otherwise, it would have been my first order upon your arrival here."

*Realisation settled in Hazen, and she licked her lips, rolling her shoulders back. Sticking out her hand, she looked Rose in the eye. Her ancestor, her blood, her past, her present, and her future. "Then help me. Fight with me. Let's take back the power—together."*

*Rose's grin was wicked, and her gold eyes shone brightly. "I thought you would never ask." And she slid her hand into Hazen's. The power that bathed the Haven was blinding.*

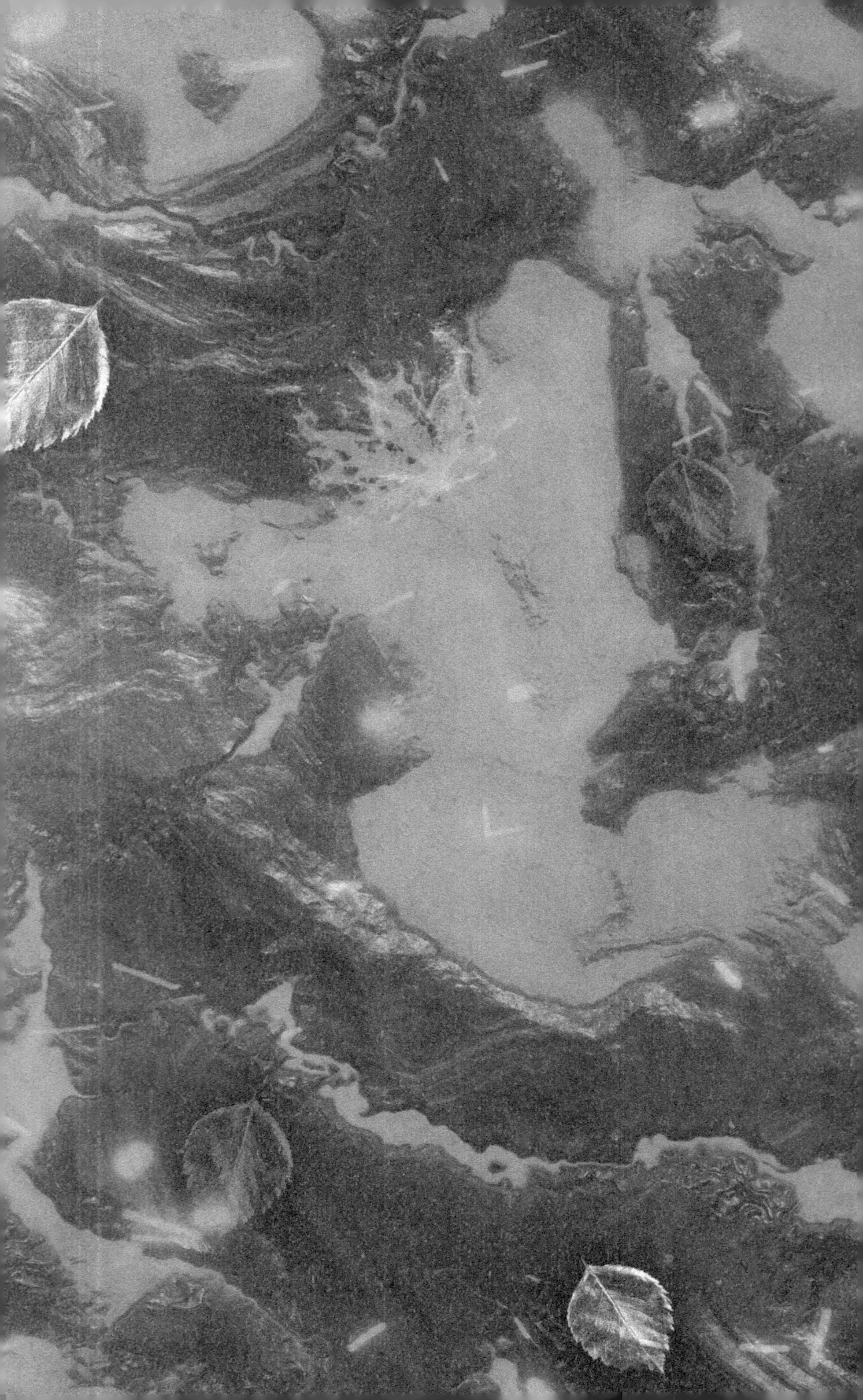

# CHAPTER 37

Bright, radiant light began to penetrate the ashen world, spearing through the limp body on the ground, covered head to foot in ash, until there was nothing but light in the bleak forest. Every shadow and crevice was laid bare. The world was bathed in it as the mass on the ground shot into the sky.

Breaking through the treetops, branches and leaves crumpling like ashen dust, Hazen launched higher and higher into the clouds like a glowing arrow. Large golden wings erupted from her back and flared wide, and she caught herself before she fell.

Power raced through her body, free and new. Something unfamiliar settled in her bones, a sense of sureness like she knew this world from the time of her birth. Rose's consciousness flowed through her, guiding the instincts that Hazen did not yet possess.

Hazen raised a hand to stare openly in awe at her glowing skin. It looked like starlight. Her wings pulsed, flapping behind her, as though she'd been doing it her entire life. Thankfully, her muscles were well trained after Åsmund's gruelling regimen, like he had known all along that she had wings and helped build the foundation for when they would appear.

Below her, the world was a graveyard. Not a soul stirred, and ash coated bodies like snow. The trees, the moor, and beyond were pale and grey, life did not exist within its borders.

A roar rattled the clouds, and Nazar's dragon dove under the dark sky, wings cutting through the air. Massive jaws snapped for her, and Hazen shot out of the way, the thin gold leather of her wings carrying her fast and steady through the air.

The dragon was close behind, its hot breath sliding along her legs. Hazen pushed herself higher. The air became thin and colder, the world a swirling abstract thing below, gravity was non-existent. A dark expanse of the universe lay ahead of her, and for a moment, she saw only the stars and vast nothingness.

Her body floated, weightless, for a breath. It was the feeling of freedom that consumed her, that pulsed through her veins and made her heart sing. She was flying.

Reality came crashing back in when a roar shook the sky at her back, and Hazen smiled to herself. Closing her eyes, wings tucking tight to her body, she fell back into the world like a falling star. Glowing and golden in the darkness.

The world spun uncontrollably, but her eyes fixed on the black dragon, its shadow wings melting in the clouds. Its red eyes narrowed on her with hunger. Black shadows erupted from its maw instead of fire, and the grin that spread on Hazen's face was deadly.

*"Now..."*

The voice in her head was commanding, both her own and not. And she listened. She grasped the power funnelling through her veins and held fast, letting it rise and rise until white fire coated her wings, hands, and arms.

And she dove right into its gaping mouth with a ruthless scream.

Darkness, shadows, and nightmares clawed for her, but they couldn't touch her. Her firelight was blinding and consuming, and she shot right through the mass of shadows and ash until grey light opened, and she ripped through the dragon.

Its scream was chilling, like the screams of a thousand beasts. But Hazen didn't halt her fall, even when the dragon imploded. Light beams from her white fire speared across its body, finally the remnants of its shadowy form fell like ashen snow.

The ground rose to meet her, and she flared her wings wide. The gold leather snapped out before she impacted, and she flipped her body upright. Landing hard and fast in one of the few patches of dead earth that didn't have a body covering it. Ash billowed around her, and she straightened, tucking her wings in.

No one was standing. Not a single life remained. The world before her was cold, decayed, and covered in a soft, downy layer of grey cinders.

Soft applause echoed in the air, and Hazen whirled. Nazar watched her with cold red eyes as he applauded her, his nearly sheer shroud misting around him as if it too was made from his shadows.

"I had hoped you would survive." His voice was twisted and cold, eyes flickering to her wings. "Ah... how I would love to *rip* those from your body." His tongue slithered out as if tasting her blood that had yet to be spilt.

Hazen smirked at him, inclining her head. "Come and try."

Nazar's amusement fell, and he lunged for her.

Hazen's feet dug into the sopping earth, and she charged towards the shade.

Shadows and firelight met in a collision of sparks that showered the battlement. Hazen was lost in a sea of darkness, Nazar's pale, sickly face nowhere to be seen. Her fire struck out, lashing against the demon claws that reached for her. Hissing filled the air, talons and claws retracting back into darkness.

Nazar was a flurry in the shadows that bounced off her light. Hazen snarled, charging at him when she saw him vanish ahead of her.

The darkness was a consuming tunnel, but Hazen didn't falter, even when she felt the bodies press under her boots. Wings flaring, she shot into the air, eyes narrowed on the patch of black before her. A fire burned hot in the core of her being, wrapping around her arm, and she shot it through the void in a blazing ball. Faces lit up the shadows for nanoseconds, withering and screaming silently, all piled atop one another before the fire passed, and they were submerged into the abyss again.

She felt those trapped in the shadows clawing for her—the souls Nazar feasted on. They were trapped within his chasm, consumed by him, and forced to spend eternity in torment.

Gritting her teeth, Hazen made her wings move faster. The air sliced her face, or maybe those were nails trying to drag her under, but she snarled and let her firelight fly again and again and again until it punched through the chasm.

Hazen tore out of the darkness, Nazar waiting for her with a menacing grin.

He lifted his hands, and twisting vines of dark magic tore through the ground and speared for her.

She dodged one twisting in front of her, but she screamed when black magic struck her stomach, her dented cuirass reminding her power-hazed brain that her bones were broken. Hazen's body twisted through the air violently, her wings unable to catch her, and the world whirled in her vision.

Crashing across the field, her body tumbled once, then twice, the bite of pain stealing her breath, and she saw stars as her head smashed against the side of a forgotten mallet.

Blinking the blur in her vision away, Hazen saw the dark vines twisting over body after body, crawling towards her. A shiver ran down her spine, making her wings twitch, and she shoved herself up onto to her knees. Pain jarred her torso, a large dent in the abdomen of her armour. Grimacing, Hazen lifted a shaking hand to the leather straps at her shoulders, holding it together. The metal fell away, and relief filled her lungs.

Hazen braced on the mallet she had hit, making to stand, but paused when she saw the fallen around her.

Ice doused the fire in her, and the glow of her power faded.

Åsmund stared up at the sky. Dead.

Rage and grief and pain spliced her, tears instantly burned her wide eyes. Hazen fell towards him, crawling to his side. Her shaking hand hovered over his still face. He was coated in cinders, disguised with the rest of the dead. His wings ripped from his body, dried blood caking the corners of his mouth, and the sky reflected in his eyes.

"Åsmund," she whispered brokenly. Hot, bitter tears raced down her cheeks, but she couldn't tell if it was from anger or grief that she cried.

Pressing her hand to his chest, hoping to feel it rise, it didn't move. His skin was as cold as ice.

Hazen sucked in a sharp breath, and the fire in her blazed, her power rising to the surface. And she *burned* with it. Leaning forward, her skin glowing against his grey body, she pressed her lips to his, tasting death, and whispered, "You were a beautiful dream." Her tears dotted his ash-coated cheeks. Gently, she closed his eyes, her chest aching and tearing in two.

Forcing herself to stand, Hazen staggered to her feet. Dressed in only her black leathers, strands of her braided hair were wild around her face, and her eyes burned with anger. She grasped onto her power, the cord of it burning hot and true in her body. She was an unending chasm of fire and light as she whipped to face the black magic.

A spear of darkness aimed for her, and she dodged the first one, spinning when the second came for her face, but the third was poised for her chest. Hazen twisted as her hand automatically jabbed out, and her fingers wrapped around the darkness. Her glowing skin a stark contrast against the writhing black vine. It burned her hand, but her lips curled back, baring her teeth, and she forced her firelight to rise until it wrapped around the vine. The shadows didn't disperse. There was nowhere for them to go but closer to themselves as the light caged them in.

With a guttural scream, she crushed the darkness with her light until nothing was left.

Nazar's red eyes darted between her and the air where his shadows had been. True shock marred his horrible face.

Rolling her shoulders back, she stalked slowly towards Nazar, who took a hesitant step back. With a single thought, a javelin of light and fire was crafted in her hands. She wasn't prey, she was the predator, and she was really fucking tired.

Arching her arm back, Hazen let the javelin fly with a wild cry. Crafting another and another and another until they sailed one after the other, straight for her mark.

His shadows shot from the ground, trying to deflect, but they were too slow. Light pierced Nazar's shoulders and both his thighs. His body launched back under the assault before being pinned to the earth. His magic sank back into the ground like a slithering serpent.

The shade struggled against the light penetrating him, the javelins creating a ring around his body, bright and burning. His demons had nowhere to run.

"How does it feel?" Hazen asked softly, stopping above him and tilting her head.

"What?" he hissed, jerking against his restraints.

Kneeling beside Nazar, Hazen grabbed a forgotten sword caked in aged blood and ash and stood, smiling faintly. "Knowing you're about to die?"

"You can't kill what is already dead," he sneered, his eyes turning bright, shadows pressing along his carved skin.

Hazen regarded him thoughtfully, nodding in understanding, before lifting the blade and looking between it and the shade as her firelight twined down the steel. "The dead can't survive without their head." She lifted the sword above her.

"Wait!" Nazar screamed, twisting in the light as if it burned him, and then he started to cackle. "It's not over yet. You kill me, but my darkness will live on! It will destroy you and this world, but we can make a deal. Make a deal with me. I will give you power beyond what you already know. I will give you the world!"

Hazen's smirk turned amused, and she arched her arm back. "That sounds like somebody else's problem."

Nazar's head rolled from his shoulders, fear frozen on his screaming face. The power coating the blade surged through his body at contact, his shadows had nowhere to flee as they were devoured. Nazar's skeletal frame imploded, and black soot scorched the earth where he had lain.

Dropping the sword, her power faded enough for fatigue to set in. Her body felt like lead, and her limbs started to shake when the fire dwindled back to that flickering ember, she stumbled. The power had consumed her, taken parts of her, and moulded itself to fit her mortal body; now, she felt hollow, stretched too thin. She glanced at her shoulder when an ache shot through it, seeing the gouges that had been cauterised by the fire; all that was left were pink scars.

A bright golden glow came from her back, and her wings disappeared.

Hazen flexed her shoulder muscles, there was a lightness to them without the wings. The soft warmth emanating from the scar on her back was the only reminder that they had been there.

With a shuddering breath, Hazen turned towards the wreckage of the world. A sob broke free the longer she stared. What was once beautiful was just a shell. Brittle bones of a stunning land. Trees crumpled to piles of downy ash the longer they stood, unable to hold their weight. The sea of bodies seemed vaster than the sea beyond the moor.

A soft wind brushed her cheeks, and when she raised her fingertips to her face, they came away wet with her tears. The air wasn't bitter any longer, the turbulent sky settled, and rain slowly began to fall. Misting across the moor, the forest, and beyond. Like the world was trying to cleanse away the destruction that watered its grounds.

Hazen found herself walking towards her general, her body trembling with pain. But it wasn't physical pain that made her shake, though she felt that too. This was emotional pain. Pain that cleaved its way down to her soul and made her feel like it was being ripped from her body.

She stood over Åsmund, his green eyes now closed, his face relaxed. And she wanted nothing more than to kneel beside him, brush the strands of his hair away, and trace the plains of his face. To memorise the stubborn, stoic general she had come to care for. But Hazen knew if she knelt to the ground, her body wouldn't have the strength to make her stand. So, she stayed, looking down at him. Her tears mixing with the soft pattering of rain.

"You were right," she whispered into the silence. "I have wings. And I wish you could have seen them." Her throat burned with the force of her emotions, and she forced in a calming breath, blinking rapidly. When she gathered her strength, she gave Åsmund one last smile, the ends of her mouth curling slightly, and spoke her last promise to him, "I will see you again in the next life."

Hazen forced herself to walk on, otherwise she would stay frozen with him in time. Her heart chipped away with every step, still she kept her eyes scanning the faces. Both Fae, undead, and creatures alike laid at rest. There was no difference in who they were or what side they fought for. They had all bled together. They had all died together.

Her feet froze beside a pair of lovers. The female's hair was midnight, spilt around her like ink, her one arm stretched protectively over the male beneath her, the other was gone. Hazen sucked in a deep shuddering breath when she noticed it was Néefar, his neck ripped out on one side. And when she walked around them, she saw Anabelle's face.

Lips trembling, Hazen gritted her jaw tightly and made herself walk on, carefully stepping over the dead. Her muscles were screaming with fatigue, but she willed herself to keep going. Warmth blossomed in her limbs, her fire, and something else, an essence lent to her, wove through her muscles and let her walk on.

She made it to the middle of the moor, the stretch of forest behind her, and the sea before her as sheets of mist and light rain coated her grimy skin. She stopped beside the long stretch of the crater that had been a river and observed her friends who lay beside it. They looked like lovers. Savven's arms wrapped protectively around Brean, her face cradled against his chest, their legs interwoven like they had embraced before they met their ends.

Hazen didn't know what to say to them. Savven had protected her, dealt with her stubbornness, trained her, and humoured her. But above all, he had been her friend. So, she did the only thing she could think of doing. Hazen dipped her chin at them, her sadness lingering in her smile as she whispered, "Thank you."

Leaving her friends, the fallen lovers, and her general behind,

Hazen trekked across the field for the last time and faced the towering remains of the forest. Ash fell in time with the rain. Hazen licked her lips, breathing deeply, smoothing a hand down her leathers and over her hair. She took one more look over her shoulder. Taking in the world she had been thrown into, had survived, had learned, lived, loved, and cherished. And the faces and memories she would take with her wherever she went. Garnering her courage, she stepped into the forest.

It was quiet, like a tomb. Her sword glinted under the grey light, and Hazen stooped to pick it up. The ruby in the eye of the dragon's head twinkled back at her. The altar was cracked in half, concaved. Even stone could not withstand the decay Nazar had brought.

Stumbling, the power keeping her upright began to wane. Hazen walked around the ruined altar, her eyes trailing the broken language etched into its top.

*'All ends have a beginning.'*

Digging deep, Hazen closed her eyes, feeling the rush of heat and fire fill her veins despite her exhaustion. Igniting a blazing path down her arms to the tip of the blade she held in her right hand until she burned brightly. The world turned translucent, and she followed the now black veins beneath the earth to where they stopped, a shimmering iridescent sheen to the air in front of her.

Stepping up to the veil, she waved her hands over it, watching it shimmer like water. Her neck prickled, and she glanced over her left shoulder. No one was there, physically at least, but the eyes of the Gods were on her now. As if they held their breaths in reverence to what was coming.

Hazen raised her eyes to the veil, lifting her sword. The polished silver was speckled with dried blood, but her reflection stared back at her all the same. She blinked, and when Hazen opened her eyes, it wasn't her face she saw anymore.

Rose smiled faintly back at her. Her gold eyes shone, and serenity filled the beautiful, angled plains of her face. "Live, blood of my blood, and live well."

Her voice filled Hazen's head, and when she blinked, Rose was gone.

The world seemed to slow, time pausing, and it felt like her life was flashing before her eyes as she arced the first blade back, bathed in firelight. All the good and bad moments, all the faces she met along the way, and the stories she was a part of. She brought it down, and the blade drew through the air like nothing was there.

And then the world went still, and cracks of light filled the air in front of her, stretching as far as she could see. Like the world was splitting before her eyes.

Her hands fell to her sides, and Hazen stumbled back, dropping the sword to the ground. The wind picked up, strands of hair whipped violently across her face, swirling ash blinding her. She brought a hand to her eyes, wiping at the cinders, gasping for breath as the air grew dense and thick, and she choked on it.

Pain filled her chest, her broken ribs screaming with every breath, and Hazen dropped to her knees. Head spinning, vision cloudy, the wind roared in her ears, drowning out the wild hammer of her heart.

Darkness enclosed her vision, and her body swayed as breathing became harder and harder until she finally fell to her side. The pain that split up her ribs at impact made her want to scream, but she didn't have enough air, and she gasped for breath instead.

The air shimmered with golden light, the cracks spreading, and in her fading vision, Hazen watched the veil explode before she was knocked into the waiting abyss.

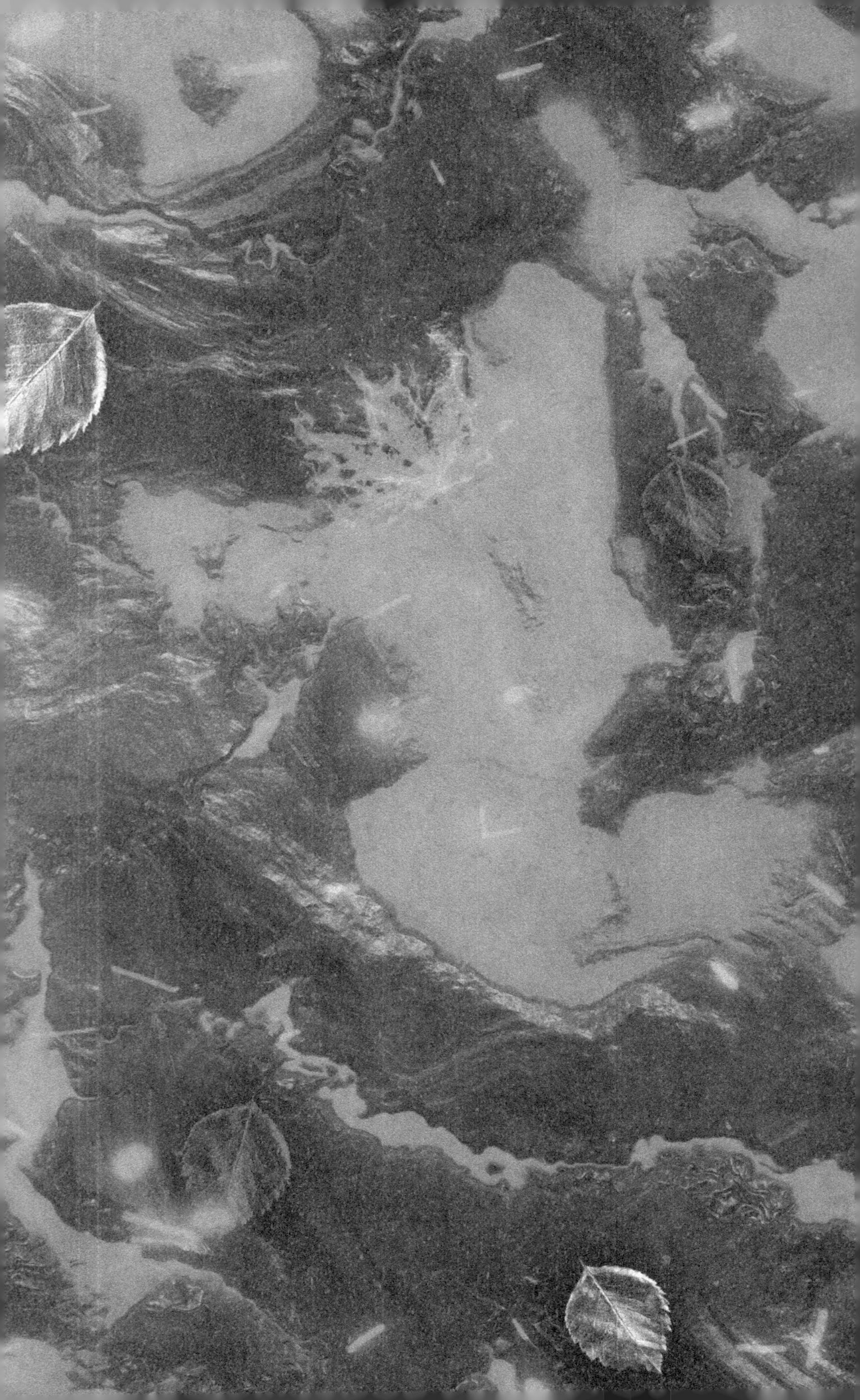

# CHAPTER 38

Terror made tiny limbs tremble. Screams and jeering pierced her ears, and Brean whimpered, smashing her hands over them to mute the sounds. She hid behind a large wooden barrel along the edge of the village square. A black cape was strewn over her shoulders and pale brown dress, its large hood hiding her unruly bright red curls.

Villagers passed her with lit torches, their faces twisted into ugly smiles. Brean shrunk into herself, eyes peaking over the rim of the barrel. They didn't notice her. She was too little, and their gazes were fixed on the Hangman's noose and the woman who stood beside it.

Still in the dark purple dress she had been wearing when they took her, though soiled and torn, hands bound in chains, her ankles shackled so she couldn't run, Brean stared at her mother with large, watery amber eyes, and her shaking got worse. Her mother wasn't the only woman there bound in chains. A line of nearly sixty females stood at the stairs leading up to their fate; the faces of some were tight with anger, while others were forlorn with fear.

Thunder clapped overhead, and Brean glanced at the storm threatening above. Where was her papa? He had shoved her behind the barrels and vanished.

Bushels of sticks tied together were piled atop one another under the Hangman's post. They planned to burn them once they were dead.

"Do not be afraid, my little love. Mama's with you." Those had been her final whispered words to her before she pressed a fierce kiss to her forehead and shoved Brean into a hay cart.

When Brean had emerged, pieces of hay tangled in her hair, soldiers had taken her mother, who had spat in their faces, snarling at them to do their worst. She watched them strike her mother across the face and shackle her before tossing her into a cart with iron bars.

Her mother had gazed at her until they vanished from view, and now Brean stared at her, wishing she could do something—protect her, take those chains off her!

She had run back to their little cottage, her feet barely keeping her upright until she ran right to her father's leather apron-clad legs and bawled until her nose was ruddy. Screaming at him what happened.

Brean's father had dressed her the next day, bundled her in her cloak, and scooped her into his large arms. Telling her she must remain very quiet as they entered the village and walked to the town square.

Now, she was watching a man walk up the stairs to the platform, pointedly ignoring her mother. He had a scroll in his hands and stood at the edge of the Hangman's stage. Opening the scroll, he cleared his throat.

The crowd quieted, listening.

"Upon this day in West Lothian County on the 16th of June in the year of our Lord 1590, his majesty King James the Sixth decrees the hanging and burning of all persons conspiring with the works of the Devil. This proceeding will follow sixty-two souls to their deaths. They will each have an opportunity to repent for their sins. May they find peace in their judgements."

The announcer's voice was carried, monotoned and loud across every head that filled the square.

After he finished, the crowd began to yell: "Burn the witch!" "Snap her neck!" "Devil worshipper!"

Hot tears tore down Brean's cheeks, and she sniffled, shaking her head. Her mama wasn't any of those things. Magic was good. It helped. The herbs she made for their neighbours, and when Brean was sick, her mama made her feel better with them. She didn't hurt anyone!

Where was Papa? Brean fanatically scanned the square, searching for his large frame, familiar red hair, and green eyes. But her head jerked when she heard her mother's name.

"Sorcha McKenzie, do you repent for the sins you have committed, lest you burn for eternity?" the announcer asked loudly, reading from the scroll.

Her mother scanned the crowd. She looked like she was trying to find someone, and Brean wanted to stand on the barrels and wave her hands in the air to catch her attention. She wanted to scream, "I'm here, Mama! I'm here!" But instead, she kept low like her papa had instructed, her cheeks splotchy and wet from tears.

Raising her chin in defiance, her mother spoke with a soft burr, barely loud enough for the crowd to hear, "I have committed no sins. I am a good mother, a good wife, and my spirit will live on with them."

The announcer raised a brow as if disinterested, but Brean could see the twisted, cruel smile on his mouth. "You refuse to repent for your works with the Devil. May you burn for eternity. Hang the witch."

The screams for her to hang were deafening, and Brean squeezed her hands over her ears again, shaking her head back and forth.

The sky rumbled overhead, and the noose was placed around her mother's neck. Her mother bowed her head as if she were being crowned, a look of resignation on her soft round face, her amber eyes and wild blonde curls shining despite what was about to come. There was no fear in her mother, and Brean slowly lowered her hands. If her mother was not afraid, then neither would she be.

*'Hang the witch' was chanted repeatedly like a song, and Brean's heart was the drum.*

*Her breaths came in short gasps, her chest heaving with each one, her eyes wide and glassy.*

*The Hangman walked to the lever beside her mother, who still stood reverent.*

*Time seemed to slow. The Hangman pulled the leaver. Brean screamed. Her mother closed her eyes. Her father sprinted from the onlookers towards his wife. "Release my wife!" he screamed as the floor opened under her. Someone swung a torch at her father's head, and he crumpled to the ground. Her mother's neck snapped, the sound cracking through the air, at the same time the thunder clapped violently. The sound etched into Brean's soul.*

*Then time really did freeze. Every face, every movement, paused in the moment.*

"So, this is your Hel? Interesting."

Brean shook, still huddled behind the barrels, as a girl older than her, no more than thirteen years, looked down at her. "Who are you?" she asked in a wobbling voice, eyes darting between the girl, her mother, and her father.

The girl held out a hand. "Stand, Brean McKenzie."

Brean, hesitating, put her hand in the girl's. When she stood, she wasn't a child but her full-grown self. The nightmare changed, shifting around her until the battlement stood on her right and merged into the day of her parent's deaths on her left.

No matter where she looked, the dead surrounded her, and Brean shuddered.

"I want to make a deal with you," the girl said directly.

Amber eyes flashed to the girl, studying her. Black nondescript gown, shoulder-length black hair, and depthless black eyes. "Who are you?" she asked cautiously.

"I am Tatius, the God of Death."

"And you want to make a bargain with me?"

Tatius gave her a bored stare. "Do I need to repeat myself?"

"No," Brean murmured, shaking her head once, eyes locked on her mother, "you don't."

Tatius followed her gaze. "You kept your secret well. Your friends never knew you were a human witch before the veil saved you."

More memories flashed in Brean's mind, but they didn't play out like her mother's execution. Memories of her running for her life as the village searched for the witch's child who was seen doing magic. Brean closed her eyes to the images, gritting her teeth.

"What do you want?" she demanded, pushing her emotions down.

Tatius's mouth tilted into a shadow of a smirk. "I need you to live. So, I'm going to bring you back. But in return, I need you to do something for me."

Brean studied the God before looking at the stretch of the battlefield to her right. Pain lanced through her when she saw the bodies they stood beside.

Savven held her to him even in death, and she swore she could still feel his warmth press into her before the world had gone black.

"Bring them back."

"What?" Tatius snapped impatiently.

Anger and pain fuelled her blood, and she turned sharp eyes towards the God. "Do I need to repeat myself?"

The God scoffed. "No."

"Yes," Brean gritted back.

"I cannot. That is not how the balance of life and death works."

Brean's eyes darted back to Savven and her. "Then no deal."

She heard the God take a long breath as if she were trying to calm herself.

"They're my family," Brean said softly, walking over to her and Savven. Kneeling, her fingers hovered over his face and traced the proud lines of his profile. "I lost my family once, then twice, and now... I can't lose them again." Brean looked up from the prince who had become a king before her eyes and her friend. "You've taken so much from me, and now you want to take more?"

"I want to give you your life," Tatius snipped, pursing her thin lips.

"But it's not a life without them in it," she countered, looking back down at Savven. "I would rather not live a life alone when I know what it's like to have a family." Brean stood, walking over to the God. "Bring them back, and I will make a deal with you."

Tatius's face softened somewhat. "There needs to be balance. Life for life."

"And this deal has a life exchanged in it?"

The God nodded once.

"Then have my life." Tatius furrowed her brows at Brean. "Bring them back in exchange, I do whatever it is you need done, but you may have my life afterwards."

"You would sacrifice your soul in exchange?"

"I would rather live a life with them in it and die knowing it was a life well lived than live without them. I don't want to be alone anymore." The last words were whispered, and her voice shook faintly, but she didn't look away from the black assessing stare of the God before her.

Tatius's eyes glazed over as if seeing something no one else could. Then she turned her head, listening to something only she could hear. She frowned, her eyes going deadpanned as she listened.

Brean raised a brow.

"Dragons," the God muttered under her breath with a shake of her head. Snapping her attention back to Brean, she briefly regarded her before nodding. "Very well, Witch. Your soul in exchange for another. But I cannot bring them all back. Only one."

Relief filled her, and Brean smiled faintly. "Alright. Now, what is it you need me to do?"

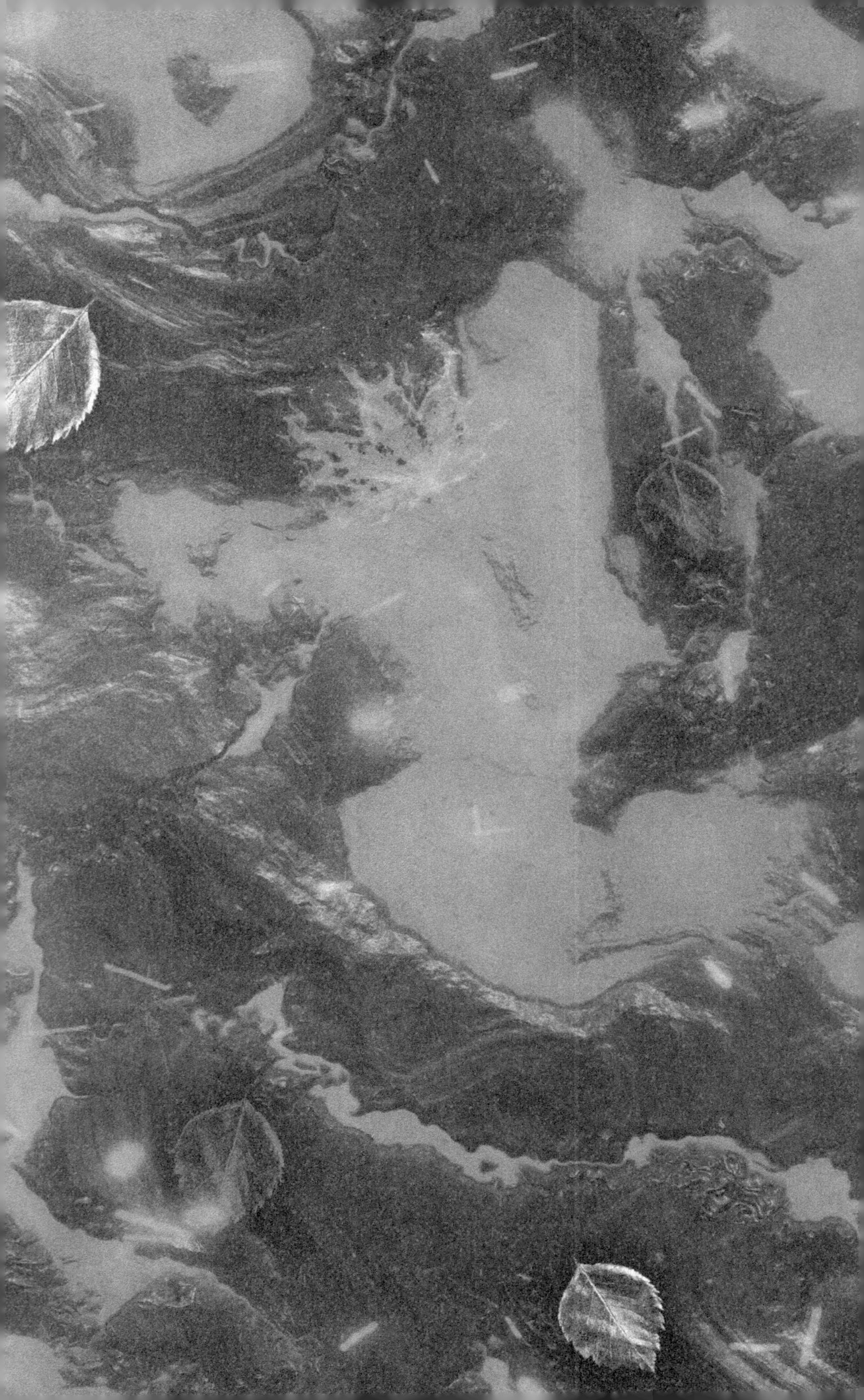

# CHAPTER 39

*Beep... Beep... Beep...*

Hazen was floating. She felt weightless as if she were drifting in a black sea.

"I'm here, my darling. I'm here," a soft female voice soothed.

*Mum?*

"Claris, we should go get some food while we wait. The doctor said we have to let her rest."

*Dad?*

"No," her mother murmured. Hazen felt her brush soft fingers over her face. "I want to be here when she wakes up."

*Beep... Beep... Beep...*

Hazen listened to the beeping for a moment. It was too loud. The smell of antiseptic filled her nostrils, and she tried to move away from it.

"Jorg! Did you see that?"

Something moved by her side, probably her mother standing.

Hazen's heart began to hammer, the beeping coming faster and faster beside her head. It was so loud in her ears.

"Hazen, love, are you awake? Can you hear us?" her father asked cautiously. His rough, calloused hand was warm around hers.

She tried to speak. The sea she was floating in brightened like the sun igniting the darkness, and she squinted against the light.

"M… Mum?" she croaked out. "D-Dad?" Gods, everything hurt, and her throat felt like sandpaper.

Blinking rapidly, the darkness faded completely, and bright fluorescent lights illuminated overhead. Hazen squinted against it, the room she was in going in and out of focus before finally settling. Her parents worried, hopeful faces hovering over her.

"Oh my God!" her mother cried, flinging her arms around Hazen. "You're awake!"

"Mum?" she asked again, tears stinging her eyes. Unknowing if this was a dream or reality.

"I'm here, love. Mummy is here," her mother sobbed into her hair, pressing kisses to her temple repeatedly. "You scared me half to death!"

Hazen brought a hand to her mother's shoulders, feeling her heat, smelling the faint remnants of her perfume, and the solid feel of her pressed into her chest. She was real. She was back home.

Her gaze found her father's, who hovered behind her mother, watching them with misty eyes. She gave him a small smile, reaching out her free hand. He took it, nodding his head once.

"You worried us, Kid."

"Sorry," she breathed, still holding her mother.

Finally, her mum pulled away, sniffling and wiping the tears from her red eyes. "What were you thinking, Hazen? Going out into that storm? They found you half frozen to death beside the forest!"

Hazen opened her mouth to say something, anything. But what could she say? That it was all just a trick by a God and some ancient lizard? Instead, she just said, "There was a dog."

Claris snorted. "Of course, you would run into a storm for a dog."

She offered her mother a small smile, trying to sit up. But when she did, the pain made her fall back to the bed. Everything was on fire anytime she moved.

"Oh! We need to tell the doctor and your grandparents!" Her mother grabbed her father's hand, ushering him away from the bed. "We'll be right back!"

They were there and gone with a click of the door.

Hazen watched the door for a long time before she stared up at the fluorescent light above. It was buzzing faintly in the now-too-quiet room. There was a small square window to her left, the sky outside was sunny and bright. The storm had passed, and all that was left was light.

Despite the clear blue sky, a storm raged in her as faces slowly filtered through her mind, one by one—once alive and now dead—smiles, laughter, butterflies, love, and family. Her eyes burned, and a pained sound wrenched from her lips.

They were all dead.

Dream. Reality. Hallucination. It didn't matter. They had lived and died, and that will remain with her for the rest of her mortal life.

As she sobbed, staring at the blue sky, her door clicked softly, and the lights dimmed. Hazen blinked rapidly. Her grandmother stood quietly at the foot of her bed. The overhead lights more bearable.

"Grandmother," she whispered.

André's mouth curled, green eyes twinkling. "Hello, Greatdaughter."

Her tears came again, and despite the pain, Hazen sat up, opening her arms. The IV in her left arm pulled, but she ignored it. She fell into her grandmother's warm embrace, sobbing into her chest.

"Oh, child," André soothed, gently running her hand over Hazen's hair.

Hazen pulled back. "It wasn't a dream?"

A small laugh slipped through, and André shook her head.

"What a wonderful dream it would have been. But no. It wasn't a dream."

"Adanessa…" The name slipped from her tongue before Hazen could stop it.

André lowered her eyes and sighed, a distant look crossing her face, before staring back at Hazen. "It has been a long time since anyone has called me that."

Shaking her head in disbelief, Hazen asked, *"How?"* How was it possible? How is she here? How did she survive? How did the world change? There were so many questions, but all she could ask was: How?

Thinking for a moment, André's pale green eyes met hers, and with a flick of her hand, the woman before Hazen shimmered and changed within a blink of an eye. She was still older and softer, and delicate lines were still etched into her skin, but she had changed. Her ears were gracefully pointed, her face a little narrower, cheekbones higher, eyes more vibrant, and her white hair seemed to shine.

"You have… you got your… how?" Again, all Hazen could ask was *how.*

André's smile beamed at Hazen. "You brought magic back to the world, Hazen."

Hazen looked out the window, not seeming any different. "Are you sure?"

"Yes, Hazen," André laughed. "Otherwise, I wouldn't be able to have my magic back from the Haven… and the memories that came with it."

If her magic returned to her, then what about… "And Rose?"

"Rose did not have a body to return to. Her spirit is finally free."

Hazen laid back, ignoring the radiating tenderness along her ribs. André helped stuff pillows behind her head so she was semi sitting up. "What about—"

Her parents and the doctor chose that moment to come into her room. The lights turned on again, blinding Hazen. She blinked rapidly, trying to stop her swimming vision.

"Oh, she's here! André is in here!" Her mother called over her shoulder, and her grandfather walked in, stuffing his phone into his pocket.

"Was just about to call you, my sweet," her grandfather said, walking over and placing a kiss on her grandmother's head. He looked at Hazen with twinkling blue eyes. "Welcome back."

Hazen frowned, eyes bouncing back to her grandmother, who sat patiently, still with her pointed ears and otherworldly beauty. But no one seemed to care or pay attention to it.

The doctor called a nurse who took blood samples, and her mother and father held hands as they spoke with the doctor about when she could be released. She faintly heard mention of bruising along her ribs and left shoulder and that she would have to ice them. But she didn't care about any of that. Hazen only had eyes for her grandmother, who leaned forward and spoke so only she could hear.

"You changed the world, Hazen. Magic has been reborn in them all. Now, they never knew a world without it."

She had been discharged the following day, dressed in a light-knit baby-blue long-sleeved shirt, jean shorts, and black trainers her parents had packed when she had been brought to the hospital. But now, back at her grandparents' home and standing alone in her room, she stared out the window to the forest beyond it. It felt weird being back in her own clothes, in her grandparents' home, like none of it had happened. She felt foreign. How funny that she had wished for home when away from it, but now being back, she missed the family she had made, the family she had left behind forever.

The towering evergreens were less foreboding under the bright blue sky and sunshine. But still, Hazen narrowed her eyes on them, trying to see if she could detect the magic that had once lain within.

When she had left the antiseptic room, and the too-bright fluorescents and fresh air hit her face, Hazen had nearly wept again. She had lived a lifetime in the world within the woods, travelling under the stars, through the sea, and across mountains. A lifetime in which she saw her friends live and die beside her.

Hazen let out a harsh breath, combing a hand through her loose hair. Her reflection watched her in the windowpane. Human. She was utterly human again, but something in her face had changed. Her eyes were a little more gold now, a sureness lighting them, and her hair was a little blonder. She felt light on her feet when she walked, despite the stiffness and echo of pain around her ribs and shoulder, her body lean from the double life she had lived. And when she had looked in the bathroom mirror earlier, checking her left shoulder, the scar was almost entirely gone. The only thing left was a faint discolouring of its lines like a birthmark, and she had carefully traced it with her fingertip—the scar on her face gone altogether.

But knowing it had been real and that the world had been changed because of it also brought a lingering sadness that clung to her bones and weighed her down.

It had been real. Which meant their deaths had been real, too.

Thoughts of her general reeled her mind. His amused green eyes, the slight quirk of his mouth, and the way he brushed her hair from her face whenever he could. Allowing himself the briefest touch of her. Or the way he had finally kissed her, and held her, and claimed her. The way his name felt on her lips. And the faith he had in her despite it going against his clan.

And then there was Savven. The exasperated roll of his eyes anytime she spoke and the faint twitch of a smile when she practised with a wooden stick as a sword for the first time.

Brean's smiling face came next, and Hazen felt a soft pinch in her heart. The witch had secrets, and Hazen suspected they had been more similar than Brean let on. More human.

And on and on it went. Every face. Every word spoken. It all replayed in her mind, and she swallowed the lump in her throat.

The storm was over. The sky was blue. The world could breathe again. But now, Hazen had to learn to live in it and with herself.

Hazen heard the doorbell ring downstairs, pulling her attention for a moment. Voices lifted to her room.

"Hazen?" her grandmother called from downstairs.

Sighing heavily, Hazen looked away from the forest and left her room. "What is it, Greatmother?" She reached the landing, and a soft, warm breeze kissed her left cheek from the open front door.

Her grandmother, dressed in a light purple sundress, who hadn't put up her glamour since she had dropped it to show Hazen in the hospital, smiled and stepped out of the way, opening the door fully to a man who took up the entire door frame. Dressed in a heather grey t-shirt stretched over a large muscled chest, low-slung jeans, and white trainers.

Hazen's heart stopped and dropped into her stomach.

Bright green eyes met hers, and a smile curled a familiar mouth.

A sound between a sob of relief and a sharp gasp left her lips, and she sprinted to the door, flinging herself at the male standing there.

Åsmund banded strong arms around her and pulled her to him. Slipping a hand under her bottom as she lifted her legs to his waist, the other tangling in her hair at the back of her head.

"You're alive!" she cried into his neck, breathing in his familiar scent. The relief that filled her was instant. Now, she didn't care if this was a dream or not. He was here, he was holding her, and he was *warm*.

"Aye, Little Dragon. I made a promise to you," he spoke in the same deep voice that she remembered, holding her tight.

She pulled back just enough to stare at his face. Light brown skin covered a sharp jawline and strong cheekbones. Green eyes with flecks of gold were framed by sun-bleached sandy brown hair curling around his face and shoulders and a small gold hoop through his right nostril. When she peaked over his shoulders, she noted his missing wings.

"In this lifetime or the next," he echoed back his words to her, studying her face as much as she was his. "You think death could keep me from you?"

Her heart resumed its beating and was racing across her bruised ribs, her lungs tightening as her eyes burned and she cupped her hand over his cheek. Åsmund leaned into her touch, kissing her palm.

"What did you do?" she breathed, dropping her forehead to his and sliding her fingers into his hair. He was alive. He was real.

"I made a deal with Death," he answered lowly, holding her gaze. "Bring me back, and she can have my immortality."

Hazen's heart stuttered. "You're mortal?"

"When you face Death, I will go into the abyss with you. My life is joined to yours now until the forever claims us."

And then she was kissing him. Fiercely, deeply, and with every fibre of her soul. He held her tight to him, the promise of never letting her go in the press of his lips.

Åsmund pulled away with a small radiant smile, his eyes dancing. "Does this mean I get two names now?"

Hazen laughed, bright and filled with a burning happiness. "I'll give you mine."

And then he was kissing her again. His lips parted hers expertly, his tongue tasting her as he claimed her as his in this world.

Even when her mother's voice came like a distant sound behind her and the sounds of her grandmother ushering her away, Hazen didn't stop kissing him. The door clicked shut behind her, and it was just the two of them outside with the world as their witness. She held fast to the man holding her, getting lost in the taste of him and the promise of tomorrow.

She would teach him how to be human, show him her world, and they would learn the new world together. The world where magic and man were one. They would figure it out *together*.

And as her general kissed her, Hazen smiled.

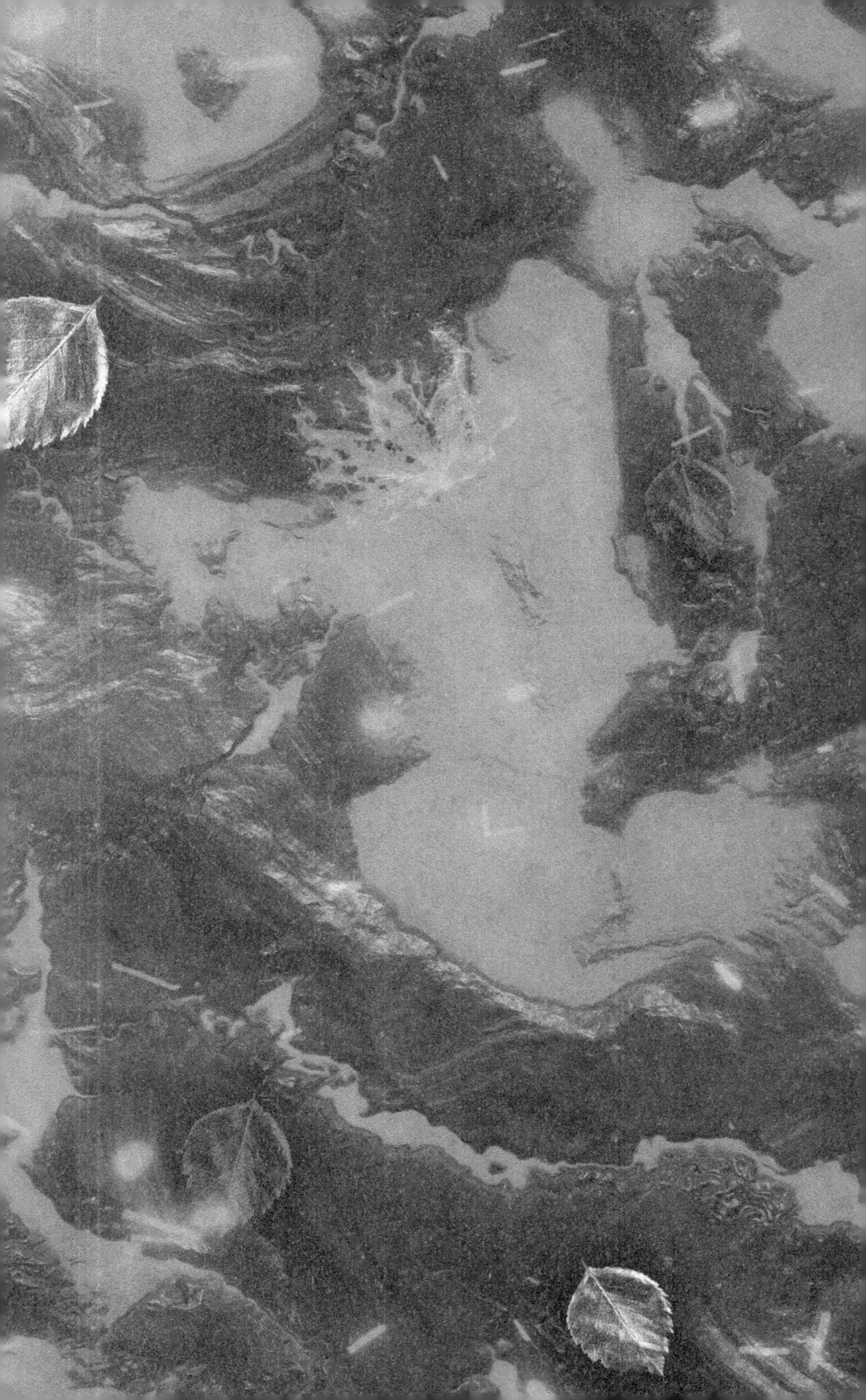

# EPILOGUE

Levina awoke with a sharp inhale. Eyes flying open and black as night. The darkness pressed in around her, and she gritted her teeth when hot pain cut between her legs. Ushering the demons down, she slammed them into the deepest regions of herself, and she felt the darkness slither away.

Her eyes became sky blue, and she blinked at the forest around her, ignoring the throbbing between her legs that was quickly vanishing and the stickiness she felt. Head darting around, she eyed her surroundings. The last thing Levina remembered was giving in to the urge to push, the pain becoming explosive and consuming. Laudin's black stare held her own as she had gritted her teeth, spit flying as she screamed and finally pushed. And then the world had gone dark.

Still dressed in the torn black gossamer gown, Levina slowly sat up, grimacing when her body ached like nothing she had ever felt before—like she had been torn in two and stitched back together.

Her hand went to her soft belly, and panic instantly rose like bile in her throat. Where was her baby?! Making to climb to her feet, her body *ached,* and she muffled her strangled cries behind her hand.

A soft cooing bubbled up beside a large weeping fern in front of her.

Levina startled and froze.

It came again, and a tiny hand waved over a large frond. Crawling on hands and knees, Levina raised a shaky hand to the leafy blade and pushed it down.

A healthy, cooing baby boy stared back at her with electric blue eyes.

Quickly sitting on her heels, Levina tore a thick strip of her gown from the hem, leaving it hanging to her knees. Wrapping the swath of gauzy fabric around her child, Levina brought her son into her arms, hot tears spilling down her cheeks.

Tiny hands reached for her blonde hair that fell around them, and her baby cooed again, grabbing the strands with a strong fist.

She stroked a finger over her son's face, awe filling her at what she had made. "You're perfect," she breathed, kissing his forehead and breathing him in.

He smelled new and perfect, and she loved him with everything within her. At that moment, she decided all the pain and suffering leading up to this point had been worth it. Staring down at his pristine little face, his ivory skin unmarked by the evil their world had been tormented with, Levina cradled him to her breast. Guiding his mouth, it took a moment before he latched onto her nipple and began to feed.

"Don't worry, I'll protect you," she promised quietly.

The forest was silent, observing them. Levina could feel magic pulsing in the world; the ache in her body was nearly gone. She looked at her wrist where the bargain had been tattooed but found it blank. Ezra was dead. The bargain was broken. Her magic and everything that made her Fae had been restored.

Levina stood carefully, her son tucked safely in her arms as he fed, her muscles relishing the flow of magic flooding her senses. With her body nearly healed, she began to walk. She didn't know where she was going or what was going to happen, only that she had to keep going. She had to survive—for her son.

"Don't worry," she whispered again. "I'm right here. Your mother is right here."

# ACKNOWLEDGEMENTS

Do you want to know a secret? I wrote The Black Forest/The Veil when I was 16. Now, before you ask about, The Keeper, I'll add that I didn't write these books with the intentions of them being a series (together). I wrote the first 80k words of The Black Forest when I was 16, and the last 20k words when I was 23.

When I was writing, The Keeper, I didn't realise I was writing the back story—the prologue—to The Black Forest, until one day I was writing a scene and Savven popped his cute head in and said, "Hi, this is my story." And I stopped, stared at my screen *realllly* hard, remembered I had this epic fantasy tucked away in my computer, and Savven was one of the main characters in it. So, I said, "Oh, okay, why not?" That's how this series was born, because I never thought I would publish The Black Forest, but here we are. Funny how life works.

The Black Forest was originally a first finished draft of 100k words, last year when I decided to do the developmental edits on it, it took me 7 months, but I ended up writing *another* 100k words into it, leaving the final product at 200k words and too expensive to print and sell as a whole, so that is how, The Veil, was born. Honestly, I'm not mad about it. I was lowkey freaking out, but I came to terms with it, and through the help of some of my friends, I was able to wrap my head around it, and make it all happen.

To make this happen, though, I had to start a GoFundMe to help with some of the cost of publishing: cover, interior, editing. It was a lot, and in this economy, it was hard to come up with those funds on my own. Thank you to the amazing souls I'm about to list below, I was able to cover most of the cover and interior of, The Veil, through those donations. So, thank you, from the bottom of my heart for all of your support, graciousness, and love:

Howard Curtin . Cathy Curtin . Hannah Curtin . Loni Joes Walsh . Derwin Williams . June Williams . Ashley Tyree . Tracy Daigrepont . Roger Nimer . Diana O'Brien . Mirjana Dougherty . Lisa Whytock . Sara Foster . Lisette Pombo . Jamie Haley . Christi Myrup . Cristobal Lander . Jazmyn M. A. Brandon-Lowe . Samantha Hansen . Joanna Rasmussen . Gina Schriefer . L. Nicole Cudworth . Rachel Ludewig . Edward Lein.

Brandy, my talented, patient, and overall amazing line editor. I've said this once, I'll say it again until I'm blue in the face and you finally believe me: You. Are. Superwoman. Being a woman, a wife, a mother, a homemaker, an editor, a friend, a crafter, a reader, and so much more is no easy feat, but you do it like its breathing, and the easiest thing in the world. Thank you for loving my novel(s), being diligent, honest, and as excited as I am about them. You're so talented, and I'm so proud of how far you've come in your editing career.

Stacey, my lovely proofreader, thank you for being so quick with the proofing, and falling in love with my novel(s). Thank you for believing in my work and wanting them to thrive in this world of readers, I truly appreciate you.

Hannah, where do I begin? You read The Black Forest *and* The Veil before they were edited and finished. You were so helpful throughout every stage, and so excited and honest with all the feedback you gave me. It was invaluable, and I'm so grateful to you. You have no idea. Thank you from the bottom of my heart.

Jazmyn, the sister our good Lord blessed me with. One, you're an amazing woman, and I want you to know how proud I am of you—it's in a book now, forever, so you'll never forget it. Two, thank you for supporting me through all of this, loving me, being my best friend, my sister, and just an overall beautiful human that God created.

Ashlyn, what an unlikely best friend I found in you. Life is a weirdly, funny, and ironic thing. Sometimes, when our lemons go a bit too sour, we get a chance to make some amazing sweet lemonade. Nothing in life is ever coincidence, God has everything timed, and beautifully planned, and he knew what he was doing. Never forget that among the rubble, there's gold to be found, and I'm glad I found you.

Charly, my designer, how do I put into words how talented you are? Telling you just doesn't seem like enough. You've come so far, and you have a whole life to hone your craft, and there is no limit. Even when you were busy you always managed to make time for me, and now there's only one book left after this one. But it won't be the end, if you're okay with that. I'll come to you for all my novels, if you'll have me, of course. But I just want to say thank you. You were the FIRST person to tell me, "Babes, your book is too big. You're probably going to have to split it." You were right. You talked me through it when I started to have a small anxiety attack, we had a work date and you proceeded to design an amazing cover for, The Veil, with me on the other end. You have no idea how much that meant to me. So, I guess thank you will have to do, because there are no words big enough.

Mrs. Williams, you call to ask about life, my books, and how everything was going with the splitting of the novels, the donations, and did everything you could, along with Mr. Williams, to help. So, thank you for being so wonderful. I'm blessed to have you in my life and in my corner.

My mum, thanks for being the garden within the mountain I could go to for peace, when the world became a little too much. For making me strong like you.

To my father... hey daddy, look, I have three books out now! I think you would really like this one. Actually, I already know you did, because you read the first draft when I was 24. You said, "Anabelle is great, but The Black Forest is my favourite. She's a fighter, like us." I didn't forget.

To me... deep breaths, Babygirl, you did it. Good job.

# ABOUT THE AUTHOR

P. S. Whytock is a thirty, flirty, and semi-thriving adult who is just trying to figure out life. She currently lives in Florida and is a Merchant Marine when she's not pretending to be an author.